Patricia Burns is an Essex girl born and bred and proud of it. She spent her childhood messing about in boats, then tried a number of jobs before training to be a teacher. She married and had three children, all of whom are now grown up, and she recently became a grandmother. She is now married for the second time and is doing all the things she never had time for earlier in life.

When not busy writing, Patricia enjoys travelling and socialising, walking in the countryside round the village where she now lives, belly dancing and making exotic costumes to dance in.

Find out more about Patricia at www.mirabooks. co.uk/patriciaburns

D0620536

Also available from **Patricia Burns**

WE'LL MEET AGAIN

Patricia Burns

Bye Bye Love

MIRA

DID YOU PURCHASE THIS BOOK WITHOUT A COVER?
If you did, you should be aware it is **stolen property** as it was
reported *unsold and destroyed* by a retailer. Neither the author nor the
publisher has received any payment for this book.

*All the characters in this book have no existence outside the imagination
of the author, and have no relation whatsoever to anyone bearing the
same name or names. They are not even distantly inspired by any
individual known or unknown to the author, and all the incidents are
pure invention.*

*All Rights Reserved including the right of reproduction in whole or
in part in any form. This edition is published by arrangement with
Harlequin Enterprises II B.V./S.à.r.l. The text of this publication or
any part thereof may not be reproduced or transmitted in any form
or by any means, electronic or mechanical, including photocopying,
recording, storage in an information retrieval system, or otherwise,
without the written permission of the publisher.*

*This book is sold subject to the condition that it shall not, by way of
trade or otherwise, be lent, resold, hired out or otherwise circulated
without the prior consent of the publisher in any form of binding or
cover other than that in which it is published and without a similar
condition including this condition being imposed on the subsequent
purchaser.*

*MIRA is a registered trademark of Harlequin Enterprises Limited,
used under licence.*

*Published in Great Britain 2009
MIRA Books, Eton House, 18-24 Paradise Road,
Richmond, Surrey, TW9 1SR*

© Patricia Kitchin 2009

ISBN 978 0 7783 0269 8

54-0409

*MIRA's policy is to use papers that are natural, renewable and
recyclable products and made from wood grown in sustainable
forests. The logging and manufacturing processes conform to the
legal environmental regulations of the country of origin.*

*Printed and bound in Spain
by Litografia Rosés S.A., Barcelona*

To Isadora,
who carries our love into the future

CHAPTER ONE

IT WAS going to be a very special day. Not that there were any clues to it when Scarlett Smith woke up. Everything seemed much the same. There was the sound of her mother's broom knocking against the skirting-boards as she swept the floors downstairs, there was the drone of a BBC accent coming from the wireless and there was the familiar smell, the one that Scarlett had grown up with, the smell of stale beer and cigarette ash. The morning smell of a pub.

But today was June the second. Coronation Day. The Queen was going to be crowned Elizabeth II of England and it was going to be extremely busy at the Red Lion. Scarlett slid out of bed, washed in cold water, pulled on an old cotton dress and a cardigan and ran down the creaking stairs to the lounge bar. Joan Smith, a floral overall wrapped round her cosy body, was mopping the floor. She looked up with a smile.

'How's my darling girl this fine morning? Not that it is fine. It's raining. Such a pity! And all those people sleeping out on the pavements in London to get a look at the Queen. It said on the news they was out in their thousands. Old people. Little kiddies. But they're all in great spirits, they said. Ready to cheer and wave their Union Jacks.'

'Must be wonderful to be up in London,' Scarlett said.

'Yes—a once in a lifetime event. The fairy tale princess becomes queen.' Her mother sighed. She leaned on the handle of her mop, a faraway expression in her eyes. Joan Smith loved a good story. A real life one featuring a real live queen was even better. Then she snapped out of it. 'Still, we're going to have a right old knees-up here, aren't we? Morris dancers, tea on the village green—mind you, it might be in the village hall at this rate—and us open all day so as people can toast Her Majesty. No peace for the wicked! Come on, sweetheart, fetch a bucket and cloth and do the bars and tables for us. Sooner we finish, sooner we can have breakfast. I got fresh eggs. Old Harry brought us in a basin last night.'

Mother and daughter worked rapidly through the lounge and public bars, wiping, polishing, setting out clean ashtrays, fresh beer mats and bar towels, straightening the tables and stools. Nobody looking on would have guessed they were related. Joan was round and dumpy, her brown hair greying, her blue eyes fading, her hands cracked and swollen and knees stiff from a lifetime of hard work. Scarlett, at fourteen, was already taller than her mother, slim and strong with big brown eyes and long dark hair pulled back in a shiny ponytail, her coltish figure starting to develop into a woman's body.

'Don't it look lovely?' Joan said as they gave a last rub to the horse brasses on the beams.

'Very patriotic,' Scarlett agreed.

The Red Lion was all dressed up for the Coronation.

Outside there was red, white and blue bunting draped from the windows and over the sign, with a big Union Jack over the door, and inside more Union Jacks and flags from the countries of the great British Empire were hung around the bars. Pictures of the Queen and the Duke of Edinburgh and the little prince and princess had been cut out of magazines, framed with red, white and blue ribbons and stuck up on any available wall space. A specially brewed Coronation Ale had been delivered from the brewery a few days ago and was nicely settled and ready to serve to any of Her Majesty's loyal subjects who cared to drink her health. Nobody could say the Smiths hadn't made an effort.

The two put away the cleaning things and Joan set about making breakfast in the kitchen-cum-living room behind the public area. It was rather a dark room, tacked onto the back of the main building and crowded with a table and chairs, sink and stove and dresser, and a sitting area of two Windsor chairs and a small fireside chair grouped round the fireplace. The big brown wireless set sat in pride of place on a small table next to the larger of the Windsor chairs. When Scarlett was little, the grouping reminded her of the Three Bears, and she would always be ready to guard her breakfast porridge against invasions of golden-haired thieves.

Joan poured tea into a large white cup, put in three sugars, stirred it and handed it to Scarlett.

'Go up and give your dad his cuppa, lovey.'

Scarlett walked carefully up the stairs. Her dad never made an appearance until half an hour or so before opening time, giving himself just enough time to check the beers, have a cigarette and look at the sports page of the newspaper before the first customers of the day came in. Scarlett tapped on the door of her parents' bedroom, listened for the muffled reply from inside and went in. The curtains were still closed and the air smelt of beer fumes. Her father had had a hard night last night. The regulars had been getting in some practice at toasting the new queen and naturally the landlord had to keep them company.

Victor Smith raised his head from the pillow as his daughter came in.

'Ah—tea—what a lovely girl you are.'

He coughed, fumbled for his cigarettes and matches, lit up the first Player's Navy Cut of the day and took a deep drag.

'That's better. Tell your mum I'll be down soon.'

Scarlett raised her eyebrows at this.

'Pull the other one, Dad.'

They both knew that pigs would fly and the moon turn blue before Victor made it to breakfast.

Victor laughed, coughed and patted her arm.

'You're getting too knowing by half, you are. Sharp as a barrowload of monkeys. What's two pints of best, a rum and black and a half of mild and bitter?'

Scarlett added them up in her head in a trice, then made up a longer round for him to calculate. It was a game they had played practically since she could count. As a result she was top of her class at mental arithmetic.

'Can't beat you these days,' Victor admitted.

Scarlett kissed the top of his head, left him to his tea and cigarette and went back to the kitchen.

'He all right?' her mother asked, whipping eggs out of the frying pan and slipping them onto a plate.

''Course,' Scarlett said.

When she was younger, she had accepted the idea that fathers lay in bed while mothers worked. Even when she'd realised that other fathers got up and cycled to farms and factories to start work at eight, or down to the station to catch a train up to London and start work at nine, she'd still accepted it because, as her mother pointed out, other fathers didn't have to stand behind a bar each evening. But as she'd grown older she'd realised that it was her mother who served the drinks, cleared the glasses, changed the optics, emptied the ashtrays and washed up. Her father supervised. That involved leaning on the bar, chatting to the customers and sampling the stock.

'Oh, but he has all the cellar work to do,' her mother said when Scarlett questioned this. 'Everybody says he serves the best pint for miles around.'

Which was true. The Red Lion and Victor Smith were famous for their beers, and he was known as a good landlord who made everyone feel at home but dealt quickly with any potential trouble. And though other dads might work harder than hers, none of them were more fun, or quicker to back you up when you needed it. All the same, she couldn't help thinking that it would have been nice to have a bit more help today.

'Here you are, poppet.'

Joan placed a blue and white striped plate in front of her. On it were piled two chunky slices of fried bread, a rasher of bacon and two large fried eggs, the whites crispy around the edges, just the way she liked them.

Scarlett sat down at the rickety table with its checked yellow oilcloth cover.

'Two eggs?' she questioned.

'Well—we need to keep our strength up,' her mother said, but she only managed to work her way through one egg herself before she pushed her plate to one side and sat holding her teacup and staring at its contents.

Scarlett looked at her. Anxiety stirred within her.

'What's the matter, Mum? You all right?'

'Yes, yes, quite all right.'

'You ain't eaten your breakfast.'

Her mother never left food on her plate. It was a waste. After years of wartime rationing, nobody ever wasted a crumb.

'I will. In a minute.'

Joan's hands were shaking. She put the teacup down.

'Mum? You've gone all pale.'

'It's all right. I'm fine. Just a touch of heartburn, that's all. Go and fetch me the Milk of Magnesia, there's a good girl.'

Scarlett ran to the corner cupboard and got out the blue bottle. She gave it a good shake and poured the thick white liquid into a spoon. Her mother swallowed it down.

'That's it. That'll do the trick.'

But still she pushed her plate towards Scarlett.

'You finish it off for me, darling. Go on, before it gets cold.'

Scarlett did as she was told, though worry made it difficult to eat.

'P'raps you ought to go to the doctor, Mum.'

'Oh, doctors—I know what he'll say if I do. Take a tonic and get some rest. Rest! Who's going to do my work if I rest, that's what I'd like to know.'

'I could, if you'd let me.'

Joan patted her hand.

'That's very nice of you, dear, but you do quite enough to help round the place already. And you got your studies. You got to do well at school. That's the way to get on in life.'

Scarlett sighed. She knew there was no shifting her mother on that point.

'Well, get someone else in, then. Just someone to serve behind the bar on a couple of evenings, so you wouldn't have to work every day. Everyone else has a day off a week, Mum. Why shouldn't you?'

Unspoken between them was the fact that Victor went to football every Saturday afternoon and to the greyhound racing at Southend every Wednesday evening without fail.

'Get someone in? A barmaid? Oh, I don't know about that, lovey. We couldn't afford the wages. Things are tight enough as it is, without starting paying other people to do what I can perfectly well do myself.'

'But Mum—'

'Look, I'm all right, see? There's nothing wrong with me that another cup of tea won't cure.'

She certainly didn't look as white and clammy as she had done a few minutes ago. But Scarlett couldn't shake the persistent anxiety gnawing at her overfull stomach. This wasn't the first time her mother had had one of these turns.

'But Mum—'

'Enough said, pet, right? I don't want to hear no more about it. We didn't come into this world to have an easy ride. You got to keep at it, like Scarlett O'Hara. She never let anything stop her. Wars, famine, whatever, she still kept right on. That's why I named you after her, Scarlett. I wanted you to be like her—fearless, not a little mouse like me.'

'You're not a little mouse, Mum.'

Scarlett had heard this story countless times before. It was one of her mother's favourites.

'Oh, but I was. Still am, really. Of course, I didn't have much of a choice. I had to look after my mum and dad, didn't I? First him and then her, both of them invalids. All those years.'

Joan sipped at a fresh cup of tea, looking inwards, back down the years. The commentator on the wireless was describing the crowds gathered for the coronation, but neither woman heard him.

'Thirty-seven, I was, when poor Mum died. Never had a job, never went out dancing with young men, never done nothing except go to the library and borrow lots of books. Didn't know how to do anything but run a house and look after invalids. And there I was, alone in the world with the rent to pay and no pension nor nothing coming in now they'd passed on, God bless them. So I thought I'd better get something doing the same thing. I couldn't be a proper nurse—I didn't have the training—but I thought maybe I could get something live-in with another invalid. And I guess I would have done just that, and been a poor old maid with no life of my own, if I hadn't—'

'—met my dad,' Scarlett said for her.

Joan smiled. Her voice was soft with love. 'Yes. Your dad. Oh, he was so handsome! Like a film star. Tall, dark, lovely black hair he had, just like yours, and those flashing dark eyes, and that lovely smile. Just waiting there at the bus stop he was. My fate. Just think, if I'd got there five minutes later, I'd of missed him, and then I wouldn't be Mrs Smith now, and you would never of been born. Just think of that! No Scarlett in this world. No wonderful daughter to love and watch over. Best thing that ever happened to me, you are.'

'Oh, Mum—' Scarlett leaned over and gave her mother a hug. 'You soppy old thing.'

'I mean it,' Joan insisted, hugging her back, stroking her hair. 'I couldn't ask for a better daughter than you. My Scarlett. *Gone with the Wind.* Oh, how I loved that book. Scarlett O'Hara was everything I wasn't—she was rich and beautiful and brave and she didn't care what she said or who she took on. And just look at you! You're beautiful and brave, and maybe one day you'll be rich.'

'Oh, yes, and then I'll have a big house with a swimming pool, like a film star,' Scarlett said.

It was a game they often played, the When I Am Rich game. Sometimes it was Scarlett who was going to become rich, by marrying a millionaire or being a beauty queen, sometimes it was Joan, who was going to win the football pools.

'Wasn't so long since you wanted a pony and a pink taffeta dress.' Joan sighed. 'Now it's a big house with a swimming pool.'

'Yes, well, I'm fourteen now,' Scarlett reminded her.

'Fourteen. Quite the young lady.'

Joan held her daughter's face between her hands and looked at her long and hard. Then she gave a nod and stood up.

'Yes, quite grown up. Grown up enough to read *Gone with the Wind.* I'll fetch it for you.'

She bustled out of the door. Scarlett started to clear the table and pile the plates up by the sink. At last she was going to be allowed to read the story that had figured in her mother's tales ever since she could remember. Since she had joined the adult section of the public library, her hand had often hovered over a copy of the novel. She had even picked it up, opened it, read the first page. There was nothing to stop her from borrowing and reading it, nothing except the amazing grip it held on her mother's imagination. It had been held out to her as a huge treat, something to look forward to, something almost as good as marrying a film star or winning the football pools, except that the sensible part of her knew that she would probably never do either of those things, whereas one day she surely would get to read all about her namesake.

'Here we are.'

Her mother came back into the kitchen and sat down at the table, breathless, holding her side.

'Oh, dear me. Those stairs. I swear they get steeper every day. There—here it is. I've read it so many times it's a wonder the pages haven't worn out.'

Scarlett took the book and ran her hands reverentially over the cover. She looked at the spine. *Gone with the Wind by Margaret Mitchell.* She opened it up and read the first line, the first paragraph, the first page. She was transported back ninety years or more to the front porch of a plantation house in Georgia. Such a strange world, so very different from her own.

Her mother touched her shoulder.

'Things to be done, pet.'

'Mu-um—' Scarlett protested. 'You can't give it to me, then tell me I can't read it!'

'Well, maybe I shouldn't of, but we got to get going, love.'

Joan had her hands in the sink. The first of many lots of washing up she would be doing today, what with all the glasses people would be using. Scarlett read one more paragraph, sighed dramatically and walked over to pick up the tea towel.

By the time Victor sauntered down the stairs the morning's chores were all done and Joan and Scarlett were glued to the wireless.

'What's all this, then?' he asked, squeezing Joan's shoulder, kissing Scarlett's cheek. 'Slacking on the job?'

'Oh, it's so wonderful,' Joan breathed. 'All the singing and that. He describes it so well. The people and the robes, all the colours. I just wish we had one of those televisions. It must be wonderful to watch it all going on.'

'It's what we do best, ain't it?' Victor said. 'Us British. We do pomp and ceremony best in the world.'

He pulled up a chair and lit a cigarette. Scarlett made her parents another cup of tea each and left them sitting contentedly, one either side of the big brown wireless, while she picked up the precious copy of *Gone with the Wind* and went to her room to change. Like everyone in the country who could possibly afford it, she had a new dress to wear for Coronation Day. It was blue cotton with white polka dots, with a tight bodice and a fashionably full skirt. She tied a long red, white and blue striped ribbon round her ponytail and then turned this way and that in front of the small mirror over the chest of drawers, trying to get a full length view of herself. What she could see pleased her. She put her hands to her slim waist and pushed it in still further, smiling at her reflection. She might not be a southern belle like Scarlett O'Hara, but today was a special day and she was going to enjoy it.

CHAPTER TWO

'Two more pints o' that there Coronation Ale, if you please, young missy!'

'Coming up, sir!'

An anomaly in the licensing laws allowed Scarlett, as the licensee's child, to serve alcohol even though she was too young to drink it. She pulled the beer carefully into the jugs, as she had been taught. It was no use rushing a good pint.

Beside her, her mother pushed a strand of hair back off her damp forehead.

'Scarlett, love, when you've done that, can you run round and get the empties? We're almost out of clean glasses.'

'Righty-oh, Mum.'

The Red Lion was jumping. There was a roar of happy voices from both bars and a pall of blue smoke hanging over everyone's heads. Nobody could remember seeing so many people in since VE day. Crowds of men and quite a number of women were packed into the two bars and children were running around on the village green outside clutching bottles of pop and shrieking. Everyone was in an excellent mood, and of course there was only one topic of conversation.

'…she looked so beautiful, sort of stately, like…'

'…and the two little kiddies, they behaved so well, didn't they?'

'That Queen of Tonga, she's a character, ain't she? Sitting in the rain there, waving away to the crowds!'

Scarlett squeezed her way between the cheerful customers. Those who had managed to get tables piled the empties up for her and handed them over.

'There y'are girl, and here's a few more. Can you manage? Oh, she's a chip off the old block and no mistake. You going to be a landlady when you grow up, young Scarlett?'

'Not on your nelly,' Scarlett said to herself. She had other ideas for her future. An air hostess, maybe, or a lady detective, tracking down ruthless murderers, or more practically, a lady chauffeur, driving rich and famous people about in a swish car.

She wriggled past her father's little group of regulars on her way out to the kitchen. Even he was on the business side of the bar this evening. He was only attending to his cronies, but at least he was doing that and he was keeping them well topped up. They were on whisky chasers, Scarlett noticed.

'Ah, here's the prettiest little barmaid in all of Essex,' one of them exclaimed as she tried to force her way through. 'Aren't you afraid some young fella-me-lad will come and whisk her away, Vic?'

Her father smiled at her between the flushed faces.

'Ah, she's still Daddy's girl, aren't you, my pet?' he said, lifting the flap in the bar to let her through.

'That's right,' Scarlett agreed. Most of the boys she knew were gangling and spotty. Not like the heroes of books and films.

There were more dirty glasses lined up on the bar. She piled those onto a tray with the ones she had collected already, staggered through into the back room and kicked the door closed behind her.

'Phew!'

It was cooler and the air was much clearer out here. Better still, there were no raucous voices calling out to her. It was tempting to linger over the washing up, spinning out the time before going back into the bar. Her school friends would all be at home or round at friends' or relatives' houses enjoying themselves this evening. They'd be playing card games or watching repeats of the day's ceremony on their new televisions, not rushing about working. She thought of the copy of *Gone with the Wind* waiting for her upstairs. How nice to be able to slip up there now and escape into Scarlett O'Hara's world and just listen to the rumble of voices coming up from below, like she used to when she was younger.

'Hey, Scarlett, my pet!'

Her father's head appeared round the door.

'Those glasses ready yet?'

'Nearly.'

Scarlett dried the last one and hurried out with the loaded tray. Her parents immediately grabbed them and started pouring fresh drinks.

'Good girl—can you do the ashtrays now?' her mother asked. 'Yes, Mr Philips? Two best bitters and a mild, was it? And a G and T. Right. Mrs Philips here too, is she? How did the children enjoy the tea? All right, sir, be with you in a minute. Yes, I know you've been waiting. Scarlett, leave the ashtrays and serve this gentleman, will you?'

Scarlett concentrated on the impatient customer as he reeled off a long and complicated round. Over on the far side of the public bar, a sing-song had started.

'Daisy, Daisy, give me your answer, do—'

Others took up the song until the whole bar had joined in.

'I'm half crazy, all for the love of you—'

'Two port and lemons, a rum and blackcurrant, half of bitter shandy, a Guinness—' Scarlett muttered to herself, adding it up in her head as she went along.

People in the lounge bar heard the singing and started up a rival tune.

'Rule Britannia, Britannia rules the waves—'

'Oh, and a pint of Coronation Ale, love,' Scarlett's customer added, shouting above the noise.

Both songs were going full blast, but the lounge bar crowd didn't know all the words to *Rule Britannia,* so they contented themselves with singing the chorus three times and tra-la-ing in between. The public bar finished *Daisy, Daisy* and started on *Roll out the Barrel.* The lounge bar lot gave up competing and joined in too. Scarlett finished her round and took the money. As she rang it up on the till, there was a crash and a thud behind her. She spun round and cried out loud. Her mother was slumped on the floor surrounded by broken glass and a pool of beer. Her face was deathly pale and her lips a dreadful bluish colour. Scarlett bent down beside her.

'Mum, Mum! What's the matter?'

'Joannie!'

Victor crouched at the other side of her, patting her cheek, shaking her arm. His face was as flushed as hers was pale.

'Joannie, what is it? Come on, Joannie, speak to me!'

Joan's eyes were staring. Jagged groans tore from her mouth as she struggled to breathe.

'What's up? What's wrong?'

People were leaning over the bar.

'Joan's had a funny turn.'

'Get her into the fresh air.'

'Get a doctor.'

One of the regulars lifted the flap and joined them behind the bar.

'Come on, Vic, let's get her out the back.'

In an agony of worry, Scarlett followed. She grabbed a cushion from one of the chairs to put under her mother's head as the men lowered her mother gently to the floor, then Scarlett crouched beside her, holding her hand and feeling utterly helpless. What could she do? She wanted so desperately to help her mum and didn't know how.

A woman came in. 'Can I help? I'm a nurse.'

Scarlett felt a rush of relief. Here was someone who could advise them.

Victor welcomed her in. As she knelt by Joan, a man put his head round the door.

'Someone's gone for Dr Collins. How is she?'

'Thanks,' Victor said. 'I don't know. She's—'

'Ring for an ambulance,' the nurse cut in. She looked at Scarlett. 'You'll be the quickest. Run over to the telephone. Do you know how to do it? Ring 999 and tell them it's a heart attack.'

Fear clutched at Scarlett's entrails. A heart attack!

Her mum was having a heart attack! Wordlessly, she nodded and sprang to her feet. She was out of the back door, round the side of the pub and across the village green in seconds, running faster than she had ever run in her life. Her lungs heaving, she wrenched open the heavy door of the telephone box on the far side of the green from the Red Lion, picked up the receiver and dialled 999. She struggled to control her breathing so that she could speak clearly.

'Ambulance—my mum—the nurse said she's having a heart attack—'

A calm female voice on the other end of the line took the details and assured her that an ambulance would be with them as soon as possible. Scarlett replaced the phone and stepped out into the summer evening again. Everything was carrying on as if nothing had happened. Houses were bright with flags and bunting for the big celebration. Across the green, the door of the Red Lion stood open and children were still playing outside. Someone cycled past and called out a greeting to her. It all felt unreal, as if she were watching it on the cinema screen. This couldn't really be happening, not to her. It was all too much, too fast. One moment she had been serving a customer, the next she'd been telephoning for an ambulance. A heart attack. It wasn't right. Men had heart attacks, not ladies, not her mother.

'Mum!' she cried out loud. 'Oh, Mum!'

She set off across the green again, ignoring the shouts of the children as they chased round her. Out of the corner of her eye she noticed two other figures hastening towards the pub. Something made her look again, and then she veered over to meet them.

'Oh, Dr Collins, thank you, thank you—it's my mum—'

'I know, I know—'

The doctor was an elderly man, past retirement age. Already he was out of breath, and the man who had gone to fetch him was carrying his bag for him. Like the rest of the village, he must have been celebrating, for he was wearing evening dress and Scarlett could smell drink on his breath. He put a heavy hand on her shoulder as he hurried along.

'Don't worry, young Scarlett—'

Scarlett hovered by his side in an agony of impatience. She knew he was going as fast as he could, but he was so slow, so slow! She wanted to drag him along.

'Come round the back,' she said as they reached the Red Lion.

She knew as soon as she and the doctor went through the door. She knew by the way they were standing, by the way they turned as she entered the room. She knew by the look on their faces.

'Mum?' she croaked. 'She's not—? Please say she's not—'

There was a ringing in her ears. Everything was blurred, everything but the woman lying on the floor, the dear woman who was the rock of her life, the one dependable point upon which everything else was fixed.

'Mum!' she wailed, running forward, dropping to her knees. She grasped one of the limp hands in hers, clasping it to her chest. 'Mum, don't go, don't leave me!'

Hands were restraining her, arms were round her shoulders. She shook them off.

'No, no! She can't be dead, she can't!'

Dr Collins was listening to Joan's chest, feeling for a pulse in her neck.

'Do something!' Scarlett screamed. 'You've got to do something!'

Two strong hands were holding the tops of her arms now.

'Now, then, that's enough,' a firm female voice was saying.

Scarlett ignored her. She was staring wildly at her mother, at the doctor, willing him to perform some miracle of medical science. But he just gave a sad little shake of the head.

'I'm sorry, Scarlett—'

'No!' Scarlett howled. Her chest was heaving with sobs, tears welled up and spilled over in a storm of weeping. Her father was there, kneeling beside her, pulling her into his arms. Together they rocked and wept, oblivious to the people around them.

'She was the best woman in the world,' Victor croaked. 'A gem, a diamond—'

Scarlett could only bury her face in his broad chest and cry and cry. It was like the end of the world.

After that came a terrible time of official things to be done. However much Scarlett and Victor wanted to shut out the world and mourn the dear woman who had gone, there were people to see, forms to sign, things to arrange. The funeral was very well attended. The Red Lion was a centre of village life. Joan had been there behind the bar all through the terrible war years and the difficult days of austerity afterwards. Everyone missed her round smiling face and her sympathetic ear.

'She was a wonderful woman,' people said as they left the church.

'One of the best.'

'Salt of the earth.'

'She'll be much missed.'

Standing by her father's side, Scarlett nodded and shook hands and muttered thanks.

'You're a good girl,' people said to her. 'A credit to your mother, a chip off the old block.'

And all the while she wanted to scream and shout and rage against what had happened. This couldn't be true, it couldn't be happening to her. Her mother couldn't really have gone and left her like this.

But she had, and there was worse to come.

CHAPTER THREE

ONE Saturday about three weeks after the funeral, Scarlett walked into the lounge bar to find her father sitting on a stool at the bar counter staring morosely at a letter. He looked dreadful. There were bags under his eyes, a day's growth of stubble on his chin and he hadn't bothered to brush his hair.

'We've got to get out,' he said.

Scarlett stared at him. 'What do you mean, get out?'

'The brewery wants us gone. They've been holding the licence for us since your mum—' He hesitated. Neither of them could bring themselves to say the word *died*. 'But they won't go on doing that for ever. They want a licensee on the premises to deal with any bother.'

Long ago when Scarlett had first learnt to read, she had asked why only her mother had her name above the pub door as licensee. She had been told that the brewery preferred to have a woman in charge and, since the brewery's word was law as far as they were concerned, she had never really thought to question it.

'But surely they wouldn't mind having your name up there now,' she said. 'You've been here for years. Everyone likes you. They all say what a good landlord you are. The brewery must know that, surely? And I could help as much as possible. We can keep it going between us.'

'It's not as easy as that,' her father said.

'What do you mean?'

Victor sighed. He dropped his head in his hands and ran his hands through his hair, making it stick up on end. Fear wormed through Scarlett's stomach. This was her dad. When things went wrong, her dad was always there with his cheery manner, making it all right again.

'Oh, we don't have to bother ourselves about a little old thing like that,' he would say. 'Worse things happen at sea.' Or, 'It'll all come out in the wash.' And generally he was right. Up till now, whatever life had thrown at them, they had coped. Surely he could solve whatever was worrying him this time?

'I can't hold a licence,' he admitted.

Scarlett stared at him. 'Why not?' she demanded.

'Because I can't, all right?'

Fear fuelled the anger that had been simmering in her ever since her mother had died.

'No, it isn't all right! You say we've got to leave here, leave the Red Lion, because you can't hold a licence? I want to know why.'

'Look, it's best you don't know.'

The anger boiled over, all the irrational resentment at what had happened, even at her mother for going and leaving them when they needed her so much.

'I *want* to know! I've got to leave my home because of whatever it is. I've got a right to know!'

Victor rubbed his face and looked up at the ceiling.

'Because—' his voice came out as a croak '—oh, God, Scarlett, this is so hard. Worse than telling your mother—'

'Go on!' Scarlett raged.

Victor still wouldn't look at her. 'Because I've got a record,' he admitted.

His whole body seemed to sag in defeat.

Scarlett did not understand at first. She gazed at her big strong dad, who used to throw her up in the air and catch her, who could move the heavy beer casks around the cellar with ease, who could down a yard of ale quicker than anyone. All at once he seemed somehow smaller.

'A record? What do you mean? What sort of—?' And then the truth dawned on her. 'You mean a police record?'

She couldn't believe it, wouldn't believe it. It just wasn't true. Her dad wouldn't hurt a fly. He was everyone's friend. He could not possibly be a criminal.

Victor reached out to her. Instinctively, Scarlett went to the safety of his arms. She was folded into the comforting familiarity of his scratchy jumper, his pubby smell. She felt his voice vibrate through his chest as he struggled to answer her honestly.

'That's about the size of it, yes.'

Scarlett felt as if she had been kicked in the stomach. Her whole view of the world lurched, shifted and rearranged itself into a darker, more frightening picture.

'What did you do?' she whispered into his neck, as visions of robbery, of murder rose in her head. Desperately, she drove them down, hating herself for even entertaining such horrors.

'Breaking and entering.'

A burglar. Her father was a burglar.

'You went into someone's house and—and stole things?' she asked, appalled. 'How could you? How could you do that?'

Wicked people did that. Her father wasn't wicked. He was the kindest man in the world. She reared her head back, needing to see his expression. Victor looked stricken.

'You think I don't regret it?' he countered. He held her by the shoulders now, his eyes boring into hers, willing her to understand. 'There's not a day doesn't go by when I don't wish I'd said no, but I was young and stupid, Scarlett. You got to remember that. It was wrong, I know it was wrong, but you got to think about what it was like then. Times were hard. It was back in the thirties, in the depression. Work was hard to come by and what jobs there was around wasn't paid well. I'd just met this girl, a corker she was, and I wanted to impress her—'

'My mum?' Scarlett interrupted.

'No, no, this was before I met your mum. But this girl, I wanted to take her out, show her a good time, and I hadn't any money. Then this mate of mine, he said he was doing some decorating at this old girl's place, and she had more money than sense and she wouldn't even notice if we took a few bits. But she did, of course. And we got caught, and I got sent down—'

He paused. Scarlett's heart seemed to be beating so hard it was almost suffocating her.

'One stupid mistake and I ruined my life. My family cut me off. My mother died while I was inside and my brother said it was from shame over me and none of them have had anything to do with me since. And of course when I came out nobody wanted to give me a job. Who wants a man with a record when there's plenty of others with a clean sheet? I was on my uppers by the time I met your mum. She turned everything round. She believed in me. She was a wonderful woman, your mum. The very best.'

Scarlett couldn't take any more. She twisted out of his grasp, marched out of the building and went for a long walk, turning everything she had just learnt over in her head. None of it made any sense. She finally found herself back home again with everything still surging around inside. It was midday opening and there were a few customers in the bar. Not wanting to speak to anyone, she ran upstairs, grabbed *Gone with the Wind* from her bedside table and hurried down to the far end of the garden. Neither of her parents had been keen gardeners, so the patch had gone wild since the days of digging for victory. Down at the far end, beyond the apple trees, was a hidden sunspot. Scarlett lay down in the long grass with the sun on her back, opened the book and escaped into her namesake's world. A little later she heard her father calling her name. She kept silent. Then she heard him scrunching down the gravel path at the side. It sounded as if he was going out. Scarlett read on, immersing herself in the burning of Atlanta.

Hunger finally drove her back inside. She walked down the garden with that faintly drugged feeling that came from living vividly inside another person's life. The back door was open, of course. Her father had locked the front of the pub but nobody ever even thought of locking their back doors. As she went into the kitchen she glanced at the clock on the mantelpiece. Six o'clock! Opening time, and her father wasn't back. She put the kettle on, made a cheese sandwich and wandered into the serving area behind the bar, munching. Should she open up? She checked the till—yes, there was enough change. She ran an eye over the stock—yes, there was more than enough for the poor trade they were doing at the moment. But open up on her own—? In the kitchen, the kettle was boiling. Just as she was pouring the water into the teapot, her father walked in at the back door.

'Scarlett! There's my lovely girl, and the tea made too. What a little treasure she is.'

Scarlett regarded him. He was looking more cheerful than he had done ever since Joan had died. Almost elated. Despite everything she had learnt that day, hope surged inside her. Perhaps everything was going to be all right after all.

'Where've you been?' she demanded.

'Southend.' He spread his hands in an expansive gesture. 'No need to worry any more, my pet. I've solved all our problems.'

'You have?'

'I have. I've got a job at one of those big places along the Golden Mile. The Trafalgar. And, what's more, there's accommodation to go with it. We've got a home and money. We're going to be all right.'

Scarlett didn't know what she felt—relief, anger, disappointment—it was all of these. On the face of it, her father had done just as he claimed. He had solved all their problems.

'But we've still got to leave here,' she said at last. 'We've got to leave the Red Lion.'

Victor's whole body seemed to deflate. 'Yes,' he admitted. 'Well, there's nothing I can do about that.'

Someone was thumping on the front door.

'Anyone at home? There's thirsty people out here.'

Victor ignored it. 'Look, I don't like it any more than you do, leaving all this—' He waved his hand to take in the kitchen, the bars, the rooms upstairs. 'I love it too, darling. Best years of my life have been spent here. But at least we got somewhere to go. That's got to be good, now, hasn't it, pet?'

Scarlett just shook her head. Up till now, some irrational part of her had held on to the hope that something might come up, that they might be allowed to stay. Now she knew it was really true. They were leaving.

'If you say so,' she said. 'Don't you think you'd better open up?'

Defeated, Victor went to unlock the door, leaving Scarlett to brood on their change of fortunes and all that it meant. It was only later that a faint feeling of guilt crept into her resentment. Her mother would not have reacted like that. Her mother would have congratulated him on his success in finding work and a roof over their heads. Sighing heavily, she made a cheese and pickle sandwich and a cup of tea and took it into the bar as a peace offering. Victor gave her a hug and turned to the little gang of regulars leaning on the bar.

'Ain't she just the best daughter in the world? A man couldn't ask for more.'

Scarlett hugged him back and then turned to pick up the empties. As long as they still had each other, they would be all right.

The next couple of weeks passed all too quickly. Before they knew where they were, Scarlett and Victor found themselves in the delivery van belonging to Jim, one of the regulars, being driven into Southend-on-Sea with all their worldly goods packed into boxes and suitcases in the back. There wasn't a lot. Hardest of all had been deciding what to do with Joan's personal possessions. Neither of them could bear to give away her clothes and of course they wanted to keep her books and ornaments, but it was things like her comb with strands of her hair still in it that had broken their hearts. In the end, they had put everything into boxes and brought it with them.

They drove along the main road towards the town, then turned down a grand avenue with big houses on either side that led eventually to the High Street. In spite of herself, Scarlett began to take an interest. There were lots of shops with shiny big windows and displays of tempting goods. There were throngs of people, many of them obviously visitors in their seaside clothes. And there, at the end of the street was the sea, or rather the Thames estuary, grey-green and glittering in the summer sunshine.

'Oh!' Scarlett said out loud.

Their chauffeur grinned. 'Pretty, ain't it? Nothing like the sea, I always say. You seen the pier before?'

'Of course,' Scarlett said.

She'd been to Southend before, lots of times, and you didn't go to Southend without seeing the pier. But still Jim insisted on acting as her tour guide.

'Royal Hotel on your right here, Royal Stores pub on your left, and there it is, the longest pier in the world. Longer even than anything in America.'

'Lovely,' Scarlett said, as something seemed to be expected of her. And indeed she couldn't help a traitorous lift of interest. The pier was an exciting sight, stretching out before her into the sea with its flags flying and its cream and green trams clanking busily up and down and its promise of fun and food and entertainment at the far end.

'Do you think you're going to like it here?' Victor asked hopefully.

'I don't know,' Scarlett said.

It was all very different from their village. It might be exciting, but it was alien. It wasn't home.

She did not have long to admire the pier. The van plunged down Pier Hill to the sea front, and here they were surrounded by noise and colours and smells. There were ice cream parlours and pubs and amusement arcades and shops selling buckets and spades. There were families and big groups of men all dressed up for a day at the sea. Through the open windows of the van came music and laughter and shouting, dogs barking and children crying, together with wafts of candyfloss, fried onions, cockles and whelks. There was no hint of austerity here. Everything shouted, *It's a new beginning; let your hair down, enjoy yourself!*

They drove along the Golden Mile. Victor was looking eagerly out of the window.

'There it is,' he said. 'The Trafalgar.'

Scarlett followed his pointing finger. Their new home was a big yellow brick Victorian building between two amusement arcades. Two sets of double doors, closed at the moment, let on to the pavement and over the larger of them swung the sign, a painting of Lord Nelson's famous ship, the *Victory*.

'Best go round the back, I suppose,' Victor said.

They drove on past the pub to the corner where the Kursaal stood, with its dome and its dance hall and its famous funfair. Round they went and up a small road that ran behind the sea front buildings. It was quieter here. There were back fences and bins and washing and a general morning-after feel. They stopped by a stack of crates full of empty beer bottles.

'I'll go and see what's happening,' Victor said, and disappeared into the back yard.

He came back with a young woman with a thin, over-made-up face and hair an unlikely shade of auburn.

'This is Irma,' he said.

Irma looked at Scarlett. 'So you're the kid, are you? You're lucky. Missus don't normally like kids living in, but we're short of a cellar man and it's high season, I suppose. Bring your stuff and don't make a noise on the stairs. Missus and the Guv'nor don't like being disturbed when they're having their afternoon nap.'

Scarlett decided then and there that she didn't like Irma and she wasn't going to like her father's employers. Glaring at Irma's back, she picked up her bag of most treasured possessions and, together with Victor, followed her through the yard. It was a concrete area, dark and damp and smelly, totally different from the back garden at the Red Lion. The building towered over them, tall and forbidding. There was broken furniture in a heap on one side and a pile of kegs waiting to be returned on the other. A skinny cat slunk away at their approach.

'The Missus says you're to have the top back,' Irma said, leading the way through the back door and along a dark passage that smelt of damp and stale beer and cats.

After a couple of turns and sets of steps and longer

staircases, Scarlett was bewildered. How big was this place? How was she ever going to find her way around it? Irma stopped outside a door that looked just like the three others on the landing. She handed Victor a pair of keys tied together with a length of hairy string.

'There y'are then. This is yours and that's hers,' nodding at the next door along. 'Guv'nor wants you down at five to show you the ropes, all right?'

'Right, yes, fine. Thanks very much, Irma,' Victor said.

Irma clattered off down the lino-covered landing.

'Well, then,' Victor said. 'Let's see what's what, shall we?'

He unlocked the door and stepped into the room. The faded cotton curtains were drawn and in the dim light they saw a single bed, a dark wardrobe, two dining chairs by a small rickety table and a chest of drawers with a cracked mirror above it. None of the furniture matched and the walls and lino and dirty rug were all in depressing shades of green, brown and beige.

'Well—' Victor said. 'It's got everything we need, I suppose.'

'It's horrible,' Scarlett said.

She stepped over to the window and drew back the sagging curtains. They felt greasy. The view from the dirty window was of the back street they had come in from. She could see Jim there, still waiting by his van. She longed to rush back down and beg him to take her back to the Red Lion.

'Want to see your room, pet?'

Scarlett sighed. 'S'pose so.'

He unlocked the other door. This room was much smaller, hardly more than a boxroom, with just enough space for a single bed, a small wardrobe and a chest of drawers all set in a line along one wall. There was no rug, no wallpaper and the curtains didn't quite meet in the middle. Scarlett hated it.

'Better get our stuff in. Mustn't keep Jim waiting any longer out there.'

Scarlett's whole body felt heavy and listless. How was she going to bear living in this horrible place? Reluctantly, she followed her father down the maze of stairs and corridors to the back door. They unloaded the boxes into the back yard, thanked Jim, and lugged everything upstairs. By the time they had got it all in, Scarlett did at least know the way.

As they unpacked, she began to feel just a bit better. The wireless was placed on the chest of drawers with her parents' wedding photo and one of herself as a baby. Their crockery and cutlery and cooking things were piled on the table. Scarlett made the single bed up rather awkwardly with the sheets and blankets and eiderdown from her parents' double one. Then she turned her attention to her own little room. Her small store of books, her old teddy, her musical box and the pink glass vase she had won at a fair were set out, her hair things and clothes were put away. A photo of her mother on a beach, laughing, went on a nail conveniently situated on the wall above the bed, while her pink and blue flowery eiderdown went on it. It should have made the room seem more like home, but somehow seeing the familiar things in this alien setting only seemed to emphasise just how different it all was.

Her father tapped on the door and put his head round. 'All right, pet? Oh, it looks better already, doesn't it? You're a born homemaker, just like your mum.'

Scarlett said nothing. She was trying hard not to burst into tears or scream with rage, she wasn't sure which.

'We'll get one of those electric kettle things in the morning, so we can brew up,' Victor went on.

It was only then that Scarlett fully realised that something was missing from their new living arrangements. 'Where's the kitchen?' she asked.

Victor looked uncomfortable. 'Well—er—there isn't one. Not as such. But, like I said, we can get a kettle. And maybe one of those toasters. You know.'

'But we can't live on tea and toast!' Scarlett burst out. 'How can we live in a place where you can't cook?'

'Well—no—I'm sure there's some way round it—'

'And the bathroom—where's the bathroom?'

Victor was on firmer ground here. 'Oh, I found that. It's down the first flight of stairs, second door on the left.'

'So it's not ours? We have to share it?'

'Er—well—yes—'

It was all getting worse and worse. Scarlett felt as if she were trapped in a bad dream from which there was no waking.

Victor shifted uneasily. 'Look—er—it's nearly five. I got to go. Mustn't be late for my first shift. Will you be all right here by yourself, pet?'

'Oh, fine, just fine,' Scarlett said with heavy sarcasm.

Her father reached out and patted her shoulder. 'There's my good girl.'

When he was gone, Scarlett went and sat on her bed. The place smelt all wrong. There were mysterious bangings of doors and muffled shouts coming from below. The tiny room seemed to close round her like a prison cell. It was all strange—strange and horrible.

She reached for *Gone with the Wind,* but even that couldn't distract her from the aching loneliness. She clapped the book shut, threw it on the bed and went out, clattering down the gloomy staircases towards the brightness and life outside.

In the downstairs passage she stopped short. Coming in at the back door was a tall fair-haired boy. He was wearing salt-stained khaki shorts, a faded red shirt open at the neck and a pair of old plimsolls. His skin was tanned golden-brown by the sun and he had a rolled-up towel under his arm.

'Hello,' he said. 'You must be the new cellar man's daughter.' He held out his hand. 'I'm Jonathan. I live here.'

Scarlett took his hand. It was warm and strong. 'I'm Scarlett. How do you do?'

His smile broadened into one of delight. 'Scarlett? Really? Like Scarlett O'Hara?'

Scarlett found herself smiling back. 'That's right. My mother named me after her.'

'Well, I do declare!' Jonathan said in a drawling southern states accent. 'Welcome to the Trafalgar, Miz Scarlett.'

Suddenly, life didn't seem quite so dreadful.

CHAPTER FOUR

JONATHAN'S first thought was that he made a very poor Rhett Butler. His first instinct was to keep her talking.

'Where are you off to?' he asked, without thinking. It sounded lame the moment it came out of his mouth.

'Oh—just out,' Scarlett said.

Scarlett—such a wonderful name. And it suited her. There was something wild and vivid about her. When his parents had said something about the new cellar man bringing his daughter with him, he'd not really thought about it. If he had any notion of what she might be like, it was a pasty-faced kid, someone who got in the way. Not a girl like this, with a challenging stare and a mobile mouth and the beginning of a woman's figure showing through her thin cotton dress.

'I'll come with you, if you like. Show you round a bit,' he offered.

'I have been to Southend before, you know,' Scarlett said.

Jonathan felt horribly rejected. He hid it with a nonchalant shrug. 'OK. If you'd rather be on your own—'

To his delight, she looked slightly flustered.

'No…I mean…I just thought you might have something else you wanted to do,' she said.

'Tell you what I do want to do, and that's eat,' Jonathan admitted. 'I've been out all day in the Ray, and I'm starving.'

'The Ray?'

Of course, stupid of him, she wasn't local, she wouldn't know what he was talking about.

'It's a channel of water out in the estuary beyond the mud-flats,' he explained. 'You sail out on the falling tide, then you can spend all day out there sailing and swimming and having races and that, and playing cricket on the Ray Sands. It's brilliant. Do you sail?'

Scarlett shook her head. Her ponytail of dark, almost black hair shivered in glossy waves.

'We lived in the country.'

'Can you swim?'

'Oh, yes. I learnt at school. I got my hundred yards certificate.'

'Then you'll have to come out with us one day. If you want to, that is.'

He found he was holding his breath. How wonderful if she said yes.

'Thanks—yes.'

He felt like punching the air. Fancy taking her out for a whole day on the water! His mind raced, turning over how to bribe his friend to let him have the boat to himself, what time they would have to start, all the things he wanted to show her. But for now he had to keep her attention.

'Are you hungry?'

She appeared to consider.

'Yes. Yes, I am.'

She sounded almost surprised. He ran over the logistics in his head. It was just about the worst time to start cooking now. He came up with an interim plan.

'Let's go and get some chips, then. Irma or Marlene might want the kitchen at the moment, but we can go in when the pub opens and everyone's busy.'

'Marlene?' Scarlett said.

'Yes, she's the other live-in barmaid. Haven't you met her yet?'

'No. Won't your mum be expecting you?' she asked.

Jonathan had to stop himself from giving a derisive laugh. His mother, expecting him? That would be the day.

'Oh, she doesn't know I'm in yet,' he said, which was true. 'You never know quite when you're going to be back when you've been out in the boat. So do you fancy some chips?'

Scarlett nodded.

'Yes, please. I'll just go and get some money.'

Suddenly it seemed very important that she didn't leave.

'Don't worry, I've got some,' Jonathan assured her, jingling some change in his pocket.

'But I—'

'Look, I'll get them this time and you can next, all right?'

She hesitated a moment, then agreed. He couldn't believe how smoothly it was going. In the past when he'd tried to talk to girls, they'd either go all giggly and silly or look at him as if he were some lower form of life. But Scarlett talked to him like…well, not quite like a friend, because there was more to it than that. He didn't know what, couldn't put a name to it, but it was there all the same.

Walking with her along the sea front, Jonathan felt ten feet tall. They could all see him with this pretty girl, all the people he knew. He glowed as the funfair attendants called out to him, the girl behind the ice cream stand waved, the elderly Italian lady winding pink candyfloss round a stick blew him a kiss. When they got to the chip shop, he was greeted like a long lost son by the big motherly woman behind the till whom he always called Aunty Marge, although she wasn't any sort of relation.

'Ah, here's our Jonno! Talk about return of the wanderer. You been avoiding us or something? Look at you, you're fading away. You need a good feed-up, you do. Douggie!' she called to the equally large man sweating over one of the fryers. 'Nice big bag of chips for our Jonno. And stick a pickled egg in while you're about it.'

Jonathan grinned. 'Thanks, Aunty Marge. And my friend Scarlett here'd like some chips as well.'

Scarlett stood up well to being scrutinised.

'Scarlett, eh? And where've you sprung from?'

'My dad's just started work at the Trafalgar.'

'Oh, so you're going to be living down here, are you? Going to be one of us. What do you think of it so far?'

Scarlett shrugged. 'It's all right,' she said.

Jonathan winced inwardly. Aunty Marge was not going to take kindly to such a lukewarm reaction.

'All right? All right? You've come to live in London's playground and that's all you can say for it? Shame on you! You've not been trying hard enough, Jonno. Go and show her all the sights. Give her a ride on the speedway.'

'I'm going to, Aunty Marge,' he assured her.

'Right.' Aunty Marge gave Scarlett one more up-and-down look. 'Pretty girl. Needs more flesh on her bones, though. Better stick an egg in hers as well, Douggie.'

To the annoyance of the queue of hungry customers, Jonathan and Scarlett's bags were handed over ahead of everyone else's. They shook on lots of salt and vinegar, Jonathan paid and they both promised to come back soon.

Outside seemed pleasantly cool after the steaming heat and overwhelming smell of boiling fat in the chip shop. He watched as Scarlett tried a chip. It was so fresh out of the fryer that she could hardly hold it. Crisp on the outside and soft and fluffy on the inside, Aunty Marge's chips practically melted in the mouth.

'Cor, lovely!' Scarlett mumbled, breathing air in to stop her mouth from burning.

'Best chips on the Golden Mile,' Jonathan claimed. 'Come on.'

He led the way across the wide road, past seafood stalls and ice cream kiosks to lean on the rails overlooking the beach. He loved this view, loved it in the winter when it was empty and windswept, and in a different way now in the summer, when it was crowded with day-trippers. Families were packed together on the pebbly sand, the mothers and fathers sitting in deckchairs with their knitting and their newspapers, the children digging sandcastles, paddling and filling pails of water. At the water's edge, a big open sailing boat was waiting for passengers to come aboard for a ride out on the sea. Beyond that, cockle boats bobbed at their moorings and, as a backdrop to it all, marching out into the sea was the pier.

'So where do you come from?' Jonathan asked in between chips.

'A village the other side of Rochford.'

'And what brought you here?'

'My dad needed a job.'

'It's just the two of you, is it?'

'Yes.'

It was obvious that she was uncomfortable, that she didn't want to talk about it. He recalled what his mother had said about the new cellar man. 'Bit of a loser, if you ask me. But what can you do? It's high season and we need someone.' He tried a different tack.

'It was nice, your village?'

'Oh, yes—' Scarlett started to tell him about it, a faraway look on her face. It all sounded pretty ordinary to him. She went on to describe the pub where she had lived, the Red Lion.

'It was such a nice little place.' She sighed, licking her finger and dabbing up the last pieces of crispy potato round the bottom of the bag. 'It had lovely old beams, and lots of horse brasses, and benches against the wall outside. My mum and me kept it all spick and span. And in the summer I always kept a nice jug of wild flowers on the bar. Just to make it look homely, like. And at Christmas we really went to town, holly and ivy and paper chains and everything. It looked really lovely. And people used to cycle out from Rochford, and even from Southend just to have a pint with us. My dad kept the best pint for miles around. Everybody said so.'

'Sounds wonderful,' Jonathan said politely. 'A proper village pub. Very different from the Trafalgar.'

He gazed out to sea, to where huge cargo ships were making their way up the Thames to the London Docks, deliberately avoiding looking at Scarlett as he asked the obvious question.

'So why did you move here?'

'Oh…well…you know…like you said, it's different. A new start.'

She tried to make out it was a good thing, but it didn't quite sound convincing.

'Right,' Jonathan said. He knew just what was going on. He gave her a sympathetic smile. 'Parents, eh? What can you do with them? They say it's all for the best and they've got your best interests at heart and all that sort of rot, but when it comes down to it, they never listen to you.'

Scarlett hesitated, then said, 'Too true.'

In front of them, the beach was beginning to clear. Mums were packing up picnic baskets and cleaning sand off tired children's feet, dads were folding away the deck-chairs and searching for lost buckets and balls. Jonathan glanced at his wrist, realised he wasn't wearing a watch and stretched across to take Scarlett's arm, turned it slightly and looked at the time. The living warmth of her arm beneath his hand sent a hot thrill through him.

'Thanks,' he said, as casually as he could. 'I left mine at home. No good wearing one on the boat, it might get ruined in the water. It's gone half past six; shall we go back and get something proper to eat? The chips made a nice *amuse bouche* but I'm dying for a proper meal.'

He could have kicked himself. It sounded so pretentious.

'*Amuse bouche?*' Scarlett questioned, her forehead creasing in thought. 'Mouth amusement?'

Jonathan laughed with relief. She hadn't thought he was trying to get one over on her.

'Well done. That's more than most people know. It's a French restaurant term. It means a little twiddly tasty bit before the real starter, or in between courses. Something to keep the appetite interested before the next main event.'

'Yes, of course,' Scarlett said airily.

Jonathan screwed up his chip paper and lobbed it into the nearest litter bin.

'Come on, the kitchen'll be all ours now.'

As they made their way back through the raucous crowds and close-packed heat of the Golden Mile, he tried to decide just where to take her. What was she going to think if they stayed in the staff kitchen? It was going to look really unfriendly, as if he thought she wasn't good enough to be invited upstairs. But his mother was so adamant about not letting staff into their private quarters. Not that Scarlett was staff, of course, but that was stretching the point a bit. He tried to assess the odds against his mother coming in and finding them there. It was high season, and it was Friday evening, the second busiest night of the week. She should be run off her feet in the bar all night. But if she was to pop up for something…no, it just wasn't worth the risk.

By the time they arrived at the dark rear of the Trafalgar, Jonathan had made his mind up. He led the way to the staff kitchen, which looked out over the yard.

'I'll just run upstairs and get some stuff,' he said. 'You won't have had time to do any shopping, will you, what with moving and all that?'

'No, well, there wouldn't be much point, would there? We've got nowhere to cook,' Scarlett said.

Jonathan was mystified. 'But this is the staff kitchen. Didn't you know that? You and Irma and Marlene share this.'

'Oh…'

He could practically see light dawning on her expressive face.

'My dad must've forgotten to tell me,' she said.

'Yeah, right,' he agreed. 'Look, make yourself at home. I won't be a mo. Perhaps you could put the kettle on for me?'

'OK.'

Mercifully, she didn't seem put out to be left there. He raced upstairs, unlocked the heavy door marked 'Private' and went into the kitchen. If only he had known he would be cooking for a girl! As it was, he would have to improvise with what was around. He opened the cream-coloured door of the American refrigerator and took out bacon, eggs and cream, then rummaged in the cupboards for pasta, onions, garlic, olive oil and ground coffee. He piled the whole lot into a basket together with the chopping board, his French chef's knife and the percolator. A glorious mix of excitement and nerves churned inside him. Supposing she didn't like his cooking? Supposing she laughed at him? But she couldn't—she mustn't—because that would mean the end of their friendship before it had hardly started.

He galloped downstairs again to find the kettle starting to whistle while Scarlett leaned against the chipped enamel sink staring out at the back yard. There was a horribly bleak expression on her face that cut right through him.

'What's the matter?' he asked, dumping the basket on the table.

Had his mother been in and had a go at her? His heart sank at the thought.

'Oh…nothing…' She straightened up, forcing a smile.

'Only you looked…well…'

'I'm all right. Really. What on earth have you got there?' She moved over to look at the contents of his basket.

'Just a few things to make a meal. Would you like to be my commis chef?' he asked. 'I'll have that boiling water in a big saucepan with salt in, please, and butter and some olive oil in a frying pan.'

'Olive oil?' Scarlett questioned. 'Olive oil's for putting into your ear when you've got earache.'

Jonathan stopped himself from laughing. It wasn't her fault. She didn't know, any more than most people in this country did.

'Mine isn't,' he said, handing her the bottle. 'Mine's for cooking, and making salad dressings.'

Scarlett made a face and looked at the French writing on it. Cautiously, she poured a small pool of oil into a pan. Jonathan got on with skinning and chopping a couple of onions. Scarlett stared at him as he sliced them expertly with a rocking motion, just as he had been taught.

'How did you learn to do that? Did your mum show you?'

Jonathan laughed.

'Mum? No, Mum hates cooking. I've got French relatives. I go to stay with them most summers.'

Wonderful summers with lovely Tante Jeanne-Marie, who tucked him under her wing with all her other chicks and made him feel loved and wanted. Racing around on bikes and swimming in the river with the cousins…

'And they make you do the cooking for them?' Scarlett was saying.

He wrenched himself back from sunny days in Mont Saint Etienne.

'Far from it! I'm allowed to help. My aunt's a wizard cook. Her brother's a chef and owns a restaurant. They're all really keen on food. It's not like here at all. They all sit round the table and discuss what they'd like to eat for the coming week, then they go to the market together and buy the fresh stuff, and they argue while they're going round even if they've agreed beforehand what they want, like, if they've bought some lamb, should they cook it this way or that, and what other things they need to get to go with it, and whether they've got the right stuff in the larder at home. It's really interesting. It makes you think about tastes and flavours and textures and how things go together and complement each other.'

Scarlett was gazing at him in amazement. Jonathan felt hot, and then defensive. Food was important. If she didn't realise it now, then he would prove it to her. He crushed a clove of garlic with the blade of his knife, chopped it into minute pieces and put it in the pan with the onions where they sizzled merrily, giving off a glorious smell.

'What was that?' Scarlett asked.

'Garlic.'

Garlic was what foreigners were supposed to stink of. Well, at least foreigners knew how to eat.

'Are you doing something French now?' Scarlett wanted to know.

'No, this is Italian, because I'm starving and there's

nothing like a big plate of pasta for filling you up,' he explained. 'Pass us the spaghetti, would you?'

'Spaghetti?'

Scarlett looked at the ingredients on the table. She was searching for the stuff that came in a tin, he guessed.

'In the blue packet,' he prompted.

She found the right thing and watched as he opened it up.

'It's like long thin macaroni,' Scarlett said.

'Same family. It's all pasta.'

Jonathan stood it in the pan, gradually pushing it under the boiling water with a wooden spoon as it softened.

'Have you got an Italian aunty as well?'

'No—I learnt this off Mrs Mancini along the road. She's only got girls, so she sort of adopted me. I was a really skinny kid, and she used to sit me in her kitchen and feed me up until I couldn't move.'

There was a time when he'd spent more time with the Mancinis than he had at home. He was always made to feel welcome there.

Jonathan chopped, stirred and tasted. He added bacon lardons, beaten eggs and cream. Finally he drained the spaghetti, mixed it with the sauce, divided it between two plates and put one down in front of Scarlett with a flourish.

'Spaghetti alla carbonara!'

'Wow—' Scarlett looked suitably impressed. 'It smells delicious.'

She picked up her spoon and fork and tried to capture the slippery pasta. Jonathan remembered the first time he had eaten spaghetti, when he was about eight, how Mrs Mancini had stood behind him and guided his hands, her comforting warm body pressing into his back.

'It's a so-and-so to eat, isn't it?' he said. 'There's a knack to it—look—'

He demonstrated. Scarlett copied, with much laughter.

'I did it! I did it!' she cried, as she managed to get the perfect amount of spaghetti twiddled round her fork. She carried it to her mouth, and her eyes closed with pleasure. 'Mmm—gorgeous—'

Jonathan relaxed. She liked it. Everything was well with the world. They ate and they talked, they found they liked the same music, the same films. Jonathan made some proper coffee in the percolator, another new taste for Scarlett, and they began a long argument over whether Rock Hudson was a better actor than Clark Gable. He was just acting out a scene to prove his point when the door opened.

'Jonathan, I thought I could hear your voice. What on earth are you doing in here?'

It was his mother. Jonathan broke off in mid-sentence.

'I was just…' he began.

But she wasn't listening. His mother was staring at Scarlett as if she were an armed robber.

'And just who might you be?' she demanded.

CHAPTER FIVE

THE newcomer was a hard-faced woman of forty or so with grey eyes as cold as pebbles and a helmet of wiry brown hair. She was staring at Scarlett with undisguised hostility. This must be the Missus, whom Irma had said mustn't be disturbed and didn't normally allow children. Scarlett disliked her on sight.

'I'm Scarlett Smith, Victor Smith's daughter,' she said, holding that cold gaze unflinchingly.

'Really?' The eyes swept over her again. 'I thought you were younger than... How old are you?'

'Fourteen.'

As soon as the word was out of her mouth, Scarlett wondered if she should have lied. Supposing her father lost his job because this dreadful woman didn't like girls her age? Two or three hours ago, before she'd met Jonathan, she would have been glad to get out of this place, but now it was different. She had a reason to stay.

The Missus's mouth closed into a straight line of disapproval.

'Hmm. You look older. Well, you're more than old enough to know where you should and shouldn't be round here. No going in the bar area during opening time, or at any other time unless you're specifically told to by me or the Guv'nor, and no going into our flat upstairs, even if Jonathan here invites you. Is that clear?'

'Very.'

Scarlett's original dislike was turning into loathing by the second. She couldn't remember ever having met such an unpleasant woman. She glanced at Jonathan. He was looking acutely embarrassed. She immediately felt overwhelmingly sorry for him. How dreadful to have a mother like that.

'Good.'

The Missus held her eyes for a few moments more, as if she knew of the resentment boiling within her and was enjoying it. Then she turned to look at her son.

'You'd better get upstairs straight away.'

'We haven't washed up yet,' Jonathan said.

'Never mind that. She can do it. I take it that's our food you've been giving her?'

'I was making her feel at home,' Jonathan stated.

'So I can see. Now you've done it, you can go upstairs.'

'Not until I've cleared away.'

Jonathan stood up and started piling the plates and cutlery. Taking his cue, Scarlett picked up the cups and saucers. She was about to take them over to the sink when a hand descended on her shoulder and held her in a grip of iron. It was all Scarlett could do not to cry out.

'You—' the Missus's voice was low and menacing in her ear '—put those down.'

'You're hurting me!'

'Mum!' Jonathan yelled.

'Put. Them. Down.'

Scarlett did so.

'You're not at your own place now, young woman. You're at my place. You can't do what you like—you do what you're told. Understood? You and your father can be out on your ear at any time. Now, go up to your room.'

She was released with a push towards the door. Shocked, Scarlett stumbled round the scarred table. Nobody, not even the scariest of teachers, had ever spoken to her like that in her life. In the doorway she paused and looked back at Jonathan. He was flushed with anger. Scarlett's courage flared. Ignoring his mother, she spoke to Jonathan.

'Thanks ever so much for that supper. It was the best meal I ever tasted.'

His tense face relaxed into a smile.

'My pleasure. I'll see you tomorrow, OK?'

'OK.'

And she made off before his mother could ruin it.

By the time she had run upstairs to her room, she was shaking with fear, anger and a sort of wild triumph. She and Jonathan had not let that witch have the last word. She slammed the door shut behind her and flung herself on the lumpy bed, her heart thumping.

'You cow,' she said out loud. 'You cow.'

And it swept over her how far away from home she was. The life she had known—the Red Lion, her friends in the village—all of that was gone for ever. Much more than that, her mother had gone. While they had stayed on at the Red Lion, it was as if she had just gone away on a visit for a while. Her spirit was in every nook and cranny of the place. Even though Scarlett had seen her dead on the kitchen floor, had been to the funeral and seen her lowered into the earth of the churchyard, still she had felt her mother there, just beyond touching. But this place was different. It was cold and hard. Her mother would never reach her here. Scarlett lay on her face and wept.

She must have gone to sleep at last, because the next thing she knew was her father bending over her. He kissed her cheek, shut the door gently and went out. Scarlett slid once more into a sleep of emotional and physical exhaustion.

When she woke again it was morning. She realised she was fully clothed and lying on top of the covers. Outside, seagulls were crying. It was the first full day of her new life. The Trafalgar was still horrible, the Missus was still a dragon, her old life was still gone for ever, but in daylight it somehow didn't seem quite as bad as it had last night. She lay there for a moment thinking about Jonathan. What a nice person he was, and full of surprises. Had he meant it when he had asked her to go sailing with him? Sometimes when people said things like that, they didn't really expect you to take them up on it, but somehow she thought that when Jonathan said something, he meant it. She desperately hoped so. With Jonathan here, her new life was bearable.

She slid out of bed to get her washing things and go to the bathroom, and noticed a folded piece of paper on the floor. It looked as if it had been pushed under the door. She picked it up, and found to her delight that it was a note from Jonathan.

Dear Scarlett,
Sorry about the way things ended tonight. I hope
you're still speaking to me. If you are, would you
like to go up the pier or something tomorrow? I'll
be in the kitchen at half past nine.
Yours sincerely,
Jonathan

He had written it last night! And he had come over
to her room to deliver it in spite of that cow, his mother.
Scarlett put her thumbs in her ears, waggled her fingers
and stuck out her tongue in the general direction of the
flat at the front of the pub. So much for her, the interfering old witch. She went to get washed.

The bathroom was as repellent as the rest of the staff
accommodation. The lino on the floor was curled and
cracked, the bath and basin had brown stains on them
where the taps dripped, there was green mould growing
in one of the corners and there were notices taped up,
all written in fierce black capitals:

Leave this room as you would wish to find it.
Staff are allowed one bath a week. Do not waste
the toilet paper. No more than three inches of
water allowed in the bath.

Scarlett flushed several lots of paper down the toilet
and washed under a running hot tap.

Once she was dressed, Scarlett thought she had
better see how her father was. She tapped on his door,
got no answer, knocked harder and finally opened it
and put her head round. Victor was still asleep. She was

just about to close the door again when he woke up with a start.

'What? I didn't…oh, Scarlett, it's you, love. Come in. What's the time?'

'Half past eight.'

'Oh—thank God. For a moment I thought…I got to be downstairs by half nine. Mustn't be late, not for my first full day.'

He felt for his packet of cigarettes and lit one up to help him face the morning.

Downstairs by half past nine! Now, there was a novelty. Scarlett had enough tact not to say so out loud, though. Her father looked dreadful still.

'I'll go and make some tea while you go to the bathroom,' she offered.

'Would you, pet? That'd save my life. Oh—but what about milk?'

'I know where to get that,' Scarlett said proudly. Jonathan had pointed out the whereabouts of the corner shop yesterday. 'I'll be back by the time you're dressed.'

As good as her word, she walked into the room with the breakfast tray just as Victor was doing up his shoelaces.

'You're a treasure,' he said.

They sat at the rickety table, Scarlett with a bowl of cereal, Victor with his cup of tea and second cigarette of the day. Washed and shaved, he looked a bit better.

'I looked in on you last night, but you were sound-o,' he said. 'It's some place this, isn't it? Bit different from the dear old Lion.'

'It's horrible,' Scarlett said.

Awkwardly, her father patted her shoulder.

'You'll get used to it. We both will,' he said, though

it sounded as if he was trying to convince himself just as much as Scarlett. 'It's just so big and…well…not exactly cosy, is it? You should see the turnover they have here! The ale I served last night! It was just non-stop from opening to closing. They come down here on the train and the charabancs and all they want is to get pie-eyed as quickly as possible. They was queuing up outside the door at six, and when the Guv'nor opened up it was like a tidal wave coming in. They was three deep at the bar before you could turn round. I never saw anything like it in my life.'

It was no wonder he looked tired. That had been Friday night. Today was Saturday, and likely to be even busier, and here he was up and dressed well before his usual time. Scarlett got up and gave him a hug. After all, they were in this together.

'You'll be all right, Dad.'

'Yeah, well—I got to be, ain't I? But thanks all the same, love.'

Scarlett glanced at the clock that used to stand on the mantelpiece at the Red Lion.

'Twenty-eight minutes past, Dad.'

Victor sighed, took one last drag on his cigarette, stubbed it out and stood up.

'Better go, then. Oh—' He looked at Scarlett with new concern. 'What about you, love? Will you be all right? I don't know how long this is going to take. I might be down there till opening time, and then it'll be well gone two before I get up here again.'

'I'll be all right, Dad,' she assured him. 'Now go on—it's time!'

She hurried him out of the door, stacked the breakfast things and clattered down the stairs. For the first time since her mother died, she had something nice to look forward to.

It didn't last long. The moment she opened the kitchen door, disappointment hit her like a brick. Jonathan was not there. With leaden feet, Scarlett went over to the sink and started washing up. In the time it took to wash the dishes, she had gone through a whole sad scenario in her head. Jonathan had changed his mind and gone off sailing with his friends, he would avoid seeing her in future and his horrible mother was going to make her life hell. Scarlett felt utterly alone.

'Oh, Mum…' she said out loud.

How desperately she wanted to feel those comforting arms around her, to nestle her head against that warm shoulder, to hear that lovely reassuring voice.

'Hello! Sorry I'm a bit late. My m—I had to do some things before I left.'

Jonathan!

Hastily, Scarlett brushed away tears with the back of her hand. But she couldn't quite control the wobble in her voice. 'Hello—'

She turned to face him, trying to smile, and saw his cheerful grin fade to concern.

'What's the matter? Has Irma been foul to you? She can be a right cow at times—'

Scarlett shook her head. 'No—'

'What, then? Has—?'

'It's nothing. I'm all right, really.'

Part of her longed to tell him everything, but it was too soon. She knew that if she talked about her mother, she would start crying and never be able to stop. She could feel it all dammed up inside her, waiting to burst out.

Jonathan came and leaned against the sink.

'You've got to be careful with Irma. She sucks up to my mum all the time, and she'll snitch on you for the tiniest thing. I've seen her get people sacked for stuff she's made a song and dance about when really it's not been that important. So watch out. Leave all this nice and tidy for a start, or she'll get in a right tizz with you.'

Scarlett nodded, not trusting herself to speak yet.

'Look…er…do you fancy going up the pier or something?' Jonathan asked.

Scarlett managed something like a real smile.

'Yes. That'd be nice.'

There was still a great black pit of grief inside her, but a day out with Jonathan was a shaft of light.

'You'd best go and fetch a mac or something, then. It looks like it might rain later.'

Scarlett stacked the clean dishes in an empty cupboard and ran upstairs, running over the contents of her wardrobe in her mind. What to wear? Her only raincoat was the grey one she wore for school. Apart from that and the rest of her school uniform, she had a couple of summer dresses, some shorts and blouses and a smart suit for best that used to be her mother's and had been altered to fit her. When she got to her room she looked out of the window. Jonathan was right, it did look pretty grey out there. The suit was definitely not right for walking up the pier. She already had on a clean cotton dress with a pattern of pink and red flowers, so she added the red cardigan her mother had knitted her.

Reluctantly, she picked up the horrible school mac. At least its pockets would be useful for carrying a handkerchief and some money. On the way down she called in at the bathroom and splashed some cold water on her face. Looking in the mirror, she practised a smile. She stood back and considered the full effect. She tightened the tie belt round her waist. Not bad. Not eighteen inches like her namesake, but it made her figure go in and out in all the right places, and who wanted to wear a corset like those southern belles? With a lighter heart, she went to join Jonathan again.

The sea front was just coming to life as they walked towards the pier. Shutters were being taken down, doors opened, premises cleaned. Just like yesterday evening, people greeted Jonathan as they went along. As they passed the Golden Cod, Aunty Marge's husband, Douggie, was opening up.

'Morning Jonno, and young Scarlett!' he called. 'Off somewhere nice?'

Immediately, Scarlett felt a little less strange. It wasn't yet like the village, where she knew everyone, but at least somebody recognised her.

'Morning! We're going up the pier,' she called back.

'That's the way, go and enjoy yourselves. You're only young once.'

Past the boating lake they went, and the full scale model of *The Golden Hind,* and up the steps to the pier.

'Walk up and train back?' Jonathan suggested.

For the first time since her mother died, the leaden feeling had left Scarlett's limbs. She had her energy back again.

'Good idea!'

They went round the pavilion, paid their entrance money and started up the long wooden walkway.

'Just think, even the Yanks haven't got one longer than this,' Jonathan said.

They marched along, first over mud, then over ever-deepening water. The wind tugged at Scarlett's ponytail and whipped colour into her cheeks, the salt air freshened her face and filled her lungs. She felt alive again.

By the time they were approaching the far end, a rain cloud was looming.

'Come on, run!' Jonathan cried, snatching at her hand.

Together they raced up the walkway, past the train station and into the first amusement arcade, just as the shower arrived. Laughing and panting, they watched the heavy raindrops dimple the water and lash against the windows.

'Made it!' Scarlett said.

Her hand was still tingling from where he had pulled her along.

Jonathan turned away from the window to look at the nearest machine. It was a miniature crane in a glass case surrounded by a sea of small fluffy animals and cheap plastic dolls.

'What would you like?' he asked.

Scarlett had tried to win something from similar things in the past. It was very difficult. Just as you got the end of the grab over the thing you wanted, it either closed too soon or didn't catch hold of the prize properly.

'A kitten,' she said.

Jonathan put his money in the slot, positioned the grab and dropped it over a white kitten with green glass eyes. The ends closed over its head.

'You got it!' Scarlett squealed.

Up went the crane. The kitten wobbled in the feeble grip of the grab.

'Careful, oh, careful!' Scarlett gasped.

She held her breath as the crane end juddered across the case to hover over the exit hole. The kitten was released from its grasp, landed on the lip of the hole, balanced for a second or two and toppled in to appear in the pocket on the outside. Jonathan picked it up and placed it in Scarlett's waiting hands.

'Oh, you're so clever!' Scarlett cried, delighted. She stroked the soft fur with her finger.

'I've had a lot of practice,' Jonathan said modestly.

The rest of the day followed on the same high note. They explored all over the various decks, listened to the band, watched the steamers from London come in, visited the lifeboat and had beans on toast and tea in a café. When the sun came out, they played deck quoits; when it rained, they laughed at their contorted images in the hall of mirrors or wandered round the amusement arcades and put pennies in the laughing policeman and the haunted house and turned little handles at furious speed to beat each other at horse racing.

At the end of the afternoon, they were leaning over the rail on the sun deck watching a steamer come alongside. The sailors threw the ropes, the men on the pier secured them, the gangplanks were run out and the passengers streamed ashore from their day trip to Herne Bay. Idly watching the crowds, one figure caught Scarlett's attention. Her heart seemed to turn over in her chest. That hairstyle, those shoulders, that walk—

'Mum!' she cried out, starting towards the steps that

led down to the lower deck, pushing people out of her way. 'Mum, wait—!'

Then she stopped short. Of course it wasn't her mother. Her mother was—

The whole happy day came crashing down around her. Her mother was dead. She would never see her again, never hear her voice or feel her arms around her. She was gone. Scarlett collapsed onto the step and wept, her grief all the more bitter for having been almost carefree only a few moments ago.

'Scarlett? Scarlett, what's the matter, what is it?'

Scarlett just shook her head and cried all the harder. How could Jonathan understand? The pain of it tore at her.

An arm came round her shoulder.

'What is it? Was that your mother? We can catch up with her, Scarlett. We can find her. It's not too late. Come on, I'll help you.'

'No, no—' Scarlett tried to shake him off. 'It's not…her. She…she died. On C-Coronation day.'

'Oh, Scarlett…' his shocked voice was close to her ear. 'I'm so sorry.'

He didn't tell her to stop crying. Instead she felt his other arm go round her and gently pull her towards him. Helplessly she sobbed on his shoulder while he patted her back and hordes of happy holiday-makers swirled past them.

At last she subsided into sniffs and hiccups. She pulled away from him.

'I'm s-sorry.'

'It's all right.'

'I've spoilt your day.'

She couldn't bring herself to look at him.

'No, you haven't. It's been a super day. Look…er…
p'raps you'd like to go home now?'

Home. Home was the Red Lion. Scarlett shook her
head.

'What, then?'

She didn't know. She couldn't stay here on the pier, not
now, but neither did she want to go back to the Trafalgar.

'I don't know.'

'Come on.'

Jonathan stood up and held out his hand. Scarlett let
him pull her to her feet. Together they made their way
towards the tram station.

CHAPTER SIX

'I ALWAYS thought there was something a bit dodgy about him,' Jonathan's mother said as she sat over her breakfast tea.

'There's always going to be something wrong, ain't there?' his father said. 'Stands to reason. Man his age, if he ain't got a place of his own, there's a reason why.'

He wiped the last of the fried egg from his plate with the last of the fried bread and sat back with a sigh of contentment.

'That was first class, Jonny lad. Done to perfection. You ain't got any more out there, have you?'

'Nope, but there's toast coming up,' Jonathan called from the kitchen.

He came into the living room with the toast rack and placed it on the table in front of his parents. The big main room of the flat had three large windows looking out over the estuary. Morning light flooded in to show off the ornate dining table and chairs, the large new three piece suite, the glass-fronted cabinet filled with china ornaments, and the modern electrical goods. There was a television in pride of place in front of the suite, its purple screen dead now as programmes didn't begin till the evening, a large wireless on the sideboard, tuned to the Light Programme, and a record player on a side table with a huge pile of dance band records stacked beside it.

Jonathan's mother helped herself to toast and spread large dollops of butter and marmalade.

'Well, yes, there was sure to be something,' she said, returning to her original topic of conversation, 'but with this one it's everything. To start with, his timekeeping's useless. I don't think he knows how to tell the time. When you tell him he's late, he gives you that daft vague look of his and says, "Oh, is it that already?" as if he's no idea. I could kill him, I really could.'

Jonathan ate his own toast, a feeling of doom settling uneasily in his stomach. She was talking about Scarlett's dad again. What if they gave him the boot? What if he and Scarlett then moved somewhere the other end of the country? It would be terrible.

'He does know how to keep the beers,' his father said, swigging down his tea. 'I'll give him that. Trouble is, he's too darn fussy. Throws stuff away! I caught him getting rid of nearly a gallon yesterday. Said it wasn't good enough. "It's good enough for our customers," I told him. "They're not here to taste the quality, they're here to get pissed. You mix that in with the next lot and it'll be quite all right. They won't notice anything wrong with it at all." You should of seen his face! You'd've thought I'd asked him to strangle his grandmother.'

'He was famous for his beers when he had his own place. People used to cycle out from Southend just to drink at his pub,' Jonathan said.

Both parents looked at him as if they'd only just realised he was there.

'Who told you that?' his mother asked. 'That girl, what's-her-name?'

'Scarlett,' Jonathan reminded her, regretting having opened his mouth. He knew just what she was going to say next. And she did.

'Blooming stupid name to give a kid.'

Jonathan said nothing. He'd already had this argument with his mother several times.

'And you know what I said about her,' she went on. 'You're not to hang about with her. Staff are staff. They're not for consorting with.'

She glared at his father as she said it. He took a sudden deep interest in the racing pages of the newspaper.

Jonathan felt sick. How could she compare what he felt for Scarlett with his father groping the barmaids? But it was no use even trying to explain. She wouldn't understand.

'You're far too young to be going around with girls, anyway,' his mother said. 'You've got plenty of friends, you should be with them, off sailing or something. Who are you watching the carnival with?'

'The gang,' Jonathan said.

It was true, he was going with his schoolfriends, but Scarlett was coming along as well. It would be the first time she would see the carnival. They planned to walk along to Westcliff and watch from the cliff gardens.

'Well mind you're back by seven. We're going to be chock-a-block here tonight and we'll need you to collect glasses,' his father said.

'Yes, right,' Jonathan agreed.

Really, they only ever wanted to know where he was when they wanted his help or didn't approve of who he was with. Most of the time they couldn't care less. Which was quite useful because ever since that first trip up the pier, he had spent practically every day of the holidays with Scarlett.

'And if you see her—what's-her-name—Scarlett— you can tell her she can earn some pocket money washing up. Flaming Marlene's got the gutache so she'll be no use to us today,' his mother said.

'Right—I'll ask her.'

'You'll tell her. There's five bob in it for her and I expect her to be there by seven, all right?'

'Yeah, yeah.'

Much to his surprise, Scarlett was delighted.

'Oh, good, it'll be nice to earn some money. And if you're bringing the glasses out we'll see something of each other.'

It was a bright summer's day as they wandered along the sea front towards Westcliff. The crowds were already out, milling around Peter Pan's Playground, buying their ice creams and candyfloss and spilling onto the beaches to swim and dig and sit in deckchairs.

'We'll go to the Never-Never Land one evening, if you like,' Jonathan said as they passed the part of the cliff gardens that were filled with models and grottos and were lit up at night with coloured lights. 'It's for kids really, but it's all right.'

'That'd be lovely,' Scarlett said, gazing across the road to where a miniature fairy tale castle stood at the entrance to the attraction.

It gave him such a thrill to be able to show her things

she'd never seen before. Together they had roamed all over town, visiting parks and shops, walking right along the sea front to Thorpe Bay in one direction and Leigh-on-Sea in the other, and testing out the beaches and the swimming in various places. He had taken her out sailing and been proud of how quickly she had taken to handling a boat. Sometimes she was sad and quiet, and nothing he could do would shake her out of her mood, but other times, like today, the real Scarlett would shine through her grief for her mother.

'Oh, I'm so looking forward to this,' she cried, her dark eyes sparkling with excitement. 'I've heard so much about the carnival, and now I'm going to see it.'

'It's the first time for me as well,' Jonathan reminded her. 'I was always over in France in the summer the last few years, and before that, of course, it was wartime.'

'Do you miss not going over there?' Scarlett asked. 'It sounds such fun, being with all your cousins.'

'I was really disappointed when Tante Jeanne-Marie wrote and said I couldn't come because they were all going down with the chicken pox,' Jonathan admitted. 'But now I'm really pleased, because this has turned into the best summer holiday I've ever had.'

'Oh, good,' Scarlett said, sliding her hand into his. 'Because it's the best summer hols I've ever had too. I thought I was going to hate it here, but then I met you.'

Guilt coursed through him as he thought of the news he still hadn't told her. He'd been on the point of it several times. He'd rehearsed it in his head. *Scarlett, you know how I want to be a chef, and the only way to get a proper training is to go to France—?* The longer he

left it, the worse it was going to be—he realised that.
He took a deep breath.

'Tante Jeanne-Marie wrote a couple of days ago,
actually…'

'Did she? Oh, there's Tommy! Hello Tommy, are the
others here yet?'

Never had Jonathan been less pleased to see his
friend. Once again, the moment had slipped away. He
would have to wait till later.

The group met up and walked over the mud flats to
meet the rising tide, had a mud fight and washed it all
off as the water got deeper, then followed the ripples
in till they reached the beach. By the time they had
dried, changed and had their sandwiches, it was time
to go and stake a claim to a space on the cliffs to watch
the carnival.

Huge crowds lined up along the pavement each side of
the esplanade and up in the cliff gardens. It seemed as if
the whole town had turned out to watch the parade, along
with all the thousands of visitors from London. You could
tell the locals because they had their ordinary clothes on,
whereas the day trippers were dressed up to the nines.

'Isn't it exciting?' Scarlett breathed, craning her neck
to see if anything was coming yet. 'Is that a band? Can
you hear music?'

A ripple of anticipation went through the waiting
crowd. Below the chatter could be heard the thump-
thump of drums. People stood up, children danced about.
Soon the music could be made out—a cheerful march—
and then the outrunners appeared, foot collectors in
home-made costumes, shaking their buckets for people
to throw in their pennies. The carnival had arrived.

Everyone had made a special effort for coronation year. Local clubs and businesses had built floats and made costumes, bands had practised all their best numbers, the Southend carnival queen and her court looked as glamorous as film stars. Scarlett and Jonathan saved their loudest cheers for *The Kursaal Flyer,* a life-sized model railway engine like something out of a western, with smoke coming out of its chimney and organ music blaring from its cab.

'Even better than it was before the war,' the family behind Jonathan and Scarlett declared.

Everyone around them agreed. Things were looking up, the war and austerity were behind them. The New Elizabethan age was starting with peace and prosperity in store.

'It was good, wasn't it?' Jonathan said as they wandered homeward hand in hand through the crowds thronging the gardens.

'Marvellous! All those costumes—I'd love to take part. Perhaps we should join one of the clubs, you know, tennis or something. It'd be fun anyway, and we'd have the chance of going in the carnival.'

'Yes…' Jonathan said, guilt once more flooding through him. He'd put it out of his head while they'd been watching the procession, but now it came back with full force. He couldn't deliberately string her along. Now was the moment. 'Look…er…Scarlett, there's something I have to tell you…'

She stopped short in the middle of the path so that the people behind nearly crashed into them.

'What? What is it?'

Her eyes were wide with alarm, her face pale.

Jonathan realised that, just as he was tuned to her every mood, so she had picked up his anxiety from his tone.

People were walking round them, grumbling. Jonathan grabbed Scarlett's arm and steered them off the path, scrambling up the steep slope between some trees till they got to a quieter spot.

'Well?' Scarlett said.

It had all seemed much easier when he'd planned it in his head. Actually saying it was different.

'I…well…I got a letter from Tante Jeanne-Marie the other day…'

'Yes, yes, you said.'

'And…well, you know how her brother's got a restaurant—'

She was already one step ahead of him.

'You're going to go and work there? You're leaving?'

She looked horrified. Worse than that, there was accusation in her eyes. How could he say he cared for her and yet do this?

'Not there—that's just it—'

If it had just been Uncle Michel's restaurant, he would have put it off, just to be with her for longer. But this—this was different.

'You see, Uncle Michel trained in Paris, at L'Ortolan d'Or. It's really famous, one of the top places. And the head chef there, the one he worked under, came to eat at his restaurant last week and afterwards they got talking and Uncle Michel mentioned me and they have a place coming up in the autumn when someone leaves and…well…'

'You want to go,' Scarlett stated, her voice flat.

All the animation had fled from her face. It was as if a light had gone out. Jonathan felt terrible.

'It's only for a trial period to start with, but it's such an amazing opportunity.' He struggled to explain. 'A top Paris restaurant. Any French boy my age who wanted to be a chef would kill to get in there. I'd be the only English boy they've ever taken. I mean, I don't know what Uncle Michel said to convince them. Perhaps he made them feel sorry for me, you know, marooned here amongst all our dire English food and that—'

'Oh, yes, well that's so dreadful, isn't it?' Scarlett flared. 'Poor old you, having to eat English food! So you're going to go to Paris and leave me here in your horrible pub with your horrible mother and father, are you? Well, thank you very much!'

'It's not horrible! How can you say that?' Jonathan responded, automatically coming to the defence of his home and family.

'It is, and they are. Your mother hates me, and I hate her, the evil old bag. She looks at me like I'm dirt under her shoe, and we have to live in those poky rooms and share that disgusting bathroom. It's all right for you— you have your nice flat at the front. Round the back it's damp and mouldy and dark and I'm not supposed to go anywhere except down to the kitchen and then Irma's there breathing down my neck like I'm going to break something or steal her food—I hate it! It's like I've got no right to be there.'

Jonathan stared at her, appalled. He thought he knew her, but he'd had no idea she felt like this about the Trafalgar, or about his mother.

'You've got no right to talk about my mother like that,' he said stiffly, uneasily aware of how his mother talked about Scarlett.

'I have, 'cause it's true!' Scarlett shouted back at him. 'You're getting away, aren't you? You're going to France, but I can't. I've got to stay here, and without you it's going to be unbearable! I hate you, Jonathan Blane! You're so selfish! I thought you liked me, but you don't, do you? All you care about is your beastly career, and being a chef. You don't think about me at all!'

'That's not—' he began, but Scarlett wasn't listening. She turned and set off down the slope, twisting and dodging between the trees.

'Scarlett!' he called, running after her. 'Scarlett, wait! Come back—it's not like that!'

But, if she heard him, she gave no sign. She reached the path, cut through the groups of people still making their way back from the carnival and plunged down the next bit of slope between thick bushes. Jonathan followed, but by the time he emerged from the bushes she had got to the esplanade pavement where the crowds were so thick that they swallowed her up. For a moment he paused on the grass, where the extra height gave him a chance to scan the milling throng of people. He caught sight of her glossy head by the side of two tall men in white shirts and raced down the last bit of the slope to force his way between the people.

'I do care,' he muttered, pushing and elbowing and getting cursed at. 'I do care. I love you.'

It was hopeless. Every other man seemed to be wearing a white shirt. The cheerful ambling crowd shifted and swirled like a kaleidoscope. He was never going to find her in this. It would be best to go back to the Trafalgar. She had to go back there sooner or later, since she was supposed to be washing up at seven o'clock.

Irma was getting her washing in from the yard as he walked through.

'Ooh, had a lovers' tiff, have we?' she mocked. 'Madam's just gone by with a face like thunder.'

'Shut up,' Jonathan growled, hiding the lift of relief.

So Scarlett had come straight back. Now he knew where to find her. He raced upstairs and knocked on her door.

'Scarlett? Scarlett, I'm sorry. Scarlett, are you all right?'

'Go away,' came a muffled voice from inside.

He tried the handle, but the door was locked.

'Scarlett, let me in.'

'Go *away*! I don't want to speak to you ever again!'

Desperately, he shook the handle till it rattled.

'Scarlett, you've got to let me talk to you.'

The door to the neighbouring room opened and Scarlett's father appeared.

'Look…er…if she says she don't want to talk to you, son, I think you'd better push off.'

'Mr Smith, I—' he began, when the next door along opened and Marlene put her head out. Her face was pale and her hair was a mess.

'Will you lot stop making such a bloody row? Some of us ain't feeling well.'

It only needed Irma to come along and the whole story would be reported to his mother. He ignored the two grown-ups and put his head to Scarlett's door, forcing his voice to be low and reasonable.

'I'll speak to you later, Scarlett. We'll work something out.'

There was no reply.

He hung about in the staff kitchen until opening time

to avoid seeing his parents, then spent a miserable hour in the flat, sitting at the window and staring out unseeing across the water. What was he going to do? The dilemma went round and round in his head. The last thing he wanted to do was to hurt Scarlett. The last thing he wanted to do was to leave her. But—but this opportunity was just too good to miss. If he turned it down, it would never come again. The day had started so well, too. They had been so happy, larking around on the beach and watching the carnival. And now this. Scarlett was locked in her room, probably crying, and he was here feeling like a complete monster, trying to find a way through.

He held his head in his hands, digging his fingers into his scalp. This was all so confusing. He'd known roughly where his life was going and suddenly Scarlett had come along and everything had been turned upside down. If this was what they called love, then it wasn't at all like all the songs and stuff. He still hadn't worked it out when seven o'clock rolled round and he had to go downstairs.

Both bars were heaving. Men were three deep trying to get served and every seat and practically all the standing room was taken. The air was already thick with cigarette smoke and the noise was tremendous.

'There you are, son,' his father boomed above the racket. ''Bout time too. Get your arse in gear and clear those tables.'

'You said seven,' Jonathan shouted back at him, and dived through the melée to grab the glasses from the nearest table.

His hands full, he scurried along the dank passage

leading to the toilets and into the small storeroom behind the bar area that had been fitted with a sink and draining board for just such busy times as this. Scarlett was already there, drying a trayful of pint jugs. She stiffened as he came in, but didn't turn round.

'Scarlett,' he began, placing the dirty glasses in the sink, 'please try and see it my way—'

'Why should I?' she retorted. 'You don't see it my way. You don't care that I'm going to be left here all alone.'

'Of course I do. I don't want—'

Scarlett thrust the finished tray at him.

'You'd best take these through. I'm not allowed.'

Jonathan sighed and carted the jugs into the bar.

It was frantic in the serving area. Irma and a temporary barmaid were in the lounge bar, Mr Smith and another temporary in the public bar area and his parents were moving between the two, keeping a watchful eye on the whole pub and serving more than the other four put together.

'Seventeen and eightpence, not tuppence,' he heard his father correct Mr Smith, as he pulled a pint for the round he was serving. His dad was good at that, adding up someone else's round and his own at the same time and getting both of them right. Bar staff found it unnerving, but it made them concentrate harder on being accurate, even when it was as busy as this. Jonathan unloaded the jugs and dived under the flap to collect some more.

The evening rolled on with no slackening of the pace. Jonathan collected glasses, emptied ashtrays and fetched supplies up from the cellar. Every time he took empties in to Scarlett he tried to reason with her, but somehow they never got further than a few sentences.

Either one of the barmaids would come to fetch a clean trayful, or his mother or father would shout for him to come and do something. Once when he came through the passageway he ran into Scarlett's father. He was leaning against the wall swigging from a flat quarter bottle of Scotch. When he saw Jonathan he hastily screwed the top on and thrust it in his pocket.

'I bought it myself,' he said.

'Yes, of course,' Jonathan replied, but a lifetime of listening to his parents discussing the shortcomings of bar staff made him wonder. Maybe Mr Smith had bought the original bottle from an off-licence. They didn't sell them at the pub, after all. But it would be easy enough to refill it from the optics. A squirt here and a squirt there wouldn't be missed in the volume they sold on a busy day but, if his parents did find out, there would be hell to pay. It was yet another thing to worry about.

He took the latest lot of empties through to Scarlett and, as he did so, the sound of angry voices could be heard above the general level of noise in the public bar. Then there was a crash and howls of rage.

'Fight,' Jonathan said, standing in the doorway through to the bar and craning his neck to see.

Unable to resist the drama, Scarlett came to his side, wiping her hands on her apron. Together they watched as Jonathan's father waded in and separated the combatants. Jonathan could feel the warmth of Scarlett's arm against his, could hear the intake of her breath. As his father threw the troublemakers out into the street, he put his arm round Scarlett's shoulders and pulled her away from the doorway so that they couldn't be seen from the bar. He gathered her resisting body to him and spoke into her dark hair.

'I'm sorry, Scarlett. I don't want to leave you, really I don't—'

Her fists were clenched against his chest. 'I couldn't bear it here without you.'

He felt as if he were being physically torn apart. 'I've got to do it, can't you see? It's my whole future. When I'm a trained chef, I shall open my own restaurant. We could run it together, you and me. It'd be terrific.'

'But that's years and years away,' Scarlett protested.

Inspiration struck him.

'You could come and join me, once you've left school. I could find you a job. We could both live in Paris. It'd be wonderful, Scarlett. Just think, both of us in Paris together!'

The stiffness went out of her and she looked up at him, her great dark eyes drowned in tears.

'Do you think we could?'

'Of course.'

Right at that moment he could do anything—anything at all. He could conquer the world. He bent his head and did what he had been longing to do almost from that first day she'd burst into his life. He kissed her sweet lips.

CHAPTER SEVEN

SCARLETT loathed Jonathan's father almost as much as she loathed his mother. He was a big, heavy-set man with a massive balding head and a belligerent manner, very different from her own gentle dad. But worse than that, there was something about the way he looked at her that she hated.

It was Marlene who warned her.

'Don't let the Guv'nor get you in a tight place by yourself. He don't know how to keep his hands to himself. And if the Missus catches him at it, it'll be you what gets it in the neck. I seen it happen lots of times. Me, I make sure there's always someone else around.'

'Right. Thanks,' Scarlett said.

It was yet another thing to worry about, along with her dad's health, starting at her new school and, hanging over it all, Jonathan's departure to Paris in the autumn. Top of the list at the moment was buying her new school uniform.

'But you got a school uniform,' her father said when she raised the subject one morning.

'I've got one for my old school. It's no use for the new one, it's the wrong colour,' Scarlett explained, handing him his cup of tea to drink in bed and locating his matches. Surely he must understand that? 'It's only the white shirts that are the same, and anyway the ones I had last year are too tight.'

It was a pity about the shirts. They were perfectly all right for another year, but they no longer did up over her swelling breasts. What she needed as well was a bra, but she couldn't possibly tell him that. The yearning for her mother came over her yet again. It would have been so nice to go shopping for bras with her mum.

'I need a skirt and a jumper and a tie and a mac and a beastly beret,' she said, blinking back the threatening tears.

'Oh, dear. That's going to add up to a pretty penny, isn't it?'

'But I've got to have them, Dad. I can't go to school without the uniform.'

It was going to be horrible enough starting somewhere where she didn't know anyone at all and everyone else had their own groups of friends. At her last school she had known everyone in her own year and quite a few of the older and younger girls.

Victor felt in the pockets of the trousers he had hung over the bedhead. He produced some grubby notes and a handful of silver.

'See how far that goes, love, and if it ain't enough, I'll see if I can get a sub off the Guv'nor.'

As he handed her the money, she caught a whiff of alcohol on his breath. It wasn't the first time.

'You been drinking, Dad?'

He avoided her eyes. 'No, no. I had one or two last night, that's all. Now, off you go and see what you can buy, there's a good girl.'

'You could come with me,' she said. 'It's your day off today, isn't it?'

Victor rubbed the back of his neck.

'Ah…well…now…I'd like to, love, but I'm really tired, you know? Trekking round the shops, it's hard on the feet. I was thinking of catching up with the shut-eye.'

'That's all you ever do,' Scarlett grumbled.

It was always a terrible job getting him out of bed in the mornings and, when she wasn't out all day herself, she would find him back in bed again between midday and evening opening times. What was more, he always had a Scotch or two then before closing his eyes. She sometimes had to take the bottle out of his limp hand and set it on the table.

Victor gave an apologetic smile. 'Your poor old dad's not as young as he used to be, you know, love. This place— it's a bit different from the dear old Lion. On the go all the time. And it's hard taking orders after being the boss.'

'I suppose,' Scarlett said.

She realised that he was having to work a lot harder. Instead of having her and her mum running round doing all the donkey work, he was having to graft himself. And his hours behind the bar were quite different too. There was no leaning on the bar or sitting on a stool yarning with the regulars, it was non-stop serving. He did look tired. The film star looks that her mother had fallen for had collapsed into a lined and weary face. The carefree air had disappeared. Just looking at him made Scarlett feel anxious, but she didn't know what to do to help him. She fell back on her mother's fix-all remedy.

'Would you like another cuppa?' she offered.

Victor patted her hand.

'That'd be lovely. You're a good girl, Scarlett. Take after your mum. You know—' he paused and sighed, staring up at the flaking grey paint on the ceiling '—I just miss her so much. I don't know what to do without her, and that's a fact.'

'I know,' Scarlett agreed.

Nothing could fill the gap left by her mother, but at least she did have Jonathan. It wasn't the same, but it was wonderful and exciting. Sometimes she felt as if she could spread her arms and fly. She had all that, and her father didn't. No wonder he was tired. She gave up making demands on him and went to get the money she had earned from several washing-up sessions. She had been saving it to get some smart clothes for the winter and a farewell present for Jonathan, but starting school in the wrong colour was unthinkable, so that had to come first.

It was as they were walking back down the High Street with carrier bags full of stiff new clothes that she realised that Jonathan was unusually quiet.

'What's up with you, don't you like shopping?' she asked. After all, it was supposed to be a women's occupation. Other girls had been out with their mothers choosing things.

'No, it's not that. At least—I'm not keen usually but it's different with you. Everything's fun when we do it together.'

Scarlett glowed with pleasure. 'That's just how I feel,' she said.

They squeezed each other's hands and smiled. But she could see that something was still troubling him.

'Come on, spit it out,' she said.

They sat down on a bench at the top of Pier Hill. The last of the summer trippers were flooding down the pier from the steamers, everyone dressed up and cheerful despite the grey day and the threat of rain in the air.

'Look…er…this is a bit difficult,' Jonathan started.

A sinking feeling of doom formed in Scarlett's stomach. Last time he had spoken like this, it had been to tell her that he was going to France.

'Go on.'

'Well…Mum and Dad, they have these downs on people. It doesn't really mean anything, but…well, at the moment they seem to have their knife into your father. They keep going on about his timekeeping and stuff—'

'That is so unfair!' Scarlett flared and, even as she said it, she knew that it was nothing of the kind. She was always having to remind him to go and start work.

'I know, but…well, it's not just that. It's…well, there's been quite a run on the Scotch and Mum marked the optics and someone's been using them out of hours—'

The feeling of doom was making her quite queasy.

'I hope they're not saying my dad's taking it?' she said, fear making her aggressive. It all added up. She hated herself for even thinking it, but he had been drinking Scotch, and there was that business of the old lady's money. 'That's slander, that is. My dad's not a thief!'

'I'm sure he's not. But if you could just…it'd be terrible if he was to get the sack, Scarlett. We wouldn't be able to see half so much of each other.'

'I'll tell him. So that he can be on the lookout for whoever it is. It's probably one of the part-timers,' she said, with far more conviction than she felt.

'Right. Yes, I'm sure it is. I just thought you ought to know,' Jonathan said.

'Well maybe you ought to—' Scarlett retorted, and stopped short.

'Ought to what?'

Ought to know that his dad was no saint. It was on the tip of her tongue. But she had no proof. It was just a feeling.

'Nothing.'

'No, go on. If you want to say something, then say it.'

There was just the same edge of aggression in his voice that she had used. She guessed it was for the same reason. He couldn't be sure of his father either.

'It's nothing. Just something Marlene said, that's all.'

'Marlene's got a big mouth and a chip on her shoulder. You don't want to listen to what she says.'

'Right.'

They both stared at the pier. They'd managed to keep the family loyalties and they'd managed not to row over their parents, but still it put a shadow over the rest of the day, blighting some of the very little time they now had left.

The first few days of September flew by. Scarlett started at her new school and, although it wasn't quite as bad as she had anticipated, still there was a lot to get used to. It helped that Jonathan came to meet her each day and walked home with her.

The illuminations were now switched on all along the sea front. There were strings and networks of coloured lights and all sorts of fantastic set pieces that appeared to move as the bulbs flashed on and off. Fountains spurted, fish jumped and splashed, plants grew, animals trotted, all in arrangements of coloured bulbs. Along the cliff gardens, trees and shrubs glowed blue, red and orange, while the Never-Never Land was a magical place of lights and fairy tale models. The summer season extended into September as trippers came down from London in their thousands to wonder at it all, and stayed on to visit the Kursaal, eat fish and chips and drink in the sea front pubs.

On busy evenings Jonathan and Scarlett were required to help out. Even Jonathan's mother had conceded that Scarlett was quick and efficient, and employing her meant that bar staff could be where they were needed most. For her part, Scarlett enjoyed quite a lot of the job. The actual washing up was dull and tiring, but she was earning some money, Jonathan was in and out of the little room all the time and it was good to be part of a team that was keeping up with the public's insatiable demands. Her father and the barmaids would use a trip to bring glasses out as an excuse for a quick break, and would stay for a few moments to have a joke with her or tell her what was going on in the bars.

On the last Saturday in September, the Trafalgar was crowded once again and Scarlett was up to her elbows in soapy water.

'They're good tippers out there tonight. That's the sixth one that's bought me one for myself,' Marlene said, whipping out her lipstick and powder compact and giving her make-up a quick once-over.

'All right for some. Nobody gives the washer-upper a tip,' Scarlett said.

Marlene squinted at herself in the little mirror,

patted her hair, gave a satisfied nod and snapped the compact shut.

'All in good time, darling. You'll be pulling it in when you're old enough.'

'I'm not going to work in a pub.'

'Ooh, hoity-toity! You think you're better than all this then, do you?'

'No. I just want to do something different.'

'We'll see.'

Marlene looked over her shoulder in a theatrical fashion and lowered her voice. 'Best have a word with your old man, dearie. The Guv'nor don't mind the odd drink or two, but he's had more than that. If he can't keep up because he's pissed, there'll be hell to pay. All right? Don't mind me saying, do you?'

And she made off, leaving Scarlett cursing.

Jonathan came in with his hands full of empties. 'What's up?'

'Oh, just Marlene being Marlene.'

Jonathan put the glasses in the sink and gave her a hug. 'Ignore her.'

'I am.' She closed her eyes and leaned against him, savouring the moment.

One of the part-timers was in next, complaining about the Missus.

'I know, she's a cow,' Scarlett agreed.

Then it was Irma. 'Ain't you got those half-pints finished yet? We're running out.'

'They're over there,' Scarlett told her, nodding at the tray. 'They've been ready ages.'

'Huh. Well, I should think so too,' Irma said, refusing to be put in the wrong.

Next her father nipped in and leaned against the draining board, lighting a cigarette.

'Gawd, my back! I could do with a sit-down.'

Even through the tobacco smoke she could smell alcohol on his breath.

'Best lay off the drink, Dad. People are noticing.'

Victor took a long drag, held it in his lungs and let it out slowly through his nose. 'It's a pub, sweetheart. That's what people do in pubs. They drink. And, besides, I need it to get me through the evening. My back's killing me and my feet aren't much better.'

'But if the Guv'nor—'

'He won't. Now stop nagging, pet. I got enough to worry about without you going on at me.'

'It's just that Marlene said—'

'Marlene's a sour little tart. Now let a man have a fag in peace, for Gawd's sake.'

Through the open door, the Missus's voice could be heard. 'Vic! Get your arse back in here.'

Victor groaned and shifted his weight back onto his feet. 'No peace for the wicked.'

Jonathan came in and out a few times more, and then Scarlett had another visitor.

'Hello, darlin'. Workin' hard? That's what I like to see.'

It was the Guv'nor. Nerves crawled across Scarlett's back. She shrank a little closer to the sink.

'Bit more here for you to do.'

He placed a couple of pint jugs in the water, then ran his hand over her bottom, closing it about one cheek.

'Get off!' Scarlett spat, twisting out of his grasp.

He gave a chuckle deep in his chest.

'Now then, sweetheart. You know you like it really.'

He stepped behind her, pinning her against the draining board with the weight of his body. His hands came round to cover her breasts.

'Very nice,' he approved, fondling.

'*Get off!*' Scarlett shouted. 'Get off or I'll—'

One big hand clamped over her mouth. She could feel him hardening against her back.

'No need to make a fuss, darlin',' his voice said in her ear. 'We wouldn't want anyone getting the wrong idea, would we? Not when we're just having a bit of fun.'

Scarlett jabbed backwards with her elbows, kicked at his shins. It seemed to have no effect on him.

'Ooh, it likes to fight, does it?'

The hand on her breast squeezed tight. Scarlett's cry of pain was stifled in her throat.

'Let's just keep it nice and quiet, shall we? After all, you wouldn't want your dad to get the sack, now would you?'

Scarlett's hand closed round the handle of a pint jug. Without thinking, she picked it up and jabbed it backwards over her head and into the Guv'nor's face. There was a cracking noise.

Everything seemed to happen at once. The Guv'nor gave a roar and slackened his hold on her, Scarlett wriggled free only to find herself grasped by the arm and slapped across the face, making her ears ring. And then the room was full of people shouting. Jonathan was there, and his mother, and her father. The Guv'nor was shouting loudest of all. There was blood running down his face from a jagged cut on his forehead.

'The little cat! She glassed me!'

'He was touching me!' Scarlett screamed.

Her father got to her and put his arms round her. 'It's all right, baby, it's all right—'

'That little tart, I knew she was trouble,' the Missus was saying.

'Don't say that!' Jonathan yelled, and rounded on his father. 'How can you do that? How dare you?'

'And you can shut your trap—'

The Missus took charge of the situation. 'You go upstairs and I'll see to that cut,' she said to her husband. 'You lot can all stop gawping and get back to work and you, Vic—you can collect your cards in the morning, and I want you out by midday, you and that little madam. Is that understood?'

'No!' Jonathan yelled. 'No, you can't do that.'

'I can do whatever I like,' his mother informed him grimly.

Beside her, Scarlett's father was drawing himself up to his full height.

'I'm not letting my daughter stay in this place a minute longer. We're going right now.'

CHAPTER EIGHT

'YOU can't do that!' the Missus stated, standing in the doorway with her hands on her hips, her head thrust forward.

'You can't stop me,' Victor told her.

For the first time since that dreadful day when her mother had died, Scarlett saw the old Dad back, the man who could make decisions rather than just be pushed along by events.

There was uproar again, with Jonathan begging them not to go, the Guv'nor telling them to sling their hook, the Missus telling them that if they did they weren't getting any wages.

'I'm not letting my daughter stay in this place a moment longer,' Victor said. 'You can stick your wages where the sun don't shine. My little girl's safety comes first. Come on, Scarlett, we're leaving.'

With his arm still around her, he brushed past the Missus and headed for the stairs. Behind them Scarlett could hear Jonathan arguing with his mother, and soon after his footsteps on the stairs behind them.

'Stop—Scarlett—Mr Smith—you mustn't do this—'

'Jonathan—'

Scarlett twisted out of her father's hold and flung her arms round him as he caught up with them. They clung to each other.

'Oh, Scarlett, I'm so sorry, so sorry—'

Still shaking with shock and anger, she sobbed on his shoulder. 'I don't want to leave you.'

It had all happened so quickly, it was hard to take it in. All she knew was that she and Jonathan must part.

'I don't want you to go. We must be able to do something.'

They stumbled up the last steps and onto the landing. Her father was already unlocking his door.

'Mr Smith, please—you don't have to go right this minute—' Jonathan tried to reason.

Victor opened the door and paused on the threshold.

'I'm sorry, son. I've no argument with you, but we simply can't stay, and that's all there is to it.'

'If you'd just let everyone cool down—'

'They can cool down as much as they like. They can beg me to stay, but it won't make any difference.'

'Dad, please—' Scarlett begged.

Her father looked at her, his eyes full of sorrow. 'Scarlett, love, do you really want to stay where that man could do that to you again?'

Scarlett felt as if she were being ripped apart inside. Her body crawled with dread and loathing when she thought about what had happened, what might have happened if she had not gone on the offensive. She never wanted to see the Guv'nor or the Missus again, but neither did she want to part from Jonathan.

'No—' she whispered.

'But you can't just go—' Jonathan cried.

Her father unlocked her door.

'Get a bag, love. You know, stuff for tonight.'

Hardly knowing what she was doing, Scarlett picked up a few random objects and put them into a shopping bag. Her legs and arms didn't feel as if they belonged to her. It was like swimming through mud. Before she knew what was happening, she was at the back door. She could hear Jonathan's mother yelling at him to come back at once.

'Go on, son,' Victor said.

'I'm coming with you, at least until you find somewhere,' Jonathan insisted. 'I can't let you just disappear.'

It was cold outside in the September evening. Once out on the dark back street, Victor's resolve seemed to crumble a little.

'I suppose we'd better look for a guest house,' he said, gazing vaguely down the street as if one would instantly appear before him.

'There's loads just round the corner,' Jonathan said. 'One of them'll have a vacancy.'

It was easier said than done. The streets of small houses leading back from the sea front were full of places advertising rooms, but nearly all had *No Vacancies* signs up. The landladies of the first two they tried simply took one look at the bedraggled little group on the step and shut the door in their faces. The next only had a double room. The one after told them that they only took respectable couples.

'Flaming cheek,' Victor growled. 'What do they think we are?'

They finally found two rooms in a corner property that smelt strongly of damp and disinfectant.

'Not you,' the landlady said to Jonathan as he tried to come in too. 'I'm not having any funny business here.'

They were all of them too weary to argue any more.

'Come back in the morning,' Jonathan called, before the door was shut. 'I love you.'

The landlady snorted and showed them to two chilly rooms on different floors.

''Night, Scarlett, love,' her father said, giving her a brief hug. 'It'll all look better in the morning, you'll see.'

'Right,' Scarlett said, but in her heart she couldn't believe it.

She sat down on the lumpy bed, feeling utterly alone. How had all this happened? How had she come to be practically begging people to give them a bed for the night? How could her mum die and leave them to this? For a long time she just sat, trying to make sense of it all. It was only when she needed to go to the bathroom that she realised she had not brought any washing things with her. Neither had she brought a nightdress. Her shopping bag contained her teddy, her hairbrush, a cardigan, the photo of her mother and *Gone with the Wind*.

She dragged her tired body downstairs to the bathroom, used the toilet, washed her hands under the cold tap and rinsed her mouth out with water. Back in the room again, she felt the menacing quiet closing in on her, emphasized by distant sounds of revelry from the sea front. She took off her shoes and socks and dress and reluctantly got between the sheets of the bed. The events of the evening were still replaying endlessly in her head, making sleep impossible. She propped her mother's picture up against the foot of the bed and hugged the worn old teddy to her, but somehow it failed to comfort the way it had used to when she was little. She picked up the book, the precious gift from her mother, and opened it at the marker. Yankee soldiers were invading Tara. The story wove its spell. Soon her sorrows were submerged in her namesake's travails. She read and read until her eyes closed and *Gone with the Wind* slid unheeded onto her lap.

In the morning they ate the greasy breakfast provided by their landlady, packed up their things again and walked out onto the street. It was ten o'clock on a wet Sunday. Nothing was open. They had nowhere to go.

'Jonathan said to go back to the Trafalgar,' Scarlett said.

'I'm not setting foot in that place,' her father told her.

'But our things! We can't leave them behind!'

Besides, she was desperate to see Jonathan again.

After some wrangling, Scarlett simply took charge and set off for the sea front. Her father waited at the corner while Scarlett went to the back of the pub. At the yard gate, she hesitated. The building that had always seemed grim now looked positively threatening. But the need to be with Jonathan drove her on. She walked across the gloomy yard. The back door flew open. It was him.

'Scarlett! I knew you'd come!'

They raced to hug each other. It was so good to feel his strong arms around her, his slim body close to hers.

'Are you all right?' Jonathan asked, scanning her face.

'I am now.'

'I was so worried about you last night. Listen, I've thought about it and it could be worse. We can spend the day together as usual, can't we, while your dad looks for a new job? Is there anything you want from your room? I can go and get it for you, and then when your dad finds somewhere, we can get a taxi and take all your stuff round. As long as he gets something round here, it'll be all right, we'll still be able to see each other. He is going to stay in Southend, isn't he? He's not going to move away?'

'I don't know. He hasn't said.'

'He mustn't. There are loads of pubs round here. He's sure to get a job in one of them, even if it is the end of the season.'

Scarlett's spirits began to rise again. It was all right. She still had Jonathan and her father would get another job and she would never have to see Jonathan's horrible parents again.

'Of course he will,' she agreed.

She sent Jonathan up to fetch her mac, then the two of them went hand in hand to meet Victor.

It was a strange day. Jonathan did his best to take her mind off things, taking her round to the Mancinis for delicious coffee, Italian biscuits and Mrs Mancini's welcoming warmth, then on to the Gliderdrome to go roller skating. Part of her enjoyed it, storing it all up inside her memory for when Jonathan went away. But always nagging at her was anxiety about her father— was he all right? Had he found a job? And above all was the lost feeling of not having a home, as if she was somehow detached from real life. Where was she going to be that night? She had no idea. So she laughed louder, skated faster, tried to lose herself in the moment.

They met up with her father in a café at the end of the afternoon. Scarlett knew the moment he came through the door that his search had not been successful. The slump of his shoulders said it all. He sat down at the table with them, lit a cigarette and ordered a tea.

'Nothing,' he sighed in answer to Scarlett's questioning look. 'I've been right the way along the sea front. Nothing at all.'

'Oh—' Scarlett said.

She looked out of the window. It was raining again. They had no roof over their heads. She had to go to school in the morning.

'I really don't want to go back to that awful place again,' she said.

'No—' Victor agreed. 'It was pretty grim.'

'It won't be difficult tonight. It's Sunday,' Jonathan pointed out. 'And if we start looking now, you could find somewhere much nicer.'

'Yes, right.'

'I need to get more things from my...from the Trafalgar,' Scarlett said.

'That's no problem. Just tell me and I'll fetch them,' Jonathan offered.

'They're...it's...like...personal stuff,' Scarlett said, blushing.

She couldn't get him to go through her underwear. And then there were her washing things, and her school satchel, and her uniform.

'We'll wait till opening time, then we'll sneak in,' Jonathan decided. 'Why don't we go and find you a decent guest house now?'

Victor rubbed his hands over his face. 'Just wait a bit, will you? Give a bloke a chance to catch his breath.'

He felt in his jacket pocket, produced his quarter bottle of Scotch and tipped a generous slug into his teacup.

'And don't you look at me like that, love,' he warned Scarlett. 'I need it. I've had a bloomin' awful day.'

It was much easier to find a bed for the night, and they managed to get what they needed from their old rooms at the Trafalgar. Mrs Mancini agreed to look after their bags for them the next morning while Scarlett went to school and Victor went job-hunting. It felt like a very long day for Scarlett. She couldn't concentrate on anything and got told off several times, but at last the purgatory was over and she was free to hurry out and join Jonathan. Once again they went to meet Victor at the café, and this time he was there before them. As he saw them, he pulled his face into a semblance of a smile.

'Oh, dear,' Scarlett muttered. She gave him a kiss and sat down beside him at the table. 'Hello, Dad, how did it go?'

'Well, I got a job,' he said.

'Marvellous! I knew you would. Where is it?'

'Place called the Brickmaker's Arms. Back of town.'

'I know,' Jonathan said.

'Is it a nice place? What are the landlord and landlady like?'

Her father shrugged.

'Oh—all right. You know. Not like the Lion, of course, but then nothing will be.'

'No.'

They were both silent, in mourning for their lost life.

'The thing is—' Victor began. He paused, looking down at his hands as they rested on the table, the usual cigarette burning between his fingers. 'The thing is, it's not live-in. I been all over town, asked everyone. The only ones with live-in could only let me have one room.

There was nowhere for you, love. So I had to take this one. It pays a bit more, so we'll get ourselves a little flat.'

'But that'll be lovely! We won't have to share with anyone. We'll have our own front door. Our own kitchen and bathroom,' Scarlett enthused. No more horrible notices on the bathroom walls. No more Marlene leaving her stockings to dry over the bath. No more Irma breathing down your neck to hurry up with the cooking and not make a mess.

'Won't that be wonderful, Jonathan?'

'Top hole,' Jonathan agreed. 'When do you start, Mr Smith?'

'Day after tomorrow.'

Scarlett's first euphoria faded a little. 'We'll still have to stay in a guest house till we find a flat, I suppose. Can we afford it, Dad?'

Victor gave her a weary smile. 'We're going to have to, ain't we, love?'

They went back to the place they had been to the night before and negotiated another couple of nights. Then they smuggled some more of their possessions out of the Trafalgar. Jonathan looked acutely uncomfortable as he helped them carry out the bags.

'Look…er…you're going to have to get the rest of your things out pretty quick, I'm afraid. Mum and Dad are going to want your rooms.'

'I'll look for a flat tomorrow,' Victor said. 'You tell them that, son. They'll have their rooms back.'

It was only when Jonathan had left them and Victor was flopped on the bed as Scarlett hung some of his clothes up, that he told her some more about his efforts at job-hunting.

'I soon saw it was no use asking along the sea front. They'd put the word out.'

'Who? Jonathan's parents?'

'Who else? Got on the telephone, didn't they? Rung up all the other sea front pubs and warned them off me.'

Scarlett stared at him, shocked. It made her feel quite breathless, as if someone were standing on her chest. 'That's just so mean!'

'That's the sort of people they are. Once they got their knife into you, they never take it out. I got to say, love, I know you're very fond of young Jonathan, and he seems like a decent boy, but just watch it, eh? Blood will out.'

'Jonathan's not the littlest bit like them. He doesn't look like them and he doesn't act like them,' Scarlett stated with absolute certainty.

'Yes, well…' Victor said. 'Let's hope this new place is better. Seems all right. New start, eh, Scarlett love?'

'New start,' Scarlett agreed.

Perhaps it was all for the best. She was seeing almost as much of Jonathan and when he went away to France it would be much nicer to be living in a proper flat than at the Trafalgar.

'Won't it be odd, living somewhere that isn't a pub?' she said.

But Victor had already fallen asleep.

For a couple of days, she held onto the dream of an improving future. Victor started at the Brickmaker's Arms and said that he thought that it would be all right when he got used to it. On Thursday morning the local paper came out. Scarlett got up early and bought one so that she and Victor could look at it over breakfast, and put circles round all the furnished flats she thought sounded nice.

'Look at this, *Flat of four rooms,* three pounds, five shillings. Or this one, *Furnished flat, two adults, three pounds including electricity—*'

Victor let her ramble on for a while as he chewed his way through the hearty breakfast their landlady had set before them.

'You'll go and look at them this morning, won't you, Dad?' she insisted.

'Look…er…to be honest, Scarlett love, I'm not sure we can afford any of these. It's a bit of a shock to see how much they're charging for flats these days. It's a while since I looked at rents, what with all those years at the Lion. But I'll see what I can do, all right?'

'Well…yes…I suppose so…' Scarlett said reluctantly. 'I suppose anything's better than bed and breakfast. Just as long as you find us something by this evening. It's horrible not having a home.'

'I know, love, I know. I'll find us something, I promise.'

What he found was two attic rooms at the top of a terraced house that had seen better days. A smell of boiled cabbage met Scarlett as she came in the front door with its cracked stained glass panels. Victor introduced her to their prospective landlady, Mrs Thurlow, a squat figure of indeterminate age in a floral overall and a headscarf tied like a turban, who looked her up and down.

'She looks a clean enough girl. Is she quiet?' she asked Victor.

'Oh, yes, very quiet,' her father answered.

'Only the last people up there annoyed my other tenants with the noise.'

'We won't be any trouble,' Victor assured her.

'You better not be.'

She led them up stairs with brown lino tacked to the treads and brown varnish on the woodwork.

'Bathroom,' she said, indicating a door on the landing with frosted glass in two of its panels, and took them up a further, narrower set of stairs to the top of the house. She opened another door, varnished brown like all the rest. 'There you are.'

Scarlett stepped inside. She found herself in a living room with a sloping ceiling and a little window set into the gable end. There was greenish lino and a rag rug on the floor, a put-u-up sofa and fireside chair by the small gas fire, a drop-leaf table and two dining chairs.

'Kitchenette,' Mrs Thurlow said, indicating an alcove by the chimney-breast.

It consisted of two low cupboards side by side. Their tops were covered with checked oilcloth and on them were a double gas burner and an enamel bowl.

'Where's the tap?' Scarlett asked.

'You get water from the bathroom.' Mrs Thurlow opened one of the cupboard doors and revealed a galvanised bucket. 'Put your waste in here and take it back down to the bathroom.'

Before Scarlett could comment, she marched across the room and opened another door.

'Bedroom.'

Scarlett looked in. It was much smaller, with a skylight window, a double bed pushed against the wall, a bedside table and a single wardrobe.

'This can be yours, Scarlett, love,' Victor said. 'I'll have the put-u-up.' He put a hand on her shoulder and whispered in her ear. 'It'll do us for now.'

Scarlett looked at her watch, a souvenir from the golden

past. She remembered the day her dad had given it to her, the day the eleven plus results had come out. They'd all been so excited in the days leading up to it, herself and her classmates at junior school. There had been a lot of boasting about what would happen if they passed the all-important exam to get to the grammar school.

'I'm getting a bike, a blue one with twenty-four inch wheels,' one of the girls had claimed.

'I'm getting a real gold watch,' her best friend had said. 'I've already seen it in the window of the jewellers in Southend.'

'I'm getting a watch too,' Scarlett had said. 'My dad promised.'

But when the results had arrived, she'd found that she had not got a grammar school place. She wasn't the only one. Out of the forty-two children in her class, only eight had passed, but one of those eight was her best friend. She'd paraded round the playground glowing with success, already wearing the gold watch. Scarlett had been sick with disappointment and envy. But when she'd got back home that afternoon, her dad had been waiting for her in their living room at the back of the Red Lion.

'I got something here for you, love,' he'd said, handing her a slim parcel wrapped up in brown paper.

Scarlett remembered how she had brightened up a little and immediately started to tear off the paper. Her parents had watched her, smiling. There inside was a small box, and inside that a pretty lady's watch with a red leather strap. Delight had welled up inside her.

'But I didn't pass,' she'd said.

Her dad had wrapped her in his strong arms, hugging

her tight. 'It don't matter. You tried your hardest and that's what counts. And anyway, you'll always be number one with your old dad.'

And she had realised that he was right. It didn't matter so much after all about the grammar school, not so long as she had someone who believed in her.

Now she rubbed her finger lovingly over the glass. It was already nearly five o'clock. Her dad had to go to work at six. It was take this place or face another night at the guest house.

'Yes,' she agreed. 'It'll do us for now.'

When they went back to the Trafalgar the next day for the rest of their things, they found them thrown in a heap in the back yard in the rain.

CHAPTER NINE

'COME on, lad, get that veg on those plates.'

'Coming up, chef.'

Jonathan gritted his teeth and placed the watery boiled potatoes beside the overcooked lamb chops lying in their pools of floury gravy. He added cabbage that had been boiled to death and tired-looking carrots, then hit the button that rang a bell to summon the waiters.

'Table six,' he said to the elderly man who eventually arrived.

'They'll want more gravy than that,' the waiter said.

Jonathan wasn't surprised. The gravy would help disguise the tastelessness of the vegetables. He poured some more on from the big pot that was used for all the dishes, regardless of what kind of meat it was going on, then wiped the rim of the plate carefully as he had been taught by his Uncle Michel. The waiter sighed in an exaggerated manner as he did this, and behind him the chef snorted with impatience.

'Stop farting around, lad, and get the next lot out. I've got plates piling up here.'

'Right, chef.'

He turned his attention to a beautiful Dover sole that had been grilled into submission, and gave it a dollop of grey cauliflower cheese.

This place confirmed all his prejudices about English cooking. And this was supposed to be one of the best restaurants in town. He gave the mashed potato another beating to get it to a lump-free fluffiness. That at least the chef approved of. He had tried cooking the other vegetables so that they were not reduced to mush, but had been told that people didn't like them half raw. When he had suggested serving fish with anything other than the standard stodgy parsley sauce, he had been told that people didn't like foreign muck. Likewise when he had asked why the chef never put wine or fresh herbs in his cooking. Sensing Jonathan's disapproval, the chef took every opportunity to put him in his place.

'You're here as the apprentice, not the bleeding sous chef. I'm only letting you do the veg because I'm short-handed. Now get on with chopping them bleeding onions!'

If he'd only been in a kitchen like this, he would never have even thought about becoming a chef. Nobody here had any love of food. Everything was put into either fat or water, ruined, smothered in gravy or parsley sauce and dumped on a plate. His Uncle Michel would weep to see the good quality ingredients coming in at the back door and the horrible travesties going out to front-of-house. It made him even more certain that he had to take up the place at L'Ortolan d'Or.

'You—Mr bleeding Know-it-all! Two Windsor soups. Get your finger out!'

'Chef!'

Jonathan got the plates from the warmer and ladled

the brown soup from the huge pan on the stove. It smelt like school dinners. Soon, soon, he would be away from all this. Soon he would be working in a proper kitchen with people who had dedicated themselves to good food.

He tried to explain how he felt to Scarlett. They were sitting on the put-u-up in the living room of her flat.

'Thank goodness I'm only working there lunch times. It would drive me mad to have to do the evening shift as well,' he said.

'It'd drive me mad being here all alone every evening,' Scarlett said.

They were both silent for a moment or two, remembering that in just a week she would be here all alone. Jonathan put an arm round her and gathered her up to him. Scarlett leaned her head on his shoulder. He kissed the top of her head, feeling the spring of her glossy hair beneath his lips, smelling its sweet warmth.

'You know I don't want to leave you,' he said.

'Yes, yes. So you've said before.'

'It's just that…it's like getting a place at the Slade School of Art. Or the Paris Conservatoire. They're artists at L'Ortolan d'Or.'

'I know. I'm glad for you. Really I am. But I still don't want you to go.'

He put his other arm round her and held her close.

'I'm going to miss you terribly.'

Sometimes he didn't know how he was going to bear it. It felt as if he was about to tear a piece out of himself.

'Me too.'

He hoped she wouldn't cry. He hated it when she cried. It made him feel like a monster. It was bad enough just looking round the cheerless room and knowing he

was leaving her here in this place. She had tried her best
to make it homelike. She had cleaned it all up and hung
pictures on the walls and put a pretty cloth on the table,
but nothing could disguise the ugliness of the furniture
and the smell of old cigarettes. He worried about how
cold it was going to be in the winter. Already it was
chilly. Scarlett's father hadn't left money for the gas
meter, so they were both wearing thick jumpers to keep
warm. And this was only early October. What was it
going to be like by Christmas?

'Did your dad say anything about moving to somewhere better?'

'Not yet. He's got to pay back the sub he got off his
boss when he started. Then we'll start looking.'

'Yes, right,' he said.

She caught the scepticism in his voice and flared up.

'We will, you'll see! This is just temporary.'

'Of course it is,' he agreed, and this time she
seemed mollified.

When he thought of the big comfortable flat above
the Trafalgar with its warm fires and its new furniture
and all its modern electrical stuff, he felt guilty. Why
should Scarlett have to put up with this dump? It wasn't
fair. When he thought about the reason why she was
now living here, he felt even worse. He still wasn't
speaking to his father. There had been a monumental
row between his parents at the end of the evening when
Scarlett and her father had walked out. His mother had
kept up a pretence of loyalty in front of the staff, but
once they had been behind the door of the flat, all hell
had been let loose. Insults had been screamed, cups
thrown, ultimatums given out. But, at the end of it,

because the Smiths had gone and left the rest of them in the middle of a very busy Saturday evening, somehow it had all become their fault. The reason they had left had become blurred. What had remained was their disloyalty. Loathing them had brought his parents back to an uneasy unity.

'You'll tell me when you do, won't you?' he asked. 'You will write to me? I'll write to you as soon as I get there, and tell you all about it.'

'Send me a picture of the Eiffel Tower.'

'I will, I promise. And you'll write to me?'

'Of course. I said I would, didn't I?'

'Promise me.'

'I promise.'

'That's all right, then.'

Except that it wasn't all right. A letter would never be as good as holding her like this. Jonathan bent his head to kiss her cheek, and she moved her head so that their lips met. He wanted to do more, to find what her soft body felt like underneath that jumper, but the thought of what his father had tried to do to her held him back. It made everything soiled and dirty. So they kissed and cuddled and talked endlessly about themselves and their hopes and dreams, until it was nearly time for Mr Smith to come home.

'See you tomorrow,' Scarlett said as they reluctantly parted.

'I'll meet you from school,' Jonathan promised.

They had to snatch every moment now. Each one was precious.

The days and then the hours galloped by. Jonathan spent his last evening with Scarlett and went back home to where his suitcases were packed and ready in the hall.

He didn't think he would be able to sleep that night, what with the pain of parting from Scarlett and his excitement and trepidation over what was to come. Tomorrow he would be in Paris. Tomorrow night he would be sleeping at the house of a French family a couple of streets away from the restaurant. The next day he would start work. Was he going to be up to it? What exactly were they expecting him to be able to do? Was his grasp of French going to be good enough when the orders were coming in and the going got tough? It was over a year now since he had last had to use it. Most of all, was Scarlett going to be all right? He hated thinking of her alone each evening in those miserable rooms. If only he could take her with him.

He lay awake worrying for what seemed like hours, only to be surprised when his mother came in to wake him up.

'Come on, Jonny. We don't want to miss the train. I've got the breakfast on.'

This was it. Today was the day. Once up, he found that he was ravenously hungry, and wolfed down the fry-up his mother placed in front of him. Uncharacteristically, she fussed round him.

'Have you packed your washing things?'

'Yes, Mum.'

'You've got your passport in your inside jacket pocket?'

'Yes, Mum.'

'And your tickets and your money? You've got the francs all right?'

'Yes! For heaven's sake, Mum. I did it all last night.'

'I know you said you did, but all you really wanted to do was to get out and see your friends.'

'I had to say goodbye, didn't I?'

He'd been deliberately vague about exactly who he was saying goodbye to.

'And you're sure you know which platform the Paris train goes from at Dunkirk? And what to do when you get to Paris?'

'Yes! I'm not stupid, you know. I can find my own way about.'

'But it's a foreign country. They do things different there.'

Jonathan sighed. Even though her brother had married a Frenchwoman, his mother had never really come to accept that normal life was lived over the Channel. It might just as well be the far side of the moon, inhabited by little green men.

His father came in.

'All ready, son?'

'Yup.'

'Big day, then. Start of your new life.'

'Yup.'

He gulped down the rest of his tea and went out of the room. If his father thought he was going to stage a big reconciliation, he was mistaken. He fiddled around checking the tickets and counting the francs until it was time to go. He wished he was doing the whole journey by himself, but his mother had insisted on going up to London with him and seeing him onto the boat train at Victoria.

His mother came in.

'Jonny, the taxi's here. Are you ready?'

'I've been ready for ages.'

'What are you doing in here, then? Come and say
goodbye to your father. And Jonny—' she lowered her
voice '—say it properly, eh? We've had enough sulking
round here.'

Sulking? Was that what she called it? They were so
unfair, the pair of them.

With difficulty, Jonathan shook his father's hand and
spoke to him in something approaching a polite tone.

'Work hard, son. It's a wonderful opportunity you've
got. Good of Michel to arrange it for you.'

'Yes, I know.'

'And don't forget to have some fun as well. Work
hard and play hard, that's the way to do it. After all, you
know, Paris—'

He gave him a man-to-man type wink.

'Right.'

For one horrible moment, Jonathan thought his father
might be about to make sure he knew the facts of life.

'Got to go, Dad.'

They lugged the suitcases downstairs to the waiting
cab, Jonathan stiff in his new jacket and trousers, his
mother done up in one of her tailored suits with a
matching hat and gloves. Irma and Marlene came out
to wave goodbye. For the length of the short journey to
the station, Jonathan could feel only relief that he had
escaped. Once inside, he stood by the cases as his
mother queued to buy the tickets to London.

'Jonathan—'

He spun round, his heart thumping. It wasn't a dream.
There she was, in her school uniform, her hair neatly
plaited and her beret perched on the back of her head.

'Scarlett!'

They flung their arms round each other.

'You came to see me off. I'm so glad.'

'I couldn't not come.'

'But what about school? You'll be so late.'

'I don't care. This is more important.'

His mother's voice cut through their brief reunion. 'What on earth are *you* doing here?'

'She's come to say goodbye,' Jonathan said. As if it wasn't perfectly obvious.

His mother sniffed her disapproval. 'Well, get it over with, then. We're going onto the platform. The train leaves in five minutes.'

'I've got a platform ticket,' Scarlett said.

'You clever thing! You think of everything.'

Grim-faced, his mother got hold of a porter and marched beside him to make sure he didn't drop the suitcases. Jonathan and Scarlett followed behind, arms round each other. They stood on the platform while his mother banged on the window of the carriage behind them, trying to make Jonathan get on board.

'It's only until Christmas. The time'll fly,' Jonathan said, though he hardly believed it himself.

'It won't. It'll seem like a hundred years.'

'I'll think about you all the time.'

'Will you?'

She looked up at him, her dark eyes swimming with tears. Jonathan felt as if his heart would burst.

All down the platform, doors were being slammed shut.

'I love you, Scarlett.'

Her chin was trembling. 'Do you? Do you really?'

'I'll always love you.'

She swallowed. Her voice was gruff with unshed tears. 'And I'll always love you. Always and for ever.'

At the end of the platform, the guard blew his whistle. Jonathan's mother let down the window in the carriage door and called at him to get in at once. Jonathan ignored her. Her kissed Scarlett's full lips.

The train gave a jolt and began to move.

'Jonathan! Get in *now*!' his mother yelled.

He tore himself away and ran to jump onto the moving train.

'Always and for ever!' he called, pulling the door shut, leaning out of the open window.

Scarlett was running down the platform, waving. She ran right to the end and stood there. Jonathan waved back until she was out of sight, oblivious to his mother's efforts to make him sit down.

He finally collapsed onto the seat. Opposite him, his mother was looking thunderous.

'Well,' she said. 'That was a fine display. Thank God you're going away. A few months in Paris will soon cure you of that little madam.'

Jonathan stared back at her.

'You just don't understand,' he said.

CHAPTER TEN

DEAR Scarlett,
Here I am in Paris. I hope you are all right. It was
awful leaving you at the station like that. If only
you could have come with me.

Except that it wouldn't have worked, Jonathan
realised. He didn't like to think what Madame Dupont,
his landlady, would have said to his turning up with a
girl in tow.

The boat crossing was pretty rough. There were
people being seasick all over the place, but I
enjoyed it. I stood out on deck with spray flying
up from the bow. It was really exciting. It took the
captain three goes to get into the harbour and by
the time we got in the train to Paris had gone, so
we had to wait for the next one. I found my way
to the Duponts' place all right, but of course I
was late and Madame wasn't very pleased.

Two days on, he was beginning to realise that
Madame was never very pleased about anything. But it

hadn't been a very good start. He looked round the stark little room that was to be his foothold in Paris. It had been Madame's son's room before he'd left home. Jonathan wasn't surprised he had gone. It wasn't very comfortable. There was a narrow hard bed, a large gloomy *armoire*, a chest of drawers, also gloomy but not matching, and, on the walls, faded rose paper and a large and rather terrifying picture of the Sacred Heart of Jesus—Madame was very religious.

I was pretty nervous about starting at the restaurant, so I was up miles too early and went for a walk just to make sure I knew the way there. This is a very posh area of Paris, and most of the buildings are very grand, but the Duponts' apartment is sort of round the back in a big block. My room faces inwards into a tiny central bit. I think it's called a light well, but not a lot of light comes into it. But anyway, it is nice and near the restaurant, so I found it all right and got there in good time. It's an amazing place, all red and gold and marble. I can't believe I'm working there.

If only he wasn't working with Leblanc. He didn't mind being put on vegetables again. After all, this was Paris and he wasn't going to be asked to boil them to death. He didn't mind spending all his time prepping. He knew that all that cleaning and chopping was a necessary part of the process. But Leblanc was a bastard.

Jonathan paused again, wondering just what to tell Scarlett. He didn't want to moan to her the moment he arrived, especially after insisting that he had to come.

I've been put with the veg chef, a bloke called Leblanc. I don't think he likes the English very much.

When Leblanc wasn't mocking Jonathan's accent or pretending he didn't understand what he said, he was complaining that the English were stupid, that Jonathan was doing everything wrong and that he had better things to do than explain every little thing to a dumb boy.

But I'll show him. I'll learn quicker than any French apprentice they've had in the kitchen, then he'll have to eat his words. I was getting really fed up with him by the end of service this evening, but the pastry chef came up to me when his back was turned and said not to mind Leblanc and that he was a miserable old devil and the same with everyone. 'But he is the best vegetable chef in Paris. To learn, you have to suffer,' he said. So there you are.

He paused again. It was the quiet time of the day, between lunch and evening service, and he had three hours to himself. He wanted to get this letter finished, find a post office and send it off to Scarlett. He knew she would be waiting for it. But what else to write? He'd never written to a girlfriend before. It was a bit different from writing a thank you letter to his grandparents for a birthday present. He wrote a bit more about the kitchen and the people in it, but then wondered if Scarlett would find that boring. He stared out of the window. There was nothing to see but another window staring blankly back at him. He knew nobody in Paris except the men in the restaurant kitchen, and they were all much older than him. For the first time since his arrival, he felt horribly alone. He gazed at the paper. Did Scarlett feel the same way?

> *I miss you terribly. It's like a big space inside me. I think about you all the time. I wouldn't mind anything, not Leblanc or Madame or not knowing anyone, if only you were here too. Please write back as soon as you can and tell me how you are.*
> *Love,*
> Jonathan XXXXX

He read the letter through, decided it sounded daft but would have to do, and set out to find a post office.

It was raining again. It had been raining all week. There were drips coming through the ceiling in three places. Scarlett emptied the bowls that she had placed under them into the bucket. Soon she would have to go downstairs and empty the bucket. She shivered and went to get a cardigan to put over the jumper, blouse and vest she was already wearing. Luckily, the ceiling in her bedroom was sound so there was no danger of her bed or any of her precious possessions getting wet, but it was very cold in there, even colder than in the other room, so she picked up her small bundle of letters from Jonathan and took them back into the main room. The clothes-horse was in front of the feeble gas fire with a selection of underwear draped over it, steaming gently. Scarlett moved it slightly to one side so that some of the warmth reached her and settled down on the hearthrug to reread the letters.

The last one was a good deal more cheerful than the first two or three. Jonathan had met a boy a year or so older than himself who lived in the apartment below him, and through him had made friends with a little group. Together they roamed over Paris, played football, listened to records and went to the cinema. He was still not getting on with Leblanc, but he was being trusted to make salads and dress them properly.

Scarlett looked at the flickering blue flames of the fire, wondering just what to write back. The flat was far too dismal to write about, her battle with the washing and drying too depressing. She'd not even attempted to lug the sheets downstairs and trample them in the bath this week, as she knew she would never get them dry.

Writing to Jonathan was her biggest solace, even though it did make her miss him even more. She fetched her writing pad and sat cross-legged by the damp socks and pants.

Dearest Jonathan,
I'm glad to hear you've made some friends. It must be nice to have some people your own age to go around with. You're lucky to meet someone so quickly. The girls at school have only just decided that I'm worth talking to. I wasn't sure that I wanted to talk to them after they've been ignoring me all this time, but one of them, Margie, is really quite nice and said she was sorry she

hadn't tried to make friends before. So things are
looking a bit better.

The only trouble was, now she was worried sick
about being invited to anyone's house. How could she
accept when she couldn't possibly invite them back to
this horrible flat? But what excuse could she give for
not accepting? It was all so different from when she had
a proper home. She had always been happy to invite
friends to the room behind the Red Lion. It had been
warm and cheerful and comfortable and her mother
would always have a cake to offer to visitors. Not like
here. She couldn't bear to let anyone see how she lived.

We're practising carols at school for the concert.
I'm in the choir. That makes something to go to
after school every day now, so I don't get in till
nearly five, and just have time to make something
for Dad's tea before he goes off to work.

Sometimes she felt guilty about doing this, but it was
warm and clean and dry at school, whereas it was chilly
and damp at home, and her dad always seemed to be
gloomy. Or, worse still, drunk. It worried her that he
went off to work drunk. How long would it be before
his new boss got fed up with it?

It won't be long now till you're back for
Christmas. I can't wait to see you again.

The restaurant would be closed for the few days
between Christmas and New Year and Jonathan was due

to come home on a flying visit. It was the only thing about Christmas that she was excited about. Otherwise she was dreading the end of term. Holidays meant being at home all the time. Even if she didn't like all the teachers or enjoy all the lessons, at least there was a pattern and a purpose to each day when she was at school. And there were the school dinners. They might not be that tasty, what with the gristly meat and the lumpy custard, but they were proper hot meals. It meant she only had to make beans on toast or a sandwich for tea. All in all she wasn't looking forward to being at home and, as for Christmas Day itself, it threatened to be truly dreadful.

I don't know what we'll be doing then. It used to be so lovely at the Red Lion. We always put up lots of paper chains and stuff and made it look pretty, then on the day we had family time and presents in the morning, then we went in the bar and talked to all the regulars while they had their Christmas drinks, and then we had our dinner in the afternoon.

It was going to be horrible here in the flat. But, most of all, it was going to be horrible without her mother. It wouldn't have mattered where they were if her mother had been here. Scarlett felt the familiar lump forming in her throat, the sense of loss overwhelming her. How were they going to get through the festive season without her? The only thing that made it bearable was the thought of seeing Jonathan again, even if it was only for a couple of days.

*I expect Dad will have to work over midday. I
suppose your family will want you to be with them,
but if you could get away it would be lovely. I
think it's going to be very lonely here.*

The flames on the gas fire began to flicker and fade.
'Damn!' Scarlett said out loud.

The money had run out again. It didn't seem to last
five minutes. Normally when this happened she just
went to bed, but this evening she needed to get the
washing dry, or she would have no clean knickers or
socks for school tomorrow. She looked in the jam jar by
the cooking ring. Only coppers. Why did her father do
that? He took the shillings and left pennies. Pennies
were no use for the meter. She went into her room and
looked in the shoebox at the back of the wardrobe where
she had hidden the money she earned working on
Saturdays at the corner shop. She wasn't supposed to
be working, of course, as she wasn't yet fifteen, but
why should she take any notice of the rules when she
needed the money and Mrs Sefton at the shop needed
the help? And it meant another day out of the flat. Still
feeling disgruntled at having to use her money for heat,
she fed the meter and huddled up by the fire again to
finish her letter to Jonathan.

Dear Scarlett,
 *It's really cold here at the moment. Everyone says
spring is just around the corner, but it doesn't feel
like it. I hope you're all right. Christmas seems so
long ago now, doesn't it?*

Looking back, it seemed as if he had spent most of his brief break in trains or on the cross Channel ferry. But it had been worth it, worth all the travelling and the row with his parents when they learnt that he was rushing off as soon as he got home, worth it all to hold Scarlett in his arms again. The trouble was, it had all been over so quickly. Scarlett and Southend, and even the Trafalgar and his parents, were a different world. Paris and the Ortolan were his reality now.

I've got a new nickname—P'tit Salade. One of our customers said I made the best salad in Paris! I was really pleased when the waiter told me, but of course I get teased something awful over it.

He paused, wondering whether to explain the layers of meaning behind the name. *Petite Salade* was Ortolan slang for mistress. When the kitchen staff asked what customers they had in, the waiters would sometimes give that dismissive puffing of the lips that the French did so well and say, 'Nothing but a bunch of uncles.' 'Uncles' were middle-aged men who came in with their young mistresses. The mistresses, especially if they were not so young, were all watching their weight. They ignored the wonderful menu, with all the exquisite delights it offered, and asked for a little salad.

He decided against it. It was difficult to convey to Scarlett just what the atmosphere was like in the kitchen. He had tried to explain at Christmas, when she'd asked what was so wonderful about preparing vegetables all day. You had to experience it—the pressure when service got really busy, the satisfaction of a difficult job

well done at the end of a long evening, the cursing, the
obscene jokes, the tension between the kitchen and
front-of-house. The head chef, Monsieur Bonnard, was
a perfectionist of the first water. Anything that did not
meet with his approval was thrown in the bin. 'Fit only
for pigs!' he would yell, clouting the unfortunate sous
chef across the ear. His underlings might mutter about
him behind his back, but they accepted the punishment.
Bonnard was a master. He had three Michelin stars. He
was entitled to hurl insults or even knives. They were
proud to be working for him.

*Monsieur Bonnard himself congratulated me over
it. Mind you, he said I wasn't to let it go to my
head. One compliment doesn't make a chef. But
it's a start. Of course, Leblanc wasn't very happy.*

*We had a very important customer come in yes-
terday—General de Gaulle himself! After he had
eaten, he asked if he might thank Monsieur Bonnard
personally. Just think, I have made a* rémoulade *for
the president of France! It is a great honour.*

That was one of the big pluses of working at a pres-
tigious restaurant. They had lots of famous guests. The
stars of French cinema came in, people whom Jonathan
had seen on the silver screen with his friends. A *grande
dame* of the theatre came in regularly with her little
poodle and sat at her own special table with the dog
opposite her on its own chair. Ministers of state decided
new legislation over their five course dinners and bottles
of Petrus. And then there were the Americans. They
were a mixed blessing. The waiters considered them

philistines, on a par with the British, unless they proved themselves otherwise, but they did spend a fabulous amount of money.

The other day a party of Americans came in. They generally don't speak French, but Monsieur Duchamp, the maître d'hôtel, has pretty good English. The trouble was, he was at a funeral, and nobody else front-of-house could understand them. They were getting impatient, so I was called out. I had to put on a jacket and bow-tie double-quick and go and take their order. They spoke with those drawly southern accents, like in Gone with the Wind. *It made me think of you. Anyway, they were so glad to have someone who could understand them that they left me a massive tip. On top of that, the sommelier was really pleased when I persuaded them to have the wine he recommended, which is super because now I'm in his good books and I really want to learn about wine and he's brilliant. What he doesn't know isn't worth knowing. When he found I could ask intelligent questions, he was willing to talk to me.*

The incident of the Americans plus the compliment about the salad had changed the general attitude towards him in the restaurant. He was no longer the stupid English boy, M Bonnard's odd choice, but someone who might actually make himself useful. He was still teased and treated as the bottom of the heap, but he was beginning to prove himself.

The best news of all is that I'm to move to patis-
serie. That means learning all the different
pastries and the dishes you can make from them.
When I next come home I'll make you some
yummy fruit tarts or profiteroles. *You'll love them!*
But not half as much as I love you…

Dear Jonathan,
Thank you so much for the lovely card. It is so
pretty, I have stuck it up on my wall next to the
postcard of the Eiffel Tower and I look at it every
morning and every evening and think of you over
there in Paris. The scarf is beautiful. I wear it all
the time I'm not at school. I think it's the nicest
birthday present I've ever had.

In fact, it was the only birthday present she had that
year. Her father had completely forgotten and she
hadn't told anyone at school because she couldn't invite
them to a party. The card and present from Jonathan had
just about redeemed a day that had almost been as
dreadful as Christmas. Once more she had cried herself
to sleep, longing for her mother and the life they had
used to live.

I could leave school now that I'm fifteen. If I got
a job, we could afford a better flat, but I really
want to stay on till the end of the summer term and
take the exams and get a certificate to show I'm
not stupid.

Scarlett sucked the end of her pen. What she really wanted to do was to stay on the extra year till she was sixteen and take O levels. With O levels she could do anything. She could get an office job up in London and catch the train each morning wearing nylons and high heels. She longed for nylons and high heels.

Some of the girls in her class were planning to leave at the end of term and learn shorthand and typing. Typists, they claimed, earned more than clerks, and if you had good shorthand as well, you could get to be a secretary and have your own desk and telephone.

'And get to marry the boss,' one of them said.

The rest shrieked and giggled, but they all secretly liked the idea. After all, working was only something you did to fill in the time before you got married, and marrying the boss was definitely a step up from the boy next door.

Scarlett quite liked the idea of being a typist, even though she had no idea what it really entailed. But lessons cost money, more money than she could earn at her Saturday job. And it was no use asking her father. It was bad enough getting the rent money out of him each week, plus a bit extra for food.

I'd really like to be an actress or an air hostess. I got a book out of the library about careers for girls, and I'm too young to apply to be an air hostess yet. They like you to have some knowledge of first aid and to be able to speak a foreign language, so I've joined the Red Cross and I'm learning all about bandaging and how to treat people for shock, which is quite interesting, but the woman running it is a right bossy cow. She keeps calling me Crimson instead of Scarlett. Everyone laughs obediently as if it's a huge big joke. I expect it's the same with your Little Salad. Or do they call you something different now you're in the pastry department? As for the foreign language, I did learn a bit of French at my last school but they don't do it at this one. We have to do sewing instead. I hate sewing. Anyway, I thought that when you come home next time you could teach me some French. I'm so longing to see you again. The summer seems such a long way away.

August. It would be August before he could take a break. Nobody important stayed in Paris then, Jonathan told her, so the restaurant closed for the month. Some of the staff got jobs in restaurants or big hotels by the sea, but Jonathan was coming back to Southend. It was like a great beacon ahead of her, lighting the dark times. But it wasn't even Easter yet, and it seemed an interminable wait. She hardly knew how she would get through it.

CHAPTER ELEVEN

'Blooming history.'

Scarlett stared at the pages of the textbook, trying to make sense of it. She really couldn't work up any interest in the Great Reform Act, but she had to get this homework done this evening because they were short of textbooks at school and she had to pass hers on to another girl tomorrow morning.

As she tried to work out what to write down in her exercise book, she heard a banging noise downstairs as the front door was shoved open. She didn't take much notice. There was always someone clattering up and down the stairs, or playing music or thumping on the walls and shouting for some quiet. Then she realised that the heavy footsteps were coming up the last set of stairs to their floor. She glanced at her watch. Eight-thirty. It couldn't be her father, not halfway through the evening. She looked at the door, trying to remember if she had locked it. They were an odd lot in some of the rooms. One or two she definitely did not want in her flat. Then she heard a familiar cough, and the door handle rattled.

'Scarlett? Scarlett, open the door.'

'Dad?'

Her stomach sinking with foreboding, Scarlett went to let him in. Victor lurched through the door, bringing a wave of whisky and beer-flavoured breath with him. He staggered across the room and collapsed onto the put-u-up.

'What's happened? Why are you back here so soon?' Scarlett demanded, though she knew the answer already.

Victor dropped his head into his hands.

'Bastards,' he mumbled. 'Bastards. Don't give a man a chance. Working in a pub and they won't let you have a drink. Bloody ridi—ridic—'swhat a pub's for, drinking.'

Scarlett stared at him, appalled. How could he be so stupid? How did he even manage to get so drunk so early in the evening?

'You've gone and got the sack, haven't you?' she accused.

Victor looked up at her as she stood over him, hands on hips. He seemed startled by her reaction.

'No good working there anyway. Never did like it. Mean lot,' he said.

Anger boiled up inside Scarlett. Things had been bad enough, but they had managed. Now they were a whole lot worse, and all because he wouldn't stop drinking.

'How could you? You know how difficult it was to get that job, and now you've gone and lost it. Of course they sacked you. How can you take money in that state? You don't know what you're doing.'

Victor was gaping at her.

'Now then, girl. 'S only a little drink. Little drink never hurt no one.'

'Little drink! How much have you had? And how much did it cost? We're out of gas money again, and you've been drinking whisky chasers.'

'No—no—only a beer or two—' Victor protested.

Scarlett snorted her disbelief. Not for nothing had she been brought up in a pub. She knew the smell of Scotch. Furious, she used the strongest weapon at her disposal.

'What would Mum have thought of you?'

The moment the words were out of her mouth, she knew she should not have said them. Victor seemed to crumple before her eyes. He put his elbows on his knees and held his face in his hands. To Scarlett's horror, she saw his shoulders shake.

'I know…I know…I failed her. The most wunnerful, wunnerful woman…'

Harsh sobs were torn from his throat.

Scarlett's anger evaporated, leaving her shaken and frightened. How had this happened? How had her big strong father turned into this broken creature? She put her hand out and stroked his head.

'It's all right, Dad,' she said soothingly, as if talking to a child. 'It's all right. You'll get something else.'

'No, no—'s not all right. Lovely girl like you. I should've done better. Lovely girl. Best daughter in the world—'

It was all too much. Scarlett could only fall back on her mother's failsafe remedy. She went to her secret cache of money and got yet another shilling.

'I'll make some tea,' she said.

Later, after she had left her father snoring on the put-u-up, she took out the letter she was writing to Jonathan. She usually took two or three days over them, stringing out the pleasure of confiding in him. What was she going to say to him about this? Loyalty to her father along with a sense of shame stopped her from writing about what had just happened, however much she wanted to share the bad news with someone. She felt very alone. She put the writing pad away again and got into bed. For a long time she lay awake, turning her next move over and over in her mind. Perhaps it would all turn out all right. Perhaps her father would get another job within a few days and she would be able to stay on at school, at least until the end of the summer term. Perhaps.

It was not to be. Every day when she left for school, Scarlett gave her father a cup of tea and asked when he was going to go and look for another job.

'Today. I'll go later on today,' he promised. 'No use getting anywhere at this time in the morning.'

Which was true enough. When she got in from school, he shook his head and sighed and said he had looked all over and there were no vacancies anywhere. Scarlett sympathised and asked where he had been and suggested looking further afield. Then on Friday, coming home a different way from school, she passed a pub where her father had said he had asked for work. Outside on the pavement was a blackboard with 'Experienced barman wanted' written on it. She marched home. Victor was lying on the put-u-up with a bottle of beer in one hand and a cigarette in the other.

'I thought you said you'd asked at the Grapes,' she said.

Victor looked shifty. 'What? The Grapes? Er…yes, yes, I think so.'

'And they didn't have anything?'

'Er—no.'

'Well they have now. There's a notice outside.'

'Oh. Well, things must have changed, then. That's good. I'll go back and ask again. Good girl. Clever of you to spot that.'

Scarlett gave him a considering look. She didn't like to suspect him. After all, the notice could have been put there only that morning. She went round to the corner shop and bought a packet of peppermints from Mrs Sefton, then made toast and jam for tea.

'I didn't get anything nicer because we've got to have enough to pay the rent tomorrow,' she explained.

She chivvied Victor into combing his hair and polishing his shoes, gave him a clean shirt and a peppermint and shoved him out of the door at ten to six.

'You'll be there for opening,' she told him.

Half an hour later, he was back.

'They wanted someone younger,' he explained.

The next morning, Victor called from the other room as Scarlett was getting ready to go out to her shop job.

'Yes?'

'Er…do you think Mrs Sefton'd let you have a sub from your wages?'

Scarlett knew just what was coming next. Anger warred with resignation within her.

'Why?' she asked.

'Well…er…we haven't got quite enough for the rent.'

'Why's that?' she said, though she knew the answer perfectly well. He wasn't earning, but he'd still spent a full week's beer and fags money.

There was a mumbled er-ing and ah-ing from the other room, and something about the bastards giving him the elbow. Scarlett stared at the wardrobe where her small cache was hidden. That was her money. But the rent had to be paid. Still sharp in her mind was that time when they had walked out of the Trafalgar, and the dreadful feeling of having nowhere to call your own. Even this nasty little flat was better than nothing.

'How much do we need?'

'Er…not a lot…'

Exasperated, Scarlett stumped out to where Victor was sitting up in bed with this second cigarette of the day.

'How much, Dad?'

He fiddled with the blanket, avoiding her hot eyes.

'Ten and six.'

'Ten and six! That's more than a small sub. I don't earn that, Dad. It's only a Saturday job.'

'I know, love, I know. But…oh, well, maybe the old cow will let us owe a bit. Just this once.'

It was a quarter of their week's rent. If they got behind this week, and her dad didn't get a job next week, where would they be? Out on the street.

'I've got a bit saved up,' she admitted.

Relief flooded Victor's face.

'You're an angel! A guardian angel! I'll give it you back as soon as I get paid.'

Before she could stop herself, Scarlett asked, 'And when's that going to be?'

She could see the hurt in his eyes and knew she shouldn't have said it. Her mother would have been horrified to hear her talk like that to her own father.

'As soon as I've paid the old vulture her rent, I'm going out and I won't come back till I find something,' Victor promised.

Scarlett the child wanted so desperately to believe him. Scarlett the young woman had her doubts, and hated herself for it. She bent down and kissed his head.

'That'll be good. Must dash, I promised Mrs Sefton I'd be early today. 'Bye, Dad!'

Her doubts were justified. They had only her Saturday job money to keep them in food and gas all week, so there was nothing for the rent. Their landlady told Victor that they could have one week on tick, but after that they were out.

'There's plenty more want a nice little place like this,' she told him.

Victor agreed with everything she said, and went downstairs to borrow cigarette money from one of the other tenants.

'It'll soon be Easter, and then the seasonal jobs'll start,' he told Scarlett.

Lying awake with her stomach growling with hunger, Scarlett fought against coming to the inevitable conclusion. They couldn't hold out till Easter, not without borrowing so much that they'd never catch up with themselves. And it was no use asking her father to get a factory job. He wouldn't last a week having to get to work at eight. She stared at the ceiling, where the feeble light from the street lamp shone through the threadbare curtains and illuminated the flaking whitewash. All her dreams of becoming an air hostess were just that— dreams. Nor would she be a typist or a clerk in an office. She would have to leave school now and get whatever job paid the most.

'Why don't you try some of the shops in the High Street?' Mrs Sefton suggested when Scarlett explained the situation. 'That's a nice career for a smart young girl like you. You're good in a shop. Anyone'd be glad to have you. I'll give you a reference.'

'Oh, you don't want to do that,' her friend Margie at school said. 'The pay's rubbish. Get a factory job. You go to one of them new places making electrical stuff and do piece work. That's what my sister does. She earns loads. And they got canteens.'

It was the thought of a decent meal that did it. After school that day, Scarlett trekked out to the edge of town where the new factories had gone up, stopped at the first one with a vacancies sign outside, took a test to prove she had nimble enough fingers for the work and got the job.

'Can you start tomorrow?' the woman in Personnel asked her.

'All right,' Scarlett agreed.

And that was it. Walking home, she felt elated. She was a grown-up now. She had a proper job with the proper wage. No more school. No more stupid homework about the Great Reform Act. She was taking her place in the world of work.

'You didn't have to do that, love,' her father said when she told him.

But they both knew that she did have to. That evening they had nothing but bread and margarine for tea, and that had been put on the slate at Mrs Sefton's. They both knew how disappointed her mother would have been that Scarlett had left school, but neither of them said anything more on the subject. It was too painful to pursue.

The next morning Scarlett got up at seven in order to walk out to the factory. The personnel officer gave her a clocking-in card and handed her over to a hard-faced middle-aged woman wearing a navy-blue overall and a headscarf. On her large bosom was a badge declaring that she was Mrs Laver, Forewoman.

'I hope you're neat with your fingers,' she said, looking Scarlett up and down.

'They gave me a test yesterday and I passed it,' Scarlett said.

Mrs Laver snorted her contempt at tests.

'I've had enough of you kids spoiling whole consignments.'

She showed Scarlett where to push her card into the clock to prove that she had come in on time, and place it on a rack under S for Smith. Then she showed her the cloakrooms and handed her a nylon overall several sizes too big.

'Roll the sleeves up. You brought a headscarf? Right. Tie it over your hair. You don't want to go getting it caught in the machines. You used any sort of machine before? No? Why aren't I surprised?'

The factory was huge, with racks of components, power lines and rows of girls at machines stretching off into the distance. What struck Scarlett the most was the noise—the whirring and clattering, the thudding and vibrating of hundreds of small drills and riveters and punches.

'Toilets over there,' Mrs Laver said, waving an arm.

Scarlett looked to where she was pointing and saw brown-painted doors in the high wall at the side of the building, but she wasn't really concentrating. It had just struck her why she disliked this woman so much. She reminded her of Jonathan's mother. It wasn't the way she looked, it was her manner. She could feel herself wanting to disagree with her at every turn.

'Canteen at the end. Get someone to show you at dinner time. Tea break at ten-thirty. Trolley comes round to your bench.'

They were walking down the floor now, and the noise was getting louder as more and more women and girls turned on their machines and got started on the first consignment of the day. All of them were dressed in navy nylon overalls like the one Scarlett had been given, and they would have looked spookily like robots attached to their machines if it were not for the different coloured headscarf each one wore, turning her into an individual.

'I'll put you on something simple to start with. It's piece work here, did they explain that to you?' Mrs Laver shouted above the row.

'Yes.'

She followed the forewoman down a row of women to where a machine lay idle, and sat on the seat in front of it. Mrs Laver showed how to take a small plastic shape from the container to her left, place it on a metal holder on the machine and operate a foot lever that brought a head with six sharp points on it down to punch through the thin membrane over six holes in the plastic shape. She then had to take the shape off the holder and toss it into another container on her right.

'Now, do you think you'll be able to do that?' Mrs Laver asked.

Scarlett couldn't believe she was seriously asking this.

'No, that's far too difficult,' she said, revelling dangerously in the sarcasm.

Mrs Laver glared at her. 'You're not at school now,

my girl. No larking around and cheeking the teachers here. You don't work, you don't get paid. Got it?'

Scarlett nodded. She got it all right. She placed a piece on the holder, brought the six-pointed head down and lifted it up again. Six holes appeared.

'That all right?' she asked, showing it to the forewoman.

Mrs Laver looked closely at it, and seemed disappointed that she couldn't find any fault.

'It'll do, I suppose. Now, get on with it. There's five thousand of them things to be done by the end of the day. If you don't get them done, you don't get your bonus. Got it?'

She knew she ought to say, Yes, Mrs Laver, but just couldn't get the words out.

'Loud and clear,' she answered.

Beside her, she thought she heard smothered giggles from the next girl.

Mrs Laver snorted. 'I'll be back to make sure you're doing them properly,' she warned.

Scarlett couldn't think what could go wrong. She looked at the full container. Five thousand. OK. That shouldn't be too much trouble. She reached for the nearest one and got going.

The girl next to her leaned over and shouted above the noise, 'Wotcha! I'm Brenda.'

'Scarlett.'

'No kidding? Scarlett? Like Scarlett O'Hara?'

'It was my Mum's favourite film.'

Try as she might, Scarlett couldn't quite keep the catch out of her voice. Brenda didn't seem to notice.

'Yeah, that Clark Gable. Bit of all right, eh? Don't know what she saw in Lesley Howard, though. What a drip! You wouldn't catch me mooning over him, not with Clark Gable around.'

'Nor me,' Scarlett agreed.

'You like films?'

'Love them.'

'Me and all. Look—' she glanced behind her dramatically, as if they might be overheard in all the racket going on '—you don't want to cheek Mrs Laver. I know she's a pain in the backside, but if she takes against you she can make your life hell here. To start with, you'll never get any of the decent jobs. Like, you're never going to make anything on that one. It's only one piece, so the rate's rubbish. You keep your nose clean and you'll get to do some of the five-bit pieces. They pay really well. But if she don't like you, she'll come along and say what you've done is no good and your pay'll get docked, see?'

Scarlett saw.

'Thanks, Brenda. You're a pal.'

'Don't mention it.'

Scarlett got on with her consignment, determined to get them done within time. Reach, place, push the lever, lift, throw. Reach, place, push the lever, lift, throw. After an hour, the pile in the left hand bin hardly seemed to have gone down at all. The parts in the right hand bin hardly made one layer. Determined not to be beaten by something so ridiculously simple, she kept going.

By the time the tea trolley came round, her shoulders were beginning to ache. Brenda glanced at what she had done.

'You're never going to get them done by the end of the day at that rate,' she said. 'You having a bun with it?'

'What?'

'With your tea.'

'Oh—no, thanks. I'm not hungry,' Scarlett lied. Her stomach growled at the thought of a big sticky bun, but she couldn't afford any extras, not until she had got her wages and paid off the rent arrears plus what she had had to borrow from Mrs Sefton to get her through this first week.

Both girls stretched their arms and flexed their shoulders as they walked along the row to where the elderly tea lady had stopped with her trolley. The other women and girls were joking amongst themselves and with the tea lady. Brenda joined in. Nobody spoke to Scarlett. Mrs Laver marched by and chivvied them all back to their places. Brenda was still chatting to the girl on her other side. They went into gales of laughter over something. Scarlett felt very alone. This was worse than her first day at the new school. She sipped her thick tea and picked up an unpunched plastic piece. She might as well get on. At least then she would be earning some money.

Brenda stopped shrieking with her neighbour and came and leaned over her shoulder.

'Look, mate, you got to get moving,' she said through a mouthful of Bath bun. Scarlett could smell the delicious sugariness of it.

'But I'm moving as fast as I can,' Scarlett protested.

'Nah—look—you got to be getting the next bit while you're throwing the last one. Move both hands at once, like.'

Scarlett saw what she meant. It cut a quarter of the time off the entire process. She practised it slowly a couple of times, then speeded up.

'That's brilliant!' she said. 'Thanks a lot.'

Brenda shrugged. 'It was Doris what showed me. Her over there—' She indicated a small middle-aged woman in a pink headscarf. 'She's the top earner. She sometimes takes home four pounds fifteen a week.' Her voice was awed.

'Wow,' Scarlett said.

Four pounds fifteen would go a long way. As she attacked the heap of plastic pieces again, she started to plan what she would do with so much money. But after a while her brain seemed to stop working. It was as if the machine had taken over her mind. The same small phrase went round and round her head in time with the simple task she had to perform. All proper thought stopped.

A large hand dipped into her right-hand bin and picked up a piece.

'You're pressing too hard.' Mrs Laver was looming over her.

Scarlett glared up at her. 'What do you mean?'

'You're pressing the foot pedal too hard. The holes are too big. See?' She thrust the piece under Scarlett's nose.

'No, I don't see,' she said. And she couldn't. The holes were already in the piece. She was just clearing the thin bit of plastic that remained over them. How could she be making them bigger?

'Don't make trouble, girl. Do it lighter or I'll have to reject the whole lot. Get it?'

Scarlett dearly wanted to tell her where to put the whole lot, but the thought of four pounds fifteen got in the way. She needed that money.

'Right,' she agreed.

'I hope you have. You're only on trial, you know.'

'Right.'

'Right what?'

'Right, Mrs Laver.'

Scarlett waited till the woman had gone off to annoy someone else, then tried different levels of pressure on the pedal. She looked at the resulting pieces. They all looked the same to her. She went back to doing it the way she had been. They still looked the same.

'Interfering old cow,' she muttered.

Now she had wasted all that time when she could have been whizzing through the consignment. She went into overdrive, trying to catch up. She was so intent on getting the work done that she did not notice machines shutting down round her until Brenda spoke to her.

'Blimey, you're a bit keen, aren't you?'

'What?'

Scarlett looked up. All around her, women and girls were standing up and stretching and gathering up their bags.

'Don't you want your dinner?'

Scarlett looked at her watch. Twelve o'clock.

'You bet.'

'Come on, then. If you don't hurry, we'll have to queue for ages.'

Scarlett followed her to the toilets, where they had to queue first to get into cubicles, then to wash their hands. Then they hurried right through the long building to a double door at the end, passing groups of women chatting to each other as they all headed in the same direction. The double door led into another large space filled with long tables and the smell of cooking. Brenda was right, they did have to queue for ages.

'Smells like school dinners,' Scarlett said.

'Tastes better, though,' Brenda told her. 'Canteen here's really good. That's why I stick it out. It's nicer working at a smaller place, but you don't get the food, and my mum's so tired by the end of the day you're lucky to get tea, let alone dinner.'

Scarlett didn't want to get onto the subject of mothers.

'You worked in lots of places, then?' she asked.

'Three since I left school. Rawlings first. Blimey, that was awful. You think Mrs Laver's a tartar, you should of met the old bat they had there. Then I went to TS Novelties. That was good, but the money was rubbish…'

Brenda could talk for England. Before they reached the head of the queue, Scarlett had learnt about all her jobs and all the people who worked there, her mother and her six younger brothers and sisters and all the places she had lived. A lot of them sounded even worse than Scarlett's flat. At least they didn't have rats, and there was a bathroom, even though they did have to share it with all the other tenants.

They reached the counter and chose from steak and kidney pie or toad-in-the-hole. Scarlett went for the pie. It smelt delicious. Not quite as good as her mother's, of course, but the best thing she'd had on her plate for ages. She added carrots, cabbage and mash and took a Bakewell tart and custard for pudding. All that slaving over the hole-making machine seemed well worth while. She paid out of the money she had borrowed from Mrs Sefton, picked up some cutlery and followed Brenda to a couple of spare seats at one of the long tables.

'We got one of them prefabs now. It's heaven. Of course, it ain't big enough, not for all us lot, but who cares? We got our own kitchen and bathroom and everything. My mum can't get over it.'

'What about your dad?' Scarlett asked through a mouthful of pie. No mention had been made of him.

Brenda shrugged. 'Oh, him. He run off ages ago with this war widow. She's welcome to him. Good riddance, that's what I say. We're better off without him.'

Scarlett stared at her, shocked. 'How can you say a thing like that about your dad?'

Brenda immediately took umbrage. 'What's it to you?'

'You shouldn't talk about him that way.'

Jonathan's parents were pretty awful, but he was never disloyal to them. Her own father… She turned her thoughts away from her own father's failings.

'I can talk about him any way I want,' Brenda blustered. 'And it's none of your business anyhow. Blimey! I look after you and show you what to do and all you do is criticise.'

Part of Scarlett knew she should back down and apologise. She was the new girl round here. She needed friends.

'Family's important,' she insisted. 'Maybe it's different when you've got lots of family. I don't know. I haven't got lots of brothers and sisters like you. There's only me and my dad. We have to look after each other.'

To her humiliation, she found tears standing in her eyes.

'You still ain't—' Brenda began, then caught sight of Scarlett's expression. 'What happened to your mum?' she asked.

'She died of a heart attack. On Coronation Day.'

The tears were threatening to spill over. She brushed her eyes with the back of her hand.

Brenda dropped her knife and fork and put her arms round her. 'You poor thing! That's dreadful. I dunno what I'd do without my mum. And you're only a kid, ain't you? This your first job?'

Scarlett nodded.

'Well, look, if anyone gets at you, you tell me, right? There's some right cows round here. I'll be your big sister.'

'Thank you.'

The afternoon seemed to go on for ever, with only another short tea interval to break the monotony. But Scarlett managed to finish her consignment and start on the next. At five she clocked out with the rest and took the long walk home. She was tired, the job had been boring in the extreme and she had to do it all over again tomorrow, and next week, and all the weeks after. But she was earning money and she had found a friend. It wasn't all bad.

CHAPTER TWELVE

1955

'GOODBYE! Good luck! *Á bientôt!*'

Jonathan leaned out of the window of the Dunkirk train, waving and calling. On the platform, his gang of Parisian friends waved back. Hortense jumped up and down and blew kisses, her small face anxious for a last promise.

'*Au'voir*, Jonathan! Write to me!'

Jonathan avoided her eyes. He liked Hortense. She was fun and pretty and he liked being with her as part of the group, but she was far too clingy. Most of all, she wasn't Scarlett.

The train was pulling away. Hortense sent a last kiss, Jonathan gave a last wave. The end of the platform passed by. He was really off. He sat down, slightly embarrassed, amongst fellow passengers who were already immersed in books and newspapers.

He took a deep breath. So this was it. Goodbye Paris, goodbye Ortolan, hello national service. One important part of his life has finished, the next was about to begin.

And in between there was two weeks of home, his parents, his Southend friends—and Scarlett. He patted his jacket, where he kept a photo of her in his inside pocket, but didn't need to take it out and look at it. Her face was imprinted in his mind and his heart. Scarlett laughing as they ran through the rain, Scarlett crying as they parted, Scarlett poised on a breakwater, about to dive into the water, Scarlett toiling over the dirty glasses. A store of memories that had helped him through his lonely days and stayed with him as he'd fashioned a place for himself at the restaurant and made friends in Paris. Nothing Hortense or any other girl could do would ever erase Scarlett from his heart.

The Paris suburbs were trundling by. The city that he had grown to love was going about its daily business, but he was no longer part of it. He was going to miss it, but there were new adventures to come. He knew something of what to expect. Older brothers of his English friends had made much of the horrors of basic training, of bullying drill sergeants, of forced night marches, but had also enthused about the comradeship and the new skills learnt. 'It'll make a man of you,' was what everyone said. Well, at least he was used to being away from home and getting on with strangers, which put him ahead of most boys of his age.

Monsieur Bonnard had advised him to make the most of his skills.

'I do not know how the English army works,' he'd said. 'All these military types are quite mad, and the bureaucracy treats you as a number. But in the army of France, a young man who had trained at the Ortolan d'Or would always be assigned to the kitchen of the highest officers' mess. The English, of course, they know nothing of good food. They may send you to be a tank-driver.'

Jonathan felt that he would much rather be a tank-driver than serve up mince and lumpy mash in a canteen. But who knew where the army in its wisdom would send him? In the mean time, there was a brief respite at home to look forward to.

When he finally got back to Southend he found that life at the Trafalgar was going on much as usual. The main bar had been painted since Christmas and his parents had yet another new cellar man to complain about, but otherwise nothing much had changed. The sea front was just opening up and getting ready for the new season as he strolled along it the next day. It felt odd to be back. Even though Mrs Mancini and Aunty Marge had both welcomed him with open arms and told him how big and handsome he'd become, still he didn't feel quite part of the place. He wondered if he belonged anywhere now. He wasn't a real Parisian, but neither did he feel quite like a real Southend boy any more.

At half past four he got out his old bike and cycled through the town towards a new industrial estate. He hated to think of Scarlett having to work at soulless factory jobs. In the year or more since she had had to leave school, she and her friend had slaved at three different places, each one more boring than the last. Now they were working for a firm making cheap jewellery. As he powered along the familiar streets, the odd sense of not being part of real life lifted. This was what he had been waiting for. All the rest was just filling in time. Excitement flooded through him, edged with doubt. It was five months since he had last seen Scarlett, and then only during his brief Christmas break. Had she changed in that time? Would she still like him?

He found the right road, and then the right building. Ten to five. He was in good time. He waited by the main gate, his whole body aching in anticipation of holding her again. The first few workers came out, hurrying by in order to be at the head of the queue for the bus. Then a few more emerged, and then a flood of people, mostly women and girls, laughing and chattering. He scanned the faces. He thought he saw her and his heart leapt, only to crash with disappointment. It wasn't her, it wasn't even like her, just someone with similar dark hair. Some of the girls called out to him.

'Hello, handsome!'

'Going my way?'

Jonathan smiled vaguely but didn't reply.

And then there she was, pushing through the crowd, her face shining with delight.

'Jonathan, Jonathan!'

'Scarlett!'

He raced forward to meet her, catching her in his arms as she flung herself at him, holding her tight, rocking her from side to side.

'Oh, Scarlett, it's so good to see you!'

Oblivious to the whistles and catcalls, they kissed long and passionately.

'You don't know how long I've dreamed of doing that,' he told her.

'I do,' she said. ''Cause I have as well.'

Jonathan knew he was home at last. He was complete because he was with her.

Arms round each other's waists, they walked along the road together, a small island of pure happiness amongst the stream of factory workers anxious to get home. There was so much to catch up on, neither of them could talk fast enough. There was all the news they had told each other in letters to go over, and all the small things that hadn't been written, and every so often they had to stop and gaze at each other and kiss and say, 'I can't believe you're really here at last.'

Jonathan couldn't stop looking at her in wonder. She was still the same Scarlett, but she wasn't the young girl in white ankle socks and a ponytail who he had first met nearly two years ago. She was a lovely young woman, and she was walking next to him. He was the proudest man on earth.

They arrived at last outside the house where Scarlett's flat was, the flat that was supposed to have been just for the meantime, until they got something better. Scarlett looked uncomfortable.

'Look…er…I'll just pop in first. You wait here,' she said.

Jonathan knew why. She couldn't be sure whether her father would be there or not. It was a quarter to six and he should have left for work, but if he hadn't it would be because he was either asleep or drunk or both and she was embarrassed about him.

'OK,' he agreed.

At least Victor was working again—for now. It was one of a string of temporary jobs he'd had recently. None of them seemed to last more than a couple of weeks. Jonathan looked about him as he waited, and came to the same conclusion that he always did, that Scarlett should not be living in a street like this. It was really rough and neglected-looking. She deserved much better. One day, after he had done his national service, after he had established his career…

Five minutes later, Victor came out of the front door. Jonathan was shocked to see how much he had changed since Christmas. He looked really haggard and un-healthy, and he had lost a lot more hair, but it was the way he held himself that was most telling. He was round-shouldered and shuffling, as if he was apologis-ing for simply being there. When he saw Jonathan, he tried to straighten himself up and smile.

'Ah…er…Jonathan. Yes. Nice to see you. Scarlett's been looking forward to you coming home.'

Peppermint-flavoured breath wafted over Jonathan. He held out his hand.

'I've been looking forward to it too, Mr Smith.'

'Good. Yes.' Victor's grasp was brief and weak. 'National service next, is it? That'll make a man of you.'

'Yes, so they all say.'

Victor's eyes had already slid away from his.

'Well, got to go. Mustn't be late.' He was just turning away when he suddenly appeared to change his mind and swung back to look Jonathan in the face again. 'Look, you treat her right, d'you hear? She's a good girl. Like her mother. Her mother was a wonderful woman.'

Jonathan could hardly believe his ears. He was being warned off by this disaster of a man.

'How about treating Scarlett right yourself?' he flared. 'How about giving her a proper home instead of this dump, and letting her go to school instead of having to slave in that factory just to pay the rent and keep you in booze and fags?'

Victor shrank away from him, fear and loathing in his eyes.

'All very well for you,' he muttered. 'Bloody Blane. He started all this—your father. It's all his fault.'

Guilt jolted through Jonathan. It had been his father's fault that the Smiths had had to leave the Trafalgar. But that wasn't the whole story.

'It's not his fault that you drink too much,' he said.

Out of the corner of his eye, he saw Scarlett hurrying out of the front door. The words died in his mouth. She had never admitted to him that her father was a drunk, though they both knew it. It was the only forbidden territory between them.

'You leave him alone!' she cried.

To his amazement, Jonathan realised that she was speaking to him.

'Look, I—' he began.

But Scarlett wasn't listening to him. She was taking her father by the arm and gently turning him away from the house.

'Go on, Dad, don't mind him. It's time you left. You'll be late if you're not careful.'

She watched him as he shambled off down the road. Then she rounded on Jonathan.

'How dare you talk to my dad like that? How dare you?'

'Because it's true.'

He was in too deep now to back out and, besides, he felt passionately about this.

'He should be looking after you, not the other way

round. It's not fair. It's like you're the mum. You shouldn't have to be checking up on him and making sure he's all right and paying for things for him. He should be doing that for you. That's what fathers are for.'

Scarlett flushed with fury. Hands on hips, she faced him down.

'Oh, and your father's perfect, is he?'

She had him on his weak spot now. It still made him feel sick to think of what had happened that last night the Smiths had worked at the Trafalgar.

'No,' he admitted, 'of course not. But at least he works hard and keeps a decent roof over our heads. I don't have to keep him.'

'Well, it's easy for him—' Scarlett started.

But Jonathan was on the defensive now, and it drove him on.

'No, it isn't. He started with nothing. He was an East End boy who started work when he was fourteen and he's worked his way up to running the Trafalgar. That wasn't easy at all. That was blooming hard work for years and years, and he still works all hours.'

'Well, bully for him,' Scarlett shouted. 'Three cheers. Just don't get at my dad, see? He's all I've got, and if you don't like him, you'd better just clear off!'

'Oh, fine. If that's what you want, then I will. I was just thinking of you, but that doesn't seem to be good enough!' Jonathan retorted.

He grabbed his bike and cycled off down the road as fast as he could, his head pounding and his chest heaving with rage. He charged round the corner, narrowly missing a van, and raced on without noticing where he was going. He was halfway home before he even started to cool off. He slowed down a bit as doubts began to surface. Maybe he shouldn't have gone off at the deep end like that. Maybe he should have kept his mouth shut. It was true that Victor was a rotten father. He still believed that. But telling him so to his face, and telling Scarlett what he thought, perhaps wasn't very bright of him. But then Scarlett shouldn't have said those things about his father…

Jonathan finally came to a halt at the top of the cliffs. What had he gone and done? He groaned out loud and hit his head against the handlebars.

'Idiot! Idiot!'

He'd been looking forward to this great reunion with Scarlett for so long. How had it all gone so wrong? Just half an hour ago he'd been the happiest person alive. He couldn't believe how he'd plunged from being on top of the world to down in the depths in such a short time. One thing was clear—something had to be done, at once. He couldn't bear for her to be angry with him like this. He glanced at his watch. His mother was expecting him back at seven. She and his father were leaving the pub to the staff to run for the evening and his aunts and uncles and cousins from London were coming down specially. They were to have a big family meal together to welcome him home. But making it up with Scarlett was more important than being on time for his parents. He cycled back to Scarlett's road.

A short time later he was holding the Smiths' doorbell down with his thumb. He waited. Nobody came to the door. He tried it again. Still no reply. Was the bell working properly? Nothing else in this house seemed to. He stepped back and looked up at the small window in the gable that let light into the Smiths' flat.

'Scarlett!' he yelled. 'Scarlett! Come down and let me in!'

He thought he saw a face at the window, but it was gone so quickly that he couldn't be sure. He waited again, but still the front door remained shut. He pressed one of the other bells at random. A middle-aged woman with bright orange lipstick and her hair up in curlers answered the door. She looked him up and down with suspicious eyes.

'Yes?'

Jonathan put on his best smile. 'I'm terribly sorry to disturb you, but could you let me come in? I'm trying to visit the Smiths on the top floor, but I don't think their bell's working.'

'Well, I don't know. We can't let any old Tom, Dick or Harry in here, y'know.'

Jonathan could feel desperation pounding inside him. If she didn't move he was going to have to just push her out of the way.

'I'm not any old Tom, Dick or Harry. I'm a friend of the Smiths. I've been coming here ever since they moved in.'

The woman looked unconvinced. 'I never saw you before in my life.'

'Look, just let me in, will you? It's important. It's a matter of life or death!'

'Oh, well, I suppose—'

The woman took half a step back. Jonathan seized the chance, squeezed past her and ran up the main stairs and up again to the Smiths' flat. He banged on their door.

'Scarlett, it's me! I'm sorry. I was wrong. Let me in, Scarlett!'

From inside the flat he heard a muffled voice. 'Go away. I don't ever want to see you again.'

It was terrible. It was like the end of the world.

'Scarlett, I'm sorry. I shouldn't have said all that.'

A male voice floated up from the first floor landing. 'Too much bleeding noise round here. Put a sock in it!'

Jonathan ignored it. He slapped his hand on the door. 'Scarlett, open up.'

'Go away.'

'You don't mean that.'

She couldn't mean that. She mustn't.

'I do.'

'Scarlett, come on. I've said I'm sorry. Don't ruin everything. I love you.'

There was silence on the other side of the door.

'Scarlett?'

Then he heard movement. The lock clicked and the door opened. She looked dreadful. Her face was blotchy and her eyes were red from crying. Jonathan stepped into the room.

'Come here,' he said, and took her in his arms.

She clung to him fiercely, her head buried in his shoulder. He kissed her hair, felt its silkiness and the hard warmth of her skull beneath. It was all right. They were safe. He felt as if he'd just pulled back from the edge of a high cliff.

'Say that again,' Scarlett said.

'Say what?'

'You know.'

'I love you.'

'Really truly?'

'Really truly.'

Some of the tenseness went out of her. She looked up at him. Her eyes were still full of tears.

'I love you too. So much. Sometimes I can't bear it. But my dad—he's all I've got, and I'm all he's got. We've got to stick by each other. You must see that.'

Jonathan thought of his own parents. They might seem distant, he might not get on too well with them, they might appear to put the pub and making money before him, but they were always there. He knew that he could rely on them. And, beyond them, there were the London relatives and the French relatives, a back-up family. It was hard to imagine having only one person in the world related to you, but that was how it was for Scarlett. Of course she had to stick by her father, however useless he was.

'I do see,' he said.

She raised her face to his then, her sweet lips opening to his. Still wrapped around each other, they shuffled over to the one armchair and collapsed onto it. They kissed again and Jonathan ran his hands over her new womanly curves, covered only by a light skirt and blouse. It was a long time before he remembered that his family and a celebratory meal were waiting for him at home, and even then he only left reluctantly.

'I'll be back tomorrow,' he promised.

Cycling back to the Trafalgar, he didn't care how much trouble he was in. Scarlett loved him, and that was all that mattered.

It was the start of two magical weeks. Scarlett had taken her annual holiday to be with him, and they visited all their old haunts together, went to the cinema when it rained and spent a day in London looking at the tourist sights.

'Whenever I see a picture of Tower Bridge or Buckingham Palace now, I'll think of you,' Scarlett said.

The time went all too quickly. Before Jonathan could believe it was possible, it was their final evening together. With the last of his money, he took Scarlett out for a romantic candlelit meal. She was enchanted.

'I've never been anywhere like this before,' she breathed.

All through the meal she held his hand and gazed at him over the table. Under the table their feet met and played. As they waited for dessert, she kicked off her shoes and ran her stockinged feet up and down his legs. Jonathan hardly noticed that the food was rubbish by Ortolan standards. It was Scarlett that he wanted to devour.

They finally stumbled outside into the cool darkness and wrapped their arms round each other. Scarlett sighed and snuggled against him.

'That was so, so wonderful—' she sighed '—it was the best evening I've ever had.'

Jonathan drew her into the shelter of a handy doorway and kissed her. Her mouth opened hungrily. He held her face in his hands, concentrating on her lips, her mouth, his senses reeling as her tongue slid over his. Intoxicated, he realised that she wanted him just as much as he wanted her.

'Scarlett, Scarlett,' he gasped as they came up for air. 'You are so gorgeous. I love you so much.'

'I love you too,' she said. 'I don't want you to go away. I want you to stay here with me for ever.'

'I don't want to be anywhere else,' he told her.

But they both knew he had to go.

Somehow, they walked back to her street, stopping frequently to kiss long and passionately. But, however much they drew out the journey, they arrived at last at her door. Inside the porch, Scarlett leaned against the wall and pulled him to her. Jonathan felt the soft sweet curves of her body pressed to his with only a few layers of clothing between them. She pulled at his shirt and ran her hands up the bare skin of his back.

'Kiss me again,' she begged.

On fire, he did so, until both of them were breathless. Scarlett's nails dug into his flesh.

'You can come in,' she whispered. 'My dad won't be back yet.'

Jonathan groaned. His body was crying out for hers. But a last vestige of sense held him back. She was only sixteen. He was going away.

'I mustn't,' he managed to say. 'I want to, but I mustn't. I love you too much.'

'Always and for ever?' she asked, her voice cracking.

'Always and for ever,' he agreed.

CHAPTER THIRTEEN

1956

'BLIMEY, bit hot out here, ain't it?'

A squaddie who Jonathan hadn't met before came and leaned beside him on the railings of the troop ship.

'Better than being down below. It's like a bloody furnace down there. At least there's some breeze up here,' Jonathan said.

'Yeah. Nothing like a bit of fresh air. Smoke?' The man offered an open pack of cigarettes.

'No, thanks.'

'Blimey, what's wrong with you?'

Jonathan had often got this reaction from the others.

'Bloke I worked for told me it spoils the taste buds,' he explained.

Monsieur Bonnard and the Ortolan seemed a very long way away now, but his influence was still strong enough to stop him from smoking.

His companion shrugged. 'Cheap round,' he said, and lit up. He chucked the dead match overboard into the green water of the Suez Canal. 'Funny to think that back home it's winter, ain't it?'

'Yeah. They're all suffering rain and snow and here we are in sunny Egypt,' Jonathan said.

He wondered how Scarlett was coping with the leaks and the damp in that crummy flat of hers. When they got to Aden, he would be able to post the letters that he had been writing to her.

'Rum place this, ain't it?' his companion said. 'All them camels and palm trees and that. Like the pictures they used to show you at Sunday school.'

The two of them gazed idly at the slowly passing scenery. Flat-topped houses with minute windows huddled in groups, as if propping each other up. Goats and hens foraged in refuse heaps. A man in a long white shirt was riding a tiny donkey laden with bundles of sticks. Two women covered from head to foot in black were carrying pots on their heads.

'Sure is,' Jonathan agreed. 'Really foreign.'

'At least the bleeding ship's not rocking about no more. God, I hate ships.'

'I used to think I liked them, until I got on board this one,' Jonathan said.

He had felt pleasantly superior to the men who were chucking up from the moment they'd got on board. He'd never been seasick, not even on the cross Channel ferries in winter. But being battened down below on a troop ship crossing the Bay of Biscay was another thing altogether, especially during a storm. The smell alone had been enough to turn his normally tough stomach, reducing him to a groaning wreck.

'We got the Indian Ocean to do yet,' his companion said gloomily.

'Yeah, but before then we've got Aden. Two days off

the boat! I can't wait. I'm going to get in that water and swim and swim. Get all the sweat and dirt off me then lie on the beach.'

'It's one great big bleeding beach out there, mate.'

They both looked at the desert as it stretched out as far as the eye could see beyond the fringe of habitation by the canal.

'As long as they let us off this ship, I'll be happy. I've never been so bored in all my life,' Jonathan complained.

The long days at sea were broken by nothing but drills and inspections.

'Yeah, but look at it this way, mate. They're paying us for doing sweet FA. That's got to be good, ain't it?'

'Better than basic training,' Jonathan agreed.

The basic training had been every bit as gruelling as he had been warned, but he had survived it and come out the other end to find himself posted to catering training. For a while he had harboured hopes of getting to the kitchens of the officers' mess, as Monsieur Bonnard had said he should. A sergeant had spotted his ability and sent him on a B2 and then a B1 course, and all had seemed set for a recommendation for an A1 course, and promotion. But then some strange quirk of army organisation had come into play, and here he was on a ship bound for Malaya.

'Anything's better than that, mate.'

'Oi, you two—'

Jonathan looked round. Three men sat in the shade of a lifeboat. One of them was shuffling a well-worn pack of cards.

'Fancy a round of pontoon?'

'Might as well,' he agreed. After all, the scenery wasn't that riveting. One camel was very much like another.

The two day break at Aden was over all too quickly, and then it was the long haul across the Indian Ocean. The days settled into a routine of inspections, drill, nasty food and long stretches of time playing cards and listening to the limited selection of songs played over the ship's radio. After the ninety-ninth repetition, even *Rock Around The Clock* failed to excite them. Everyone slept a lot. And then at last they sailed into Singapore.

Jonathan had hoped that he might get another break there, and get a chance to look round, see the sights, maybe even get to the famous Raffles Hotel. Some of the men were sent to a camp outside the city, but his contingent were loaded into lorries and sent off for acclimatisation before jungle warfare training started.

The one bright spot was that, by some miracle, a letter from Scarlett was waiting for him. Not only had it got there before him, but the postal system delivered it right into his hands. Jonathan devoured her words. She had changed her job again, the landlady had had the worst leaks fixed but the flat was still damp, she and her friend Brenda had taken to listening to Radio Luxembourg together and singing along with all the latest records but what she really wanted was a record player. For a while he almost forgot the heat and the insects, and imagined himself back in the cold streets of Southend in winter. Best of all were the last few lines, where she told him how much she loved and missed him, and ended with a row of kisses across the bottom of the page. He folded the letter up and hid it at the bottom of his kitbag.

A few days later, he tried to reply. He had sent off all the letters he had written on the ship, but now there were his first impressions of Malaya to get down. He read through his letter to Scarlett, flapping with his hand at the insects flying round his face and crawling over his legs. It seemed a pretty feeble effort. It did not convey the excitement of all the new experiences he had been bombarded with this last week. The only thing that was familiar was the hut. Wherever you were in the world, it seemed, you lived in a standard British army hut. Otherwise, it couldn't have been more different from Catterick or Aldershot. Outside, it was pouring with rain like he'd never seen before, straight down like stair-rods. You could hear it hammering on the roof of the hut. But it wasn't cold, like the rain back home, it was warm, and made the air steamier than ever. He looked at the faces of the men sprawled on the adjacent bunks. They were bright red and running with sweat. He supposed he must look the same. The acclimatisation hadn't yet worked. They were in a kind of limbo, strangers in this new land of humid heat and lush vegetation, yet so far away from home that sometimes it was hard to believe that it was still there. There was only his photo of Scarlett and the letter from her to remind him, a thin thread connecting his old life with this strange and fascinating new one.

Across the hut from him, another man was sitting with a notepad on his knees, sucking the end of his pen.

'Difficult, isn't it?' Jonathan said to him. 'I mean, how can you tell them what it's like here? It's just so different from home.'

'Just say it's like bleeding Tarzan, mate. But no bleeding Janes, worse luck.'

It was like a Tarzan film, the jungle thick with huge

trees, exotic greenery, hanging vines and stinging insects. He'd not seen any monkeys yet, but you could hear them calling from the trees, and when they lit the lamps in the evening, huge moths fluttered round them, as big as his hand.

'You writing to your girl?' someone asked.

'My mum,' Jonathan lied.

The men around him snorted in disbelief.

'No use trying to hang onto a girl when you're out here, mate. They're not going to wait for you, are they? They're not going to stay in of a Saturday night. They'll be off out on the pull, all dolled up to the nines. No, mate, you want to give her the push, whoever she is. Once we're through with this jungle training lark, get yourself fixed up with a nice little native girl. Plenty of them keen enough to have a British soldier for a boyfriend.'

'I thought the Malays wanted us out of here. Isn't that why we're here—to fight the guerrillas and protect British property?' Jonathan said, keeping well off the subject of girlfriends being unfaithful.

'That don't mean the girls don't like us. We got money, ain't we? Give 'em a few little presents and they're putty in your hands.'

All around the hut there were guffaws and boasting as the men imagined what the girls might do for them. Jonathan looked at the date on the letter he was trying to write. It was nearly Scarlett's birthday! Seventeen. Back in cold, wet Southend, Scarlett was about to be seventeen. She'd been more beautiful than ever when he'd seen her before being posted. Surely nobody could look at her without wanting her as much as he did? The other men's words of warning echoed in his head. How could he keep the other boys away from her from this distance? There was nothing he could do but tell her he loved and missed her and hope that she continued to feel the same.

He need not have worried. Back in Southend, his only rival was Elvis Presley. Scarlett had taken a day off from working at the corner shop so that she and Brenda could go to the record shop in the High Street and listen to him. They stood in the booth and requested *Heartbreak Hotel* until they were told to buy it or go. Brenda bought it.

'But you haven't got a record player,' Scarlett pointed out.

'No, but Tony at work's got a radiogram.'

'You don't like Tony at work.'

'I never said that. I just told him I wasn't going out with him. But maybe I'll change my mind.'

Scarlett never could understand Brenda when it came to boyfriends. As long as she had someone on the go, she didn't seem to mind who it was.

'He's creepy,' Scarlett objected.

'He's not!'

'I wouldn't be seen dead with him.'

'Oh, you, you've got eyes for nobody but your flaming Jonathan. That's daft, if you ask me. Fancy waiting around for some boy who's out in wherever-it-is when you could be going out and having fun with somebody here.'

'I don't want anyone else,' Scarlett told her.

'That's what I mean. Daft.'

They were never going to see eye to eye on that one. Scarlett had noticed that Brenda's mum was putting

on weight. She didn't think much of it until she started
wearing a maternity smock. Then she just had to raise
the subject. She waited till one evening when she and
Brenda were listening to Radio Luxembourg on the
brand-new radio that Scarlett had saved up for. It was
her pride and joy, far clearer and more modern-looking
than the old thing they had brought from the Red Lion.

'I thought you said your dad had left ages ago and
you never saw him,' she said.

'Yeah, he did, and we don't.'

They both nodded their heads to *Why Do Fools Fall
in Love?* Brenda sang along.

'But…your mum…well…she's wearing a smock.'

Brenda stopped singing. She gave Scarlett a hard
look. 'Yeah, what of it?'

'So—is she having a baby?'

'Yes, she is, as it happens. Anything else you want
to know?'

What Scarlett really wanted to know was—who was
the father, if it wasn't Brenda's mum's husband. But the
look on Brenda's face stopped her from asking. You
had to be careful with Brenda.

'I just wondered, that's all. It's going to be a bit
crowded at your place, isn't it? I mean, there's eight of
you already, all jammed into your prefab.'

'Yeah, well, with a bit of luck we might get a proper
council house. They're lovely, them council houses. Loads
of space. Mind you, I'm still getting out as soon as I can.
I'm fed up of living at home and looking after the little
'uns. It's always me as has to see to them, and now with
this new baby, Mum's going to be more tired than ever.
Just as soon as someone asks me to marry them, I'm off.'

'What—anyone?' Scarlett asked.

'Anyone decent. Rich would be nice. Handsome would be nice. But as long as he can get me away from that lot, that's it.'

'What, even Tony?'

Brenda made a rude noise. 'Oh, him! I'm fed up with him. I'm chucking him next time I see him.'

'Good idea,' Scarlett said. That at least was something they could agree on.

CHAPTER FOURTEEN

SCARLETT put Jonathan's latest letter safely in her pocket. It was no use, however hard she tried she couldn't picture his world, beyond its being very hot and very different. It had been bad enough when he was in Paris, but at least then he had only been across the Channel. Malaya was so far away. Just trying to imagine the climate was impossible. But at least he was safe. Instead of being sent into the jungle to fight guerrillas, someone had realised that he was in the catering corps and he was now running the kitchen at an army hospital.

Here in Southend it was summer, but she still needed a cardigan over her blouse and skirt when she cycled to work in the mornings. Jonathan spoke of being boiling hot in the middle of the night, and things rotting from the damp. It sounded more like a different planet than a different country.

The work she was doing didn't help. There was nothing about it to engage her mind at all. It was similar to her very first job, and involved riveting bits of electric plugs together. Sometimes she felt so bored she wanted to scream or attack someone or throw something into a

machine and wreck it. All the petty dislikes and rival-
ries that seethed in practically every place she worked
were due to the grinding sameness of the days. Having
a feud with someone made for some drama. Getting one
over on them made a point to the long featureless days.
What made it even worse was not having a television.
Everyone discussed what they'd seen the evening before
and she couldn't join in. She couldn't see that she and
her father would ever be able to afford a set. It was difficult enough paying for the essentials plus her new
radio, without finding enough for TV rental and licence.

At least today she was going to Brenda's for tea,
which was something to look forward to. They could
have a good chat and watch TV there. In spite of having
no husband bringing in wages, Brenda's mother still
managed to have a TV set.

'I'm fed up,' she told her friend as they cycled home
at the end of the day.

'You're always blooming fed up.'

'I'm not.'

'You are. And I'm getting fed up of you being fed up.
You're no fun at all.'

'Oh.'

That really jolted Scarlett. Thinking about it, it was
hard to remember when she'd last had fun, apart from
having a laugh with Brenda and the girls at work, or
with Brenda and her new boyfriend Chris, though that
was always a bit uncomfortable since she was the gooseberry all the time. Everyone seemed to have a boyfriend
and they all went out on Friday and Saturday nights
while she stayed in. Jonathan, on the other hand, seemed
to be having a whale of a time. Every week at his

hospital there seemed to be a party. Leaving parties, twenty-first birthday parties, beach parties. Any excuse, it appeared to her, to get together and have a knees-up. And, of course, being a hospital, there were lots of nurses, so it wasn't just the lads having a drink. There was dancing.

'I don't mean to be,' she said. 'Bet you don't dare do this!'

She took both hands off the handlebars and steered by shifting her body weight from side to side. The road sloped downwards, not quite a hill, but enough to get up a fair speed. Scarlett spread her arms out and shrieked with fear and excitement as she hurtled towards the main road at the bottom. Behind her, she could hear Brenda screaming at her to stop. At the last minute, she grabbed the brakes and skidded to a halt, just as a lorry went by. Brenda almost crashed into her. Laughing and gasping, she turned to her friend. The blood was coursing round her body. She felt alive again.

'That fun enough for you?' she asked.

'You're mad, you are,' Brenda told her. 'You nearly got yourself killed.'

'Better than being bored to death.'

'No need to get bored to death. Come dancing with me on Friday night.'

Scarlett scooted across the road before the next car came along, closely followed by Brenda.

'I don't want to play gooseberry to you and Chris, thank you very much,' she said.

'You don't have to. I'm giving him the elbow,' Brenda told her.

They cycled along side by side.

'You're joking! Last week you said he was the love of your life.'

'Yeah, well—maybe he wasn't. I just sort of looked at him last night and it was like…like the lights had been turned off, you know? And I thought to myself, what am I doing with him? He's not good looking and he's not clever and all he talks about is motorbikes. It wouldn't be so bad if he had a motorbike, but he hasn't. He just talks about them. So I'm not in love with him any more.'

Scarlett shook her head. She could no more stop loving Jonathan than she could fly. Missing him was a constant ache.

'But you wanted to marry him.'

'I know. Mad, ain't it? Lucky escape. So—I'm a free woman again. You going to come dancing or not?'

Scarlett had always refused before, but in her pocket was Jonathan's latest letter, full of those parties.

'I've got nothing to wear,' she said, which was true.

'That's easy. Borrow something of mine,' Brenda offered.

'Could I?'

''Course! What're friends for?'

'Brenda, you're a darling!'

Once decided, she found she was really looking forward to it. By Friday evening she was in a fever of excitement.

'You're very cheerful. What's up?' Victor asked, as she sang and danced while getting the tea ready.

'Aren't I always cheerful?' Scarlett said.

'Well—not like this, all of a twitch. You going out somewhere?'

Scarlett was surprised. She hadn't realised that he noticed her changes of mood.

'I'm going to the Kursaal ballroom with Brenda.'

'Oh—' Victor nodded slowly, turning it over in his mind. 'Well, you be careful. How are you getting home? Don't go accepting any lifts from men in cars.'

Scarlett was touched. He did care. It might seem sometimes as if he hardly noticed she was there, but he still loved her as much as he ever had.

'We'll get a bus, or walk.'

'But it'll be late at night.' Victor put down his cup of tea and looked at her as she tucked into her beans on toast. 'I worry about you. You're a young woman now. You got to be careful.'

Scarlett felt a spurt of impatience.

'You worry about me! What about you? Look at you—you look ill. And you know why? It's because you drink too much and don't eat enough.'

Anger clouded Victor's face.

'I only drink what I need, right? And it's not your place to tell me what I should or shouldn't do. I'm your father— you should listen to me. You watch out for yourself this evening. I know what young men are like, I was one myself once. They'll all be after you, pretty girl like you.'

For once, Scarlett backed down. He was thinking of her, after all.

'I'll be all right. I'm used to fending off the boys at work. Brenda and I are just going for the dancing. I'm not looking for a boyfriend.'

Bored with the conversation, she swallowed down the last of her toast and started chivvying Victor into getting off for work.

Once he was out of the way, she could concentrate on getting herself ready. Rushing up and down to the bathroom and in and out of the two rooms of the cramped little flat, singing bits of her favourite songs and practising dance steps, she set about transforming herself from factory girl to dream dance partner. She put on powder and a new bright red lipstick, brushed her hair up into a fashionable style and pulled on new stockings, making sure to get the seams dead straight up the backs of her legs. Then came the clothes—a scoop-necked white blouse of her own that fitted her figure perfectly and a bright green circular skirt of Brenda's with a can-can petticoat underneath. The layers of gathered net in the petticoat made the skirt stick out and swirl round her when she turned, emphasizing her small waist, which she cinched with a wide elastic belt.

She studied the finished effect, turning this way and that in an effort to see herself in the small mirror. She was amazed. How sophisticated she looked! She patted her hair, put her hands to her waist to make it even smaller, puffed out her chest. Yes, she looked the part. This was going to be fun.

By the time Brenda arrived, she could hardly contain herself. She scampered downstairs to open the door. For half a beat the two girls looked at each other, then squealed their delight and hugged.

'You look wonderful. Really glamorous!'

'So do you. Like a film star!'

Arm in arm, they set off for their big night out, clattering along the road in their high heels, giggling at the slightest thing.

The ballroom was amazing, with pillars holding up

first floor galleries and a wonderful display of flowers round the stage. Scarlett gazed about her, taking it all in.

'Isn't it beautiful?' she breathed.

Now she was here, she couldn't think why she had resisted coming all this time. The band was already playing, the crystal ball was revolving and out on the famous sprung floor, couples were dancing. All around was a buzz of excited chatter as the girls sitting round the sides watched the dancers, commented on their prowess and eyed up the young men. The young men, other than the brave ones dancing, seemed to be mostly at the bar, nursing their beers and eyeing up the girls from a safe distance.

'I can't wait to get dancing,' Scarlett said, looking at the quickstepping couples with envy. Her feet went tap-tap in time with the music.

'Got to get someone's attention first,' Brenda said. 'Anyone'll do, just to get out on the floor. Then we'll be seen.'

She was sitting up straight with her bust shown off to its best advantage, trying to look available and casual at the same time, all the while scanning the room for talent.

'Don't look now, but there's two boys coming our way,' she hissed at Scarlett, and then, in a bright, chatty voice, '...and what about her over there, then? I wouldn't wear blue and green together like that, not never nohow, I mean—oh!' She broke off with exaggerated surprise as two young men stopped in front of them.

'Wanna hoof it round, then?' one of them asked.

Scarlett looked up and smiled politely. Both of them were about twenty-one, with thin faces, badly fitting suits and their hair brushed into fashionable DAs. She wasn't very impressed but before she could say anything, Brenda had answered for both of them.

'Don't mind if we do.'

And off they went, shuffling round the floor to a slow foxtrot. It felt odd to be held by someone other than Jonathan.

'I'm Ray,' Scarlett's partner said.

'Scarlett.'

Ray snorted with laughter. 'Get away! That's a good one, that is.'

Scarlett was used to this reaction. 'Take it or leave it,' she told him.

'I'll leave it, thanks. I'll call you Sue.'

'I shan't answer to it.'

They made their erratic way round the floor in a state of armed stand-off. Scarlett was disappointed. This was no more exciting than practising with Brenda. Ray obviously rated his own dancing, judging by the way he pulled her around and tutted when either of them stepped on the other's foot, but Scarlett didn't think much of his style. After the long walk from home, her feet were already beginning to hurt. She wasn't sad when the music ended.

'Hey, you're quite a girl. Another?' Ray asked.

Scarlett looked at him in amazement. 'No, thanks,' she said and stalked off back to where she and Brenda had been sitting.

'What was yours like? Mine was quite nice,' Brenda said.

'Useless,' Scarlett told her.

The next one was much better. He was called Pete and he danced with confidence.

'I haven't seen you here before, have I?' he asked.

'No, it's my first time.'

'I thought so. I'd've noticed a smasher like you. You enjoying it?'

She was now. Dancing with Pete was a pleasure.

'Yes, it's good. But what I'm really waiting for is the rock 'n' roll. It's miles better than this old-fashioned stuff.'

'Yeah, too right!' Pete agreed. 'This is tame, isn't it? Can you jive?'

'You bet!'

She and Brenda had practised for hours.

'Oh, great. Will you jive with me? The rock 'n' roll band should start in about half an hour.'

He seemed nice enough, so Scarlett agreed.

While the strict tempo band was playing, the general mood was calm and the dancers polite and well-behaved. But then they took a break and a small group of guitarists, a drummer and a double bass took the stand. The whole atmosphere in the ballroom changed. The young men who had been standing in the bar came flooding onto the floor, the girls who had so far been wallflowers perked up and looked hopeful, everyone fizzed with anticipation.

A young man with a guitar slung in front of him came up to the microphone.

'Ladies and gentlemen—chicks and guys—'

A roar of delight broke from the crowd. Entranced, Scarlett watched to see what was coming next. She didn't notice Pete approaching until he was at her side.

'Ready to rock 'n' roll?' he asked.

'Oh—yeah—you bet!'

Almost at the same moment, the young man at the

mike asked the same question. 'Are you ready to rock 'n' roll?'

'Yes!' howled the crowd, whistling and cheering.

'Then let's go!'

Scarlett found herself whirled onto the floor with a torrent of couples as the familiar song began—

One, two, three o'clock, four o'clock , rock!

At first Scarlett tried to sing along, but almost immediately she hadn't enough breath. She needed all the oxygen she could get for dancing. Back and forth, round and round, spinning and stepping, she danced, a whirling doll in Pete's expert hands. The ballroom became a blur. There was only the music, the insistent rhythm and the demands of the dance until, with the last dying fall of notes, Pete gave her one final turn under his arm and clasped her to him. Laughing and gasping, Scarlett clapped and cheered with the rest of the dancers.

'Enjoyed it?' Pete asked.

'Oh, yes!'

'You're a fabulous dancer.'

'Thanks, so are you.'

'Another?'

'OK.'

The band struck up *Shake, Rattle and Roll*. Once again, Scarlett was whirled and spun. At one point Pete took both her hands as she faced him and straddled his legs. In a flash, Scarlett understood. She let her feet slide along the floor and went through Pete's legs with her body just inches from the ground, while Pete stepped neatly over her, swung round and pulled her upright again. It was all done in seconds. Scarlett squealed in delight and Pete yelled 'Yeah!' and then they were turning and spinning again.

Scarlett was in a breathless blur of excitement. The band kept up the intoxicating beat, different boys asked her to dance and she was whirled round with various degrees of skill. She forgot all about Brenda, Jonathan and her sore feet. There was only the rock and roll and her own vibrant body. When the music finally stopped, she felt as if she were coming down to earth from a different planet.

'Why are we stopping?' she asked her partner. She couldn't remember what his name was. Maybe he hadn't told her.

'End of the set,' he said.

All around her, people were shouting for more. Scarlett joined in loudly.

But the singer just waved in acknowledgement, thanked them and left the stage.

'Drink?' Scarlett's partner asked.

'Yes, please!'

Now she thought of it, she was parched. She gulped down the half pint of lemonade he brought her in one go. Then she decided she'd better find Brenda.

Her friend was sitting with a Teddy Boy in full rig—draped jacket, drainpipe trousers and bootlace tie.

'Having a good time?' she asked.

Scarlett flopped down on the chair beside her. 'Am I! I want to go dancing every week for ever!'

'Told you,' said Brenda with cheerful satisfaction.

'…and can you do fish and rice and one of those steamboat things for Saturday night?' Jonathan asked.

'Ah, yes, Mr Jon, that no problem,' the Chinese storekeeper said.

Of course it was no problem. The Chinese could get you any sort of supplies or services you might need, and Jonathan had the best trade goods going—British army stores. By some quirk of the system, he was issued with seven days' worth of meat plus the Friday fish, which left a day's supply of tinned steak and kidney and corned beef each week, which the Chinese were eager to get their hands on. Catering for a party was easy with such riches.

This week it was another twenty-first. One of the nurses—June, the small fierce one—was arranging it for her friend. In effect, this meant asking Jonathan to do the catering while the rest of the men brought the beer. All June had to do was to ask everyone who wasn't on duty, put up some decorations and have a whip-round for the present.

The party food set in motion, Jonathan went about finishing lunches for the day. His kitchen here was pretty primitive. He cooked on wood-burning stoves which were a devil to control, temperature-wise, and his pastry had to be rolled out on dampened flour sacks to keep it even slightly cool. It was a far cry from the cold marble surfaces of the patisserie in the Ortolan. But he liked it here. The strangeness had worn off. The heat, the humidity, the lush vegetation, the Chinese and Malay people were all familiar to him now. He felt at home.

'Hey, Jonno—!' Another of the nurses stuck her head round the kitchen doorway.

'Hello, Irene. What's up?'

'Can you be an absolute angel and do me an omelette for a special patient?'

'For you, Irene, anything.'

'You're a darling.'

'I know.'

'Coming for a drink in the NAAFI this evening?'

'Yeah, when I finish the birthday cake.'

'Ooh, cake. Wonderful. I adore your cakes. I would marry you for your cakes.'

'You'll have to join the queue.'

Irene gave a tragic sigh. 'Story of my life. I'll send an orderly for the omelette in about ten mins, OK?'

'Right you are.'

Whistling, Jonathan checked the huge pot of spuds that his Malay kitchen porter had peeled, made sure the bacon and onion pudding was steaming properly and stirred a great vat of gravy. The patients could rely on getting good solid English cooking to help them get better. All was well with the world. If it weren't for the letters from Scarlett that still arrived every week, he might have begun to wonder whether Southend still existed. It was so far away, and he had done so many new things since he'd left, that England seemed like a different world, vague and insubstantial. Only a continual gnawing sense of loss kept him linked with it, the feeling that, without Scarlett, something of himself was missing.

CHAPTER FIFTEEN

'It's all right, don't worry. I've found another job,' Victor said, as Scarlett came in from another boring day's work on an assembly line.

Scarlett dropped her bag on a chair. It was hot outside and the flat was unbearably stuffy. She went over to the kettle. As usual, her father had not bothered to fill it up after he had used it. She banged it down on the gas ring. She was far too cross to be pleased with him for finding work.

'Well, thank goodness for that. I can't think why it was so hard. It's high season, after all. Everyone's crying out for bar staff.'

It would be so much nicer to be working somewhere down on the sea front in this sunny weather. Waitressing or selling ice creams was far more pleasant work than assembling parts for electrical goods, but it was only for the summer and it didn't pay so well. One of them had to have a regular income.

'They all want pretty girls behind the bar, don't they?' her father said. 'Here, give me that kettle. I'll go down and fill it.'

Scarlett flopped down at the table, seething. She stared out of the window at the ugly street. Pretty girls, indeed.

'What they want is people who are sober,' she said out loud, hardly caring whether he heard her or not.

They also wanted people who could get to work on time, add up correctly and not drop things. You only had to take one look at her father to know that he wasn't going to be the world's best employee. In the old days at the Red Lion, Victor would not have dreamed of taking on someone in the state he was in now. She heaved a sigh. At least he had got something, but how long was it going to last? They had been here so often now, and the gaps between jobs were getting longer each time.

'Where is it, anyway?' she asked, as Victor came in with the kettle.

'The Oaks.'

'Oh, yes, I know.'

She and Jonathan had been there on that last wonderful leave before he'd gone off to Malaya. It was quite a large place, a bit on the rough side, with a big room at the back where they had new bands and skiffle groups performing. She was so involved with remembering that evening that she didn't ask just what sort of job her father had got there. At least he was working again, that was the main thing. She would now have enough money left over at the end of the week to go dancing. She told Brenda the good news the next day.

'Oh, well, that's good, I suppose. Only my Phil said his mate Alan'd like to make up a foursome, so you won't have to pay anyway,' Brenda said.

'You know I don't like foursomes,' Scarlett told her.

She had been on two or three before that Brenda had

set up, and had always ended up having to fend off some awful boy with sweaty hands.

Brenda looked annoyed. 'I don't know what you're saving yourself for. Your precious Jonathan's not going to know, is he?'

It was true. What was more, Jonathan's letters were full of girls' names. He wasn't going out with any of them, and he always said how much he missed her, but sometimes she felt he was slipping away from her.

'No, but—'

'I think you're daft. Look at all those gorgeous men you've turned down. That Pete, for a start. He's got to be the best dancer on the floor of a Saturday night, but you won't go out with him. I would, if he asked me.'

'Well, you're not me, are you?' Scarlett snapped.

Brenda responded by sulking for the rest of the day.

It wasn't till the weekend that Scarlett realised her father wasn't working as a barman. During the week she was always up and out before he was even awake, so she had no idea what he was doing during the day. But on Saturday she didn't get up till later, and was surprised to see him stirring as she was about to leave for Mrs Sefton's shop.

'You're early,' she said to him.

'Yeah, well—got to be in by ten.'

She didn't have time to find out more, but as she walked down the road to the shop she wondered if her father had landed a cellar man's job again. He would have to be earlier for that, so that he could see to the pipes and the casks before opening time.

'You're looking cheerful, dearie,' Mrs Sefton said as she went in. 'Had a good time last night, did you?'

'Wonderful! I never stopped dancing all evening.'

Mrs Sefton shook her head. 'And here you are, all ready for a day's work, and you'll be out dancing tonight as well, I'll be bound.'

'You bet.'

'My, my, what it is to be young and full of energy. I was able to do that once. Not any more. Now then, dearie, there's a lot of tins to be fetched in.'

Scarlett carried cases of baked beans and fruit cocktail through from the shed in the back yard where Mrs Sefton kept her stock. Yet again she thought about getting a better paid Saturday job. Mrs Sefton hadn't put up her wages since she was fourteen. But she did let Scarlett buy some foodstuffs at cost price and often gave her ends of ham or day-old bread.

'Your dad's got another job, then?' she asked as Scarlett stacked the shelves.

'Yes, at The Oaks. I'm wondering if he's got the cellar man's job. It'll be good if he has. He'll earn more.'

And it would be good for him, she thought, though she didn't say it. He'd have more pride in himself.

'Well, you tell him to come in and pay off his slate, dear. I don't mind him running up a bit, seeing as he's your dad, but I don't like it getting too big.'

'Right,' Scarlett said, gritting her teeth. He'd told her he hadn't got anything on tick. Why did he have to lie to her, and especially when he knew she would find out? It made her so mad.

On Sunday she finally got to speak to him.

'So what sort of job is this at The Oaks?' she asked. 'Cellar man?'

Victor busied himself with rolling a cigarette. 'Not exactly.'

'Well, what then?'

'General sort of stuff. You know.'

'Just bar work, then?'

'Yes.'

'Only I wondered why you were going in by ten of a morning.'

'Plenty to be done at a big place like that. You should know. It's the size of the blooming Trafalgar.'

She couldn't get anything else out of him. In the end she gave up. She had the weekly wash to do by hand in the bathroom downstairs before she could go out and enjoy her one day off.

Then, three weeks later, she got to find out for herself. It was Friday and Victor had been unwell for a couple of days.

'What about your wages?' Scarlett asked.

'Oh, they'll give them to me when I go in.'

'Blow that for a lark, Dad. What about the rent? I'll fetch it before I go out this evening.'

Victor was very reluctant for her to go, coming out with all sorts of excuses. But Scarlett brushed them aside. They needed that money and, if she didn't fetch it, Victor would start running up a tab at Mrs Sefton's again. She got on her bike and cycled off along the back streets towards The Oaks. It was a lovely late summer evening and it was nice just to be out of the flat and wheeling easily along. Young men coming home from work whistled after her as she passed by.

As she rolled into the car park of The Oaks, she could hear music coming out of the open doors of the big room at the back. A guitar was strumming and someone was singing *Rock Island Line* in the nasal style of Lonnie Donegan. He broke off, there was laughter and a roll on the drums, then the song started again. A rehearsal was in progress.

Scarlett parked her bike and made her way through the back corridors until she found a bar. A woman in her thirties was running a bar towel over the beer pumps.

'We're not open yet,' she said.

'I know. I'm Victor Smith's daughter. I've come for his wages.'

'Victor—? Oh, you mean Vic. The pot man.'

'I…er…yes…' Scarlett said, stunned.

Her dad was the pot man? That was the lowliest job in the pub. Most places employed a pensioner to do it. It involved picking up the empty glasses and emptying the ashtrays and any other dirty work going, like…and then she realised why he was working from ten in the morning. He went in to swab out the toilets.

'Well, you're a turn-up, to be sure,' the woman was saying. 'I would never of guessed you was his daughter, a bright pretty girl like you. I suppose you don't want a job here, do you?'

'I'm under age for bar work,' Scarlett told her.

'Pity. Still, I suppose you wouldn't want to anyway. It's hard to get decent quality staff here. I'll go and fetch his envelope.'

She was back in a couple of minutes holding a small brown wage packet.

'How ill is he? Is he going to be back tomorrow? Only I can't keep him on if he's not going to be reliable. There's plenty willing to do his job.'

'He's had a stomach upset,' Scarlett told her.

The woman made a sceptical face. 'Stomach upset, is it? Nothing to do with whisky chasers, I suppose?'

Scarlett glared at her. The cheek of it! Her father had been really poorly.

'No, nothing to do with them. He wanted to come in today but he wasn't well enough,' she stated, and reached over the bar and took the envelope from the woman's hand. 'Thank you. He'll be in tomorrow, don't worry.'

And she made off, fuming, with the landlady's parting shot of, 'He'd better,' ringing in her ears. She blundered along a badly lit passage, opened a door and found herself in the music room. It looked scruffy and tawdry in daylight, but Scarlett hardly noticed. There, on the stage, was a rock 'n' roll band consisting of two guitarists and a drummer. A home-made banner above their heads proclaimed them to be Ricky and the Riptides. But it was not that which held Scarlett's attention. It was the guitarist who was also the singer. He was a slim young man with dark hair and a brooding face and a mouth as sensual and snarling as Elvis Presley's. He was halfway through *Singing The Blues* and as he saw Scarlett enter the room he immediately targeted her with his dark gaze and sang to her. Scarlett was transfixed.

The song ended with him striking a final chord. Scarlett clapped with shining enthusiasm. The singer—surely this must be Ricky himself?—gave a mocking bow.

'Thanks, babe. Join the fan club.'

That brought Scarlett to her senses. She wasn't falling at his feet.

'I'll join yours if you'll join mine,' she told him.

Ricky laughed. 'Which band are you in, babe?'

'You don't have to be in a band to have them queuing up for you,' she said.

The Riptides hooted and whistled.

'That told you, Rick.'

Ricky ignored them. It was as if they didn't exist. The only two people in the room—in the world—were Ricky and Scarlett.

'What's your name, sweetheart?'

'Scarlett.'

She left the doorway and walked casually to the centre of the room, where she stood with a hand on her hip and a challenge in her eyes.

'And please don't say yours is Rhett. I've heard it all before.'

She was enjoying this. She knew she looked good and she knew she was holding her own with Ricky. At least, she was so far. There was something about him—an air of danger—that called out to her. She had to test herself against it.

'Oh, Ashley, Ashley!' the drummer warbled in a very bad southern states accent.

'I've heard that too,' Scarlett said without taking her gaze off Ricky.

Ricky's brooding eyes ran over her with open appreciation.

'What would you like us to sing for you, Scarlett?'

'*Be Bop a Lula*,' Scarlett said without hesitation. It was her current favourite. She listened out for it every night on Radio Luxembourg.

Ricky gave a slight nod. 'OK. *Be Bop a Lula* it is.'

He clicked his fingers to set the beat, and counted the band in.

Scarlett stood just where she was in the middle of the floor, watching and listening. However much she tried to stay cool, she couldn't help moving her shoulders to the beat. And, however much she tried to resist it, she found Ricky fascinating. Everything about him—his stance, his voice, the way he held his guitar, the look in his eyes—drew her in. The song flowed around her. The thud of the drum went through her chest. She fought against the spell.

The last notes died away and Scarlett gave half a dozen claps, her head to one side as if assessing the performance.

'You're not as good as Gene Vincent,' she said.

'No one's as good as Gene Vincent. He's the greatest. But we're the best band singing his songs in Southend,' Ricky claimed. 'You coming to hear us play tonight?'

Scarlett knew she shouldn't. It was like standing on the edge of a precipice. If she jumped she might fall, but then again she might fly. Either was dangerous.

'I'm going dancing,' she told him.

'There's dancing here.'

'I'm going down the Kursaal.'

'Why? We're much better than that square stuff down there.'

'I'm going with my boyfriend,' she lied.

Ricky did an imitation of the famous Elvis thrust. 'Has he got what I've got?'

'All that and more,' Scarlett said. 'Thanks for the performance. Bye.'

She turned and walked towards the outer door, swinging her hips as she moved. She knew she looked good from the back in her tight Capri pants with her long dark ponytail bouncing on her shoulders. There was a thud behind her as Ricky took off his guitar and jumped down from the stage. He ran and slid to a halt in front of her. Scarlett felt a spurt of triumph. She was enjoying this game.

Ricky put his hand into his jacket pocket and produced a couple of tickets. He gave one to Scarlett.

'We're playing at the Rugby Club dance next Saturday. You might like to come along.'

Scarlett glanced at it, shrugged and shoved it into her pocket with her father's wage packet. 'I might. And, there again, I might not,' she said.

Ricky gave her a knowing smile. 'Just think what you'll be missing if you don't.'

'Yeah, a whole lot of trouble.'

She stepped round him and went out of the door. Once round the corner and out of his earshot, she jumped up and down and gave a squeal of exhilaration. That had been fun! She felt alive and tingling all over, like she did when doing the rock 'n' roll. She sang *Singing The Blues* and *Be Bop a Lula* all the way home.

All the next week she thought about the Rugby Club dance. Would she or wouldn't she go? She couldn't make her mind up. She knew she shouldn't. Ricky had 'bad boy' written all over him. But that was the attraction. None of the boys she met at the Kursaal tempted her in the least, however good-looking or charming they were. She enjoyed dancing with them, but that was all. Her heart was Jonathan's. It had been from the moment she'd met him. She could dance with Pete and the others all evening long, but when she went to bed it was Jonathan's arms she imagined around her.

She told Brenda all about it.

'Give it a whirl,' she advised. 'I would.'

'I know you would. But what about Jonathan?'

'What about him? He's on the other side of the world, ain't he? He can't stop you.'

'I know he can't stop me, but that's not the point—'

'You want to live a little, mate. You're only young once, y'know.'

'But I love Jonathan.'

'Well, then, you're safe, ain't you? You're not going to fall for this other bloke. Just go along and have a laugh.'

It all sounded fine. Brenda wasn't saying anything that Scarlett hadn't thought of for herself.

On Thursday a letter arrived from Jonathan, with an account of a Chinese wedding he had been to. It was so strange to think of him being part of something so very alien. And it was still so long until she would see him again. Scarlett took out the ticket and looked at it again. After all, where was the harm in it? She wouldn't even be dancing with Ricky, seeing as he and the band were playing. She would just go along and hear him sing.

Saturday evening saw her changing into her one and only dance dress. She had saved up for weeks to buy it and it was her pride and joy. Made of blue nylon taffeta, with a tight bodice, sweetheart neckline and yards of gathered skirt, it made her feel like a princess. The ponytail looked far too unsophisticated for such a special dress, so she pinned her hair into a bun on the top of her head. Lots of make-up and white stilettos finished the look.

It felt odd to be going out all by herself, but Scarlett wasn't going to let that get her down. Now that she was committed to this evening, it was a big adventure.

She found the Rugby Club and joined the throng of noisy young men and women queuing at the door. The clubhouse was hardly more than a large hut, but there was a real sense of occasion amongst the people going in. They had all been looking forward to this and were out to enjoy themselves. What she hadn't bargained for was how posh they all were. Horsy laughs and middle-class accents came at her from all around. Scarlett just lifted her chin a little higher. She was more than a match for this lot. She had on her dance dress and she felt wonderful.

Inside, the club had been decorated with streamers and balloons to make it look festive, the bar was in full swing and a small stage had been made at one end for the band. And there they were, Ricky and the Riptides, giving their all to *Hound Dog* while couples danced and non-dancers clapped and tapped their feet and all around people were drinking and greeting each other. Scarlett felt a great burst of excitement. It didn't matter that she was a stranger here. The star of the show had invited her and that was enough. She stood at the edge of the small dance floor, looking at Ricky, waiting for him to see her.

When he did, a grin of triumph passed rapidly over his face. So, he thought he had won this round. And maybe he had. She was here, after all. That had to prove something. Scarlett immediately turned to the girl who happened to be standing next to her and struck up a conversation. She wasn't going to let Ricky think she was just going to gaze at him all evening.

'It's good, this, isn't it?' she said. 'I haven't been to one of these dances before.'

'Oh, you'll love it,' the girl said. 'Everyone always

has such fun. And the band's terrific, isn't it? It's the first time we've had them. The committee wanted some boring old trio doing ballroom stuff. They're such a bunch of squares! The boys in the team all said they wanted something with a bit of life. "Give us rock 'n 'roll", they said.'

Hound Dog came to an end. Everyone clapped and whistled. A beefy young man came up to Scarlett's new acquaintance and handed her a lemonade. Scarlett turned her back on the stage and chatted to both of them while Ricky thanked the audience and announced the next number.

'Excuse me.'

Another even beefier young man joined them, a pint jug of beer clasped firmly in his large hand. 'Are you Mike's new girl?' he asked Scarlett.

'No.'

'Oh, good. Would you dance with me, then?'

He wasn't good-looking or remotely charming, but he would do to prove to Ricky that she wasn't waiting around for him.

'As long as you're not welded to that,' she said, nodding at the beer glass.

'Welded to—? Oh! No—I'm sorry, would you like a drink? I should have asked—'

'Let's dance first,' Scarlett said.

This one was going to be easy to control. Not at all like Ricky.

It was as Brenda had said that first time Scarlett had gone to the Kursaal. You just had to get yourself seen on the floor and then it was easy. All the young men who hadn't come with a girlfriend soon realised that

Scarlett was unattached and from then on she hardly sat down. Every now and again she glanced at Ricky to make sure he had noticed how popular she was. If he did, he gave no sign.

When the interval was announced, Scarlett's last partner went to buy her a lime and soda. While he was caught up in the queue at the bar, Ricky appeared at her side.

'Hi, babe. You couldn't keep away, then?'

'Seemed a shame to waste the ticket,' Scarlett said.

'Yeah, right. What about this lot, then? Right bunch of posh cretins.'

'They're very nice.'

'Ah, come on. Grown men who hang onto each other's shorts and roll in the mud together? Where's their style?'

Looking around, Scarlett had to admit that, when it came to style, Ricky won hands down.

'There's more to life than style,' she argued.

Ricky gave a disbelieving smile. 'Admit it, babe, you're just dying for a bit of excitement.'

The trouble was, he was right. Just being near him made her insides churn and her legs go to string. She was repelled by and attracted to him in almost equal amounts.

Her last partner came back with her drink. Ricky casually draped his arm over Scarlett's shoulders. The rugby player's eyes flicked from Ricky to Scarlett and back again.

'She's with me, mate. I've bought her a drink,' he said.

Ricky stared back at him. He didn't look aggressive. He simply had arrogance oozing from him. 'I don't think so, *mate*,' he said. Reaching out, he took the glass and gave it to Scarlett. 'Thanks for looking after her for me. Bye.'

The weight of his hand on her shoulder, his arm across her back was doing strange things to Scarlett. She tried to speak, swallowed, tried again. Her voice came out as a squeak. 'Thanks. I…I'll dance with you again later.'

The rugby player said nothing. He hunched a shoulder and went off in the direction of the bar.

'Oh, dear. He didn't like that, did he?' Ricky remarked. 'How d'you like the music, babe?'

Scarlett took a swig of her drink. The pause gave her time to gather her senses a little. 'Not bad,' she said.

Ricky lifted his hand and ran the back of his finger-nail down her spine. Scarlett practically groaned with painful pleasure.

'I like you,' Ricky told her. She could feel his hot breath on her neck. 'You've got plenty of go in you.'

'Doesn't mean to say it's going for you,' Scarlett countered.

'Oh, I think it is. What would you like me to sing for you in the next set?'

'*Heartbreak Hotel,*' she said. It was the first thing that came into her head.

She was glad when it was time for him to go back and play again.

At the end of the evening she was going to slip away before the band had finished, but she was thwarted by one of her earlier partners grabbing her and insisting that she had the last dance with him. Then there was a huge scrum of girls in the cloakroom and by the time she had found her raincoat there was Ricky waiting for her.

'The others are taking the van home,' he told her. 'I'm taking you.'

This was it. Decision time. She tried to think of Jonathan, but he seemed so vague and far away that she could hardly conjure him up in her mind.

'I don't think so,' she said, making a last effort.

'I do think so,' Ricky stated.

She was caught like a rabbit in the headlights.

They set off for her road with Ricky's arm once more slung round her shoulders. As they went along, he held her closer, so that she either had to fold her arms or put one round his waist. She folded them. Every now and again he leaned over and nuzzled the back of her neck. Her efforts at stopping him were very half-hearted.

They reached the corner of her street.

'I live down here. You don't have to come any further,' she said, trying to back out of his grasp.

In answer, Ricky put both arms round her, pulled her to him and fastened his mouth on hers.

Months of being faithful to Jonathan swelled up and burst inside her. Her young body answered the urgency in his as she clung to him, her mouth and lips and tongue devouring his. The world spun around her until there was nothing but the hot pleasure of his kiss and the yearning down the whole length of her body.

They came up for air, gasping and panting.

'God, Scarlett, you are so hot,' Ricky growled.

Scarlett knew she ought to stop, but wanted it to go on.

'I've got to go,' she said.

'Not yet.'

He kissed her again, bruising her lips against her teeth. Scarlett dug her nails into the back of his neck, making him stop for a moment.

'Bloody hell. You wildcat,' he yelped, and backed her against the blank side wall of the end house.

It was only when he started reaching under the many layers of her net petticoat that Scarlett came to her senses. It was now or never. She must stop.

'No!' she said, struggling to get free from the weight of him pinning her to the wall. 'No. Let me go. I want to go home.'

'Don't tell me you're not enjoying it.'

Ricky gave her one more bruising kiss, then released her.

'Till the next time, babe,' he said with a laugh in his voice.

Scarlett tottered down the road on her stiletto heels and turned in at her gate. He was still there on the corner. He knew where she lived.

She hurried upstairs to the sanctuary of the mean little flat, shut the door behind her and leaned on it, panting. She was safe, for the time being. She had pulled back from the edge.

But when she went to bed, her unsatisfied body kept her awake long into the dark night.

CHAPTER SIXTEEN

RICKY turned up at the flat on Thursday evening.

'Oh!' Scarlett said as she opened the door. 'What are you doing here?'

It was a shock to see him there at the top of the attic stairs. Someone else in the house must have directed him up.

'Nice welcome, I must say,' Ricky responded.

All that week she had been wondering if he would get in touch. Now he was here, dangerously close to her territory, lounging against the landing rail with his hands in his trouser pockets and his brooding eyes running over her body. She wasn't sure that she wanted to see him again after all.

'What do you want?' Scarlett asked.

'Well, I ain't come to deliver the milk, have I?'

'Ha, ha.'

Scarlett was acutely conscious of the musty smell of the hallway and the fact that, behind her, there was no-one else in the flat. She didn't want Ricky to know she was all alone.

'Come on,' he said. 'Stop mucking about. Get your bag, we're going out.'

'I told you, I've got a boyfriend.'

'So what? Give him the elbow. You know you want to.'

'No, I don't.'

'Come out with me anyway.'

Just looking at him was doing odd things to her insides. She recalled what it felt like to be kissed by him and nearly reached out to him then and there.

'I'll ask my dad,' she said, and shut the door in his face.

She turned up the radio to mask the fact that there was no father there to ask, and stood biting her lip and trying to come to a decision. Go out with Ricky or not? She looked at the table, where Jonathan's latest letter lay, waiting for her reply. If she went out with Ricky, she would have to lie to Jonathan. She took a deep breath, marched to the door and opened it about a foot.

'He says no,' she told him, and shut the door again before he could get another word in.

A mocking laugh came through the flimsy wood.

'I'll be back, babe.'

She spent the rest of the evening wondering whether she had done the right thing.

On Friday and Saturday evenings she went dancing, but found that somehow the shine had gone off it. The boys were boring and stupid. Even her old friend Pete, the ace dancer, annoyed her. She kept catching sight of young men she thought were Ricky, only to be disappointed.

On Sunday afternoon, just as he had promised—or just as he had threatened?—Ricky was back.

'Come on, babe,' he said. 'I'll take you down the speedway.'

It was a beautiful afternoon and the point in the week when Scarlett felt most alone in the world. She had nothing but *The Billy Cotton Band Show* on the radio to keep her company at a time when everybody else was with their families having Sunday lunch with all the trimmings.

'All right,' she said, before she could persuade herself otherwise.

As they walked down the street, she asked why he wasn't at home with his family.

'My mum and dad have gone to my gran's.'

'But didn't they want you to go with them?'

Ricky made a dismissive noise. 'Yeah, but I wasn't going to. Mad old bat. And she smells. Said I had better things to do.' To prove it, he pinched her bottom.

Scarlett yelped and slapped his hand. 'Get off!'

He didn't know how lucky he was to have a grandmother, she thought. If only she had more family, she wouldn't feel so very alone in the world.

Going to the sea front with Ricky was a strange experience. Everything was so familiar, but being there with him instead of Jonathan made it utterly different. It was as if a line was being drawn between now and the past. Young Scarlett, with her plaits and her white ankle socks, lurked there, just the other side of the line. She laughed and held hands with Jonathan, she cried for her mother. It made Scarlett realise how much things had changed. She still missed her mother every day, but the grief was blunted. She still missed Jonathan, but he was far away. She no longer expected anything from her father, who started each day now not just with a cigarette but with a drink as well. She was on her own. And here was Ricky, who could have any girl he wanted, going out of his way to chase her.

She could see other girls eyeing him up wherever

they went, even girls who were with their boyfriends. It made her feel very superior. She was the chosen one, the lucky girl with the boy who looked like a singing star. The boy who might well turn out to be a singing star. Ricky had no doubts on that score.

'We're getting known in Southend, but that's just the start,' he told her as they licked their ice creams. 'Next we got to play up in London. The Two I's coffee bar, that's the place to be. That's where Tommy Steele got discovered. All we need is for an agent to hear us play and we're made. Rock 'n' roll's the thing, babe. It's our music. It belongs to us.'

'Oh, yes,' Scarlett agreed. 'Once I heard Elvis, all that stuff by Johnny Ray and Perry Como was dead. It's really square.'

But Ricky wasn't interested in her opinion. All he needed was his own, which he aired at length.

After the speedway they went on the big wheel. When their chair stopped right at the top to let someone on at the bottom, Ricky rocked it until Scarlett squealed. Then he got hold of her and kissed her. Fear made her all the more responsive.

When they got off, he looked around Peter Pan's Playground with that James Dean sneer.

'This is tame. Let's go to the Kursaal and ride on the Cyclone. That'll make you scream.'

It did make her scream. The vertiginous drop made her feel as if her stomach had been left behind on the top. After that he took her in the Caterpillar. By the time they came out, her legs would hardly hold her up.

They had frothy coffee at the brand new coffee bar that had opened up in the High Street. Ricky fed money into the jukebox and told her about the singers he had chosen and why they were the best, and why the Riptides would soon be up there with the established stars. Right on cue, a couple of girls behind them started squeaking and whispering.

'Look, it's Ricky from Ricky and the Riptides!'

'I saw him the other week. He's really good.'

'Looks all right and all.'

As they left the coffee bar, Ricky gave them a passing wave.

'Hi, babes.'

The girls dissolved into delighted giggles.

Scarlett drank it all in.

Ricky delivered her back to the flat at about teatime.

'You inviting me in, then?' he asked.

Even in her weakened state, Scarlett knew better than to fall for that one. She'd already broken one of the rules of courtship—no kissing on the first date. In fact she'd more than broken it in allowing not just a quick touch on the lips but proper deep kisses. But ask a boy in when you were all by yourself? Oh, no.

'You must be joking,' she said, reaching up to give him a peck on the cheek. 'Thanks for—'

She got no further. Ricky wrapped his arms round her and kissed her passionately. Behind them, the tenant of the downstairs front room rapped loudly on the window. Ricky waved two fingers.

'Come on,' he said. 'You know you want to.'

Her body wanted to. Her head was more than aware of the dangers.

'No,' she insisted. 'I don't know what you think I am.'

'I think you're the hottest babe I ever met.'

'Oh, yeah? And how many girls have you said that to?'

'Only you. You're the best.'

Somehow, she managed to get free and once more slam the door in his face.

Of course, playing hard to get was the surest way of sharpening his interest. But it was a game two could play. Ricky would be all over her, asking her out, taking her to gigs with the band, even bringing her flowers and chocolates, then he would disappear for a week at a time, leaving her wondering whether he would ever show up again.

One Saturday evening at the end of September, Scarlett was dancing at the Kursaal as usual when she glimpsed him through the crowd. As always when that happened, her insides turned painfully. She looked again, expecting to find she was agonising over a perfect stranger, and found that it really was him. What was more, he was wrapped round a common-looking girl with a very low-cut blouse and too much make-up. She was gripped with murderous jealousy.

'Look at that!' she hissed at Brenda. 'He's here— Ricky's here—with that little tart.'

'Swine,' Brenda said.

'I'll scratch her eyes out!'

She really wanted to. Her fingers ached to pull the girl's hair out, to do her some damage. She stepped forward. Brenda caught hold of her.

'Don't give him the pleasure,' she counselled. 'He'd love that, wouldn't he? Two girls fighting over him.'

'I don't care. How dare he two-time me?'

Brenda had the sense not to mention Jonathan's name at this point. Instead, she gripped Scarlett's arm even tighter.

'Don't be a bloody idiot. He'll have you just where he wants you then, won't he? Give him a taste of his own medicine. Dance with Pete or someone.'

Enough of the rage dissolved for Scarlett to see that she was right. She danced every dance, and when she was with Pete she made sure that Ricky was close enough to notice how brilliantly they performed together. It felt like the longest evening she had ever spent there. She left early, before Ricky could see that nobody was taking her home, and waited for the last bus weeping tears of anger and disappointment. Her evening had been ruined. Her enjoyment of the Kursaal had been ruined. She would never feel the same way about it again.

'I hate you, Ricky Harrington,' she muttered to herself. 'You've spoilt everything.'

Footsore and exhausted, she let herself into the flat. A revolting smell hit her. She fumbled for the light switch and cried out loud. Her father was slumped on the floor in a pool of vomit. She rushed forward, turning her ankle painfully in her high heeled dancing shoes. She kicked them off, bent and got her hands under his armpits to drag him away from the mess. It was heavy work, as he was a dead weight. She managed to get him out of the worst of it, found a newspaper to put under his head and went downstairs with a bucket to get some water. At first she couldn't decide what to do first. Clean up her father or clear up the sick? He was still unconscious and the smell was making her heave, so she decided on clearing up. She toiled up and down the stairs with newspapers and cloths and buckets, scraping and scrubbing until the smell of bleach overlaid that of vomit. Then she got yet more clean water. She eased her father's soiled shirt and jumper off, then gently wiped the mess from his face and hair.

'Oh, Dad,' she wailed. 'What have you done to yourself?'

She tried to remember the strong, happy father who used to hug her and her mother and joke with the customers at the Red Lion. Where had he gone? This defeated man with his shabby clothes and bloated face was a different person. As she washed him, he began to regain consciousness, first moaning, then muttering odd words. He seemed afraid.

'It's all right, Dad. You're safe, you're at home,' she told him.

Victor opened his eyes. He stared at her blankly.

'Joan. Where's Joan?' he croaked.

Tears welled up in Scarlett's eyes. 'It's Scarlett, Dad. I'm here. Can you get up?'

She tried to help him up but he made no effort to move.

'No, no. Leave me. I want Joan.'

Scarlett opened up the put-u-up and tried again.

'Come on, Dad. You can't stay there on the floor. You'll be more comfortable in bed.'

By degrees she managed to get him off the floor and on to the bed. She covered him with a sheet and blanket and placed the bucket beside him. She stroked his damp head.

'There's a bucket there if you feel ill again, all right? Now you go to sleep. It'll look better in the morning.'

She went down to the bathroom one more time to scrub the smell out of her hands. Then she fell into bed and cried herself to sleep. She had never felt more alone.

The morning brought fresh trials. Victor woke with a

massive hangover and insisted on hair of the dog to help cope with it. Scarlett made him tea, which he refused, then found the last drop of whisky in a flat bottle in his jacket pocket and went and flushed it down the toilet. After a massive row, Victor slammed out of the flat.

'You're no daughter of mine!' he shouted through the door, and stumped off down the stairs.

Scarlett wrenched the door open again.

'Don't you dare come back drunk!' she yelled at his departing back.

Which brought complaints from three of the neighbours.

'Oh, shut up!' she snapped at them, and went back inside.

She looked round the dreary flat—at the gloomy greenish lino, the rickety furniture, the patches on the peeling walls where it got damp in winter. It was horrible, horrible, horrible. And so was her life.

'You got to do something, girl,' she said out loud. 'You can't go on like this.'

The first thing was to find a better flat. She ran a comb through her hair, put on some lipstick and went off to the newsagent's to get a *Southend Standard.* Just making the decision made her feel a hundred times better. With the paper under her arm, she started to walk back with something like a spring in her step. Perhaps when they moved, her father could be persuaded to turn over a new leaf. Then, if he could hold down a better job, she could get away from doing factory work and try something less well paid but more interesting. Just as she had come to this conclusion, a van pulled up beside her.

'Hey, babe!'

It was Ricky, in the TV repair van that one of the Riptides had the use of.

Scarlett hardly paused in her stride. 'I've got nothing to say to you.'

'Oh babe, you know you don't mean that.'

Ricky stopped the van and got out. He jogged round in front of her. He was dressed in a snappy suit and tie and carrying a bunch of pink carnations.

'For you,' he said, holding them out to her.

Scarlett thrust them back at him. 'I don't want them.'

'Ah, babe, you're not jealous, are you?'

'Don't flatter yourself.'

Scarlett made to dodge round him, but he sidestepped back into her path.

'You haven't really got a boyfriend, have you?'

'I have!'

'So where is he, then, if you're not with him on a Saturday night?'

He had never been that interested before and, when he had asked, Scarlett had fobbed him off with some glib answer.

'Busy,' she said.

'Too busy to go out with a cracking bird like you? He don't deserve you.'

'He's…tied up.'

'He's inside, ain't he? Doing time.'

That shocked her.

'He's not! He's on his national service.'

'Where?'

'Malaya,' Scarlett admitted.

'Malaya! Blimey, he's not much use to you there, is

he? Look—' for once, his voice became serious '—be my girl, Scarlett. Come out with me. I got the van, look. We can go for a ride right along the sea front and have lunch in a café, all nice, like. What do you say?'

After the dreadful time she had had with her father, it was just too tempting.

'All right,' she said.

Which opened up the second part of Ricky's campaign.

CHAPTER SEVENTEEN

JONATHAN sat on a folding chair outside his hut with Scarlett's latest letter in its envelope in his hand. Giant moths fluttered round the hurricane lamp on the table beside him and from the dense greenery beyond the compound came the night sounds of animals. His surroundings were so familiar now that he hardly noticed them. What concerned him was the letter.

A couple of nurses coming off-duty waved to him as they passed.

'Hey, Jonno, coming to the teashop?'

'Yeah, in a minute,' Jonathan answered.

He took the letter out and read it again. It was difficult to pinpoint why it made him so uneasy. It was just—wrong. And it wasn't the first time. This feeling had been growing in him for a few weeks now. There was something Scarlett wasn't telling him.

He gazed in the direction in which the nurses had disappeared. The teashop was a cross between a bar and a café in a little bamboo hut just outside the compound. It was run by a whole Chinese family and offered tea, *dim sum* and home-brewed beer as well as a break from army life. Jonathan sighed, put the letter in his breast pocket and got up. It was no use sitting here brooding. That wasn't going to solve anything.

The usual gang was sitting round a low table, swigging beer, sipping jasmine tea and snacking on plates of steamed Chinese delicacies by the light of red tasselled lanterns. Chinese music tinkled from the gramophone. A place was found for Jonathan in the circle and a beer put before him. The conversation was mostly about the forthcoming cricket match between the hospital team and one from a camp a few miles away. Tactics were being aired. Jonathan tried to join in but his heart wasn't in it.

The girl next to him, Judy, touched his knee.

'What's up, Jonno?' she asked. 'You're not with us at all, are you?'

'Nothing,' Jonathan said automatically. Then on impulse he changed his mind. 'Well, yes, actually there is something. I don't know whether you can help me.'

He and Judy were old allies. She had a fiancé back in Scotland to whom she was fiercely faithful, so they tended to pair up on the strict understanding that it was friendship only.

'For you, my pet, anything. Or almost anything.'

Jonathan glanced at the rowdy group. He didn't want them listening to this. One whiff of gossip and his worries would be all over the compound.

'Let's get away from this lot,' he said.

To a chorus of 'Ooh—' and 'Look at them!' from the others, they decamped to a small table in the corner, and Jonathan explained his concerns.

'I'm wondering whether it's her father,' he said. 'He's

a drunk. He doesn't look after her like a father should. In fact, if anything, she looks after him.'

'If that's it, why don't you ask her?' Judy said. 'If she's worried, she'll be glad to tell you about it.'

'It's difficult. We had this big row about him, you see. He's all she's got in the world by way of family, so she defends him. In fact she said that if I couldn't accept her father, I could sling my hook.'

'Mmm—' Judy pursed her lips and considered the situation. 'Even so, if she hasn't anyone else to turn to, she might really need to talk to you but after what she said she doesn't know how to start. If you were to write something like, "You sound very worried. Is everything all right at home?" Not mentioning her father by name, just sort of opening the door, so to speak.'

'Yes—' Jonathan turned it over in his mind. 'Yes, that might do it.'

But somehow he didn't really feel any better about it.

Judy leaned forward. 'Look, Jonno, you don't think it's anything else, do you?'

'Like what?' he asked sharply.

'Well, shout at me if you like, but I've seen her photo, and she's a very pretty girl, your Scarlett. And you say she goes dancing every week.'

'So what are you saying?' Jonathan asked, though he knew perfectly well.

Judy just raised her eyebrows a little and looked at him.

'Scarlett loves me,' he told her.

'Well, then, you've nothing to worry about, have you?'

'No.'

Except that the nasty little suspicion just wouldn't go away.

* * *

Scarlett fought Ricky off in the back seats of cinemas, in the van and outside dance halls and pubs. Each time it got more difficult to say no. But what she did hold out on was letting him in to the flat. As long as she kept him out of there, she felt she was safe.

'So your precious Jonathan's out of the picture, then?' Brenda said.

'No!' Scarlett said. 'Ricky's just a bit of fun, until Jonathan comes back. I love Jonathan. I always will.'

'But you don't mind two-timing him?'

'I'm not two-timing him.'

'Looks like it to me.'

'Well—he goes out with all those nurses to parties and things.'

'But does he snog them in car parks?'

'I don't—!' Scarlett began.

Brenda snorted. 'I've seen you,' she said. 'I bet you ain't told him about Ricky.'

Guilt surged through Scarlett. Brenda had hit it right on the button. She had not told Jonathan about Ricky. She used to mention Pete and the other boys at the Kursaal, but she had never once let Ricky's name drop.

'I bet there's things he doesn't tell me,' she said.

'Oh, well, if you two really love each other like you say you do, then that's all right, ain't it?' Brenda said. But there was an edge of sarcasm to her voice.

'Yes, it is,' Scarlett said.

But she was becoming increasingly confused. Going out with Ricky was a roller coaster ride. There were evenings of wild excitement and days of guilt and worry. It wasn't like going out with Jonathan. They didn't talk much. They weren't utterly engrossed in each other.

The only time she had Ricky's full attention was when he was snogging her. And he was wearing her down. Her body cried out for his touch. Even as she batted his hands away, she wanted him to carry on, to go further.

Then Jonathan's letters would arrive, full of tales of his strange and distant life on the compound, but always ending with a declaration of his undying love. Reading them, she was sure she did still love him and knew that she shouldn't be going out with Ricky. It was playing with fire. The trouble was, she was becoming as addicted to Ricky as her father was to alcohol. The more she had of him, the more she wanted.

After a gig at one of the sea front pubs, they walked home together. Scarlett felt quite ill as they passed the Trafalgar. A sharp longing for times past pierced her heart. Things had been simple then. She and Jonathan loved each other, and that was all that mattered.

'Let's go along the cliffs,' Ricky said.

The cliffs were full of places where the grass was long and the trees gave cover. Even now, in autumn, there would be courting couples taking advantage of the friendly dark.

Scarlett looked over at the broad frontage of the pub. Up there was his parents' flat. Jonathan's home.

'No,' she said. 'I'm tired. I want to go straight home.'

In answer, Ricky steered her round the sea side of a shelter. Under the fancy roof, he kissed her expertly and ran his hands down her back and over her buttocks.

'Now then,' he said, 'you don't really want to go home yet, do you?'

'Yes, I do.'

Scarlett tried to wriggle free, but Ricky backed her

against the side wall of the shelter. With his body pressed against hers, Scarlett could feel her resolve falling away. Ricky kissed her again, covering a breast with his hand, running his thumb across her nipple. Scarlett couldn't suppress a moan of pleasure.

'No, you don't,' Ricky said.

She could hear the wolfish smile in his voice.

'We'll go for a little walk on the beach,' he told her.

With his arm firmly round her waist, he guided her down the nearest steps and onto the pebbly sand. Scarlett's high heels sank in, making it difficult to walk. She took her shoes off and carried them in one hand. It was quieter here, away from the traffic and the throngs of noisy drinkers coming out of the pubs. The smell of salt and seaweed fought with the wafts of chips and candyfloss and onions. The multicoloured lights of the illuminations reflected in the puddles on the glistening mud, and beyond them the pier strode out into the sea with lights strung along it like a giant necklace. The pebbles were cool under Scarlett's bare feet.

Ricky stopped and kissed her again, gripping her buttocks and pulling her against him. She could feel him, hard and eager, against her groin, awakening an answering flame.

'God, but you're fantastic, babe,' he said in her ear. 'I want you so much I can't stop thinking about you. You're on my mind all the time.'

Scarlett's legs were so weak that it was easy for him to pull her down on the sand with him. Before she had time to protest, his mouth was fastened on hers and his hand was inside her blouse, pulling down her bra strap, exposing her breast, cupping it with his hand, stroking and squeezing.

He stopped for a moment, sitting up to strip off his jacket, which he rolled and put under Scarlett's head.

'Now—' he said, 'you're going to like this, babe. You're going to love it.'

And she did. From the moment he slid his hand up her thigh and explored between her legs, she was helpless, swept away on a hot tide of desire. She cried out with pain when he entered her, but soon the need and the pleasure overcame it, until both of them collapsed in a slippery, satiated heap.

'Christ, babe,' Ricky said hoarsely, pushing the hair back from her hot face. 'You were a virgin, weren't you?'

'Yes.'

'You're a natural, babe. We gotta do this all the time. You're just amazing.'

Scarlett said nothing. She was feeling so many different things that she couldn't take it all in. But most of all she knew that there was no going back now. She had done It with Ricky, and nothing would ever be the same again.

For once, Ricky noticed that she was unnaturally quiet.

'You all right, babe?'

'I think so.'

'You did enjoy it, didn't you? I said you would.'

'Yes.'

There was no denying that. She was only now beginning to notice that she was sore and bruised.

'That's all right, then. Come on, we better get going.' He sorted out his clothing and handed her a clean handkerchief. 'Here—d'you want this?'

Dazed, Scarlett realised that real life had been going

on all the while she had been in some other place with Ricky. Drunks were still rolling along the sea front. The chip shops were still frying. Embarrassed now, she cleaned herself up with the offered handkerchief and felt about for her knickers and shoes and bag.

Ricky stood up and pulled her to her feet. Scarlett clung to him, wobbly and disorientated, and they made their way back up the steps and joined the homegoing crowds milling about on the sea front. Ricky was in top spirits.

'God, you are just the greatest, babe,' he said.

He put his arm round her waist and sang all the way back to the flat.

After that, there was no point in putting up any resistance. Every evening that he wasn't playing with the band, Ricky came round to the flat. While he was with her, Scarlett gave herself up completely to this new and amazing pleasure. At all other times she was in turmoil.

The rules of the game, as outlined by the girls in every factory she had worked at, were that you didn't give in. Boys were only after one thing and, though they didn't like it when you refused, they did at least respect you. Once they got what they wanted, they lost interest. More often than not they boasted to their friends about you, and then you lost your reputation. Scarlett lived in fear of Ricky losing interest and on top of that was ashamed of how much she enjoyed making love with him and worried that this meant she was a bad girl.

Then there was the guilt. It was all too easy to deceive her father, who still thought she was an innocent young girl, but it made her feel bad. What made her feel worse was deceiving Jonathan. She knew she should tell him what was going on, but couldn't bring herself to do so.

She couldn't bear to hurt him, or to destroy everything they were to each other. But it made writing to him a nightmare. She put it off until she got a letter from him wondering if one of hers had gone astray as he hadn't heard from her, and asking if everything was all right at home.

And then she missed a period.

She was never late, so she knew straight away that something was wrong. Overheard conversations amongst the older women at work gave her plenty of clues as to why she had tender breasts and a bloated stomach. For a while she held on tight to the fact that she was not sick in the mornings, but she knew really that this was no help. Not everyone had morning sickness. That didn't mean that she wasn't… She refused to actually put a name to it.

'You're quiet,' Brenda complained. 'Can't get a word out of you. What's up?'

'Nothing,' Scarlett told her.

Perhaps it would all go away. Maybe she was just late. Just because she had been regular up till now, it didn't mean it couldn't change.

'Ricky given you the push?'

'No.'

But what would happen if she had to tell him? She couldn't see Ricky as a father.

The problem dominated her life, pushing out all the minor worries.

By November she knew there would be no reprieve. She took a morning off work and went to the doctor, who confirmed it and worked out the due date. It was official. She was having a baby.

'And what about the father?' the doctor asked, looking at her disapprovingly over the tops of his glasses.

'What about him?' Scarlett said.

'Does he know about this child?'

'Not yet.'

'Then I suggest you tell him straight away. There are arrangements to be made.' His gaze hardened. 'You do know who the father is, I hope?'

'Of course I do!' Scarlett said. 'What do you think I am?'

It was the first indication of what was to come.

Walking home in the drizzling rain, Scarlett considered all the people she had to tell. Ricky. Her father. Jonathan. Oh, God, how was she going to tell Jonathan? It was going to break his heart. She had been such an idiot. How could she have done this? Tears of shame and regret trickled down her face with the raindrops. She reached her road and looked down it. Going out with Ricky had distracted her from looking for somewhere better. What if he didn't stand by her? They wouldn't even be able to afford this horrible flat without her wages. She would be stuck in one room with a baby and her father. It didn't bear thinking about.

For several long minutes she stood at the end of the street, tempted to just walk away and keep walking. For the umpteenth time she wished for her mother. She needed someone to turn to more than ever before. And then it struck her how terribly upset and disappointed her mother would have been to find that her one daughter was an unmarried mother, and something changed inside her. At least her mum would never know. She might hurt all the others around her, but she couldn't hurt her mother. Scarlett took a long shuddering breath and straightened her shoulders.

'Come on, girl,' she said out loud. 'Let's face the music.'

It was her father's day off. He was sitting listening to the radio with a drink in his hand. Scarlett's announcement seemed to sober him up instantly.

'You're *what*?' he yelped, getting up out of his chair. 'It's that singer, ain't it? That Ricky? The little bastard, doing that to you! I knew he was no good. My God, when I get my hands on him, he won't know whether he's coming or going. I'll wring his bloody neck. How dare he touch my little girl?'

Scarlett didn't like to tell him that she hadn't exactly been forced.

'Have you told him yet?' Victor asked.

Scarlett shook her head.

'When are you seeing him again?'

'I don't know. Tomorrow, probably.'

'I'm working tomorrow. This has got to be sorted out. Where does he live?'

Scarlett gaped at him.

'We can't go round his house, Dad!'

She knew where he lived. She had even been past his house on a couple of occasions, but she had never been invited inside to meet his parents.

'Oh, yes, we bloody well can. What time does he get in from work?'

However hard Scarlett tried to persuade him that it would be best to tell Ricky quietly by herself, Victor wouldn't back down.

'I know these young lads. They'll wriggle out of it if they possibly can. No, we got to get him in front of his parents. They'll bring him into line.'

Defending his chick had a wonderful effect on Victor.

He washed, shaved, cleaned his shoes, looked out his one suit and brushed it and had Scarlett iron him a shirt. By the time they set out for Ricky's house, he looked a different man from the one who couldn't get up in the morning without a drink. However much she was dreading this confrontation, Scarlett was glad to have him at her side. For the first time in ages, she felt she had a proper father. If it hadn't been for the desperate circumstances, she would have been delighted.

Ricky's parents lived in a neat terraced house in Westcliff. The privet hedge was clipped, the front path was swept and the brass knocker and letter box were polished. A small thin woman in a frilly apron with tightly permed pepper-and-salt hair opened the door to them.

'Yes?' she said, looking coldly from Victor to Scarlett.

'Mrs Harrington? This is my girl, Scarlett. Your boy Ricky's been taking her out.'

Ricky's mother made no move to ask them in.

'Yes?' she repeated.

'Well—' Victor shifted uncomfortably. Scarlett felt her fleeting confidence in him begin to seep away. 'Well…er…we got things we need to talk about. Things that's better said inside. Sitting down, like.'

'I don't know who you are,' Ricky's mother said.

The man who used to run the Red Lion surfaced. Victor introduced himself and held his hand out. Ricky's mother did not appear to be impressed, but she grudgingly let them in. She showed them into the front room, where a green moquette-covered three-piece suite was placed round a television set with a lamp on top of it in the shape of a crinolined lady. A small coal fire burned in the grate, but it had been recently laid and wasn't yet giving out much heat. Scarlett and Victor perched uneasily on the sofa while Mrs Harrington fetched her husband.

'This is George. I'm Betty,' she said.

Mr Harrington was an older version of Ricky. He nodded silently at Scarlett and Victor and sat down in the chair nearest to the fire, staring resentfully at them.

Victor cleared his throat. 'Well…er…'

'I hope this is important. I was eating my tea,' Mr Harrington said.

'I'm sorry—' Victor began.

Scarlett wanted to disappear into the stiff sofa. This was going to be dreadful. Her father was backing down before they had even started.

But Victor managed to bring himself up to the mark.

'But yes, it is important. Very important.' He plunged straight in to the business in hand. 'Your son's got my girl in the family way, and I want to know what he's going to do about it.'

Mrs Harrington squawked with shock and horror.

'My Ricky? With you? I don't believe it. He's a good boy.'

Mr Harrington just sat there, stony-faced.

'It's true. She's been to the doctor's and everything. It's due in June.'

Mr Harrington finally spoke. 'You sure it's Ricky's?'

Scarlett was outraged. This was the second time she had been doubted and she wasn't having it. It was bad enough being pregnant without everyone assuming she was a bad girl.

'Of course it's his. What are you saying? I've never been with anyone else in my life.'

At that moment, there was the sound of a key in the door. Everyone's heads swivelled round as footsteps came into the hall. Scarlett felt ill.

Mr Harrington broke the silence. 'Richard! Come in here.'

Ricky stepped into the room. He caught sight of Scarlett and Victor and stopped dead.

'Bloody hell. What are you doing here?'

'Ricky! Language!' his mother exclaimed.

'We got some sorting out to do here, son,' his father said. He gave Scarlett a hard look. 'This girl—'

Victor interrupted. 'You got my Scarlett in the family way, and I want to know what you're going to do about it,' he said loudly.

'I…what…you're never…' Ricky stuttered.

He looked round at all the eyes fixed on him. For one terrible moment, Scarlett thought he was going to deny all knowledge.

'Is it yours, son?' his father asked heavily.

'Mine?' Ricky shifted his shoulders. Then, to Scarlett's amazement, a cocky grin appeared on his face. 'Of course it is. Nothing wrong with the old equipment, is there, babe?'

All three adults looked shocked.

'You little—' Victor growled.

Scarlett put a hand on his arm, afraid that he might get physical.

'It's all right, Dad.'

'No, it ain't all right—'

'There's no need for that sort of talk, son,' Mr Harrington told him.

Ricky rolled his eyes. 'Blimey, I only—'

'You'll have to get married, of course,' Mrs Harrington stated.

'Married?' Ricky looked horrified. 'I don't know about that.'

'You've admitted to it. You're the one what indulged in immoral behaviour. Now you got to bear the consequences, and give this child a name,' his father said.

'Though everyone will know. A seven month baby. I don't know how I'm going to hold my head up. Nothing like this has ever happened in my family before,' his mother ranted.

'Young people today. Got no shame. Wouldn't have happened in my day,' his father stated.

'Girls in our day knew how to behave,' Mrs Harrington agreed, glaring at Scarlett.

Victor flared up at this. 'My Scarlett's a good girl. She got led astray by your son.'

'Bloody hell!' Ricky exploded, producing gasps and cries of shock all round. 'I tell you something, it'll be worth it just to get away from here. Nag, nag, nag all day long. Don't do this, don't say that. Take your shoes off, chew your food proper, watch your tongue. I've had enough of it, you hear? Scarlett and me'll get a place and do what we want, won't we, babe? All night and all day, and no one to tell us we can't.'

Scarlett hardly heard the furore that this produced. She sat staring at the flames as they began to lick round the coals. Married. She was going to be married to Ricky. A huge dark weight seemed to settle on her, filling her with dread. She knew it would be the wrong thing to do. Ricky was not the man for her. The only person she wanted to spend the rest of her life with was Jonathan. But inside her was Ricky's baby.

There was no way out.

CHAPTER EIGHTEEN

THE wedding was quick and very unromantic. Ricky's mother took charge and insisted that they married in church.

'I don't hold with them registry office things,' she said. 'I don't care what they say, I don't think you're properly married at them places. It's bad enough having to rush things like this.'

She did relent a little in her attitude to Scarlett when she realised that her daughter-in-law to be didn't have a mother to guide her.

'All the same, you should of known better,' she kept saying.

That seemed to be everyone's opinion. Ricky didn't come in for much blame at all. It was all Scarlett's fault for giving in to him. Some joker at work made up a new nickname for her—the Scarlett Woman. She heard it whispered wherever she went.

She hardly slept the night before her wedding. She harboured wild thoughts of running off and finding a ship to take her to Malaya and Jonathan. But imagining telling him that she was carrying someone else's baby put paid to that. She was caught up in what everyone else had decided was the right thing to do, and the only alternative was to have the baby all by herself, which still wouldn't bring back the old days with Jonathan. In the end she did what she had known she was going to do all along. She got up and put on the dress she had borrowed from one of the girls at work.

Mrs Harrington had been scandalised that she would be wearing white when she wasn't a virgin.

'You're the one that wants to keep up appearances,' Scarlett told her.

So here she was, wearing a nylon satin dress that didn't really fit her. The fashion for tight bodices and tiny waists was not kind to the pregnant woman. The girl she had borrowed the dress from was much fatter than her, so though it went round her expanding belly all right, the rest of it was far too large. She sighed and plonked the head-dress and veil on her pinned-up hair. It hid the worst of it.

Brenda arrived. She was also dressed in borrowed finery, a lemon-yellow bridesmaid's dress from the same source as Scarlett's.

'You all right?' she asked.

'No.'

'For Gawd's sake! He's a bit of all right, your Ricky, and he ain't made any fuss about getting married, has he?'

'Why should he? It's his baby too, you know.'

'Yeah, but it don't always follow that they admit it. I bet there's a lot of girls round this town ready to step into your shoes right now.'

'They can have him. It's Jonathan I want.'

'You should of thought of that before you let Ricky put you up the duff,' Brenda told her.

Which was so true that Scarlett was silenced.

Victor, Scarlett and Brenda took a taxi to the church. Victor was dressed once more in his suit and buoyed up with a bottle of whisky in his pocket. By the time they arrived, it was Scarlett who had to support him up the aisle.

A disapproving vicar intoned the service in a bored voice. Scarlett and Ricky repeated the vows, the register was signed, and there they were, man and wife. They all went back to the Harringtons' for a buffet lunch, where Victor drank most of the beer and went out for more whisky and Ricky's family looked more and more appalled at the whole set-up. The happy couple escaped as soon as they could for a one night honeymoon in Clacton, where Scarlett spent most of the time in tears. She still hadn't told Jonathan.

Jonathan had a bad feeling about the letter the moment it arrived. It had been nearly a month since Scarlett's last one, and that had been very brief, telling him that everything was fine at home and if he meant was her father a problem, he was quite all right, thank you very much. Jonathan had been regretting asking about him ever since Judy had advised him to try. After all, what did Judy know? She was very nice and kind, but she had never met Scarlett or her father. She couldn't understand how loyal Scarlett was to him. He stood holding the latest letter, turning it over and over in his hands. Good news or bad, he knew it was best to get it over with, but he needed somewhere quiet to read it.

'Another hot one from the girlfriend?' someone in the hut asked.

'Yeah. Not for your eyes, mate,' Jonathan said.

He thrust it into his pocket, where it burned all morning long.

It wasn't until the lunches had been served and cleared away that he had ten minutes to himself. He sat on a packing crate under the palms behind the kitchen and tore it open. The first thing he noticed was a new address in Westcliff, then that the letter itself was very short.

My dearest Jonathan,
I'm sorry I haven't written for so long. An awful lot has happened these last few weeks and I didn't know how to tell you.

As you can see from the top, I've moved. It's a nice flat on the ground floor with two bedrooms and a proper kitchen and everything. Well, there isn't a bathroom but there's a toilet out the back that no one uses but us and we can wash in the kitchen. It's really lovely having my own sink with my own tap and not having to go downstairs for water all the time like at the last place. We have to boil a kettle for hot water but that's not a problem. I've got a real cooker as well, with an oven and everything. The kitchen's very poky, you can hardly turn round in it, but it is a real kitchen, not just a corner with a gas ring and a bowl like I had before.

I had to clean the whole flat right through when we moved in. You should have seen the mess! The last people kept dogs there and it was all covered with hairs and muddy paw-prints and worse. The smell! I don't know how people can live like that. We got the first week for free because of it though

*so it was worth the effort. Brenda was a real angel
and came and helped me.*

*Jonathan, I don't know how to tell you this. I've
been putting it off and putting it off and now I've
got to tell you because it's not right not to. The
reason why I've moved is because I got married
last week. Jonathan, I'm so sorry. It all happened
so quickly. I always thought that when you came
back, well, you and me, but it's too late now. I
know this is going to be a terrible shock for you. I
hope you won't hate me because I still care a lot
for you and it's making me really upset to think of
you reading this. I've tried lots of times to make
this letter not so bad, but I don't know what else
to say, only that I'm sorry and please don't hate
me.*

Love,
Scarlett

At first Jonathan was so shocked he just stared at the
words on the page.

'No,' he said out loud. 'No. You can't do this to me.'

He read the whole thing through again slowly in the
vain hope that he might have misunderstood. But no,
there it was. Scarlett had got married. A terrible physical
pain tore at his guts. This could not be happening to him.
Not his Scarlett. He dug his knuckles into his eyes,
trying to keep the tears at bay.

How could she do this? How long had it all been going
on? Who was this man who had taken her away from him?

He thought of all the opportunities he had had here—
the nurses, the Malay girls, the Chinese girls. He had

turned them all down because he knew Scarlett was waiting for him at home. Or at least, he had thought she was waiting for him at home. Clearly she hadn't. But to string him along like this! All the time pretending everything was all right, then to tell him she was married. He felt utterly betrayed.

A murderous rage came to his rescue. He couldn't stay where he was a moment longer. Not caring what the consequences might be, he walked out of the compound through the hole in the wire at the back and went and got very drunk at a bar.

At some point in the evening he fell into the arms of a Malay girl who took him back to her village. After that he remembered nothing until he was finally arrested by the military police the next day and put on a charge. He didn't care. Nothing mattered, now that Scarlett was no longer waiting for him back home. The future was blank.

His senior officer read him a lecture on ruining his unblemished record. Jonathan couldn't feel anything much about it. It was his own sense of responsibility to the patients he was feeding that kept him doing his job properly. The routine of the kitchen held him together and made a pattern to each day.

He vented his feelings in a blistering letter to Scarlett that ran into several pages. He felt slightly better having written it, as if an abscess had been lanced. For days afterwards he wavered between regretting having sent it and being pleased that Scarlett should be made to feel bad about what she had done. Either way, the deed was done. He did not expect a reply.

It was Judy who put the pieces together again. At first she was sympathetic, then she became stern.

'You're drinking far too much,' she told him after a going-away party.

'Everyone drinks at parties,' he said.

'Not as much as you do. You're not just drinking to be sociable like the rest of us. You're drinking to forget.'

'So? It works.'

'And how do you feel this morning?'

'All right.'

He hurt so much all the time that a headache was almost a welcome distraction.

'Liar. You've got a huge hangover. I can tell. And do you remember what you got up to last night?'

Jonathan didn't answer. He could recall the first part of the evening, but the rest was a blur. He had some unexplained cuts and bruises but he had woken up in the right bed.

'You got very aggressive, you challenged Mike to a fight and then you fell over a table and passed out. The lads had to carry you home. You'd better thank them, because if it weren't for them you'd be up on another charge.'

'Oh.'

He hadn't realised he had been quite that bad.

Judy put a hand on his arm. 'I seem to remember you saying that your Scarlett's father was a drunk, that he didn't look after her properly.'

'Yes.'

Just the sound of her name was like a kick in the stomach.

'Do you want to end up like him?'

'I'm not in the least like him!'

'Maybe not yet, but this is how it starts.'

Jonathan refused to believe her. Only later did he turn

it over in his mind and admit that drinking was no way out. More than that, the last person he wanted to be like was Victor Smith. He went on the wagon. At least then he felt he was in control of himself, if not of his life.

When he was just getting over the first shock, he met Agatha at a wedding. The daughter of a Dutch father and a Chinese mother, she was small and exquisite, with pale gold skin, Chinese features and startling blue eyes. In a classic rebound, Jonathan fell willingly under her spell. She was charming and funny and when she was with him she gave him her absolute attention, making him feel as if he was the only person in the room that mattered.

She invited him to her home to meet her family. Jonathan arrived in a borrowed Jeep to find that she lived in a vast bungalow surrounded by an exotic garden and run by what seemed like an army of servants. He was taken aback. He knew that Mr Van der Post ran a successful company exporting Malay silk and artwork and importing western electrical goods. What he hadn't realised was just how well off the family was.

A uniformed houseboy conducted him to a broad veranda at the back furnished with comfortable cane chairs and hammocks and hung with baskets of orchids.

'Jonathan!' Agatha slid elegantly out of the hammock she was lying in and came towards him with both hands outstretched. 'Come and meet my parents.'

He was introduced to a tall blond man with skin turned brick-red by years of tropical sunshine. He grasped Jonathan's hand and studied him closely as he shook it. Jonathan looked steadily back at him. He wasn't going to be intimidated by this man. Mr Van der Post was evidently satisfied with what he saw, and in turn introduced his wife. Mrs Van der Post was a surprise. Jonathan had expected her to be in traditional Chinese clothing with her hair in a bun, but instead found himself looking at a woman wearing a western hairstyle and the latest Paris fashions.

'How do you do?' she said, in the same prettily accented English as her daughter. 'Agatha has told us much about you.'

Two younger sisters, not as lovely as Agatha, came forward to say hello. The only son of the family was away at school.

Lunch was served at a spacious table further along the veranda. Jonathan found himself questioned about his family, his education, his ambitions. All were met with polite nods but no great enthusiasm. It wasn't until he described his dealings in surplus army food supplies that Mr Van der Post became enthusiastic.

'Good, good. You have a business brain,' he commented. 'That is the way to get on in life—see an opportunity and exploit it.'

From then on the atmosphere around the table lightened. Mr Van der Post appeared to decide that Jonathan was acceptable and conversation became more general.

After lunch the four young people swam in the large pool, then played doubles on the tennis court. When the time came for him to leave, Agatha took Jonathan for a walk round the garden before he set off. They stopped to kiss under the cover of a jacaranda tree.

'My father likes you,' she told him. 'You must come again.'

He was soon a regular visitor.

The weeks flew by. The end of Jonathan's time in the army was fast approaching. As he lay awake at night, he tried to come to a decision about his future. His senior officer had offered him promotion if he signed up to stay on in the army. That one was fairly easy to dismiss. He had enjoyed army life, but he did not want to make a career of it. Far more tempting was the prospect of staying on in Malaya. He was fairly confident that if he asked Agatha to marry him, she would accept. Her father would readily find him a job in his business and he would be able to enjoy a very pleasant way of life. But was that enough? If he was really clear-eyed, he knew that under the surface attraction, what he felt for Agatha was nothing compared to what he still felt for Scarlett. And then there was the third option—going home. Without Scarlett there to welcome him, England seemed a grey place, foggy and cold. And so he wavered, until people started talking about his going-away party and he knew he had to make his mind up. He went into town on his day off and bought a sapphire and diamond ring. Sapphires would match Agatha's eyes.

On the morning he was due to see her again, a letter arrived, not from England, but from Paris. It was a brief note from the great Monsieur Bonnard, informing him that though a place at the Ortolan was not free at the moment, should one become available, he would be welcome to apply.

It was like a light coming on in his head. How could he have forgotten his first ambition, or all that time painstakingly learning his art at the Ortolan? What about those coveted Michelin stars? He would never be comfortable as the boss's daughter's husband in a trading company, and he would never be truly Agatha's with Scarlett still in his heart.

He hid the ring at the bottom of his kitbag and started counting the days till he could board the ship for home.

CHAPTER NINETEEN

1957

'IF YOU keep on picking her up every time she cries, she'll never learn,' Ricky's mother said, not for the first time.

'She's hungry,' Scarlett said.

'Well, she'll have to learn to wait, won't she? She won't starve to death.'

From the big pram in the hall, the wailing grew louder, making Scarlett's guts clench and her breasts ache. It was only a couple of hours since the baby had last been fed and if Ricky's mother hadn't been there, Scarlett might have rocked the pram to get her off to sleep again. But having her mother-in-law tell her to do something was enough to make her do just the opposite.

'Poor little scrap. I can't just leave her. She'll get herself in a right state,' she said, and went to pick the baby up.

Her daughter's small face was screwed up and her body trembling. Scarlett laid her gently over her shoulder and touched her soft fluff of hair with her cheek. For a few beats the baby stopped crying, comforted by her mother's body. Scarlett was overwhelmed by the rush of love and tenderness, fear and terrible responsibility. This perfect creature was hers to care for. It was both wonderful and terrifying.

'You'll spoil her.'

Ricky's mother was glaring her disapproval from the doorway.

Scarlett glared back over the baby's head. If that woman thought she was going to take charge, she was mistaken.

'She's two weeks old. She's hungry,' she said.

And she's mine. Mine, not yours.

'She's old enough to learn,' Ricky's mother insisted.

Scarlett walked past her and went into the bedroom. Sitting on the sagging double bed with its pink candlewick bedspread, she undid her blouse. This was something else her mother-in-law disapproved of. Breast-feeding was old-fashioned and mucky. The baby should be on a nice clean bottle, where you could see exactly what she was getting.

'The midwife says breast-feeding is best,' was Scarlett's killer argument. Ricky's mother tried to dispute even that, but Scarlett simply wouldn't listen.

The added advantage was that Ricky's mother found the whole process embarrassing, and never followed her into the bedroom when she was feeding. She had her daughter safely to herself for as long as she stayed in here. She put the baby to her breast, gasping as the hard little gums seized her sore nipple. She gazed in awe at the tiny face, so fierce in its concentration. Though still soft and undefined, the nose, the chin, the shape of the forehead, were all hers. The blue eyes with their fringe of dark lashes already had a touch of brown to them. Her daughter was going to be a mirror image of herself. It was strange and breathtakingly wonderful.

'You're so beautiful,' she murmured. 'How did I manage to make something so perfect?'

She could hear her mother-in-law clattering around in the kitchen, no doubt finding something that needed cleaning. Since Scarlett had come home from her ten days in hospital, Mrs Harrington had been round every day. She said she had come to help, but Scarlett looked on it as interference. It was hard enough learning to cope with motherhood without having that old bag sticking her nose in and finding dust and dirt to tut over. At least having the baby had resolved what Scarlett should call her. 'Mrs Harrington' was too formal, but 'Betty' was out as being too informal. Scarlett refused to call her Mum or even Mother. As far as she was concerned, that title was reserved for her own darling mother. But now the baby was here, Mrs Harrington was Nana. It was a title that everyone was happy with.

Scarlett stayed in the bedroom for as long as she could, but she had to come out eventually to change the baby. Her mother-in-law was waiting for her.

'I can't find much food in the place,' she said. 'What are you giving Ricky for his dinner today?'

'I'm going out to the shops now,' Scarlett said.

It was already gone eleven o'clock and Ricky would be back for his main meal of the day at twelve-fifteen. He only had a bare hour for dinner, so it needed to be on the table and waiting so that he could eat and cycle back to work for one o'clock. What with all the feeding and changing, Scarlett hadn't had time to do much else.

'Now, if you were to keep to a routine with the baby, you wouldn't be in this fix,' Mrs Harrington said.

'The baby has to come first,' Scarlett said, taking off the rubber knickers, unpinning the bulky terry nappy. Such a lot of fabric round such a little body. The baby seemed to like it with the air on her. Scarlett put the soiled one with the others in the bucket under the sink to soak, cleaned the baby up, smothered her bottom with petroleum jelly and folded a fresh nappy.

'It's neater if you do it the way I used to with Ricky,' Mrs Harrington said.

'This is how they showed me in hospital,' Scarlett said.

'I don't know. These modern ways—'

Scarlett carefully pinned the nappy together, putting her fingers next to the baby's body so as not to jab her.

'There!' she said. 'All nice and dry. Now, we're going out in the pram to get Daddy's dinner. Say bye-bye to Nana.'

'He can always come round to us, if it's too much for you,' Mrs Harrington said. 'Just until you get into a routine.'

Scarlett went into the hall and laid the baby in the shiny coachbuilt pram that the Harringtons had bought for them. She covered her with a sheet and a pink satin quilt and straightened up. She looked her mother-in-law in the eye.

'I'm Ricky's wife and this is his home. He comes here for dinner,' she stated.

Without waiting for a reply, she picked up her purse and key and a string bag and put them in the zip bag attached to the pram, then started manoeuvring the big vehicle out of the front door and down the step. Mrs Harrington could do nothing other than follow her.

'I'll come round tomorrow and make sure you're all right,' was her parting shot.

'I'm fine,' Scarlett said, and set off up the road.

Once away from her mother-in-law, she felt the tension slip away from her.

'That's got rid of the old bag,' she said to her sleeping daughter. 'Now, what are we going to get for dinner? It's got to be something quick.'

She ran over the contents of the larder in her head. As far as dinner ingredients went, there were eggs and a few tins of stuff. She glanced at her watch. She really did have to get a move on. Then, as she neared the corner, she caught a whiff of frying from the chip shop.

'That's it!' she told the baby. 'Eggs, chips and peas.'

And there it was, ready for Ricky as he came in the door. He was not impressed.

'Call this dinner?' he said, poking the chips with his fork. 'Where's the meat and gravy?'

'I didn't have time, what with seeing to the baby,' Scarlett told him.

'My mum always does a proper dinner.'

'I bet she didn't when you were a baby.'

'And you know I don't like these peas. Why don't you get the marrowfat ones?'

'I'll get some, all right? And I'll go out again this afternoon and get something to cook for tomorrow. If your parents had only bought a fridge instead of that great big pram, I'd be able to keep fresh stuff longer.'

'You don't buy a fridge for a baby.'

'Well, maybe you could buy one instead of a new guitar.'

'I gotta have a new guitar. It's for my career.'

'And I gotta have a fridge if you want meat and gravy dinners.'

They glared at each other across the table set in the front bay window.

'Well, ask your flaming father to buy it.'

For once, Scarlett was silenced. Her father was living with them in the flat. The theory was that he paid them for his room and board, which helped towards the rent of the flat. In practice, Scarlett was lending him money out of the housekeeping halfway through the week, because she knew that if she didn't give it to him, he would borrow it from someone else or run up a slate at whichever off-licence still didn't know he wasn't to be trusted.

Ricky pushed the last of his chips into his mouth.

'You finished it, then,' Scarlett said. 'It can't have been that bad.'

'It fills a gap,' Ricky admitted. 'No pudding, I suppose?'

'No. If you want pudding, you'll have to go back to mummy.'

Ricky did one of those lightning changes of mood that always took her by surprise. He stood up and reached out to her.

'Hey, babe—'

Glad not to be at odds with everyone, Scarlett snuggled into his embrace.

'I don't half fancy you when you're angry,' Ricky said.

He closed a hand over her breast. Scarlett flinched.

'Bloody hell! I forgot. I dunno whether I can stand this, babe. I thought when the baby was born I'd get your body back again.'

'Another four weeks yet, that's what the doctor said,' Scarlett reminded him.

She wished she'd lied and said it was longer. The last thing she wanted at the moment was Ricky anywhere near her. Her stitches had hardly healed.

'I'm gonna explode if I wait that long, babe. I still want you all the time, even with all this fat on you.'

He ran his hand over Scarlett's wobbly belly, just to prove the point. She put her face up to be kissed. This was where her power lay. Ricky might like his mother's cooking, but he liked sex better. As long as she could get back to fancying him again, she was going to win every time.

'No good getting excited now. You've got to get back to work,' she reminded him.

Ricky groaned with frustration. 'OK, OK.'

No sooner had he set off on his bike than the baby started crying again. Scarlett left the washing up and went to lift her out of the pram. It was time for another feed.

For the fourth time in as many weeks, Jonathan reached the top of Scarlett's street. Try as he might, he could not resist the pull of the place. So far, he had not gone any further than the corner. From here he could see her house. He had counted the almost identical square bay windows in the long row of terraces and was sure he knew which one hers was. It was stupid to keep doing this, he told himself. He only had one day off a week, and he should be using it to catch up with old friends or make new ones. Anything rather than keep reminding himself of what might have been. The trouble was, it was all very well for his head to tell him that when his heart said otherwise. So here he was, staring down the road at where she lived yet again.

It was a nicer street than the last one she had lived in. The more charitable part of him was glad of that, while the jealous part hated her husband for being able to take her away from that last dreadful place. Husband. He still hadn't got used to it. Scarlett's husband. How could she do that to him?

This was it, he decided. He would go and have it out with her. If he didn't, he was going to spend his life wondering why. With a new sense of purpose, he marched down the street and up her front path to the two doors set in one porch. The ground floor flat, she had said. He knocked on the door nearest to the bay window.

A shape could be seen through the obscure glass. His heart turned over. It was her. The door opened and there she was, as beautiful as ever, but white-faced with shock, staring at him open-mouthed.

'*Jonathan!*'

'Hello, Scarlett.'

For a long moment they just gazed at each other. She had put on some weight, but it suited her. Her face was softer and her figure more womanly. Jonathan clenched his hands, resisting the urge to hold her in his arms. He swallowed.

'Aren't you going to ask me in?'

'I…yes…of course…come in…' she stuttered, stepping back.

He walked past her into small hallway. The space was so restricted that he could feel the heat of her body as he passed.

'Go in,' she said, shutting the door behind him.

He went in to the front room. It was a standard sitting room with an old-fashioned three-piece suite, a dark oak sideboard and a matching dining set all crowded in. The only thing that obviously hadn't been rented along with the flat was the television set in the corner.

'You got the TV you wanted, then,' he said, and cursed himself. It sounded vindictive.

'The Riptides bought it for us.'

'The what—?'

'The Riptides. The rest of the band. Ricky and the Riptides. Brian works for a TV repair company. I think he got it cheap. It's second-hand.'

Jonathan pounced on the relevant part of this statement. 'And Ricky is—?'

'My…my husband.'

'Right.'

There was a brief, tense pause, then both of them spoke at once.

'Scarlett, I can't understand—'

'I never meant for it—'

They both stopped.

'You say.'

'No, you.'

Scarlett stood biting her lip, looking acutely uncomfortable. Jonathan wasn't sure whether he most wanted to kiss her or shout at her.

'What happened?' he asked.

In answer, she turned and walked out of the room, waving at him to follow her. They went down the hallway, through a minute kitchen where what smelt like mince was simmering on the stove and out into the rather overgrown back garden. A row of nappies were drying on the washing line and there, under an apple tree, was a big green pram. Scarlett leaned over it, smiling at the baby asleep there. Tenderness lit her face. There was no doubt that the child was hers.

Jonathan stared at them while a storm of emotions swept through him.

'When—?' he managed to ask.

'Three weeks ago.'

'Three weeks?' His bewildered brain battled with the maths. 'So you were—?'

'She was the reason I had to get married, yes.'

He wasn't sure whether this made it worse or not. Either way, this really was the end of any tiny chink of hope he might have had. Scarlett married was bad enough, Scarlett married with a child was tied for life.

'What's her name?' he asked, and was surprised to hear such an ordinary question come out of his mouth.

'Joanne.'

'Joanne?'

Their eyes met for a long moment.

'I'm sorry,' she said.

He turned away. He should never have come. He started towards the gate leading to the alleyway down the side of the house, but she ran and touched him on the arm. He stopped dead.

'Please, Jonathan—don't go—I can't bear it—'

'It's no good, Scarlett.'

'Just—don't leave like this. Stay a while, please. Tell me what you're doing.'

'I shouldn't.'

Nothing was going to make it better. And yet when she pulled at him he followed her and sat down with her on a rickety bench at the end of the garden. He knew it was dangerous, sitting there just inches away from her.

'When…when did you get back?' she asked.

'Six weeks ago.'

'You look very brown.'

'Yes, well, it was hot there.'

This was bizarre, making conversation like this, as if they were chance acquaintances.

'What are you doing now?'

'I'm working at the Dorchester for the time being. It's a big hotel in London.'

'Do you like it there?'

'Yes, they've got French staff so they understand good food. It's nice to get back to restaurant cooking after doing all that bland stuff for the army hospital. And they're a good crowd. We have a few laughs.'

'Good, I'm glad. That you've found somewhere you like, I mean.'

There was so much he desperately wanted to ask her—when had she met this Ricky? Did she love him? What was so bloody wonderful about him? Above all, why hadn't she waited for him? He would have waited for her till the end of time.

He stood up.

'Oh, yes, don't bother to worry about me. I'm just fine. Hunky-dory.'

Scarlett gasped. She looked as shocked as if he had slapped her face.

'Jonathan, please—'

'It's no use, Scarlett. I shouldn't have come. I won't—'

'Hello, and who have we got here?'

He heard Scarlett gasp again as he turned towards the newcomer. A young man a couple of years older than himself was strolling across the grass with his hands in his pockets. Everything about him was fashionable, shiny—and cheap. So this was the man who had taken Scarlett away from him. All his hatred seemed totally justified.

'Oh—Ricky—you're early—I wasn't expecting—' Scarlett twittered. 'This—er—this is Jonathan. A—er—a family friend.'

Ricky nodded. 'Afternoon, mate. Scarlett's not mentioned you before.'

'I've been away. National service.'

'Oh, right. It's a bugger, ain't it? Happiest day of my life when I got out. Did you get caught up in that Suez stuff?'

'No, I was out in Malaya by the time it started up.'

'Malaya?' A nasty smile spread over Ricky's face. He tipped his head back, looking Jonathan up and down. 'So you're the boyfriend who was in Malaya. Well, mate, I'm sorry but you're a bit too late. She's spoken for.' He reached out for Scarlett, putting an arm round her waist. 'My dinner ready, babe?'

Something snapped inside Jonathan. He hit out with all his force, punching Ricky square on the jaw. Then he turned and walked away, leaving them both in confusion.

CHAPTER TWENTY

SCARLETT woke up. It was pitch-dark and cold. She listened for the sound of the baby breathing. Yes, everything was all right. She was about to turn over and go back to sleep again when a thin wailing started up from the cot. Scarlett lay rigid. Would Joanne settle if she ignored her, or should she get up now and pick her up before Ricky woke up? Before she could make her mind up, the wailing escalated and Ricky stirred. Scarlett slid out of bed and made her way over to the cot.

'Shh, shh, it's all right, Mummy's got you.'

She hauled the baby out of the cot and cuddled her. She was hot and fretful and snuffly.

'Bloody hell, Scarlett, can't you keep her quiet? She's been awake all night.'

'She can't help it, she's teething.'

Scarlett rocked the baby to and fro. It was freezing out here with only a nightdress on and she was desperate for sleep. She shuffled back to bed with Joanne in her arms. Maybe she would settle if she was in bed with her.

Ricky groaned. 'No, not in here. You know what happened last night. She kept both of us awake. I got to go to work in the morning and I got a gig in the evening. I need my sleep.'

Scarlett needed her sleep too. Her body was crying out for it, so much so that she didn't have the energy for yet another fight.

'All right, I'll put her in the pram,' she said, raising her voice to be heard above Joanne's.

'If your flaming father wasn't here, she wouldn't be in with us, she'd have a bedroom of her own.'

'Yes, well—'

'I'm stuck here with a screaming kid and a bleeding alcoholic, and I'm supposed to feed them both!'

'For God's sake—stop whining and go back to sleep!' Scarlett snapped.

She grabbed her dressing gown from its hook behind the door and went out into the hallway with Joanne still struggling and crying on her shoulder. Without putting the light on, she lay the baby in the pram, where she screamed even louder, then manoeuvred it backwards through the living room door. There was still a hint of warmth left in the remains of the fire, enough to give a faint comfort. Scarlett stood as close as she could to the grate and rocked the pram on its bouncy springs as she sang *Bye Baby Bunting* over and over again.

For what seemed like half the night she stood there, shivering and rocking and singing, until at last the exhausted baby fell asleep. Not daring to stop moving the pram, Scarlett leaned over and made sure she was properly covered up. Then she gradually reduced the rocking. She stopped, and waited. There was a snuffle from Joanne.

Please, please, go to sleep! Scarlett pleaded silently.

The snuffling stopped.

Scarlett crept to the door. It was no use going back to bed. The moment she got there, Joanne was sure to wake up again. She felt for her coat and Ricky's on the pegs in the hall, took them down and went back into the living room. Then she curled up on the sofa with the coats on top of her and fell immediately into a deep sleep.

The next thing she knew, something was poking at her. Reluctantly, she swam upwards into groggy wakefulness. Ricky was digging her in the shoulder with his finger. She tried to focus on his face. He didn't look pleased.

'Come on, shift y'self. Get the breakfast on.'

Scarlett couldn't believe it. Joanne had slept right through to half past seven. She hurried out to the kitchen and put the kettle on for tea and Ricky's washing and shaving water, but no sooner had she lit the gas than Joanne woke up.

The next hour was a nightmare of trying to feed and change the baby and make Ricky's fried egg and beans and toast all at the same time. As Ricky went out of the door at twenty to nine, neat and smart in his working suit, he turned and looked at her.

'You really oughta smarten yourself up, babe. You look a right mess.'

'Oh, thank you so much,' she said, refusing to be squashed in front of him.

But when he had gone she went and looked at herself in the bedroom mirror. A pale, puffy face with dark smudges under the eyes looked back at her. Her hair straggled down unbrushed, and she was still wearing a crumpled nightdress and a well-worn dressing gown with a streak of baby sick down it. She had to admit that Ricky was right. She did look a mess. But she was only halfway through getting dressed when Joanne started crying again. And then there were the nappies to boil up and the fire to sweep out and re-lay.

She had just about managed to get herself looking tidy when she looked at the clock and realised that her father should be up by now. She went and banged on his door.

'Dad! You awake? You've got to get a move on, it's nearly ten o'clock!'

When shouting failed to get any reply, she went in. Her father appeared to be deeply asleep. She shook his shoulder. It was essential he got to work. If he lost this job he might never get another.

'Dad, wake up.'

Victor groaned and shook her off, turning over so that his back was towards her. It took a lot more shaking and persuading to make him sit up and put his feet to the floor. He sat on the side of the bed with his head bowed, bracing himself upright with his arms. He looked dreadful. Scarlett felt awful, making him get up when he was plainly feeling bad, but she knew that if she gave in this once, he would soon take to lying in bed until he needed to get out and buy some drink. She lit a cigarette for him and put it in his mouth.

'There you are, Dad. I'll heat you some water for washing and make you a cup of tea, right? It'll be waiting for you on the table.'

From the living room, she could hear Joanne grizzling. She hurried back to see to her. The baby was sitting up in her pram with plenty of toys and rattles to keep her amused, but she didn't seem to be interested in any of them. Her cheeks were bright red where her teeth were breaking through. The moment her mother came into the room she starting crying in earnest.

Scarlett picked her up and jiggled her in her arms.

'The only thing that's going to keep you quiet is going for a walk, isn't it?' she said to her. 'But we can't do that yet. We've got to get Grandad off to work and put your nappies out on the line and by the time we've done that we'll have to get Daddy's dinner on. And I don't know when I'm going to get to tidy this place up. It looks like a bomb's hit it.'

Her father finally shambled in and drooped over his cup of sweet tea. Scarlett had long ago stopped offering him even a slice of toast for breakfast. All he could face in the morning was tea and whisky, or whatever alcoholic drink he could get hold of. Lately he had taken to British sherry, presumably because it was cheaper. Scarlett chivvied him into his coat and hat and out of the front door. Outside, it was raining.

'You wouldn't send a dog out on a day like this,' Victor said, giving her a resentful look.

'It'll be warm and dry at work,' Scarlett told him.

'You're heartless,' Victor accused, and started up the street, hands in pockets, shoulders hunched, leaving Scarlett feeling wicked.

When Ricky came in at dinner time he was in a foul mood. 'There's ten bob missing from my wallet,' he said.

With a sinking feeling, Scarlett guessed where that had gone.

'Are you sure?' she asked, serving up large dollops of mashed potato to go with the sausage and onion.

'Of course I'm sure. You don't just lose that much.'

It was no use suggesting he might have forgotten where he'd spent it. Ricky was very careful with his money.

'No,' she said. 'How much gravy do you want?'

'Lots.' Ricky wasn't to be distracted. 'You know who's had it, don't you? Your bloody father, that's who. He's a bloody parasite, Scarlett. And you make it easy for him. You run around after him, you give him subs out of the housekeeping. I bet these are bloody beef sausages and not decent pork ones, ain't they? We can afford pork sausages if you don't go giving your father money to piss away all the time.'

The trouble was, Ricky was right about the money. It was very hard managing the housekeeping and giving her father money so that he didn't borrow it from other people.

'He pays his rent. We wouldn't be able to afford this place without him paying for his room,' she said.

She picked up the plates and walked through to the living room. Ricky followed her, still talking.

'That's bollocks. He's costing us more than he pays. We could get a proper lodger in that room, and then we'd be quids in.'

Fear gripped Scarlett. What would happen to her father if Ricky turned him out? He couldn't look after himself. He'd end up on the street. It didn't bear thinking about. She plonked the plates down on the table and whipped round to face Ricky.

'He's my father, right? He's family, and families stick together, and that's an end to it.'

'Bloody ain't an end to it, not when he's nicking money out of my wallet. I tell you, Scarlett, it's got to stop. It's shape up or ship out for your dad.'

He sat down and started eating his meal. Scarlett was so angry she couldn't face hers.

'If he goes, I go,' she stated.

Ricky gave her a cold look, his jaws chewing on a large piece of sausage. He swallowed. 'Please y'self,' he said.

At that point the baby started crying again. Scarlett picked her up and went into the bedroom. Her head was throbbing. What was she going to do about her father? She couldn't see a way out.

When Ricky slammed out again and went back to work, the silence of the flat seemed to close around Scarlett. Outside, it was still raining, but even going out in the rain seemed better than staying in. She dressed Joanne warmly in several layers of cardigans, a knitted bonnet and mittens and strapped her into the pram, where she peeped over the top of the rain apron with round brown eyes and looked happy for the first time that day. Then she put on her own mac and a pair of wellies and set out, marching up the road to keep warm. At once she felt better. She could breathe out here.

Without really thinking where she was heading for, she crossed over the London Road and kept going. It was only when she saw the Thames estuary between the houses that she knew where she wanted to be. The sea front. Soon she was hanging on to the pram as they went down the steep slope to the esplanade. She breathed in the salt air. It was a pretty dismal prospect. The tide was out, leaving a mile of grey mud, beyond which was the gleam of grey water. The rain was so heavy you could hardly see the hills of Kent on the other side. As it was winter, nearly all the small boats were laid up and every one of the little shops and kiosks

was closed. But still the feeling of openness lifted
Scarlett's spirits. Overhead a seagull soared, squawking.
Scarlett smiled up at it.

'This is more like it, isn't it, pet?' she said to Joanne.

The baby smiled and gurgled back at her and batted
at the plastic ducks on her pram with her mittened
hands. They were almost the only people braving the
weather. There were a couple of dog-walkers and an old
man wheeling a bike, but everyone else seemed to have
had the sense to stay at home. Scarlett marched along,
telling Joanne about the carnival and reliving her
memories as she did so. It all seemed a very long way
off now, that first wonderful summer with Jonathan. It
was difficult to imagine sunshine and colour and crowds
of noisy people in this grey December landscape.

'Soon it'll be Christmas,' she told the baby. 'Your
first Christmas. We'll have a tree and everything. I
suppose we'll have to go to your nana and grandad's for
Christmas dinner, but at least it'll put your daddy in a
good mood. He likes your nana's cooking much better
than mine. And I suppose it's better than having them
all sitting round criticising what I've done.'

And then her mind went off on a different train of
thought. December. It was the first week of December
and she hadn't had her period. She'd not really got back
to being regular since Joanne had been born but,
thinking about it, she couldn't actually remember when
she'd had the last one. She tried to pin it to an event, and
could only come up with Ricky's birthday in October.
She'd had one then, and he'd been really fed up about
it. Surely she'd had one since? The more she thought
about it, the more worried she became. There had been

other signs, but she had thought they were just the result of being tired all the time with Joanne teething, plus she had recently stopped breast-feeding. But what if it wasn't just that? What if she was pregnant again? She did some sums in her head. There would be less than fifteen months between them. How on earth was she going to manage? Just the thought of boiling and drying two lots of nappies made her feel quite desperate. But, most of all, whatever would Ricky say if she told him she was having another baby? He didn't seem to like Joanne much, resenting the way she took Scarlett's attention away from him. He would be much worse if she had two babies to care for.

'It's not Scarlett, is it?'

She was so engrossed in her own worries that she hadn't noticed the young man on the dinghy rack. He was making sure that one of the small boats on the wooden platform above the beach was securely covered against the rain. Scarlett stopped short and looked at him. It was one of Jonathan's sailing friends.

'Graham! You gave me quite a turn. I was miles away. How are you?'

She felt a flush of embarrassment rising up her neck and face. How much did Graham know? He was sure to take Jonathan's side.

'Oh, fine, fine. I'm working for my dad now, but I just came down to make sure the boat was all right.'

They both paused, silenced by the presence of the pram and the fact that, the last time they had met, Scarlett and Jonathan had been inseparable.

Scarlett swallowed. 'Have—?' she started. Her voice came out as a squeak. 'Have you seen Jonathan?'

'Not recently.'

She just had to know. 'Is he all right?'

Graham was stony faced. 'What do you think?'

Scarlett bit her lip. 'Is he still working at the Dorchester?' she persisted.

'No, he's gone back to Paris again. To the place where he was before.'

'The Ortolan?'

'Yeah, that was it.'

'Will you—do you think he'll be home at Christmas?'

Graham shrugged. 'I expect so.'

'Could you—would you remember me to him?'

Graham sighed and shifted uncomfortably. 'I dunno, Scarlett. It's difficult. He was pretty cut up when—you know. He still is. I don't know that he'd want me passing on any messages from you.'

A great weight of shame, guilt and regret was pressing down on Scarlett's chest, almost suffocating her.

'I know. It was just—'

How could she possibly explain to Graham what had happened when she didn't understand it herself?

'I must have been mad,' she said feebly.

'That's what we all thought. He's a good bloke, is Jonno.'

'I know—' Scarlett said again.

A good bloke. What an understatement. Jonathan was the best. The love of her life. And she had thrown it all away.

She couldn't bear to stay with Graham a moment longer.

'I've got to go,' she said.

She practically ran away from him, not stopping till she was passing under the pier. She found herself on the Golden Mile. Everything here was at its lowest ebb, the bright colours looking cheap and tawdry in the rain. The amusement arcades were shuttered, the ice cream parlours locked. Most of the Italian families had gone home for the winter. Scarlett looked at the familiar facades. There was Aunty Marge's chip shop. There was the Mancinis' café. She turned away from the section of the beach where she had lost her virginity to Ricky and gazed at the Trafalgar. Solid and ugly, it stared back at her. Up on the first floor were the windows of Jonathan's parents' flat. In three weeks he might be there, looking out of those windows at the pier and the sea. Would he be thinking of her, remembering the wonderful times they had had together? One thing was for sure, he wouldn't be coming to see her again.

Tears streamed down Scarlett's face, mingling with the raindrops.

'Oh, Jonathan,' she said out loud, 'I'm sorry, so sorry.'

But she knew that no amount of regret was ever going to put it right. She turned the pram round and headed for home, and an uncertain future.

CHAPTER TWENTY-ONE

'Is HE out, then?' Victor asked.

'Yes, he's off playing with the band. They've got bookings in London,' Scarlett said.

She lumbered after Joanne, who was trying to open the sideboard doors.

'No, pet. Not in there. Come and play with your toys.'

The toddler screamed in protest and sat down hard on her well-padded bottom. The contents of the sideboard were far more fascinating than any toys. Scarlett scooped Joanne up and placed her in the playpen, where she rattled the bars like a caged lion cub.

'She's got a mind of her own, all right. Just like you at that age,' Victor said. He returned to his first line of thought. 'So is he back tonight?'

'No, they're staying over at Brian's cousin's place in Walthamstow, then he's doing another one tomorrow. He's got time off specially.'

She had told him all this only yesterday, but he had obviously forgotten.

Victor smiled and settled himself more comfortably on the sofa. 'Nice with just the three of us.'

Scarlett had to admit that it was, as long as her father remained reasonably sober. These days there seemed to be nothing but rows when Ricky was around, and it was getting harder and harder to defend her father's behaviour when the rows were about him. But today was her father's day off and Ricky was away. There were plenty of chores to be done, but the pressure of getting the midday meal ready in time was off. It almost made the day into a holiday.

'Let's have a cup of tea in the garden,' she suggested.

They had one rather decrepit deckchair which lived in the outside toilet. Scarlett set it up for her father and spread a spare blanket on the grass for herself and Joanne. She made a pot of tea and put the tray on top of the coal bunker, well out of Joanne's way. It wasn't quite Buckingham Palace, but it was fine for a little party.

The garden was a wilderness. Earlier in the summer, Scarlett had cut the lawn most weeks, doing it on her knees with a pair of shears as they didn't have a lawnmower. But now she was so huge with the next baby she couldn't summon the energy to do it. It was one of the many things they argued about. Ricky hated anything to do with the garden and said that Victor ought to do it, seeing as he didn't do anything else that was useful. Victor was clearly quite incapable of any sort of physical effort, so Scarlett told Ricky that he shouldn't be asking an old man to do something he could easily do himself. Ricky just snorted and said that Victor wasn't old, just drunk. In the meantime, the garden grew more and more untidy and the next-door neighbour, a keen gardener, constantly complained about the weeds growing in from their side.

But today there were to be no arguments.

'There you are, my pet,' she said, giving Joanne a bottle of diluted orange drink. 'Your nana would say you had to drink it from a cup, but you're much happier with your bottle, aren't you?'

Joanne smiled and happily glugged away at her orange.

'You're a good little mum,' Victor said, smiling at the baby. 'Your mum would of been proud of you.'

'Mum wanted me to stay at school and get a good job before I got married,' Scarlett said sadly.

'Ah, but she would of loved being a granny. She loved kiddies. Wanted more herself, but it wasn't to be.'

'Pity,' Scarlett said.

How much easier it would have been if she'd had a brother or sister to share the burden of caring for her father. They were both silent for a few moments, remembering the woman they had loved so much.

'We don't see much of that friend of yours nowadays. What's-her-name? Brenda,' Victor said.

'No. She's got other things to do.'

She had hardly seen Brenda since Joanne had been born. Brenda wanted someone to go out dancing and chasing boys with, and clearly Scarlett was no use for that any more, so other girls had taken her place as Brenda's best friend. And then, when she did come round, either Joanne was making a fuss or Victor was drunk or Ricky was arguing about something, so it wasn't a very welcoming atmosphere. Scarlett missed the hours of talking about pop stars and records and films, and the gossip about who was going out with whom.

Joanne dropped her bottle and got to her feet, using Scarlett as a steadying post. Scarlett and Victor watched with pride as she toddled off the blanket, tripped on a tussock of grass, picked herself up and stumped off towards the old Anderson shelter.

'She's a grand little kiddie, isn't she?' Victor remarked.

Scarlett heaved herself to her feet and went to rescue her before she fell in the stinging nettles. As she did so, she felt a nagging pain in her back.

'Oh, God,' she said.

'You all right, love?'

'Yes.'

She knew just what it was. It was a week or so early, but the pain was unlike any other. She waited to see whether it was just a twinge or the real thing. By midday she was sure. They were coming every fifteen minutes.

'I've got to get moving,' she said.

'What?' Victor was dozing in the sunshine.

'Got to get Joanne round to the Harringtons'. Good thing I got everything packed the other day.'

She had it all planned out. Much as she disliked having to do so, she had arranged to leave Joanne with her mother-in-law while she was in hospital. She looked at Victor. How nice it would be if she could trust him to take Joanne to her nana's while she waited for the taxi. As it was, Victor needed looking after himself. She was afraid that if Ricky came home and found him dead drunk, he would turn him out. She heaved Joanne and her things into the pram, together with her hospital bag.

'You'll be sure to get yourself up and out tomorrow morning, won't you, Dad?'

'What? Are you off somewhere? What's happening?'

Scarlett groaned with exasperation. 'The baby's coming, Dad. I've got to get to hospital.'

Victor finally realised what was going on. He got up and held her. 'Good luck, my darling. You just get on with what you got to do. Don't you worry about me, I'll be just fine.'

Scarlett knew just what would happen the moment her back was turned. He would take whatever booze he had hidden about the place out into the garden and quietly drink himself senseless.

'You'll make sure you eat properly, won't you? There's milk and cereals and beans and bread. You can manage those all right.'

'Yes, yes, don't worry. Now, off you go.'

He was looking distinctly nervous. Scarlett guessed he was afraid she might give birth then and there. She gave him a kiss and set off, not without misgivings, but right now she had to leave him to his own devices. She had more urgent matters to take care of.

Even in this extremity, Ricky's mum was less than delighted to see her.

'I thought you had another couple of weeks. I've got my Mothers' Union meeting this afternoon and you know I don't like to miss it. Still, these things were sent to try us, I suppose. You'd better sit down. I'll go next door and see if I can use their phone, seeing as it's an emergency.'

Scarlett collapsed into the nearest chair and doubled over as a contraction gripped her. Thankfully, the taxi that Mrs Harrington had phoned for was quick to arrive. Her mother-in-law gave her an exasperated look.

'Have you got enough money for the fare?'

Scarlett shook her head. Mrs Harrington sighed dramatically and pressed two half crowns into her hand.

Joanne clung to her mother, wailing, but Mrs Harrington peeled her off.

'That's quite enough fuss from you. You've got to learn to behave yourself, young lady,' she said, holding onto the struggling toddler. 'When Mummy comes back, she'll have more than enough to cope with, without you playing up.'

Scarlett felt as if she were being torn in half. She had to go to hospital, but she hated leaving Joanne with this woman.

'Be kind to her, please,' she begged as she plumped down on the back seat of the taxi. 'And you will tell Ricky what's happened when he comes home?'

She couldn't be sure that the message would get through from her father.

'Of course I will. Whatever do you take me for?' Mrs Harrington asked, speaking loudly over Joanne's screams.

Scarlett worried all the way to the hospital. But, by the time she got to the maternity ward, things were so far advanced that she had to leave it all behind her. The midwife scolded her for leaving it so late, got her into a gown and rushed her straight into the labour ward. By eight o'clock that evening, baby Simon was born.

At evening visiting time the next day, Mr and Mrs Harrington arrived with Joanne, a card and a bunch of carnations. Mrs Harrington, in full grandmother mode, bent over the bassinet to admire her new grandson.

'Isn't he just beautiful? What a lot of hair! Is he feeding yet?'

Scarlett answered all the usual questions and gave Joanne lots of attention. It was strange how huge Joanne seemed now. She had always thought of her as a baby, but now she was the big sister. What with coping with her and replying to all Mrs Harrington's ideas as to who the baby looked like, it was a while before she could ask about what was worrying her.

'Does Ricky know?'

All down the long ward, other mothers had their husbands with them, except for one poor unfortunate unmarried mother who only had a couple of friends to support her.

'Oh…well…it's difficult to contact him, you know. That relative of Brian's they're staying with isn't on the telephone, and of course we aren't either, as you know. He'll be back tonight, so he'll find out then,' his mother said. 'Now, we mustn't tire you. You've got to get your rest and get better, so I think we'll run along now.'

There was a big drama from Joanne, who didn't want to be parted from her mother, and then they were gone, leaving Scarlett feeling uneasy. Why did Ricky have to go away just when she needed him? He ought to be here.

The next day Mrs Harrington came in the afternoon without her husband.

'Is Ricky coming this evening?' Scarlett asked.

'Oh, yes, I'm sure he will,' Mrs Harrington replied. 'Joanne's been such a good girl, haven't you, darling? She's eaten up all her dinner for Nana and she slept really well last night and didn't wake Nana up till nearly seven this morning.'

'Oh, good. That's nice. So Ricky knows about the baby, does he?'

'Oh, yes. And she sat on her potty like a good girl. That's splendid, isn't it? You want to get her trained as soon as possible. Washing two lots of nappies is going to be a handful.'

Mrs Harrington chattered on, relating every minute detail of Joanne's behaviour. Scarlett was relieved to hear that she was not pining too much and even let herself get sidetracked into discussing the merits of different brands of teething rusks, but she still hadn't had a straight answer to her question about Ricky.

'Nana, when did you speak to Ricky?'

Mrs Harrington looked flustered. 'Well, dear, I haven't actually spoken to him as such.'

Scarlett's head felt like cotton wool. Something wasn't making sense here.

'But he is home, isn't he?'

When he got home last night and found that she and Joanne weren't there, he would have guessed what had happened and gone round to get the news from his parents, even if he didn't ask her father.

'Well…er…' Mrs Harrington looked acutely uncomfortable. She took refuge in speaking to Joanne rather than Scarlett. 'Daddy's not actually back yet, is he, darling? But I'm sure he will be soon.'

'He was only supposed to be away for one night!' Scarlett cried.

'Well…yes…but I suppose he must have got held up somewhere. He'll be back this evening, don't you worry.'

Scarlett had to be content with that.

By Saturday, Scarlett had reached the tearful stage and Mrs Harrington had run out of excuses. Ricky had not been home, nor had he visited his parents, nor had he been to work. Mrs Harrington sat on the hard chair by Scarlett's bed and wrung her hands.

'I don't know what's happened to him! I sent George round to Brian's and Alan's parents' houses, and they're back, but Ricky isn't.'

'But don't they know where he is?' Scarlett cried.

Mrs Harrington shook her head. 'Some man came to see them play on Wednesday evening, and he and Ricky went to a coffee bar together afterwards. The others waited and waited for him, then they came home to Southend, and they say Ricky turned up at about three in the morning at Brian's cousin's house and got his case and went with this man. He wouldn't tell Brian's cousin where he was going, just that he was going to…to…what did he say? Hit the big time. That was it. Hit the big time. Brian seemed a bit cut up about it.'

Scarlett had no time for Brian's problems. 'But he will be coming back, won't he?' she asked, in between sobs.

Mrs Harrington was almost as upset as she was. For once they were in accord. 'Of course he will, dear. Of course he will,' she said, tears starting in her eyes.

Joanne, finding herself ignored in this crisis, started wailing as well. Scarlett cuddled her close and laid her cheek on her dark hair. It was some comfort to hold her small body, but not enough to quiet the fears that were multiplying inside her.

Brenda came to see her, bearing flowers, grapes and a blue matinee jacket.

'What do you mean, disappeared?' she asked, when told about Ricky.

'He was supposed to be playing in London some-where on Tuesday evening and somewhere else on Wednesday evening, and come home Wednesday night, but instead he went off with some man who came to see them play and no one's heard of him since.'

'Oh, he'll be back,' Brenda said. She sat on the bed and put her arms round Scarlett. 'Hey, what's all this crying about? You're usually the brave one.'

'I'm sorry, I c-can't help it,' Scarlett sobbed. 'What am I going to do if he doesn't come back? What are the babies going to do without a dad?'

'He'll be home. He's got to come home, he can't just go off like that,' Brenda said.

Scarlett managed to get the better of her tears. She was so pleased to see her friend again. Brenda was the only person she could open her heart to, and she needed to talk.

'I don't love him, you know,' she confessed. 'Not the way I loved—love—Jonathan. Not at all, really. But I need him. The children need a father. We need someone to pay the rent. If I'm left with two babies and my dad to look after, what am I going to do? I can't leave them and go back to factory work, and I can't take them with me. How are we going to live?'

'You'll have to go on the dole, like my mum did,' Brenda said. 'It ain't much, but you won't starve. But it won't come to that. Come on, cheer up. He'll be in here with a big grin and a bunch of flowers and you'll wonder what all the fuss was about.'

'I hope you're right,' Scarlett said.

By the time she was due to leave hospital the following Friday she was rested and recovered physically, but in a state of emotional turmoil. Ricky was still away. Nobody had heard from him—not his parents, nor his friends, nor his workplace. Victor organised himself enough to take the long bus ride out to the hospital and confirmed that Ricky had not been home and hadn't so much as written a note of explanation.

'Do you want to come back to our house, just until Ricky gets back?' Mrs Harrington asked when she came to meet Scarlett and take her home.

'No, thank you. I want to be there when he arrives,' Scarlett said. What she didn't admit was that she couldn't possibly leave her father any longer. He had been ten days on his own now. She doubted if he'd had a proper meal in all that time.

She sat in the back seat of the taxi with Joanne trampling her lap and wound round her neck while Nana held her new grandson. It was wonderful to be with Joanne again. She had missed her terribly in hospital. But everything else about her situation filled her with trepidation. Ricky had to come home. He had to.

At the door of the flat she hesitated. She couldn't possibly invite Ricky's mother in. God knew what sort of a mess the place was in. She leaned forward and made herself kiss her mother-in-law on the cheek.

'Thanks ever so much for all your help, Nana. I don't know what I would of done without you.'

Which was perfectly true.

It took a bit more before Mrs Harrington took the hint, but in the end she put Scarlett's case inside the door and handed her the baby.

'You know where I am if you need me,' she said.

Scarlett could tell from her voice that she had taken offence, but there was no helping that. She just couldn't let her in.

'Thanks,' she said again.

What with having a new baby, Ricky disappearing,

not knowing how her father was and now her mother-in-law looking hurt and upset, Scarlett felt as if her head would burst. It was all too much. But she did have to stay on the right side of Ricky's mum.

Joanne was already toddling into the hall. Scarlett had a brainwave.

'Come here, darling. Say goodbye to Nana.'

For once, Joanne responded and came back to her. Scarlett squatted with the baby still in one arm and put the other round Joanne.

'Thank Nana for all she's done, looking after you.'

The little girl looked up at her grandmother. 'Nan-nan,' she said obligingly.

Mrs Harrington softened.

'It's been lovely having you, darling. A real pleasure.' She looked at Scarlett. 'Ricky was lovely at this age.'

What a pity he had changed so much.

The thought was so strong that Scarlett wasn't sure whether she had said it out loud or not. She glanced at Mrs Harrington. She was still smiling at Joanne, who was now hanging onto Scarlett's coat like grim death.

'I'm sure he must have been,' she managed to say.

She finally closed the door on her mother-in-law and carried baby Simon into the living room. The place reeked of stale drink and ashtrays. Dirty plates, cups and glasses stood on the floor and furniture, some of the cups with mould growing in them, all with fag-ends piled up on them. An old pair of shoes and a dirty shirt had been left in the middle of the floor along with an untidy pile of newspapers.

For a long moment, Scarlett just stood and stared at it all. It was all so disgusting. Then Joanne went toddling over to the nearest cup and started investigating it. Scarlett clicked into action, snatching it out of her hand.

'No, darling. Dirty.'

Joanne squawked in protest.

'We'd better get all this mess cleared up. No one else is going to do it,' Scarlett told her.

She laid the baby down in the pram, opened the windows to let some fresh air in and went to see if her father was still in his room. He wasn't, though the room was even worse than the living room.

'Well, at least he's gone to work. That's one good thing,' Scarlett said.

She was only halfway through setting things to rights when Simon woke up hungry. Scarlett put Joanne in the playpen, where she threw a tantrum, and sat down on the newly swept sofa to feed the baby. Weariness flooded over her.

'Not much of a start for you, is it, baby?' she said to Simon, as he champed greedily at her breast. 'You've got a home that stinks worse than a pub on a Sunday morning and a dad who's done a bunk. I wonder if he's ever coming home?'

CHAPTER TWENTY-TWO

Two weeks after she returned home with Simon, Scarlett was still waiting for Ricky to appear. And the rent was overdue. There was only one thing for it—she would have to swallow her pride and borrow it from Ricky's parents.

'Just until he comes back,' she explained to them.

If she had been expecting trouble, she was pleasantly surprised. Mr Harrington immediately reached into his jacket pocket for his wallet and handed her two five pound notes.

'Get y'self up-to-date. You never ought to get behindhand with your rent. That's your roof over your head, that is,' he told her. 'We don't want Richard to come back and find he hasn't got a home any more.'

'I know,' Scarlett said dutifully. 'That's why I was so worried about it.'

'I don't know what Richard's playing at, going off like this. It's not what he's been brought up to do, I can tell you that.'

It was the longest speech Scarlett had ever heard him make.

Mrs Harrington was practically in tears. 'I don't know what's happened. I'm sure he's not staying away on purpose. He must be hurt or lost his memory or something. I'm going out of my mind with worry.'

Another two weeks further on, and Scarlett had lost hope.

'If he was coming back, he'd be here by now,' she told her father.

'We're better off without him,' Victor said. 'You're much too good for him, love.'

'We're not better off, that's the point,' Scarlett said. 'All I've got is my family allowance for Simon. We're just about managing with the Harringtons paying the rent, but I can't go on asking them for money.'

She bit back the obvious, which was that if Victor had a decent job and didn't spend what little he earned on drink, they wouldn't be in this fix.

'I haven't paid the HP on the fridge for four weeks now. They're sending me nasty letters,' she added. 'It took me ages to persuade Ricky we needed one, and now I can't afford to keep the payments up. You know what that means—they'll come and take it away.'

As if to underline what she was saying, the radio went dead.

'That's the electric run out again. Have you got a shilling?' Scarlett asked.

Victor went through a pantomime of feeling in all his pockets. 'Sorry, love. I did have some. I don't know where it went.'

Scarlett sighed. 'Dad, we both know perfectly well where it went.'

She looked in her purse and found another shilling,

but she needed that for food. Already their diet was down to absolute basics. She hadn't bought any meat for a fortnight.

'I suppose there's not much point in having a fridge if we can't afford to run one.' She sighed. 'At least then we needn't use the electric during the day, though it'd mean not having the radio on. I do love my radio.'

Victor made a vague noise of agreement and started rolling himself a very slim cigarette, as if trying to prove that he was making economies as well.

'And then there's the coal,' she said, following her own train of thought. 'We'll have to buy some more soon, the evenings are already beginning to draw in. It's not like when it was just us. I've got to keep the children warm.'

'Oh, yes, you got to keep them warm,' Victor echoed.

It was like talking to herself.

'What do you think, Dad?' she asked. 'What can we do? We're on our uppers. I'm going to have to go on the dole.'

That did shock him. In the days when they had the Red Lion, they had despised people who took from the state when there were plenty of jobs to be had.

'You can't do that, Scarlett. Only scroungers go on the dole.'

'We've got to eat and we've got to pay the rent. I've got the kids to look after; I can't go back to work. Even if I did, I'd only earn half of what Ricky brought in, so that wouldn't be any use. It's not fair, the way they pay men more than us.'

'Oh, well, it's women's work, ain't it?' Victor pointed out.

'If we can't pay the rent, we'll have to move. It'll be back to somewhere like the last place,' Scarlett said.

Voicing it out loud made it seem one step nearer. A feeling of doom crept over Scarlett. This flat had no bathroom or hot water and only an outside toilet, but it was a hundred times better than those two rooms in the attic. How could she possibly cope with nappies in a place like that?

'Perhaps Ricky's folks'll cough up,' was all Victor could suggest.

But, before she could bring herself to ask them, the Harringtons came to see her. They made sure it was an evening when Victor was at work. Scarlett was puzzled. They never visited in the evenings. She sat them down in the living room and made tea, thankful that she did have both gas and electricity working at the moment, having taken some money off her father and hidden it from him.

Both Harringtons sat on the edge of the sofa, as if afraid it might contaminate them if they relaxed into it. Ricky was not mentioned. His mother couldn't even speak his name without bursting into tears. She gave her husband a look.

'Go on, George.'

Mr Harrington cleared his throat. 'We…er…we came to ask you something…'

'Just a temporary arrangement. Until…until…' Mrs Harrington said, and stopped, a catch in her voice.

'Until things get back to normal,' her husband explained.

'An arrangement about what?' Scarlett asked. She had a bad feeling about this already.

'We can't go on like this,' Mr Harrington said. 'We'd like to, but we're not made of money, see? And now it's over five weeks and it looks like…like…'

'He's not coming back,' Scarlett filled in.

Mrs Harrington got out her handkerchief and dabbed her eyes.

'Oh, don't say that. He will come back, I know he will.'

Mr Harrington patted her knee awkwardly.

'Well, until then, until he does, we've got to decide what to do about you and the kiddies and this flat. Like I said, we can't afford to go on paying the rent for ever, so we thought the best thing is for you to move in with us.'

Scarlett thought about their tight little house, where there was a place for everything and everything was in its place and polished to within an inch of its life, where there were doilies and table napkin rings and vases of plastic flowers, where jokes were frowned upon and fun disapproved of and the very air tasted dead. She knew her soul would shrivel up and die there.

'We've got two spare bedrooms, one for you and one for the kiddies,' Mrs Harrington put in. 'It's not what I want, but duty comes first. Those kiddies are my grandchildren, and we've got to see they're brought up right.'

Put like that, it all sounded very sensible and far too good an offer to refuse.

'I see,' Scarlett said miserably. How could she refuse a decent home for her children?

'Of course, certain standards will have to be kept. My standards. Under our roof, you'll have to do things our way.'

Scarlett said nothing. She felt like a mouse looking into a trap. Then something occurred to her.

'What about my dad? This is his home as well.'

Mrs Harrington's mouth pursed up until she looked as if she had sucked a lemon.

Mr Harrington looked grim. 'I'm afraid we haven't got room for him. He'll have to make his own arrangements,' he stated.

Scarlett felt a huge relief. This was her let-out.

'Then I can't come. My dad needs me. I'm all he's got.'

The Harringtons argued for quite some while, but there was no room for compromise. Scarlett wouldn't move without Victor and the Harringtons refused to have him in their house. They got up and stalked out of the door.

'Don't say we didn't try to help,' Mr Harrington said.

Mrs Harrington paused on the step and fixed Scarlett with a cold stare. 'Those kiddies are my grandchildren. If they're not properly cared for, I'm going to the authorities.'

Her words sent an icy fear through Scarlett. But she stood her ground and faced her mother-in-law down.

'I can look after my own children, don't you worry.'

'We'll be back and make sure you do,' Mrs Harrington retorted.

Scarlett slammed the door on them and marched back into the living room, where her legs suddenly went weak and she had to collapse onto the sofa.

'How dare they? How dare they?' she said out loud.

One thing was for sure—she now had to take action.

The next morning, she loaded both babies into the big pram and walked into Southend. After a long wait in a dreary building, surrounded by poor and depressed-looking people, she was called up for an interview. The hatchet-faced woman at the desk took her details. The problem was that Scarlett didn't fall into any category. She wasn't a widow who could receive a pension, she wasn't a divorcée with a maintenance agreement. She was a deserted wife with no way of proving she was alone and no idea where her husband had got to. When she unwisely revealed that her father was living with her, the situation got worse. As he was working and there was nothing physically wrong with him, he was deemed able to support her. Scarlett pointed out how small his wages were. The woman suggested that he got a better job.

'He can't get a better job. He's only hanging onto this one by the skin of his teeth,' Scarlett said. 'I'm not leaving here till you sort something out. I've got two babies to feed and keep warm. I don't care about myself, but I need something to keep them until their father comes back.'

Simon obligingly woke up and started crying. Scarlett threatened to breast-feed him then and there. The woman snorted with disgust and said that she supposed something could be done under some regulation or other. Eventually, Scarlett left with an emergency payment and the promise of an allowance book in the post. The weekly amount was horribly small, but it was better than nothing. Scarlett emerged into the open air in triumph. She had kept her little family together.

The next step in her campaign was to get her hands on Victor's money. On Friday she pushed the pram all along the London Road to The Oaks to collect his wages herself.

'I'm going to do this every week now. Don't give them to him and don't let him have any subs out of it,' she told the landlady.

She then hid the money at the back of the cleaning cupboard and gave her father a small amount each day.

'I can't live on that,' Victor protested.

'You're not living on it. You're living here—food,

gas, electric and everything. This is just pocket money and it's a darned sight more than I get,' Scarlett told him.

'But it's not enough—I got expenses.'

'Yes, and we all know what they are, don't we? Fags and booze. You're killing yourself, Dad. It'll do you the world of good to cut down.'

'Call yourself my daughter? You're heartless!' Victor accused.

But Scarlett stuck to her plan.

Over the next few weeks, it became clear that more had to be done. The men from the hire purchase company came and took the fridge away. Neighbours complained to her that Victor was forever trying to borrow money off them. Then the television broke down and Scarlett couldn't afford to have it repaired.

'Stupid thing,' she said, scowling at it as it sat lifeless in the corner of the room.

The television had stopped her from feeling so lonely in the evenings. It was even better than the radio, though all the advertisements for things she couldn't afford did make her feel even poorer. Then she remembered Brian, the Riptide who had bought it for them. She found four pence for the phone, went up to the call box on the main road and phoned the repair shop where he worked. He sounded surprised to hear from her, but promised to come round one evening and have a look at the TV for her. He arrived two days later.

'You not heard from Ricky, then?' he asked.

'No, have you?'

'Not a word. Bastard, walking out like that. We got another singer but he's not as good. We're just The

Riptides now. We're all equal now we ain't got Ricky acting the star.'

Scarlett wished it was that easy to replace a husband. She made Brian some tea while he got the back off the TV and poked around inside it. He spouted a lot of technical terms that Scarlett didn't understand, put the back on again and switched it on. It lit up.

'Hooray!' Scarlett said. She felt cheerful for the first time in weeks.

The screen was still fuzzy, but Brian fiddled with some of the controls and at last a clear picture appeared.

'That's wonderful. Thanks ever so much, Brian.'

Brian gave her a funny look. 'Well, you said you wanted a favour.'

'I know. Like I said, Ricky left us high and dry. I couldn't afford to get it repaired. I hope you don't mind me asking like this.'

It was embarrassing, having to admit to her poverty, especially to Brian. She never had liked him much.

'I don't mind. Not when one good turn deserves another.' He leered at her.

'What?' said Scarlett.

Brian took a step nearer. 'I always did fancy you, Scarlett, but Ricky always got to all the best birds first. But he's gone now, and I bet you're missing a bit of the other, ain't you?'

Scarlett realised what he was on about. 'No,' she lied, stepping backwards.

Brian made a lunge at her, grabbed her in his arms and tried to kiss her.

Scarlett twisted her head away. 'Get off! Get your filthy hands off me and get out!'

Brian just laughed. 'Oh, come on—you know you want it. Ricky always said how hot you was. Begging for it, he said.'

He forced her backwards so that they fell onto the sofa.

'Come on, Scarlett—a favour for a favour.'

Scarlett struggled and kicked and scratched.

Brian laughed. 'Ricky said you was a wildcat. You love it really, don't you?'

'I do not. Get off!'

Scarlett's flailing hand touched the fire-irons on the hearth. Her fingers closed round the first handle, she wrenched it away from the stand and brought what turned out to be the shovel down hard on Brian's head.

'Bloody hell! You bitch!'

As he put his hand to his head, he shifted enough for Scarlett to wriggle from underneath him. Using two hands now, she swung the shovel at him again, this time aiming between his legs. Brian saw the blow coming, squawked in horror and jumped up. Blood was running down his neck from the cut on his head.

'Pack it in, Scarlett! Look what you done to me!'

Scarlett made a threatening movement with the shovel.

'Get your stuff and get out before I make it worse.'

He shuffled over to the television, which was still happily telling them about a washing powder that washed whiter, grabbed his repair bag and made for the door. Scarlett realised she was enjoying this. A feeling of power surged through her.

'This is the last time I do anything for you,' Brian said resentfully.

Scarlett couldn't believe what a coward he was. He could easily overpower her if he tried.

'You shouldn't try and take advantage,' she told him. She exchanged the shovel for the poker and advanced on him, ready to strike again. 'Out! Out of my house!'

'Bitch!' Brian spat, and made off down the front path.

Scarlett slammed the door on him and leaned against it. Her heart was racing and her chest was heaving. She felt more alive than she had done for weeks. She laughed out loud.

'Got you, Brian Hopkins!' she shouted.

The incident had given her a surge of energy. She turned off *Emergency Ward 10* on the TV, found her old favourite, Radio Luxembourg, on the radio and sang along with the music as she gave the floors the best polish they'd had since well before Simon was born.

By the time Simon needed his next feed, she was pleasantly exhausted. She flopped on the saggy sofa and watched him as he chomped away, his little face fierce with concentration.

'It's no good, this not having any money,' she told him. 'It means people think they can push you around. And I tell you something, that blooming Brian's really made me think. I'm not going to be taken advantage of like that any more, and I'm not going round asking for favours. I've got to earn some money somehow, and I've got to do it with you and your sister around.'

Her attention wandered to the television, which was now trying to persuade her to buy a new vacuum cleaner.

'That'll be the day,' she said to Simon. 'Just imagine, a vacuum cleaner and a washing machine and the fridge back! I'd hardly have to do any housework at all. It'd be like one of those American places you see on the films.'

It was an impossible dream. She took Simon off the breast and laid him over her shoulder to wind him.

'Perhaps we'll settle for the fridge back,' she said as she rubbed his back. 'I really miss that. But first we've just got to get enough to live on, and have more than just beans or eggs for dinner. I tell you what we'll do, we'll go and look at the ads in the newsagent's window tomorrow morning.'

Simon gave a big windy burp. Scarlett laughed.

'There's a clever boy! So that's decided, then.'

When he was fed and changed, she laid him down in the drawer she was using as a crib, then bent over the cot and kissed Joanne on the forehead. The little girl was deeply asleep, her arms spread on the pillow. Scarlett was overwhelmed with a wave of love. They were so sweet and so helpless. They depended completely on her.

'Things will get better, my darlings,' she promised them. 'We won't be poor for ever.'

The next morning saw her on the street corner, studying the postcards on the newsagent's board. Amongst the things for sale and rooms to let and kittens wanting a good home, there were only four jobs going— one for a hairdresser's apprentice, one for home work addressing envelopes and two for cleaners.

'Better go for the cleaning,' Scarlett told the babies. 'Let's hope they'll let me bring you along as well.'

She made a note of the addresses and set off. The first woman took one look at the pram and refused to even consider employing Scarlett.

'I've got a nice home. I don't want sticky fingers all over it,' she said.

The woman at the second address was more accommodating.

'That's all right, just as long as you can get the work done,' she said. 'Shall we try it for a week and see if we suit?'

Scarlett was all too ready to agree. It was arranged that she should work for three hours every Monday, Wednesday and Friday morning. Scarlett wheeled the pram back home feeling elated. She had started to take control of her life again.

CHAPTER TWENTY-THREE

THE cleaning money made a real difference. If it hadn't been for Victor, Scarlett might have been able to manage. But her plan to control how he spent his wages failed. Neighbours started waylaying her in the street and knocking at the door.

'I don't like to bother you, dear, but your dad borrowed five shillings from me three weeks ago and he still hasn't paid it back.'

'Look, this ain't good enough. You help someone out and then they welsh on you.'

'I asked him for that half-crown back I lent him, and he said you take all his money off of him and I ought to ask you.'

Scarlett apologised to all of them, told them never to let Victor have any money, however sad a sob story he told them, and paid out her precious earnings. On the third Friday since she had been doing the cleaning job she found that, instead of being able to buy some mince and make the cottage pie she had been looking forward to, she had just enough in her purse for a few vegetables and yet another tin of baked beans.

'I'm turning into a blooming baked bean,' she told Joanne.

The little girl just grinned at her and went on banging saucepans with the wooden spoon.

'And you need some toys. You've only got your rattles and stuff. You need some bricks or one of those push-along dog things. I can't even afford to go to a jumble sale now. And God knows how many more times these shoes'll take being repaired, even if I can afford to have them done, that is.'

She tried to tackle Victor.

'Dad, you've got to stop borrowing money off the neighbours. That Mrs Thompson is ever so sweet; she finds it hard to say no. It isn't fair, she can't afford to sub you. She's only got her OAP.'

'What else can I do?' Victor asked. 'I flog myself to death working six days a week, and you go and take all my money off of me.'

In the end, Scarlett had to give in and give him more of his wages each day. It was better than having to pay back other people.

There was worse to follow when she went to work the following Monday.

'I'm afraid I'm going to have to let you go,' her employer said.

'What?' Scarlett said.

'It's the babies. I really can't be having them here with you every time.'

'But you said you didn't mind!'

'I know, but now I've found a woman who'll do the same work as you and her children are at school. I'm sorry, but there it is.'

'That is so unfair!' Scarlett objected. 'I need the money. I work just as hard as someone without children.'

But the woman was immovable.

Furious, Scarlett trekked down to the newsagent's again. There were no suitable jobs at all amongst the postcards. She walked all the way back up to the London Road to the newsagent's there and found three requests for cleaners. When she went to see them, one turned out to have found someone already. The others wouldn't let her bring the babies with her. By now it had started raining and Scarlett's left shoe was letting in water. Simon was dry enough under the hood, but Joanne, sitting at the bottom of the pram, had only Scarlett's old school mac round her and was grizzling as the rainwater made her face wet and cold.

'We'll go home and get dry,' Scarlett told her.

She was in unknown territory now, in the grid of streets between the sea front and the main road. She crossed over the railway line and found herself walking along a parade of small shops with a pub at the corner. The shops just made her depressed, because she knew she couldn't afford to spend anything if she wanted to put money in the gas and electricity meters. She glanced at the pub as she passed. The Horse and Groom. It was nicer, she decided, than most of the town pubs she knew of. Not as nice as the Red Lion, of course, but then no pub would ever compare to the Red Lion. A notice in one of the windows caught her eye. *Cleaner wanted. Mornings. Good wages.*

'Might as well try it,' she said to Joanne.

She looked at her watch. Just before opening time, so someone would be there and the children would be let in. Perfect timing. She banged on the door. A white-haired woman with merry eyes and a sweet smile opened it. Scarlett explained that she had come about the job.

'Oh—good. Come in, dear. You're soaked! Yes, bring the pram as well. What sweet babies. How old are they?'

Scarlett told her. 'And before we get any further, I'd better tell you that I've got to bring them with me to work.'

'Oh, that's all right dear,' the woman said, gently pinching Joanne's cheek and smiling at her. 'I love kiddies. It'll cheer the place up a bit. Look, why don't you come through to the back and I'll put the kettle on.'

Before Scarlett knew what was happening, she was sitting at the kitchen table sipping tea and eating chocolate biscuits while Joanne guzzled a plastic beaker full of orange squash and got chocolate round her mouth.

'This is lovely, Mrs—er?' Scarlett said. She couldn't remember the last time she'd had a chocolate biscuit.

'Cartwright, dear. But call me Nell—everyone does.'

'Nell, then. It's so nice in here. Friendly and cosy.'

'Thank you, dear. We like it. Bert and me, we've had this pub for forty years. We was youngsters when we took it on. Not much older than you. Ooh, they was hard days then. No one had any money. Not like now. People seem to do nothing but spend these days.'

'Mmm,' Scarlett said. She didn't do a great deal of spending.

Nell got a cloth and wiped Joanne's chocolatey hands and face.

'Ooh, isn't she just gorgeous! I could eat her up. My daughter lives up north, so I hardly ever see my grandchildren. Three of 'em, I've got—a girl of five and boys of eight and ten—but I ain't seen them for nearly a year,' Nell said.

'Nan-nan,' Joanne said, responding to Nell's twinkle.

'Oh, bless her! She called me Nan! What a little poppet! And doesn't she look like you, a proper little picture. And what about the little one? Does he look like his daddy?'

Nell was irresistible. Scarlett found herself explaining all about Ricky and her predicament, while Nell shook her head and made sympathetic noises. Before she was finished, a bald man in his sixties put his head round the door.

''Ello, 'ello, 'ello! And who have we got here?'

It was Nell's husband, Bert, come to open up the bar.

'This is Scarlett, love, and her little ones. She's our new cleaner.'

'Oh—do you mean I've got the job?' Scarlett asked. They hadn't discussed that at all.

'Well, yes, dear. If you want it, that is. Not everyone wants to work in a pub when they can get a place in a nice house. Would you be able to do Sundays?'

Right at that moment, Scarlett would have agreed to anything. Being at the Horse and Groom was like coming home.

It was the start of a new era. Each morning Scarlett got up early and gave the flat a tidy round, fed and changed Simon, then got Joanne up, washed and dressed. After that she made breakfast, took her father a cup of tea and then bundled the babies into the pram and set off for the Horse and Groom. The smell of ashtrays and spilled beer that greeted her as she went in the door was not repellent, as it might have been to many people—it was the smell of her childhood, rich and reassuring. It was hard work cleaning the two bars and the toilets, but she enjoyed it. It was satisfying to see the gleam on all the surfaces when she had finished, the dark patina of the woodwork, the bright glow of the brass-topped tables and the glitter of the mirrors. She set all the chairs and stools straight, put the beer mats out neatly and made sure the colours of the bar towels went together well.

All through the winter she got out on time each morning and was at the pub by half past nine, pushing the pram through rain and frost and snow, working even when she had a streaming cold or when one or other of the babies was teething and breaking in to her sleep. She didn't want to let Nell and Bert down. They were like the grandparents she had never had. At Christmas, they gave her a turkey and the babies extravagant toys. Scarlett burst into tears and kissed them. It was the best Christmas she had had since her mother died.

Late in February, Bert strolled in to talk to her as she polished the beer pumps.

'You done bar work when your folks had their place, didn't you?' he asked.

'Oh, yes. I can pull a good pint, I can,' Scarlett told him.

'I thought as much. And you can add up?'

He reeled off a round of drinks. Scarlett looked at the prices around the bar and added them up in her head.

'Eleven and eight pence.'

'Right! Well done. I thought you was quick on the draw. You see, old Ivy what does evenings, she's leaving at the end of the month. Going to live with her son in London. And what we wondered was, would you like to take on two or three evenings bar work as well as the cleaning? Truth to tell, we need someone young and pretty behind the bar. Someone to bring the customers in, like, and you'd be ideal.'

Three evenings' work! Scarlett's brain whirred, calculating what she could do with the extra money. She could buy new shoes for Joanne instead of having to go to jumble sales. She might even be able to replace the fridge.

Then she faced the practical difficulties.

'I'd have to find someone to babysit,' she said.

'Well, you do that and let us know, all right?'

It was more difficult than she'd thought possible. None of the neighbours wanted to take it on, not on a regular basis. Scarlett didn't want a series of youngsters coming in, not if they didn't know much about looking after babies. And then there was her father. One of the days Bert wanted her to work was Victor's day off. She couldn't trust him not to fall asleep and not hear if one of the children woke up, but neither could she ask someone else into the house to mind them if her father was going to be lying around the place drunk. But she did very much want that job. After going over and over all the possibilities for hours, she came to a very hard conclusion—she was going to have to ask Ricky's parents.

George and Betty Harrington were not exactly welcoming when she turned up on their doorstep on Saturday afternoon.

'Oh, it's you. What do you want?' George asked, looking her up and down.

Scarlett stared back at him. She had her line of approach worked out.

'I want to talk to you. Can I come in?'

'Who is it, George?' Betty appeared behind him in the narrow hallway. 'Oh. It's you.'

'I've brought the children, I thought you might like to see them.'

Of course, it worked. They couldn't possibly turn their grandchildren away. Scarlett parked the pram on the front path, heaved Joanne down, then lifted out Simon. She gave Joanne a little push on her back.

'Go and say hello to Nana and Grandad.'

Joanne was proud to show off her new word. She toddled up to her grandparents. 'Eh-yo!' she said, smiling broadly. The Harringtons' grim expressions melted. Soon they were sitting in the frigid front room drinking tea and eating biscuits—sensible tea fingers, not messy chocolate digestives like Nell's. Scarlett handed Simon to Betty and prayed he wouldn't make a fuss. He didn't always like new faces. Simon looked unsure. For one heartstopping moment, Scarlett thought he was going to screw up his face and scream, but Betty chucked him under the chin and he broke into a smile, displaying his two little teeth.

'Oh, hasn't he grown! He looks just like Ricky, doesn't he, George?'

Scarlett didn't think he looked a bit like his father, but held her tongue. She waited while Mrs Harrington cooed over the children. Then the questions started. Had she got them into a proper routine? Was she making them both sit on the potty? Was she teaching Joanne to say 'Please' and 'Thank you'? Did she take them for a proper airing each day? As she needed to get her mother-in-law on her side, Scarlett answered yes to everything. To distract them, she asked the Harringtons if they had heard from Ricky. The grim faces returned.

'Not a word,' Mr Harrington admitted.

'It's breaking my heart.' Mrs Harrington sighed.

'Poor Simon's never seen his father, and Joanne's forgotten she ever had one,' Scarlett said to rub it in.

'It's a crying shame,' Mr Harrington stated.

'I'm doing my best to give them all they need, but it's hard,' Scarlett told them. She explained about the cleaning job and the offer of bar work. 'I can't take it up unless I can get the children looked after those evenings. It'd make all the difference.'

She paused, letting the words sink in. George and Betty looked at each other.

'So you want to be a barmaid? That's not what I'd call a respectable line of work. Not exactly what I'd want for my grandchildren's mother,' Betty said.

Just in time, Scarlett stopped herself from saying that having a rock and roll singer for a father hadn't done them much good.

'It's all I'm qualified for. And it's a very respectable pub,' she said.

To her surprise, Mr Harrington agreed. 'I've heard it's a quiet sort of place.'

'I want so much to support them myself and not live on the dole,' Scarlett added. 'Anything's better than that, surely?'

Mrs Harrington was still looking prune-faced. 'I'd like to help,' she said, 'but I really don't think I could be at your flat when your father was there.'

Scarlett's heart sank. She had always known that this was the weak spot.

'I'm not sure I want my wife away from home three evenings a week,' Mr Harrington said.

'You could both come,' Scarlett suggested. 'I've got a TV still.'

'George likes his own chair and his own fireside. He isn't really comfortable anywhere else,' Mrs Harrington explained.

It was stalemate.

'I really need that job, and there's no one else I can trust with the children,' Scarlett said.

'Well—' Mrs Harrington's fingers trailed longingly over Simon's chubby legs, lingered on each one of his tiny toes. Then her expression cleared. 'They could come here,' she suggested. 'We could get a couple of cots and they could sleep in the back bedroom. You could come and collect them in the morning.'

Scarlett hated the idea. 'I couldn't possibly put you to all that trouble,' she said.

'We know our duty, don't we, George?'

Mr Harrington made a throat-clearing noise that could have meant anything.

In the end, Scarlett had to agree. It was either that or not take the job.

Parting with the children three nights a week was heart-wrenching. Scarlett never got used to it. She dreaded handing them over to the Harringtons. On top of that, there was Mrs Harrington's disapproval to face. She always gave Scarlett an up-and-down look, followed by a sniff. Often she would comment on her appearance.

'What's all that muck on your face?' she asked.

Scarlett put her hand to her cheek. 'What? It was all right when I left home.'

'If you call all that paint all right, I'm sure I don't.'

'It's only a bit of lipstick and powder. Everyone wears those,' Scarlett said.

'Not if they're respectable, they don't.'

However often Scarlett pointed out that plenty of ladies of Mrs Harrington's age wore make-up, and every young woman did, even librarians and teachers and people like that, Mrs Harrington never approved.

Her other grouse was what Scarlett chose to wear to work.

'You're not showing yourself in that blouse, are you?' she would demand, and once again Scarlett would have to justify herself.

It all made an already stressful situation much worse.

Once at the Horse and Groom, she was usually so busy that she didn't have time to miss the children too much. The pub was a friendly place, a proper local, not at all like the Trafalgar. The regulars were delighted to have an attractive young girl behind the bar and con-gratulated Nell and Bert on finding her.

'Nothing against old Ivy, but she wasn't a patch on Scarlett here. She's a sight for sore eyes, she is.'

Scarlett soon learnt everyone's name and what they drank, and set about pulling their usual for them as they came in the door. By the end of two weeks, she knew their likes and dislikes, their families and football teams, their ailments and their hobbies.

'Trade's gone up by a quarter the evenings you're here,' Bert told her at the end of her first month. 'I think you're a bit of a hit.' He mimed hitting a bell like David Jacobs on *Juke Box Jury* and went, 'Ping!'

'I knew she would be,' Nell said.

'So we thought we ought to give you a bit of a rise,' Bert concluded.

Scarlett was delighted. It was almost worth the pain of parting with the babies, the horrible emptiness of the flat when she got back of an evening.

Not long after, Bert went down with gout and was in such pain that he couldn't move. Scarlett took over the cellar work, making sure the beer was settled and ready, cleaning the pipes and putting on the new casks.

'She's a proper little marvel and no mistake,' Nell reported back to Bert. 'You needn't worry about the beers. The regulars are more than happy about how she's keeping them.'

'I was well trained by my dad,' Scarlett said. 'He was always very proud of the quality of his beer. That was one of the reasons he hated working at the Trafalgar. They used a beer saver there.'

Bert made a face. 'I won't have them things. I wouldn't insult my regulars by using one. They come to me for good beer, not stuff that's been spilt and put back in the cask.'

'Quite right too,' Scarlett agreed.

Bert gradually got better, but he still let Scarlett do some of the cellar work, nodding approvingly from a stool at the bar as she pumped a new ale through.

As spring turned to summer, they celebrated Joanne's second birthday. Nell made a cake with pink icing and two candles and she and Bert gave the little girl a doll's pram and baby doll. Joanne was delighted and trotted round the pub with it, bumping into stools and tables.

'We got a proposition to put to you,' Bert said as they watched Joanne's chubby little person race past.

'That sounds interesting.'

'Yes, well, we ain't getting any younger,' Nell said. 'We're both finding the standing behind the bar a bit much, what with Bert's gout and my varicose veins.'

Scarlett looked at them in alarm. 'You're not thinking of retiring, are you?'

'Well, sort of,' Nell admitted.

Scarlett was horrified. Now she would have to get another job, just when she thought she'd found a safe haven. She would never find employers as kind as Bert and Nell.

'The thing is,' Bert explained, 'we'd like to take more of a back seat, like, and we thought you might consider being the manageress. We've been thinking about it for ages, but we could only do it if we found the right person. Now, you're a real grafter, and you know your way about a bar and, most of all, you're good with the customers, so we think you'd be ideal. We'd have to talk about wages and that, and we'd still do some work so that you could have time with the kiddies.'

'Oh—!' Scarlett exclaimed, overwhelmed. No one had ever put their trust in her like this before. 'I don't know. I mean, I'd love to, but—'

The complications of looking after the babies raced through her head. How could she possibly do a good job here and be a proper mum? How could she bear to leave them with the Harringtons every night, even supposing the Harringtons would agree to have them?

'—it's the children,' she said.

Bert and Nell looked at each other and smiled.

'Ah, well, that's the clever part. There's the flat on the top floor.'

'Ivy's flat?'

'Ivy's flat. We've been wondering what to do with it. I mean, we don't want any old Tom, Dick or Harry living up there, not when you have to go through the back of the pub to get there. If it had a separate entrance, it'd be different. But anyhow, there's room up there for you and the little 'uns. There's no bathroom, mind, but there is a toilet and there's a nice little kitchen and three rooms. Then in the evening we could leave the doors open and I could listen out for the babies.'

It sounded wonderful. A job and a home and built-in babysitting. Scarlett couldn't believe it. She would be able to support her children herself and still have time to be with them. Best of all, she wouldn't have to leave them at the horrible Harringtons' any more.

And then she came down to earth with a bump.

'What about my dad?' she asked.

Nell gave a sigh. Bert looked embarrassed.

'Look, love,' Nell said. 'From what you've told us, your dad's a drinker, right?'

Scarlett nodded. It was no use denying it. She'd often told them how worried she was about him, how he was in danger of losing even the bottom-of-the-heap job he had, how she had to stop him from borrowing from the neighbours.

'A drinker in a pub's no good,' Bert said. 'I seen it so many times. If he was upstairs there in the flat and he needed a drink, where's he going to go? Down the off-licence? I don't think so. He's going to come down to the bar, and then you're going to be put under pressure to slip him a free one.'

'I wouldn't do that—!' Scarlett cried.

'I know. You're dead honest, you. But you'd be piggy in the middle between him and us, wouldn't you? And no offence to your dad, but it'd be a temptation, wouldn't it, having all this drink down here? He'd be down here taking a sly one.'

'He wouldn't—' Scarlett began, but stopped. If her father could spend everything on drink and still try to get subs off the neighbours, he could well get desperate enough to steal.

'I seen it before,' Bert repeated. 'They can't help it, drinkers. They just got to have another one. And we don't want it to be a cause of trouble between you and us.'

If anyone else had put it that baldly, Scarlett would have been up in arms. But she loved and respected Bert and Nell enough to face the truth. They were right. Her father couldn't be trusted to live in a pub. It was so frustrating. Here was this golden opportunity and she couldn't take it. She could have wept. If only things weren't this way. If only her dad was like most men, and went out to do a proper day's work and just got a bit tipsy on a Saturday night. Nobody minded that. Why did he have to be a slave to the drink?

'I can't leave him.' She sighed. 'What'd happen to him if I wasn't there? He'd get thrown out of lodgings because he was drunk and he'd never pay the rent. He wouldn't go to work half the time and he'd lose his job. He'd end up on the street, a down-and-out. I can't let that happen to him, can I? He's my dad.'

Bert and Nell tried to persuade her that she couldn't be responsible for her father's behaviour, and for a while Scarlett was almost swayed. Her whole future would be better if she didn't have to consider him.

'Oh, it's so unfair!' she cried, thumping the table. She felt as if her head were bursting with the pressure of it all. But, even though she was tempted, she knew in her heart that she couldn't abandon her father. Years of loyalty could not just be wiped out. She would never be able to live with herself.

In the end Bert and Nell had to accept that family must come first. Scarlett agreed to do Friday and Saturday evenings behind the bar, as long as the Harringtons agreed to have the children. Bert and Nell decided not to let the flat to anyone else, just in case something should happen to make her change her mind. Scarlett went home at midday to find her father collapsed in the outside toilet, and knew that she had made the right decision. He needed her, and that was an end to it.

CHAPTER TWENTY-FOUR

THROUGH the summer months Scarlett got into a new routine. On the days when she had worked the night before, she made sure her father was all right and left him a cup of tea before going round to the Harringtons' to collect the babies. Then she pushed them to the Horse and Groom and spent the morning there, cleaning, making out orders and seeing them in and looking after the cellar. The children were quite at home there. Joanne had a supply of toys and Simon happily crawled round the floor and learnt to pull himself up onto his feet by holding onto the bench seats around the walls of the public bar. Once the pub opened, Nell would take the children into the kitchen at the back and give them a meal while Scarlett looked after the bar, and then either Nell or Bert would cover the rest of the midday opening while Scarlett had some time off.

The afternoons were family time. There was usually shopping to get, but on the days when Scarlett didn't have washing or too much housework to do at home, they went to the beach or one of the parks for an hour or so. She tried to insist that her father join the children and herself for tea, and most days he did sit down with them and eat something, always with a cigarette smouldering in an ashtray close to his hand.

After tea she chased Victor out of the house in one direction to get to The Oaks, while she piled the children back into the pram and wheeled them in the other direction round to the Harringtons', before returning to the Horse and Groom to work behind the bar all evening.

By August, Ricky had been gone for nearly a year. Scarlett had long given up any thought of his returning. If she did think of it, she found that she didn't even want him to come back. Her life was hard, and making ends meet was still difficult, but she was much happier without him. Then, two days before Simon's first birthday, she arrived at the Harringtons' to find Betty looking nervous and George more than usually grim.

'What's up?' she asked.

'Well…er…' Betty began.

'It's got nothing to do with her,' George interrupted.

'Oh, but it has! We've got to tell her,' Betty insisted.

Scarlett looked from one to the other in surprise. Mrs Harrington hardly ever contradicted her husband, or at least not in front of her.

'Tell me what?' she asked.

Various possibilities paraded themselves. Had Ricky returned? Had he gone to the USA? Was he dead?

'Nothing,' said Mr Harrington.

'We heard from Ricky,' said Mrs Harrington.

'Oh,' said Scarlett.

'Is that all you can say?' Mr Harrington demanded. '"Oh"? A lot you care, I must say.'

'I…I was just surprised. Flabbergasted. I never thought—but where is he? What's he been doing all this time?'

'Hamburg,' Mr Harrington said, with heavy disapproval.

'Hamburg?' Scarlett exclaimed.

'Hamburg,' Mr Harrington repeated. 'That's in Germany. He's got a job in Germany.'

As far as he was concerned, the Germans were still the enemy.

Scarlett made a dive for the stairs, where Simon was crawling up the first steps with amazing speed.

'Oh, no, you don't,' she said, scooping him up. Simon yelled in protest. He loved stairs. 'What's he doing in Germany?'

'You'd better see for yourself,' Mrs Harrington said. She disappeared into the back room and returned with a picture postcard in her hand. She held it out to Scarlett. 'Here.'

There were four small photos of vaguely foreign-looking buildings with the words *Grüsse Von Hamburg* written across the centre. Scarlett turned it over. There in Ricky's untidy writing was the brief message.

Dear Mum and Dad,
Got some regular spots in the nightclubs here.
Hope you're all right, and Scarlett and the kids.
All the best,
Ricky

Scarlett stood staring at it, as if expecting more to appear. Her strongest emotion was one of anger. He'd been away a whole year without once letting them know whether he was alive or dead, and then this! She looked at his mother, who had tears in her eyes.

'Is that it?' she said.

'That's it,' Mr Harrington said. 'That's all he can be bothered to send us. *Hope you're all right. All the best.* It's breaking his mother's heart. It's not how he's been brought up to behave, I can tell you that for nothing.'

For the first time, Scarlett felt sorry for Mrs Harrington. She never had taken to the woman, but she could feel for her as a mother. She reached out to put an arm round her, but Mrs Harrington brushed her off.

'Please don't touch me!' Hot-eyed, she rounded on Scarlett. 'It's all your fault! He would never have done this if it hadn't been for you! It was you he was running away from. He'd still be here now if you hadn't led him on. I shall never forgive you—never!'

'Led him on?' Scarlett repeated, outraged. 'I was an innocent young girl till your precious Ricky took advantage of me.'

Mrs Harrington's eyes flicked over her. They were stony with hatred.

'Innocent? You were never innocent. Your sort aren't. Look at you, all dolled up in your warpaint and your tight skirt, ready to go and flaunt yourself behind a bar all evening long. It's disgusting.'

'I beg your pardon? What exactly do you mean by that?' Scarlett demanded.

Joanne, sensitive to the angry voices around her, flung herself at Scarlett and hung onto her leg, wailing. Simon, who was already cross at being stopped from climbing the stairs, joined in.

'There, now look what you've done, you've upset the children,' Mrs Harrington said.

'Me? I didn't start this,' Scarlett retorted.

Then she realised just how childish that sounded. She was not in the playground now. And, what was more, the children were upset and she didn't want to leave them in a state. She didn't want to leave them at all, but she had to. She kissed Simon and handed him to Mrs Harrington, then picked up Joanne and cuddled her.

'It's all right, darling, Mummy and Nana aren't cross with you. It's all right. It's all over now.'

She glanced at Mrs Harrington, who set her mouth in a hard line, but said no more.

It took a while, but both children eventually calmed down. Reluctantly, Scarlett kissed them goodnight and set off for work.

It took a lot longer for her to calm down. The incident churned round inside her all the way to the pub. Once at work, there was too much going on to think about it a lot, though she was always aware of a nagging worry at the back of her head.

It was on the long walk home that things really started to play on her mind. If Ricky had at last made contact, did that mean he was eventually coming back? But if he had only written to his parents, maybe he wasn't thinking of returning to her. On the other hand, he had mentioned her and the children. Surely even Ricky would want to see his own children? What if he wanted to take up where he had left off? What should she do? She didn't want to live with him again, but it would be wrong to deny the children the chance to have a proper family life with a mother and a father. The questions went round and round in her head, but the answers didn't seem to be there.

Coming back to the flat was always the worst part of the day. Scarlett opened the front door and sniffed. Fresh cigarette smoke. That was one worry less, as it meant her father had got back. She paused outside his bedroom door.

'All right, Dad?'

''Right love.'

The words were slurred, but he was reacting.

'Cuppa tea?'

'No, thanks.'

She sighed and went into the kitchen to put the kettle on. It was no use making him one if he was only going to let it go cold. She washed at the sink, then with tea to fortify her, she faced her bedroom. It was crowded in here now. She had pushed the double bed against the wall, but she still had to edge round the wardrobe, the chest of drawers and the two cots. As always, her throat tightened when she looked at the empty cots. Her babies should be here, with her, not farmed out to their grandparents. She wanted to see their innocent sleeping faces, to smell their sweet breath. She wanted to see their first smiles in the morning.

She climbed into bed and lay in the dark. She was dead tired, but sleep did not come easily, for she had to face the fact that if Ricky did return, she would have to take him back for the children's sake. Nell and Bert were generous employers, but women just weren't paid as much as men. Ricky could earn enough for her to be with the children most of the time. There would be no more nights at their grandparents'. That had to be worth putting up with living with someone she didn't love.

Carnival week arrived. Scarlett, Nell and the babies watched from the cliffs.

'The first time I saw this, it was with Jonathan. I thought it was the most exciting thing I'd ever seen,' Scarlett said.

'Ah, well, it was first love, weren't it?' Nell said. Scarlett had told her all about Jonathan. 'It's all rainbow colours, first love.'

'Yeah, you're right.'

Rainbow colours. It had been like that, her first summer in Southend. She had been devastated by her mother's death and having to move out of her home, but still there had been a magic glow to those short months. Everything had been larger than life.

A horde of people in animal costumes came running through the crowd, shaking their collecting tins. Simon bounced around so much that the pram rocked. Joanne jigged up and down with excitement.

'Bears! Bears!' she squealed.

Nell gave her some pennies to put in the tins. Joanne gazed with wonder at the huge furry creatures with their human faces while Scarlett got her pleasure second-hand. If Joanne was delighted, then so was she. It was the children that counted now.

'Another couple of years and they'll enjoy the fair up in Chalkwell park,' Nell said.

'Yeah, I'll have to take them to that,' Scarlett said.

Another two years. What would she be doing then? Would Ricky be back, or would she still be on her own, trying to be a mum and a breadwinner? She watched the carnival queen and her court go by, and remembered Jonathan turning to her and saying that she was a hundred times prettier than any of the girls on the float. She blinked back tears. It was no use thinking of that. It was the past. Even if Jonathan were to come back to Southend, why would he want to take on somebody else's children? She put her arms round Joanne and hugged her chubby little body.

'Look, darling, a band! See all the boys marching!'

Simon bounced and crowed as the brass band played *Colonel Bogey*. Scarlett's heart lurched painfully as she remembered Jonathan and his friends singing rude words to it as a band had gone by that first summer. She grabbed Joanne's hand.

'March! March to the music!'

Hand in hand, they marched on the spot, Scarlett trampling on her memories. It was no good looking back. It hurt too much.

After carnival week, the summer always seemed to hurry to a close. When the nights drew in, Scarlett bundled the children up in warm jumpers on one of her evenings off and wheeled them round Never-Never Land, where Simon enjoyed the lights and Joanne marvelled at the magical displays of fairies and animals. And then it was winter, with all its difficulties of lighting fires and getting washing dry. Taking the children round to the Harringtons' in the dark and the rain seemed much worse than doing it in the light. Mrs Harrington seemed to think so as well.

'It's not right, pushing these poor mites round from pillar to post,' she told Scarlett.

'I know, but what can I do? Their father's not here to support them,' Scarlett retorted.

She knew as soon as the words had left her mouth that she shouldn't have said that.

'You could get a more respectable job, for a start,' Mrs Harrington said. 'A barmaid! Everyone knows what sort of women they are. We never had any barmaids in our family, not ever. We all had decent jobs in shops or dressmaking or hairdressing.'

'I couldn't take the children to work with me if I worked in a shop,' Scarlett pointed out.

'Yes, well, that's another thing. I don't like my grand-children spending their time in a public house. It's not a good way to bring them up at all.'

'I was brought up in a pub,' Scarlett pointed out.

Mrs Harrington looked her up and down. 'Yes, well, that explains a lot, doesn't it?'

'And just what is that supposed to mean?' Scarlett demanded.

Mrs Harrington just pursed her mouth up and looked self-righteous. 'I really don't think that's something we can discuss in front of the children.'

Fuming, Scarlett held her peace. The beastly woman was right. They mustn't argue when the babies were there.

A couple of weeks later, her neighbour from the upstairs flat knocked on the door. She was a pleasant young woman a couple of years older than Scarlett, but Scarlett didn't see very much of her because she and her husband were out at work during the day while Scarlett was out most evenings.

'Um…look…this is a bit embarrassing,' she began. 'But I thought you ought to know. There's been this woman from the welfare snooping round.'

'What?' Scarlett was horrified. 'What do you mean, snooping round after me?'

'That's right. She was here the other day just as I

came in from work, and she's been talking to the other neighbours as well, asking if we've seen anything.'

'What do you mean, seen anything?'

'Well…' the woman looked awkward. 'She was asking if we'd seen any men coming in and out.'

'Any men—?' It took several seconds for the meaning of this to explode upon Scarlett. 'You mean, like I was a prostitute?'

Her neighbour nodded, biting her lip. 'But don't worry, we all told her you was a good person and a good mum and all, how you was working so hard to look after them kids and your dad and everything.'

'Th-thank you—' Scarlett stammered.

She was reeling from the shock of it. It was one of her evenings off, but her pleasure in being able to put the children to bed in their own home was ruined. It was horrible, horrible. Who could possibly have reported such lies to the authorities? Who could hate her so much? As the evening went on, it became clear to her that the only possible culprits were her parents-in-law. It made her feel quite ill. If they were capable of doing this, what else might they do? She had to have it out with them, but she couldn't think of a way to do so without the children being upset by the angry voices. In the end she decided to ask Nell to mind them for a bit longer one lunch time.

It was impossible to hold her tongue when she took the children round to the Harringtons' the next evening, but she did manage to stay coldly polite.

'I need to speak to you. There's something we need to sort out,' she told Mrs Harrington.

Her mother-in-law's face stiffened. 'I can't think what.'

Something about the expression in her eyes convinced Scarlett that she knew exactly what.

'I'll be here at about half past one tomorrow,' Scarlett told her, trusting that Nell would agree to have the children at such short notice.

Mrs Harrington hardly said a word to her when she picked the children up the next morning. Scarlett reminded her that she would be round later. She realised that it sounded like a threat, but she didn't care. The Harringtons were threatening her life with her children, so she had to fight like with like.

Dead on time, she flung open the Harringtons' front gate, marched up their path and banged on their door. Mr Harrington opened it. For a moment she was taken aback. She hadn't expected to see him. He was usually at work during the day.

'You'd better come in,' he said.

He waved her into the stiff front room, where Mrs Harrington was waiting for her, sitting very upright in one of the armchairs on one side of the sulky-looking fire. Mr Harrington claimed his armchair on the other side. Both of them fixed Scarlett with a cold stare as she sat on the sofa. No tea was offered.

'Where are the children?' Mrs Harrington asked.

'My employer's minding them.'

Her parents-in-law exchanged a glance that said, We were right.

'Now,' Mr Harrington said, 'what's all this about, then?'

Scarlett had tried to plan this meeting, so she stopped herself from saying, You know flaming well what it's about. Instead, she launched into an explanation.

'My neighbour told me that a lady from the welfare

had been round asking questions about me. Asking whether they'd seen men going in and out of my flat. I was upset about that. Very upset.' It didn't need any acting to get a wobble into her voice. Just talking about what had happened brought the shock and hurt of it all back again. 'To think that someone should even suspect me of doing—that. It's horrible. And then to go and report me to the welfare.'

She stopped and looked at Mrs Harrington. Her mother-in-law had her hands clasped very tightly in her lap.

'If someone reported you, it must be because they thought there was something to report,' she accused.

'Well, that someone was wrong. I've got nothing at all to be ashamed of. All my neighbours know that. They'll all have told the welfare woman that. There's one or two opposite me what spend their lives looking out of their windows and they'd soon know if I was up to no good.' There was an edge to Scarlett's voice. 'So all the welfare woman will've found out is that that someone is just out to make trouble.'

'She'll have found out that you take those poor little babies to a public house each day, and that they're living in a flat with a drunkard,' Mrs Harrington stated.

Somehow 'a drunkard' sounded a whole lot worse than 'a drinker'.

'Don't you call my father that,' she warned.

'I speak as I find. He couldn't even stay sober for the wedding.'

This was true, so Scarlett ignored it.

'You've no right to call my father names,' she said.

'You've no right to be bringing up our grandchildren in a home that's morally unfit,' Mrs Harrington retorted.

'Steady on, Betty—' Mr Harrington warned.

There was a deathly silence while they all took in the implications of what had been said. Then Scarlett stood up. Her knees felt shaky, but she could not stay sitting in the same room as these people.

'I love those children more than my life,' she told them. 'They're well fed, they're clean, they're healthy and they're happy. Most of all, they're loved. So I'll thank you to stop trying to stir up trouble.'

'No one's trying to stir up trouble. We just want what's best for the children,' Mr Harrington said.

'If your precious son hadn't gone off to play his guitar in foreign nightclubs, I wouldn't have to go out to work and take the children with me,' Scarlett pointed out. 'So, if you want to carry on seeing them, you'd better think about that.'

With which she marched out of the door. Her anger took her halfway up the road. Then the full meaning of what the Harringtons were up to hit her. Shock and fear made her legs go weak beneath her and she had to sit down on a front wall. She was shaking all over. They wanted to take her children away from her!

'They can't do that,' she said out loud.

But what if the welfare people saw things the same way as the Harringtons? What if they thought a pub wasn't a suitable place for small children to be? What if they were to see her father on one of his bad days?

It didn't bear thinking about. One thing was for sure, she'd get on a train and run away with the children rather than let anyone else have them. No one was going to take them from her.

CHAPTER TWENTY-FIVE

'LOOK, we're passing Buckingham Palace,' Jonathan said, pointing at it through the taxi window. 'That's where the Queen lives.'

The taxi was an extravagance, but Corinne had brought so much luggage that he didn't see how they could lug it all through the underground and then along the streets from Tower Hill to Fenchurch Street. And besides, Corinne was still feeling the after-effects of being seasick during the Channel crossing.

Corinne followed his gaze.

'Oh, yes. It's very nice.'

'And there are the guards, see? In their red jackets and busby hats.'

Unbidden into his mind came the children's rhyme about changing the guard at Buckingham Palace. With it came the memory of the last time he had shown someone the Palace. Scarlett had been absolutely thrilled to see it.

He'd quoted the first line of the poem to her.

Scarlett had laughed and come right back with the next line.

Of course, Corinne couldn't be expected to know that. She had been brought up on Babar the Elephant, not Christopher Robin.

'Now we're going down The Mall,' he told her.

'Mmm—nice, but it is not as grand as the Champs Elysée.'

It was a pity the weather was so bad. London was not at its best in the rain. He pointed out all the places of interest on the way, but he had to admit that London did look grimy and dirty. It didn't have the elegance of Paris.

'This is St Paul's Cathedral,' he said.

'It is not as beautiful as Notre Dame,' Corinne decided.

He was glad when they turned into Fenchurch Street and pulled up outside the station. It had been a very long day and they were both getting scratchy. He paid the taxi driver and hauled their suitcases onto the pavement. Corinne looked up at the station.

'Not as fine as the Gare du Nord,' she commented.

'Well, it's not an international station, is it? It's only going to Southend,' Jonathan snapped.

He picked up the two largest cases and left Corinne to bring a smaller one and two bags. She tottered behind him on her stiletto heels, complaining that he was going too fast. He turned and waited for her, and his irritation turned to pride. She did look so chic, so very French— tall and slender with a tiny waist, her dark hair pinned up in an elegant pleat. Very lovely, and all his. His fiancée.

'Nearly there now,' he said. 'This is the last lap.'

To his relief, there was a fast train waiting at one of the platforms. Corinne sank into a window seat and lit up a Gauloise. Jonathan heaved the cases onto the luggage rack, sat down beside her and took her hand. Her pretty face was drawn with fatigue.

'Nearly home now,' he said.

'I hope your parents will like me,' Corinne said.

'They'll love you,' Jonathan assured her.

'And you, do you love me, Jonathan?'

'Of course I do.'

'Then say it, say it to me.'

'I love you, my little cabbage.'

He was glad they were speaking in French. They were getting curious glances from fellow passengers, but at least nobody could eavesdrop on their conversation. The language barrier was one of the things that concerned him about this visit. Corinne had only schoolgirl English and his parents spoke no French at all, but he would be there all the time to translate, so there shouldn't be too many problems. He was much more worried as to whether Corinne was going to like England.

The train started up and trundled through the East End with its rows of tiny impoverished houses and occasional bomb sites, then into the suburbs and the vast council estates of Dagenham and Becontree till eventually they came out into the green countryside of south Essex. The weather brightened up. There was even a little watery sunshine. When they passed Laindon, Jonathan insisted that they sat on the right-hand side of the carriage.

'We'll soon catch the first glimpse of the sea,' he told Corinne.

She was not very impressed with the muddy creek at Benfleet.

'This is not the seaside,' she objected.

'But there are boats.'

'Pff! Boats. I do not like boats.'

'You don't like ferries. Ferries are enough to make anyone feel sick. Small boats are quite different.'

He hoped she would like sailing. It was a bit early in the year, but if they got some sunny days he wanted to take her out on the water. At Leigh-on-Sea he opened the window and stuck his head out, breathing in the aroma of seaweed, shellfish, salt and mud. The smell of home. The train ran through the fishing village and then alongside the Thames estuary for a while. To Jonathan's delight, the tide was in.

'There,' he said, waving a hand at the grey-green waves and the sailing dinghies bobbing at their moorings. 'Now we're at the seaside.'

'Mmm—' Corinne brightened up and began to show an interest. 'It is very pretty. Are we nearly there? Is this Southend?'

'Just two more stations, then we're there.'

It was only a short taxi ride from the station to the Trafalgar, but Corinne seemed taken with what she saw. The cheeriness of Southend won her over.

'What is at the end? We must go and see!' she exclaimed, as they looked down on the pier.

'We will,' Jonathan promised.

The meeting with his parents went well. Corinne managed to understand a lot of what they said, she was delighted with the view from the windows of the flat and she liked the guest bedroom. His parents appeared to like Corinne and were pleased with her gifts of chocolates and cigars. Jonathan began to relax. It was going to be all right.

Over dinner, his mother asked Corinne about her family.

'I got a very nice letter from your mother, thanking me for inviting you. You're an only child too, aren't you? Like Jonathan.'

'Oh, yes. It is just me. No brothers or sisters. My mother is very careful for me.'

Jonathan smiled to himself. Careful was hardly the word. Corinne had only been allowed on this visit because they were going straight to his parents' home, and only then after an exchange of letters to make sure that their precious daughter would be properly chaperoned.

'That's only natural,' his mother said. 'Pretty girl like you, they want to make sure you're all right, don't they? Your father's got a jewellery shop, then?'

'Yes. We sell the jewellery and my father mends the watches and clocks also.'

'Nice line to be in,' Jonathan's father commented.

'Line?' Puzzled, Corinne looked at Jonathan. He translated.

'Ah—yes—it is a good business, yes.'

'And you serve in the shop?'

'Yes. I like to show to the ladies the beautiful necklaces and earrings. I like especially the diamonds.'

'We all love diamonds,' Jonathan's mother said, looking at the sparkling new eternity ring on her knobbly finger.

'Girl's best friend, eh?' his father said.

'Pardon?'

'Diamonds Are a Girl's Best Friend. Marilyn Monroe.'

'Ah! Marilyn Monroe. The song. Yes.'

'And your parents don't mind you getting engaged to a chef?'

'Chef is very good profession. Very—honoured?'

'Honourable,' Jonathan supplied. 'In fact, Mum, Dad, Corinne's parents have offered to give us some money towards starting a restaurant. That's one of the reasons we're here. I think it would be better to start a business here, where a good French restaurant would be a novelty. I'm hoping to persuade Corinne that she'd like to settle in England.'

It had the effect he wanted. His parents were impressed, delighted—and not to be outdone.

'That's very kind of them, I'm sure. But I wouldn't want them to think that we can't give you a bit of a start in life,' his mother said. She gave her husband a significant look. 'Would we, Arthur?'

'What? Oh—no—of course, we'll cough up some to get you going, son. I'm sure you'll be a good bet.'

'Cough up? Bet?' Corinne asked.

'Give us some money. As an investment,' Jonathan substituted.

'Oh, but that is wonderful! You are very good, very kind!' Corinne exclaimed. She jumped up and kissed both his parents on the cheek. 'We will be big, big success, I am sure. Jonathan is wonderful chef. Very, very talented. And me, I will be front of 'ouse and make the big welcome for everyone. Soon all of this Southend will eat with us, I think.'

'We might find it's better to set up in London,' Jonathan reminded her. He wasn't sure that Southend was ready for French cuisine.

'No, no. I don't like London. It is dirty. But this Southend is very nice. I like it 'ere.'

Jonathan decided to leave it at that for now. His parents were obviously charmed by Corinne and his pitch for their help had gone better than in his wildest dreams. The details could be settled later.

For the next few days he showed Corinne round town and introduced her to some of his old friends. Graham was married and living in a little house in Southchurch. They went to visit them.

'You know who she reminds me of?' Graham said, when the two women were in the kitchen.

'No, who?'

'Scarlett. Same height, same colouring, everything.'

'I like brunettes,' Jonathan said.

'Yeah, if you say so, mate. She's certainly a looker. I saw her, you know. Scarlett.'

Jonathan's heart gave a painful twist, leaving him shaken. He had persuaded himself that he was over Scarlett. He had Corinne now. They were engaged to be married.

'Oh, yeah?' he said, trying to sound uninterested.

'It was on the sea front, ages ago. Couple of years, maybe. It was pouring with rain and she was walking along with this kid in a pram. She didn't look very happy.'

Jonathan just had to ask. 'Did she mention me?'

'Don't remember, mate. We only passed the time of day.'

The women came back into the room and the subject was dropped, but Jonathan remained uncomfortably disturbed. Just that mention of Scarlett stirred up so many memories that it was difficult to concentrate on what the others were saying. Walking back along the sea front with Corinne, he found himself reliving the times he had walked there with Scarlett.

Try as he might, he couldn't get her out of his head.

He lay awake that night wondering about her. Was she still living in the same flat in Westcliff as when he had last seen her? Was she happy? The generous part of him hoped she was. She'd had a lot of sadness in her life, she deserved a break. And yet—and yet the vengeful side of him hoped she was regretting finishing with him. It had taken him a long time to recover from her betrayal. He had never really forgiven her.

A couple of days later he received a phone call from another of his old gang.

'Hello, Jonno. Heard you were back. And with a gorgeous French fiancée, so Graham says. Look, we thought it'd be good to all meet up somewhere tomorrow, and bring our womenfolk with us so your girl's got someone to talk to. What do you reckon? Someone said the Horse and Groom is a nice pub. Do you fancy coming along?'

Jonathan thought the evening might be a bit of a strain for Corinne, meeting so many new people at once, but her English was improving by the day and, if she was going to front their restaurant, she needed plenty of practice in conversation. He accepted.

It was Friday evening, and the pub was crowded when he and Corinne went in to the lounge bar. One of his pals jumped up from a seat and waved at them.

'Jonno! Over here!'

There were a lot of them now that most had girl-friends or wives. They had pushed three tables together and already had a round of drinks in. Two more seats were found and introductions made.

'I'll get some drinks. Anyone ready for another?' Jonathan asked.

It was only when he turned towards the bar that he recognised the young woman standing behind it. Scarlett.

His immediate reaction was one of anger. Who had set him up like this? He could feel eyes on his back, waiting for fireworks. For Corinne's sake, for his own sense of pride, he made his way steadily across the room. The other people in it hardly existed. They were just obstacles in his way. His eyes devoured Scarlett. She looked as beautiful as ever, her dark hair done up in a fashionable beehive with a long tail hanging over her shoulder. She was serving an elderly man, laughing and joking with him. Jonathan watched her sure movements, her air of confidence. She looked happy, at home, very much in charge.

She took some money from her customer and glanced round to smile and nod to those who were waiting.

'Be with you in a minute, sir—'

And then their eyes met. Scarlett put a hand on the bar to steady herself.

'Jonathan!'

'Hello. Long time, no see.' He wanted to kick himself. What a stupid thing to say. 'I…er…I didn't know you worked here. I came with the gang…' he explained.

She was still staring at him as if she had seen a ghost.

'I dreamed about you last night, and now here you are,' she said.

'Here I am,' Jonathan repeated. This was terrible. He wanted to jump over the bar, take her in his arms and kiss her.

'That's one and nine pence change, Scarlett, love,' her last customer called. 'When you're ready, like.'

'Yes, yes…'

Her cheeks flaming, Scarlett went to the till, rang up the money and gave the man his change. In the short time that took, Jonathan knew he had to tell her the situation now, at once. Leaving it any longer wasn't fair. She turned back to him. They both spoke at once.

'How are—?'

'Scarlett, I—' he stopped, then started again. 'Scarlett, I'm here with my fiancée.'

'Ah.'

'I really didn't know you were working here.'

'No, of course not.' She forced a smile. 'Congratulations. You must introduce me. Which one is she?'

There was a professional cheeriness in her voice that chilled him to the heart. Jonathan turned and indicated Corinne, who was watching him. He smiled at her and waved. Graham was right, the two women did look very similar. Corinne blew a kiss.

'She's very pretty,' Scarlett said. 'So what can I get you?'

'What? Oh—' He rattled off his round of drinks.

Scarlett set about pulling pints and pouring Martinis and Babychams, all the while asking him how he was and how long he would be staying in that artificially bright voice. Jonathan replied in the same fashion. He paid, she brought the change.

'There you are.'

He caught her wrist. 'Scarlett,' he asked urgently, 'how are you? Is everything all right? Your father—?'

'I'm fine. Just fine.' She refused to meet his eyes, looking away to the waiting customers. 'Just coming, sir. Hello, Mr Fielding, how's the wife?'

Jonathan returned to his table with the tray of drinks,

feeling as if he'd been through a wringer. Through the muddle of people taking glasses and thanking him, Corinne leaned forward.

'What is going on? Who is that barmaid?' she hissed in French.

'Just someone I used to know, from way back.'

'Were you lovers?'

'She was my girlfriend, yes, but—'

They were interrupted by one of the gang raising his glass.

'A toast!' he called. 'To Corinne and Jonathan! Long life and happiness!'

'Corinne and Jonathan!' everyone chorused.

Corinne laughed and thanked them all, leaning against him possessively. Jonathan put an arm round her shoulders, all the while conscious of Scarlett behind him at the bar.

'Thank you! Thank you! It's great to be back with you all again.'

'Speech!' someone called. It was taken up by others.

'No, really—'

'Speech, speech!'

Fists thumped the table. Eyes were watching him, mouths grinning. Corinne was looking up at him in expectation. There was no getting out of it.

'Right, well—thank you for your welcome. You might be glad to know that you'll be seeing quite a lot of us in the future. Corinne and I—' Whistles and cheers from the audience. 'Thank you. Corinne and I are planning to open a restaurant together and, as Corinne seems to like dear old Southend, it could well be here. So I hope you'll all come and eat with us and help to make it a success.'

More cheers and whistles. Someone was thumping him on the back.

'Good on you, Jonno!'

'Great news.'

Everyone wanted to know more about Corinne and about their project. Jonathan was kept busy explaining, translating for Corinne and catching up with all the personal news. When he had a chance to look towards the bar, Scarlett was chatting to a customer. For a moment, their eyes met again, but she instantly looked away.

One of his mates got up to go to the toilet. Jonathan seized his chance to find out who was behind this nerve-stretching situation.

'So what's the big idea, then?' he demanded.

'What? What do you mean?'

'Having this get-together here with Scarlett looking on. You must all be killing yourselves laughing at me.'

'Wasn't me, Jonno. I've never been here before. Bit of a shock for me, finding her here. I haven't seen her in years.'

'Shock! It was more than a bloody shock for me. You've really landed me in it. Corinne thinks there's something funny going on.'

His friend gave him a level look. 'She'll only think there's something funny going on if you act like there is,' he said. 'It was all over years ago, wasn't it?'

'Well, yes—'

Except that it wasn't. Scarlett still had the power to rake his heart.

'There you are then. Problem over.'

'Right.'

But he still couldn't enjoy the evening the way he

would have done if Scarlett had not been there. His spine prickled with the knowledge that she could at any time be looking at him.

The party broke up at the end of the evening with everyone promising to keep in touch. Jonathan and Corinne walked back towards the sea front through the quiet streets.

'Did you manage to follow what people said?' he asked.

'Yes, some of the time. It's hard when they speak quickly, or interrupt each other.'

'You'll get better with practice. Your English is already a lot better than when you arrived. But did you like them? I want you to like my friends.'

'Yes, they were very nice, very kind.'

'Good. Another time maybe we'll go out in a foursome or something, and it'll be easier for you to understand what's being said.'

'Yes, I'd like that. But Jonathan—that barmaid, that Scarlett. You say she was your girlfriend once?'

Jonathan took a steadying breath. 'That's right.'

'But there is nothing between you now?'

'Corinne, for heaven's sake! This is the first time I've seen her in—oh—three years or so. She's married. She's got a kid.'

'I see.'

Something in her voice told him that she saw far too much.

'Look,' he said, 'I've had other girlfriends, you've had other boyfriends, but that's all in the past. We're getting married, Corinne. That's the future.'

They arrived at the top of the cliffs, overlooking the public gardens that ran down to the promenade. It was a clear night, and the moon made a silver path across the glistening mud to the deep water beyond. They both stopped and gazed at it.

'So this Scarlett is nothing to you now?' Corinne asked.

'That's right,' Jonathan lied.

'And you love me?'

'You know I do.'

'Show me.'

She moved into his arms, put her face up to be kissed. Jonathan surrendered to the moment. He had to leave Scarlett behind him. She had her own life, and he had his.

CHAPTER TWENTY-SIX

AFTER that Friday evening, Scarlett held herself ready to meet Jonathan again. She did not want to be caught like last time, hardly able to meet his eyes. Sometimes she saw his friends. They seemed to have adopted the Horse and Groom as a meeting place. When one or other of them came in, she would look at the door, wondering whether he would be following them, whether he would be on his own or with the French girl, but he never came. She longed to know whether he was still in the country, but was too proud to ask. She didn't want his friends to gloat over the fact that she was still in love with him. When they bought drinks from her she was polite and friendly, as she was to all the customers, but she didn't engage them in conversation.

Then one quiet lunch time, when she had just about given up looking for him, there he was. He came straight over to the bar and started talking to her.

'You here on your own?' she asked, pulling him a pint.

'Yes, I only arrived back in England yesterday.'

So that was it. He had been in France since she'd last seen him.

'Your fiancée's not with you this time, then?'

'No, she doesn't like the crossing. She hates boats. So I'm here on a flying visit to look at premises for a restaurant. When I've got it down to the last two, she'll come over and have the final say.'

Scarlett struggled to suppress an acid wave of jealousy.

'Oh, you're opening a restaurant together, are you? That's nice. When's this going to happen?' She tried to keep her voice level and normal, but didn't quite succeed.

'As soon as I can find somewhere suitable. It's not easy. It's got to be the right size, a good position, not too expensive and have nice living accommodation. I've found one or two that are in the right place and a decent size. Look—'

He took a couple of estate agents' leaflets out of his pocket to show her. Scarlett could hardly bear to look at them. To her relief, she was called away to serve some customers in the public bar, but when she came back to the lounge bar to serve one of her regulars there, Jonathan was still sitting at the bar with the leaflets in front of him, waiting for her. She lingered over getting the one whisky for her customer, but eventually she had to come and look at the choices for Jonathan's marital home. One was on the quiet stretch of the sea front towards Thorpe Bay, the other was off the Hamlet Court Road.

'What do you think?' Jonathan pressed.

'They're both nice,' she said.

'I know that. They're both fine as restaurant premises, and they're both in areas where there's plenty of money, but what about the living accommodation? What do you think? I need a woman's view.'

Scarlett forced herself to look at the details of rooms

and sizes. It made her feel quite ill. Lucky, lucky Corinne, to be marrying Jonathan. Stupid, stupid Scarlett, who'd thrown away that chance.

'They're lovely,' she said.

Jonathan shook his head. 'I don't know. They both look a bit cramped to me. Corinne's used to living in a lovely apartment in Paris. I'm not sure she'll be happy in either of these.'

Scarlett could contain herself no longer. 'If she loves you, she'll be happy to live with you anywhere. In a garage, or a tent, anything. It doesn't matter as long as you're with the right person.'

Jonathan gave her a long, considering look. 'That's how you feel, is it? You're happy to live anywhere as long as you're with what's-his-name?'

Scarlett bit her lip. Why was he doing this to her? He had his Corinne now, he shouldn't be so bitter.

'No,' she admitted. 'It was never like that. And now, if you must know, he's left me. He went off to Hamburg to play his guitar in the nightclubs, and then just the other week I heard he was living in Liverpool.'

Jonathan looked shocked. 'He's done what? The bastard!' He reddened and apologised for his language. 'But honestly, Scarlett, how could he do that, leave you and his child?'

'Children,' Scarlett corrected. 'He left just as the second one was born.'

At that point a group of people came in and Scarlett had to go and serve them, and after that Bert came down to take over.

'I'm going home now,' Scarlett told Jonathan.

'No, don't—I mean, look, can I walk along with

you? As far as your road, perhaps? I have to—I mean, we can't just leave it like this.'

'Like what?' Scarlett asked. It would be stupid to agree; it would only lead to more heartache. But somehow she couldn't refuse. 'All right. I'll go and fetch the children and meet you outside.'

It was a beautiful summer's day. Joanne demanded to go to the cliff gardens. Simon, who copied everything his big sister did, chanted, 'Cliffs! Cliffs!'

'Do you have to go straight home?' Jonathan asked. 'I'd love a walk along the cliffs. Paris is beautiful, but I miss the sea.'

Scarlett found herself agreeing again. She was glad of the children's chatter as they walked down the street. Joanne only needed the odd word here and there to let her know that her mother was listening, giving Scarlett space to come to terms with the whirlwind of emotions that she was caught in. She couldn't make out why Jonathan had sought her out like this. Was he trying to punish her by showing off his new love, his plans for the future? Was he just treating her as an old friend? Somehow, she didn't think it was that. His reactions to what she had said were too extreme. She batted down any faint glimmer of an idea that he might still feel anything for her. She had treated him too badly, and now he was engaged to Corinne. There was no hope of reviving what they had once had.

They crossed the road that ran along the top of the cliffs and Scarlett lifted Simon out of the pram and let both children run on the grass. She kept an eye on them, but Jonathan was staring out over the mud to the deep water and the hills of Kent beyond.

'It's best when the tide's out, isn't it?' he said. 'It's the real Southend. Remember those days we had out in the Ray?'

Scarlett's throat tightened. She drew a shuddering breath. 'Yes,' she said. 'They were wonderful times.'

'You really took to sailing, didn't you?'

'Yes, I loved it. It was so exciting, rushing along like that with the wind and the waves and everything.' She hesitated, then added, 'I often think of what it was like, when I see the dinghies sailing out there.'

Simon fell over and she ran to pick him up. She kissed him, rubbed his knees and set him on his feet again. Happy once more, he toddled off after his sister, who was racing around barking, pretending to be a dog.

'You're good with them, aren't you?' Jonathan said.

'I'm their mum. I love them.'

They began to walk slowly along the clifftop, while the children ran about.

'How are things for you, Scarlett?' Jonathan asked. 'How are you managing on your own?'

'Oh, well—' Scarlett hardly knew where to start. 'It's hard work, that's for sure. I'm always tired.'

She explained her daily routine.

'—the worst bit is having to leave the children with their grandparents at night. I hate that. And I'm scared they'll try to take them away. They keep making hints, saying I'm not looking after them properly.'

'Anyone can see you're looking after them just fine. I mean, I don't know much about kids, but they're happy and healthy, aren't they? And you're with them most of the day and they're asleep at night anyway. It's not like you're leaving them alone, or with strangers.'

'I know, but if they told it from their point of view, you know, taking them to a pub every day—'

'You and I were both brought up in pubs, It hasn't done us any harm.'

'Yeah, that's true, but the welfare people might not see it like that. And then there's Dad. The Harringtons are always making a thing about him being a bad influence.'

'Ah, yes. How is your dad?'

'Slowly getting worse—Joanne! Not down the path. Stay along the top where I can see you!—I don't know how his body can stand it, all that drink. He hardly eats anything, just toast and stuff, and tea. I've practically given up making him proper meals. And he's got the shakes something terrible. I feel dreadful sometimes, sending him off to work when he obviously isn't well, but if he misses one day, then he'll miss the next, and then it'll be a week, and then he'll lose his job. I just have to make him keep going.'

'You're twenty-one,' Jonathan said. He sounded angry and frustrated. 'You shouldn't be doing all this. You should be out enjoying yourself.'

'Yeah, well, that's a nice idea,' Scarlett said. She tried to recall the very last time she'd gone dancing at the Kursaal with Brenda, but it was all a bit of a blur now. If she had known it would be the last time, she would have made more of an effort to store it up in her memory.

'But how do you manage, bringing up two kids on your own and coping with your dad?' Jonathan insisted.

Scarlett shrugged. 'I just have to, don't I? Nobody else is going to do it.'

'But what about what's-his-name—Ricky? Doesn't he send any money or anything?'

'No. But up till recently I wasn't sure where he was, not exactly. Well, I still don't, only that it's Liverpool. His parents know. They went up to see him only a couple of days ago.'

'They must tell you, surely? You've got a right to know where the father of your children is. He ought to be helping to support them.'

'I know. I tried to find out but they said he was only in temporary accommodation. They were very tight-lipped. It's my guess he's shacked up with some woman they don't approve of. They don't approve of me, mind, so if I am right then this one must be pretty dreadful.'

'If you are right, then you could get a divorce. Then he'd have to pay you maintenance.'

'I suppose so.'

'What's the matter? You're not still in love with him, are you?'

'No!' She had never been in love with him, not the way she loved Jonathan. But it was far too late to say that now. 'Like I said, I'm afraid of what his parents will do. I'm sure they want to take the children away from me.'

'They can't do that, can they?'

'I don't know. They're always saying as how I'm not a fit mother.'

'You are a fit mother. Anyone with half an eye can see that.'

Scarlett looked at the two children as they played. Joanne was capering about, waiting for her little brother, then rushing off just as he reached her. Simon kept solemnly toddling after her, determined to catch up.

'Don't tease him, Joanne,' she called. 'Let him catch you.'

The little girl stood poised for a moment, ready to defy her, then at the last minute she allowed her brother to clasp her waist. She hugged him back boisterously while Simon laughed with pleasure.

'I'm glad there's two of them,' Scarlett told Jonathan. 'They're a handful, but now they'll always have each other. Life's easier when you've got family. I'd love to have a brother or sister.'

'I know what you mean. I was lonely when I was a little kid and Mum and Dad were both working. It wasn't so bad when I got older, 'cos then I could go and play out with my friends.'

The talk drifted into safer waters. For a while it was almost like old times. They had always got on so well together. The aching sense of regret that Scarlett carried inside her was growing into a great ball. She could almost feel it pressing up into her chest. Anyone looking at them would think that they were the perfect little family—mum, dad and two children. It was how it should have been.

At the end of the gardens, she scooped Simon up and put him back in the pram and made Joanne hold onto the handle. Jonathan went into a sweet shop and bought them all ice creams. Simon got his all down himself and she had to clean him up with the old tea towel she kept in the well of the pram. They wandered up Hamlet Court Road until they came to one of the side streets.

'This is where one of the restaurants is. Or, at least, I think it's just been a café up till now,' Jonathan said. 'Would you like to come and look over it with me? I've got the key.'

That would just be too much. Scarlett shook her head.

'No,' she said. 'No, I'm sorry, but I don't think I could bear it. I'm sorry. I'll go now. Good…good luck with it.'

She walked away up the road without looking back, while the tears that had been gathering spilled down her face.

'…and Tante Sylvie is making the headdresses,' Corinne said. 'Of course, I can't tell you what they are going to be like, not now Jonathan is here, but they are very beautiful. They will set off the dresses perfectly.'

The wedding day was set for mid-November. Already it was July, and preparations were in full swing.

'That sounds lovely, dear,' Jonathan's mother said. 'Six bridesmaids! Your poor mother must be in a right tizz organising all this.'

'Tizz?' Corinne asked, looking at Jonathan.

'Fuss. Bother. To-do.'

'Oh, yes, I see. Tizz! What a funny word. I will remember that.'

Jonathan's father took him aside while the women moved onto the subject of flowers.

'So it's a full Catholic do, then? How do you feel about all that?'

'It's that or nothing. Corinne's parents are absolutely adamant, so I haven't much say. I'm going along for instruction each week, just to keep them and the priest happy.'

'Rather you than me, son. Still, I suppose they have been very generous helping set you up.'

'So have you and Mum. Don't think I'm not grateful.'

'Not much point in slaving away to earn the money

if you can't spend it on your kids, is there? You're still going to have a big mortgage and a bank loan, mind.'

'I know, but we've got to have the right place. This is going to be the classiest restaurant in the whole Southend area, Dad. I want it to be everyone's first choice for all their special occasions. I can't wait to show Corinne the shortlist. She's seen the details, but it's not the same as looking at the real thing, is it?'

Behind them, the women were deep into posies and bouquets. Jonathan looked out at the glory of the Illuminations. Thousands of coloured lights blazed and flashed. Right opposite their window a huge illuminated clown juggled red balls while dancing on his big flappy feet. Below him in the street, hundreds of evening visitors swirled in and out of the amusement arcades, the chip shops and the pubs. Downstairs the bars were heaving. You could hear the noise of the packed customers even over that of the television going full blast. Normally his parents would be down there in the thick of it, but today was special. Jonathan was home to see to the buying and renovation of his new business. Corinne would be going back to France again in a couple of weeks, but he was staying here until the wedding. Then the plan was to have just a few days' honeymoon before returning to their new home for the grand opening of the restaurant.

Everything was going his way, but somehow he wasn't quite as excited about it all as everyone expected him to be. He wasn't as excited as he thought he should be. Somewhere beneath the perfect surface, there were nagging doubts.

He tried to put them aside the next morning when he

and Corinne set out to look at the two premises he thought were most suitable for their venture. First they caught the white open-topped bus to Chalkwell to see a place opposite the park. Corinne liked the park but not the flat over the restaurant.

'It's too small and too dark. And there is a strange smell,' she said, wrinkling her nose.

'I expect the smell will go when it's all cleaned up and painted,' Jonathan said.

But Corinne was not convinced, so they caught the bus back again, past the Trafalgar and the Kursaal to the quiet end of the sea front nearer to Thorpe Bay. The building there was one of the ones that Jonathan had shown the details of to Scarlett. This time Corinne was far more enthusiastic.

'Oh, yes, it is a very pretty place. I like the railings and the steps. We could have window-boxes there with geraniums, and a tub by the door with a bay tree.'

Jonathan felt his spirits rising.

'Wait till you see inside. It's not big, but it's got everything we need.'

He fitted the key into the door and they stepped into a big dusty room that still had a couple of cheap tables and some chairs abandoned in it.

'Look, we could put six tables of four and two twos in this part,' Jonathan said, 'and then we could knock down this wall, or maybe partially knock it down, and have a bar area and a couple more tables in the back here.'

Corinne looked slowly round, nodding.

'Yes, yes. I can see it. We shall have very sophisticated colours—eau-de-nil and dark green maybe, or sky-blue and white with a touch of gold—and mirrors and candles and fresh flowers and crisp white linen.'

'Wonderful,' Jonathan agreed. 'Now, come through here and see the kitchen. It's pretty crummy, but there's space for improvement.'

It was pretty crummy. There was a large stained sink, a couple of worktops, some built-in cupboards and a capped-off gas pipe. But it was a large enough room with natural light and ventilation and a back door leading to a large yard. Jonathan could immediately see how he would divide up the space to make an efficient working kitchen.

'The toilets are horrible,' he warned Corinne.

They both looked at the Ladies and Gents cloak-rooms and agreed that, like the kitchen, they would have to be completely refurbished.

'So—the restaurant is fine, or will be when all the work is done. What about the apartment?' Corinne asked.

Jonathan led the way up a dark staircase to the living accommodation. It was on two levels, with a large sitting room overlooking the sea, a kitchenette and bathroom on the first floor and three bedrooms under sloping ceilings on the second floor. Corinne was delighted.

'Oh, yes, I can make it so pretty! We will have a sofa just here, and we will sit together in the afternoons between lunch and dinner service and look at the sea and the ships. We will be so happy, and so successful!'

Jonathan could see it all. The busy kitchen where he would produce food that would have all of Southend and the surrounding area flocking to his door, the elegant eating area buzzing with happy diners, the comfortable apartment to which he and Corinne could retreat. It was on this last point that his imagination blurred over a little and the nagging doubts crept in. He pushed them aside. He was committed now. He smiled at his fiancée.

'Shall we buy it, then?'

Corinne beamed and threw her arms round him.

'Oh, yes! Oh, I am so happy! We must go and buy it straight away!'

CHAPTER TWENTY-SEVEN

IT WAS at the beginning of September that Nell said to
Scarlett that she needed to have a serious chat.

'Oh, dear,' Scarlett said. 'That doesn't sound too
good. What's the matter?'

'Come upstairs. I've put the kettle on,' Nell told her.

Bert was sitting with his feet up reading the newspaper. He smiled at her a bit uncertainly when she came
in. Scarlett was beginning to feel distinctly unsettled.
Something was going on here. Nell brought cups of tea
and slices of brightly coloured angel cake.

'Now then,' she said. 'I'm afraid we've had a bit
of a shock.'

Fear snatched at Scarlett's heart. 'Are you all right?
You're not ill, are you, either of you?'

'No, no, dear. Nothing serious. But I suppose that's
got something to do with it, in a way. No, you see, yesterday evening we had a phone call from our daughter.'

'Our Thelma,' Bert supplied.

'Yes, our Thelma. In a right state, she was, feeding
pennies into the phone box at her end and crying. Her
husband's been made redundant. Terrible shock, it was.

That's five hundred of them all out on their ear at the same time, and no jobs going up there. Well, not five hundred jobs, anyway. Poor Thelma doesn't know which way to turn. They've got all this stuff on the HP and rent to pay and all the rest of it and she doesn't know how she's going to manage. Well, after she'd rung off, Bert and me had a long talk.'

'We're not getting any younger,' Bert said. 'And we can't do the standing, not any more.'

'And we have still got that flat upstairs,' Nell said.

Scarlett suddenly saw where this was leading. A feeling of doom settled on her stomach. She pushed the slice of angel cake away. She wasn't feeling hungry any more.

'The thing is, dear, we've got to think of our future,' Nell carried on. 'We did hope as you'd see your way to coming and living here and being a sort of manageress for us, but I can quite see how you can't, what with your dad and all. So you see, we thought we'd offer the flat to our Thelma and her Andy, and they could run the place for us. There's two of them, you see, so they could do it between them. We'd only have to fill in if it was very busy. We could retire and still live here. It'd be ideal. We've nowhere else to go if we leave here, but with them here running the place we'd be able to stay, and they'd have a home and a living.'

'I see,' Scarlett said. 'It's all very neat. Works perfectly.'

'Well, it does,' Nell agreed. 'And we had been getting a bit worried about what we was going to do in our old age. I mean, we got our pensions, but that's all. And now, with Thelma's Andy being out of work, like, it solves two problems.'

Scarlett could understand that all right. But she couldn't see a place for herself in the scheme.

'So—you won't be needing me any more?' she said.

Nell and Bert both looked very uncomfortable.

'We hate doing this to you, dear,' Nell said.

'You been a real little grafter. A godsend,' Bert agreed.

'But it's family, you see—'

Scarlett did see. It was just very hard when you didn't have any family yourself to stand by you and help you through the bad times.

'Right,' she said. 'Of course.'

'You're to stay on until you've found somewhere else. And just tell them you work here and we'll give you a glowing reference.'

'Yeah, anyone'd be pleased to have you,' Bert said.

'Right,' Scarlett repeated. 'Thank you.'

So it was back to looking at the local paper and the newsagents' windows. There were cleaning and bar jobs going, but no employers were as accommodating as Nell and Bert had been when it came to allowing the children to be with her in the mornings. She had to settle for just an evening job for the time being, and prepared to cut down on the very few extras she had come to allow herself. She bade a tearful farewell to Bert and Nell, and wished them well in their retirement.

'We'll miss you, dear, and the kiddies,' Nell told her. 'So we bought a little present for them to remember us by.'

Little wasn't quite the word to describe it. The brown paper parcel was as tall as Simon. Both children ripped the paper away to reveal a horse that moved along when you bounced up and down on it. Joanne and Simon were at first speechless with amazement, then wild with excitement. They couldn't

wait to get it home and play with it. Scarlett gave Bert
and Nell a last hug, loaded the toy horse onto the
pram and left the Horse and Groom and the happy
times she had had there.

The new job wasn't half as nice as working for Nell
and Bert. It was at a big pub just off the High Street.
There were lots of staff, so she was bottom of the heap
instead of the trusted almost-manager, the customers
weren't so nice and at times could be far too friendly
and it was further to walk to and fro. The long trek
back along the London Road at night was not pleasant.
She didn't tell the Harringtons that she had lost her job
at the Horse and Groom, but of course Joanne let it
slip, being far too young to understand the need to
cover things up.

'So you're finding it hard to keep the children, are
you?' Mrs Harrington said.

'The children never go without,' Scarlett assured her,
and went onto the offensive. 'Have you heard anything
more from Ricky? Is he settling in Liverpool?'

Mrs Harrington's mouth went into a hard straight line.

'He hasn't any fixed plans at the moment. He's considering his career.'

'And what's that supposed to mean? Is he going to
send any money for the children's winter shoes? I want
them to have proper ones that fit their feet, not any old
rubbish that might cramp their little toes.'

She managed to shame Mrs Harrington into submission. She couldn't very well suggest that Scarlett was
incapable of providing for her children when it was her
own son's fault that Scarlett was in this position. Then
she attacked while she had the advantage.

'Has he got a girlfriend up there in Liverpool? Is that why he's not contacted me, or made any move to come and see his own children?'

'No, of course not. He's a married man,' Mrs Harrington told her.

'Then perhaps he'd better remember that,' Scarlett retorted.

The children were beginning to look upset over the simmering tension. Scarlett decided to quit while she was ahead.

'Thank you for looking after them,' she said. 'It's a nice day. I think we'll go for a walk along the sea front. Get some nice healthy fresh air into their lungs.'

Usually she walked along the Westcliff part of the sea front, but today Scarlett decided to go the other way, under the pier and along the Golden Mile. They passed the Trafalgar, and Aunty Marge's chip shop, and the Mancinis' café. It was too early in the day for any of them to be open. The street cleaners were still clearing up after the evening trippers who came down to see the Illuminations and stayed on to enjoy the fun of the Golden Mile. At the Kursaal corner she paused. They had come quite a long way and it was even further to go back. Joanne would be tired long before they reached home and she would have to push both of them. But there was something calling her on. She knew it was stupid, but she'd heard where Jonathan was going to open his restaurant and she just wanted to see it.

'Come on,' she said to Joanne. 'Just a bit further. Then, if Aunty Marge is open on the way back, we'll get a bag of chips to help us along.'

The little girl ran ahead of her, shouting at the seagulls to make them take off from their lookout spots on the railing posts. They passed the gasworks and came out onto the prettier part of the sea front. And then there it was. She recognised it straight away from the description she had read on the estate agent's leaflet. There was a big *Sold* notice attached to the railings on one side of the door, and on the other side a board announcing *Coming soon—Petit France—Fine French Cuisine.* The front door was open and a builder's truck was parked outside. A sound of hammering came from within. Scarlett stood and gazed across the road at it. If only. Her life seemed to be full of If Onlys.

Joanne tugged at her arm. 'Come on, Mummy.'

'Yes, yes. In a minute.'

There was no point in staying. She turned the pram round.

'Scarlett! Wait!'

Her heart twisted painfully. There, in the doorway, was Jonathan, waving and smiling. Scarlett stood still. Jonathan ran across the road to join her. He looked bright and happy, his hair tousled and his face alight with enthusiasm.

'Scarlett, how are you? Did you come to have a look at the place?'

'No,' Scarlett lied. 'I just happened to be walking along here with the children.'

'Well, now you're here you must come inside. See it as it is now and then see the improvements as we go along.'

'You're not open already, are you?' Scarlett asked. He was wearing a navy sweater over his chef's trousers.

'Open? Oh, no, I'm just talking to the builders before I set off for work. I've got a temp job to keep the money coming in. We only signed the papers yesterday. It's finally ours! Isn't it brilliant?'

'Lovely,' Scarlett said. Somehow, she couldn't get anything near the right amount of pleasure into her voice.

Jonathan didn't seem to notice.

'It's going to be tough getting it all ready for opening in November, but as long as we've got the restaurant part done, then we can do up the apartment as we go along. I'm so excited about this, Scarlett. It's a bit of a gamble, bringing fine French cooking to Southend, but I think we can succeed. Are you coming over to look inside?'

'No,' Scarlett said. 'No, I don't think so.'

Jonathan finally realised that she was not as thrilled as he was about the new venture. He gave her a level look.

'I hoped you might be pleased for me, Scarlett. For old times' sake, you know.'

Scarlett took a long shuddering breath. 'I am pleased for you. Really I am. I know it's what you always wanted.'

This was his pet project, what he had talked of ever since she had known him—a restaurant of his own where he could use all the skills he had learnt. This was what he had worked so hard to achieve, his dream, and it was coming true at last. It made her own life seem emptier than ever.

'So why don't you want to come in?'

Pride stopped her from admitting that she was jealous—jealous of his success and even more jealous of Corinne, who was sharing it with him.

'I just don't, that's all,' she said. She could hear how sulky that sounded.

'I see.' Jonathan looked disappointed. 'I had hoped—well, never mind. Look, will you do something for me? I've had these cards printed, and some leaflets. Will you give them out to people at the Horse and Groom? People you think might be interested in the restaurant.'

'I'm not working at the Horse and Groom any more.'

'You're not? Why? I thought you liked it there.'

Scarlett explained. Jonathan looked sympathetic.

'That's rotten luck, Scarlett. It's a pity we can't offer you anything here. It's going to be just the two of us at first until it takes off. But we might be able to take you on later. I know you'd be able to turn your hand to anything.'

Scarlett looked at him in amazement. He didn't really think that would work, did he? It would be her idea of hell, working for him and that Corinne, seeing them happy together, taking orders from them. And she couldn't see Corinne being very pleased about it either. It would cause endless stress.

'Jonathan, this is the last place I'd want a job,' she told him.

He looked quite hurt.

'I thought we were friends, Scarlett. We could have worked well together.'

Scarlett nodded. The pain and regret were so overwhelming she could hardly speak. She and Jonathan would have made the perfect team. But not now, not when he was about to be married and thought of her as nothing closer than a friend. It was all far too late.

'Gotta go,' she managed to say. 'Good luck.'

'Thanks.' Jonathan pressed one of the cards into her hand. 'Take this anyway. Don't lose touch.'

Scarlett nodded, thrust the card into her pocket and started back along the sea front.

When she finally arrived home, she found a letter on the mat. She picked it up and frowned at it. She hardly ever received letters. She looked at the postmark. It was a bit blurred, but she could still make it out—Liverpool.

'Ricky,' she said out loud.

She hadn't recognised his writing.

Intrigued but wary, she walked through to the kitchen, still holding it in her hand. Why was he writing to her now, after all this time? Did he want to come back? She rather thought not. Knowing him, he would just turn up, expecting to be received with open arms. She made tea and took it in to her father, who was hardly awake, then sat the children down with a drink and a biscuit each. She took a comforting gulp of tea herself, then she tore open the envelope. The letter was short and to the point.

Dear Scarlett,
I hope as you and the kids are all right. I'm going to stay here in Liverpool as the music scene is good here. It was all over with us a long time ago, so it's best if we get a divorce. Mum says she doesn't think you got a boyfriend so you'll have to divorce me. It'll be easy because I got a girl here I'm living with. You'll have to get a solicitor and all that sort of thing. I think you can get them free if you haven't got no money.
No hard feelings,
Yours,
Ricky Harrington.

'No hard feelings?' Scarlett said out loud. 'No hard bloody feelings? After all you've done? You've got a nerve, Ricky bloody Harrington!'

Both the children were looking at her uneasily. Simon's face was already beginning to crumple.

'It's all right,' she said to them. 'Mummy's not cross with you.'

But she had to let off her feelings somehow. She went and locked herself in the outside toilet, dug her fingers into her scalp, stamped her feet and growled with fury.

'How dare he?' she shouted. 'How dare he do this to me? All those years without a word, and now when he wants to shack up with someone else, I've got to give him a divorce!'

She finally let herself out of the toilet, gave the children their dinner and embarked on a mammoth anger-fuelled cleaning spree. By the time she had finished she was exhausted and depressed. Whatever was she going to do now? She had lost the job she enjoyed, the love of her life was getting married and soon she would be a divorced woman, the sort of person people whispered about behind their hands. The future looked very bleak.

She flopped onto the sagging sofa and the children climbed up and cuddled close to her. She put an arm round each of their little bodies, drawing comfort from their soft warmth. She kissed each of their heads.

'Who's my own little darlings?' she said.

'Me!'

'And me!'

At least she still had them. Ricky wanted to divorce her and Jonathan was about to be married, but she still had her children.

Victor shambled into the room, carrying a half-empty bottle of British Ruby Sherry and a tumbler.

'Hello, Dad. Up on your day off?'

'Couldn't sleep with all that banging going on. What were you doing?'

'Getting stuff off my chest.'

Victor sat down at the table and poured himself a glass of sherry. He drank it down, rolled a cigarette, lit it and took in a deep drag. Scarlett's words finally got through to him.

'Getting what off your chest?'

'Ricky's asked for a divorce.'

Victor made a so-what expression, turning down the corners of his mouth. 'Good riddance.'

To her own surprise, Scarlett found painful laughter bubbling up from her stomach. She grinned and hugged the children closer.

'Yeah, you're right, Dad. We done all right without him. Good riddance!'

'Riddance, riddance!' Simon chanted.

Scarlett kissed him. Poor little soul. He'd never even seen his father, and now he probably never would.

CHAPTER TWENTY-EIGHT

SCARLETT trudged up the High Street. It had been a long evening. She had had a row with her boss, who had tried to insist that she undid another two buttons on her blouse in order to show plenty of cleavage. Scarlett had said that she preferred to keep the customers guessing, and was told that it was unbutton or go. Scarlett had obeyed, and had then done them up again as soon as his back was turned. On top of that, she was unpopular with some of the other barmaids because she was sent to work in the lounge bar, where the tips were best, and they felt that this was their right as they had been there longer. Scarlett didn't find the customers in the lounge bar any better than those in the saloon or even the public bar. They might wear suits and ties and speak with nicer accents, but they still considered the barmaid fair game. She had had to smile and take the salacious remarks all evening long.

'Bloody men,' she muttered to herself, as she walked past shop windows full of things she couldn't afford.

The barman working with her wasn't much better. He had put his hand on her bottom whenever he got the chance. Scarlett had retaliated by accidentally-on-purpose stepping back onto his foot with her stiletto heel. That had stopped him. She chuckled out loud, remembering. He wouldn't do that again in a hurry.

She reached Victoria Circus at the top of the High Street. Just a couple of last buses were waiting. Either would go right to the top of her road. She hesitated. Usually she walked home, saving the fare. Six bus fares a week made a lot of difference to the amount of money she had for essentials. But the horrible businessmen had been appreciative, cleavage or no cleavage, and she had a nice handful of tips jingling in her purse. To hell with it, her feet and legs were aching and she was fed up and dead tired. She deserved a ride. She got on the first bus and flopped down on a seat. What luxury!

She half dozed as the bus trundled along, waking with a start each time the bell rang. When it got to her stop and she got up, her feet seemed to hurt even more than when she had sat down. As she hobbled off the bus, she noticed the reflections of flashing blue lights in the corner shop windows, and people around her were asking each other what was going on, was it a fire?

Once on the pavement, she knew it was a fire. She could smell the smoke. Fear clutched at her heart.

'Don't let it be my house. Please don't let it be my house,' she prayed.

Heedless now of her swollen feet, she ran across the main road and round the corner into her street.

'Oh, my God!' she cried.

Halfway down on the left hand side, smoke was billowing from one of the long row of terraced houses, though from the distance it was difficult to see exactly which one. Blue lights flashed luridly through the murk. A police car, an ambulance and two fire engines were grouped at the scene. People were standing at their front gates, watching and pointing.

'Please, please no—' Scarlett cried, pounding down the road.

But, as she drew nearer, it became clear that her worst fear had been realised. It was her house. Even as she watched, a fireman rescued one of her neighbours from their upstairs window while others were directing hoses through the downstairs windows.

'Dad!' she screamed.

She burst through the ring of people watching.

'Let me through! Let me through! It's my house!'

A policeman caught her in his arms. 'No further, miss. It's dangerous.'

Scarlett wriggled and fought. 'Let me go! My dad! My dad's in there!'

But the policeman held her firm. 'You live in the bottom flat, miss?'

'Yes, yes—'

'Anyone else in there, miss? Just the one? You sure?'

'Yes, just my dad. Have they got him out?'

'Which room would he be in, miss?'

It was difficult to think straight.

'The—the living room at the front. Or the small bedroom at the back.'

The policeman relayed this information to the head fireman, who sent men down the alleyway at the side of the house.

One of the firemen helped her neighbour into the waiting ambulance. The doors closed and it made off.

'Where's my dad? Have they got him out?' Scarlett repeated.

'Not yet. The others were at the window. They're still trying to get into the downstairs. And your name is, Miss—?'

'Harrington. Mrs Scarlett Harrington. But my dad—'

'And your father's name?'

'Victor Smith. Look, what does it matter? Just tell them to get him out.'

Even from three houses away, the heat was intense. The homes on either side had been evacuated and shocked neighbours were huddled in the street, watching to see if the fire would spread, and being comforted by those who lived slightly further away from the flames. The policemen moved everyone back.

Weeping with shock and horror, Scarlett watched the flames licking through her home, heard terrible cracking noises from inside.

'Please, please, you must get him!' she begged.

Someone took over the job of holding her back. Scarlett vaguely recognised familiar voices.

'They're doing the best they can, love. We can only pray. At least the kiddies weren't in there.'

Scarlett let out a howl of anguish at even the thought of her children being in that inferno.

'They're not, are they, love?'

'No, no—but my dad—'

Motherly arms held her, voices tried to reassure her, but nothing could lessen the terrible torment of waiting to see if the men could get through to wherever it was that her father lay. Another ambulance drew up. Scarlett's eyes were streaming from tears and the effect of the smoke. People all around her were coughing. The fire had a dreadful stench to it, quite unlike the friendly smell of a bonfire. Once more the policemen moved everyone back.

After what seemed like an age, the flames started to die back and the smoke grew thicker and darker. Then two firemen emerged from the alleyway, carrying a stretcher between them.

'Dad!' Scarlett screamed, starting forward.

Two sets of strong arms held her back, for the figure on the stretcher was completely covered with a rubber sheet. Scarlett stared at it in agony.

'No!' she screamed. 'Oh, no, no, no! Not my dad, please not my dad!'

She fought to get away from the people who restrained her.

'I got to see him.'

'No, dear. Best not. Leave it.'

As the body was carried past and into the waiting ambulance, her nostrils caught the sickening smell of burnt flesh. There were gasps and groans of horror around her. Scarlett's legs gave way. She knelt in the road and vomited up everything in her stomach, then continued retching helplessly and weeping, doubled over in the street. Vaguely she registered the ambulance being driven off.

Hands helped her to her feet. Voices tried to soothe her.

'Come away, love. Come on. There's nothing more you can do. Leave them to it now, eh? Come along.'

She was too weak and shaken now to resist. Still sobbing, she allowed herself to be led away and taken into the house opposite her own. Someone helped her upstairs, eased off her shoes and skirt and let her roll into a soft bed, where she curled up in a ball of misery. Voices murmured round her, the springs of the bed creaked as someone sat down beside her and put an arm round her shoulders.

'Have a drink of water, dearie.'

Obediently, Scarlett drank. She found she was parched.

'That's right. Good girl. Now, take this.'

A pill was put in her mouth.

'And another little drink, dearie. It'll help you sleep.'

Again Scarlett did as she was told. Then she was allowed to lie down again. When she closed her eyes, she saw flames and smoke and that dreadful shape beneath the rubber sheet. She fought to stay awake. Anything rather than see that again. But the sleeping pill was too strong for her. She was dragged downwards into a drugged slumber, and knew no more.

When she surfaced again, it was light. She felt sick and muzzy and ached all over. For a moment she couldn't make out where she was and why she was still half dressed. Then she remembered. Her father was dead. Her home was ruined. She let out a groan of despair.

A head looked round the bedroom door.

'You awake, dearie? I brought you a nice cuppa tea.'

'Oh, Mrs Jenkins—'

Except for her time in hospital with the babies, it was the first time anyone had brought her tea in bed since she was a little girl. The simple act of kindness overwhelmed her. Her neighbour sat down on the bed and put her arms round her. Scarlett buried her head in her comforting chest and wept while Mrs Jenkins rubbed her back and talked to her as if she were a child.

When she finally subsided into sobs, Mrs Jenkins pulled away slightly.

'There now, it's best to have your cry out. There's your tea gone all cold. Shall I get you another?'

Scarlett nodded. 'Yes, please.'

But while Mrs Jenkins went downstairs, Scarlett slid out of bed. She just had to see what state her home was in. With dread clutching at her stomach, she padded into the front bedroom and looked across the street. She had been prepared for a terrible sight, but still the shock of it made her cry out. The building looked derelict. The windows were broken and the brick on the outside of the house was blackened with smoke. Inside, from what she could see, was just a black hole. There was no chance that anything could be saved. What hadn't been burnt would be damaged by smoke and water. It was a total disaster. She tried to think about what she should do next, but her poor brain did not seem to be functioning properly.

Mrs Jenkins found her and led her back to the spare bedroom.

'Here you are, dearie. Drink this up and you'll feel a bit better. We've all been having a bit of a turn-out, and we've got a few things together for you. Look—'

She nodded at the laundry basket and the bulging pillowcase by the bed. Scarlett examined their contents. There were sheets and blankets and towels, children's clothes and toys, a change of clothes for herself and a selection of toiletries.

'Oh—' she kept saying, 'oh, how kind. How thoughtful.'

So now she had a little more in the world than just

what she stood up in. But it wasn't the most important thing in her mind.

'Where am I going to go?' she wondered out loud.

'Have you not got any family?' Mrs Jenkins asked.

'No.'

She really was all alone now. Her father might not have been much of a support, but at least he had been there, and he had cared about her and the children, in his own way. Now there was no one.

'What about the children's granny? That's who looks after them at night, isn't it? Can't you stay with her?'

'That's exactly what I don't want to do,' Scarlett said grimly.

She could just imagine Mrs Harrington's reaction to the news of the fire. She would see it as a chance to keep the children with her for ever.

'Well, you can stay here till you get yourself settled,' Mrs Jenkins offered.

'That's really kind of you,' Scarlett said.

But she knew it wasn't the solution. The room she had slept in last night was tiny, Mrs Jenkins already had a lodger in the other spare bedroom and Mr Jenkins wasn't well and wouldn't appreciate having two noisy children charging round the place.

'I've got to go and pick up the children. My mother-in-law will think I'm taking advantage if I leave it any longer,' she said.

Besides, she needed to be with them. They were all she had now. She dressed in the ill-fitting hand-me-down clothes and stepped out of the front door, only to be confronted once more by the ruin that had once been her home. The smell of wet ash hung heavily on the air.

Scarlett bit her lip, trying to hold back another bout of tears as she fully realised just what had gone. The photos of her mother, of the children as babies, of Jonathan. The fluffy kitten that Jonathan had won for her on their first trip up the pier. Her copy of *Gone with the Wind*. Clothes and household goods could be replaced, but not those precious pieces of her past.

What was she going to say to the children? How could she explain? Simon was probably still young enough to adapt to anything as long as she was there, but Joanne was going to be very upset at the loss of her home and her toys. And how could she possibly explain what had happened to their grandfather? They were too young to know what death meant.

And, as she gazed at the scorched building, it suddenly came to her that she had been so wrapped up in her own woes that she had not even thought to ask how her upstairs neighbours were. They had been taken off to hospital, but she had no idea how badly they were injured.

'Do they know how it started, girl?' a voice said behind her.

Scarlett jumped and turned round. It was the Jenkins's next-door neighbour.

'I think I can guess.' She sighed. 'I think my dad must've gone to sleep with a cigarette alight in his hand.'

She didn't add that he probably had a bottle of spirits in the other hand that would have tipped and caught light, or that he had more likely been in a drunken stupor than simply asleep.

'Poor devil,' the man said. 'It's a bad business and no mistake.'

'Does anybody know anything about the young couple upstairs, how they are?' Scarlett asked.

'My old lady rang the hospital. They're suffering from smoke inhalation and minor burns. They'll be let out later today.'

'Thank goodness for that,' Scarlett said. 'But they've still lost their home as well.'

She felt partially responsible. It had been her father who had started the blaze.

'What're you going to do, girl?'

'I don't know,' Scarlett admitted.

She thrust her hands into her coat pockets. Her fingers touched a small card. She pulled it out.

'Jonathan!' she said out loud.

It was the business card he had given her. She turned it over and over in her hands, remembering how happy and hopeful he had been that day, looking forward to a successful future with Corinne by his side. And what had she done? She had rejected his offer to show her round his project and rejected his idea of her working with him and Corinne. When it came down to it, she had rejected his friendship. Would he respond now if she phoned him? She had to try. It was her only hope.

CHAPTER TWENTY-NINE

JONATHAN ran along the sea front to the Trafalgar, borrowed the car keys from his father with just the briefest explanation and galloped downstairs again to where the Austin was parked in the yard at the back. His mind was racing as fast as his feet, and already he had part of a plan of action in place. The rest rather depended on Scarlett and just how bad her situation was. He made his way round the back streets, wondering just what had happened. A fire was a terrible thing. He had seen the devastation it could cause when an apartment close to his in Paris went up in flames. And Scarlett had so little anyway. To lose what she did have was dreadful. But she hadn't said that either she or the children were hurt. He held on to that comfort.

He came out into the London Road close to Scarlett's turning and looked along the pavement on the other side. There she was, by the phonebox. His heart contracted in pity. Her hands were in her pockets, her shoulders slumped in misery. Never in all the years he had known her, through all the troubles she had had to face, had he seen her looking defeated, but today she looked very close to it. He pulled over to her side of the road and stopped.

At first she glanced at the car without interest. Then she recognised him at the wheel and her whole body seemed to gain some life.

'Jonathan!'

She stepped forward as he got out of the car. As naturally as breathing, they fell into each other's arms.

'Oh, Jonathan, you're here. I'm so glad you're here.'

'Of course I'm here. How could I leave you at a time like this?'

She felt right in his arms. He held her close, laying his head against hers. This was where he was supposed to be.

'I shouldn't have rung you. But I didn't know what to do—'

'Of course you should. I'm glad you did.'

He wanted to go on holding her, but they were standing in a busy street and there were things to be done. He led her round to the other side of the car and opened the passenger door for her. Scarlett flopped down on the seat. Jonathan got in beside her and put an arm round her shoulders.

'Now, tell me what happened.'

It was all a bit garbled at first, but gradually he put the story together. What it amounted to was that Scarlett had lost everything and her father was dead.

'My poor darling,' he said. 'I'm so sorry, so very sorry.'

It sounded so horribly inadequate.

'I've got to go and fetch the children,' Scarlett said.

'Right, we'll go and do that first.'

He couldn't wave a magic wand and bring her home and her father back, but he could take her to her children.

'But I don't know where to go after that. I can't tell

the Harringtons I haven't a roof over my head. They'll keep the children, I know they will. They're already very jumpy over the divorce—'

'Divorce?' This was news to Jonathan.

'Yes. Ricky wrote to me a couple of weeks ago. He's living with someone in Liverpool and now he wants a divorce. I think the Harringtons have known about her for a while, but they didn't tell me because they want us to stay married. But never mind that now. I must go and get the children.'

'Right.'

His mind was still reeling with the implications of what she had just said. This could change everything. But there was a gathering note of desperation in Scarlett's voice. He could feel her shaking with it. He had to deal with the immediate problems first.

'We'll get them and then we'll go to my place,' he told her.

'What, the Trafalgar?' Scarlett sounded horrified.

'No, the restaurant. You can stay in the flat there.' Jonathan started the car. 'Which way to the Harringtons'?'

Scarlett gave directions. 'But I can't stay at your flat,' she protested.

'It won't be very comfortable, I'm afraid. But I've been thinking on the way over here. We can borrow some camp-beds and sleeping bags and there are some tables and chairs out the back that were in the place when we took it over. I'm sure if we ask round the gang they'll have some spare household bits they could let you have. And the flat's got a little kitchen and bathroom and all the services are on, so it is liveable in, just a bit

Spartan. And you'll have to put up with the builders banging around downstairs, I'm afraid.'

'But it's your home. I can't live in your home. What will Corinne say? I'll cause you all sorts of problems.'

'Corinne won't know. She's still in Paris, remember. And I'm living with my parents at the moment.'

'But I can't just walk into your place—'

'Yes, you can. Until we can get something better organised.'

'But—'

'No buts. Have you got a better idea?'

'No,' Scarlett had to admit.

She was so down that he almost felt ashamed at winning the argument so easily, even though it was for her own good.

His next task was to deal with Mrs Harrington. She only had to take one look at Scarlett to see that something was wrong.

'What's happened? And who's this?' she asked, regarding Jonathan with open suspicion.

'I'm a friend of the family. I've known the Smiths for years,' Jonathan told her. 'I'm afraid Scarlett has suffered a terrible loss.'

'Mummy!'

The two children came rushing past their grandmother to fling themselves into her arms. Scarlett bent down to gather them to her, kissed them both and held them tight, rocking them from side to side.

Over Scarlett's head, Mrs Harrington was still glaring at Jonathan.

'If it's that father of hers, that's no loss at all to the world,' she said.

'He's still her father. She's very upset, naturally.'

Mrs Harrington made a disbelieving noise. 'I can keep the children here if you've got to go and make arrangements,' she said to Scarlett.

'No!'

Scarlett held them more tightly and backed away.

Mrs Harrington took a long breath through her nose.

'We know where our duty lies. You're still our daughter-in-law, remember, and we're still the children's grandparents.'

Scarlett nodded. Jonathan was beginning to understand why she feared her mother-in-law.

'Go and sit in the car, Scarlett,' he said to her.

Mrs Harrington switched her full attention to him. 'It was the drink, I suppose?' she said.

'In a way,' Jonathan admitted. It was no use lying. She was going to find out sooner or later. He waited till the car door had closed on Scarlett and the children. 'There was a fire at the flat. Mr Smith died in it.'

'A fire? What state is that flat in? She can't take the children back there, surely? Scarlett—!' Mrs Harrington made to step round Jonathan and go to the car. Jonathan blocked her way.

'She's not taking them there. My family have a property that Scarlett can live in for now, and that's where I'm taking them.'

Mrs Harrington gave him a hard look.

'I see. I've suspected this for some time. Friend of the family, indeed. You're her fancy man, aren't you? Just wait till my Ricky hears of this. There she was, acting the injured party, when all along she's got you in tow. I never did believe that she was on her own all that time. You're probably not the first and I'm sure you won't be the last. Flighty little madam. She never was good enough for my Ricky.'

Jonathan's fingers itched. He kept them firmly under control and stared Mrs Harrington down.

'I think you had better get your facts straight before you start making allegations like that, Mrs Harrington,' he told her. 'As I said, I've known the Smiths since Scarlett's mother died, so at a time like this, naturally I do what I can to help. My fiancée and I have a flat on the sea front that isn't being used at the moment that Scarlett can live in. She won't be bringing the children back here tonight because she's not in a fit state to go to work. She's far too shocked. I'm sure she will let you know what's happening so that you can support her at the funeral.'

He could practically see the thought processes going on in Mrs Harrington's head. The last thing she wanted to do was to pretend respect for Victor Smith, but she knew what the correct form was. Victor was a relative. You went to a relative's funeral, or risked being talked about by the neighbours.

Mrs Harrington made a noise in her throat that could have meant anything.

'Where's this flat you're taking her to? I have a right to know. Those are my grandchildren.'

'They are Scarlett's children, and they are being very well looked after. I'm sure Scarlett will be in touch as soon as she feels able to cope. Thank you for your help, Mrs Harrington. Goodbye.'

He strode to the car, got in and drove off, leaving Mrs Harrington holding onto the front gate and gazing after them.

In the back of the car, the two children were bouncing up and down with excitement. Scarlett tried to get them to sit down.

'You were wonderful,' she said to Jonathan.

'Rubbish,' Jonathan said.

He glanced at his watch. Nearly eleven. He should be at work. He saw a phone box coming up and stopped by it.

'Just got to make a call,' he said.

They weren't very happy at his workplace, to say the least. But this was an emergency, and they would just have to manage without him.

Next they went to pick up the things that Scarlett's neighbours had given her. He parked at the top of the road so that the children wouldn't see the state of their home and walked down to Mrs Jenkins's, once again introducing himself as a friend of the family.

'I'm glad there's someone to look after her, the poor thing,' Mrs Jenkins said, handing over the bags. 'But where is she going to stay? The police were here asking. They want to interview her.'

Jonathan gave her a card and promised he would ring the police. As he walked back up to the car, another chain of problems ran through his head. There would be an inquest, and then a funeral to cope with. And there was still this question of the divorce. Through the buzz of things to plan, this rang out clear and challenging. One day, sooner or later, Scarlett would be a free woman again.

'Here we are,' he said, opening the passenger door and putting the bags on the seat and the floor. He was greeted by crying from both of the children.

'I want my horsey!' Joanne wailed.

Jonathan got into the driver's seat and turned round to raise his eyebrows at Scarlett.

'I had to tell her she couldn't go home. She wants her ride-on horse that Nell and Bert gave her,' Scarlett explained above the row. She looked shattered, her face drawn and ill as she tried to comfort her daughter. It didn't help that little Simon appeared to have come out in sympathy.

Jonathan reached into the glove compartment, where his mother usually kept a supply of sweets.

'Here,' he said, handing back a bag of toffees. 'Try these.'

Soon the noise was muffled by sucking and chewing.

He drove down to the sea front and along to the restaurant, then shepherded his little flock up to the apartment. Joanne had brightened up a bit, but Scarlett still looked drained. Jonathan got a couple of the builders to carry a table and chairs upstairs while he made tea all round. The children chewed more toffees.

'Nana doesn't let us have sweets before meals,' Joanne spluttered through a full mouth.

'It's a special treat, just for today,' Jonathan told her. 'Look, I think there's some toys in this bag. Why don't you have a look?'

He sat down facing Scarlett across the shabby table. She was leaning on her elbows with her mug of tea cradled in her hands. A tear trickled down her face.

'I'll never see him again,' she said in a small voice.

'I'm sure he didn't suffer, not if he was asleep when the fire started. He would have been unconscious from the smoke,' he said. He had no idea if he was right, but he had to say something comforting.

'I hope so.' Scarlett brushed away the tears with her hands and took a gulp of tea. 'At least he'll be with Mum now. I've got to think of that. He wasn't the same man after she died.'

'I wish I'd known him before,' Jonathan said.

'So do I. I know you never thought much of him. Nobody did. But that wasn't the real Victor. You'd of liked the real Victor.'

'I'm sure I would,' Jonathan agreed.

He let her talk on for a while, remembering the good times with her father. Simon let out a howl when Joanne took the toy he was playing with. Jonathan distracted him with a wooden car from the small pile of hand-me-downs, and Simon climbed onto his knee and ran the car up and down the table, making engine noises. Jonathan looked at his chubby little hands, his intent expression. He was a nice kid. It was a shame he'd had such a rotten deal in life so far.

When Scarlett had talked herself to a standstill, he raised the question of talking to the police. Scarlett looked horrified.

'The police?'

'It's just routine. After an unnatural death, you know,' he told her, again hoping he was right. 'Do you want me to ring them for you?'

Scarlett nodded wordlessly. Jonathan reached across the table and squeezed her hand, lifted Simon off his knee and went downstairs to use the phone. The call to the police out of the way, he rang round all his friends. Half an hour later he went back up to Scarlett with a plate of sandwiches, more tea and a list.

'Someone's coming to interview you at four,' he told her. 'Do you want me to be here with you?'

'Yes, please.'

'OK. In the meantime, I've got promises of stuff from all these people. You should have more than enough to make a bit of a home here. And they all send their sympathy—the gang, of course, and Aunty Marge and the Mancinis, they were all shocked to hear your news. The thing is, do you want to come with me while I collect what they've promised, or would you rather stay here?'

'I don't know—I can't think—'

'There would be more room in the car if you stayed here, but are you sure you'll be all right?'

'Yes, yes—you go.'

He paused at the door of the living room as he left, looking back at her as she sat at the table. Corinne had spoken of them sitting there on a sofa, looking out at the sea, but it needed a very strong leap of imagination now to see that. Scarlett looked right sitting there.

When he came back with armfuls of household goods, he began to take a real pleasure in seeing the home come together. It was very makeshift and not particularly comfortable, but it was a home. His home, with Scarlett in it.

When the police officer arrived, he sat in on the interview and volunteered to identify Victor, but the officer shook his head.

'Not really possible, sir. We're going to have to look at dental records. Where would those be, miss?'

'I don't know,' Scarlett admitted. 'I can't remember the last time he went to the dentist. He was afraid of them.'

'Right. Did he have any accidents in his life? Any broken bones we could look for?'

'Oh—yes—he broke his wrist—his left wrist—about ten years ago.'

That satisfied the officer. As there did not appear to be any suspicious circumstances, he thought the inquest would be within a week or so, and then they would be able to arrange the funeral. Scarlett just nodded. Jonathan thanked him and saw him out.

And then the phone rang. It was Corinne.

'Jonathan! You said you would ring me today. Why did you forget?'

'Oh—I'm sorry, darling. I've had a lot on my mind. How are you?'

'I am fine. But you should not forget me, even if you have a lot on your mind.'

'I didn't forget you. I was just about to ring when you called,' Jonathan lied.

Corinne made an unconvinced noise, then evidently decided to let it ride. 'How is the building work going? Are the men working hard? Will it all be done in time?'

Jonathan told her what was happening in the new kitchen.

'That's good, but the apartment, will that be finished?'

Above Jonathan's head, small feet thudded across the floor. Should he tell Corinne what was going on?

'I don't know about that, darling. But that can be done as and when. The important thing is to get the restaurant opened for the Christmas trade.'

'I think I should come over and see for myself.'

'Oh, that's not really necessary yet,' Jonathan hurried to assure her. 'It will take a while to get all the basic stuff done and the kitchen fitted. You don't need to oversee that. Wait till we start the decorating and choose the furniture and stuff. That's where we need your good taste.'

'I know—but I want to see you. I miss you. Are you missing me?'

'All the time,' Jonathan said but, even as the words left his mouth, he knew they were no longer true.

'Then perhaps I will come. It's horrible here without you.'

'But it won't be long now, darling. And you know how you hate the ferry.'

Jonathan found he was holding his breath. The last thing he wanted now was for Corinne to arrive and find Scarlett there.

'Yes—well—maybe you are right. Or maybe some day I will just surprise you.'

'No, don't,' Jonathan told her. 'I hate surprises.'

Corinne gave a tinkling laugh. 'Oh, darling, you can be so boring! But I love you.'

A small hand tugged at Jonathan's arm. 'Uncle Jonathan—'

Scarlett urged in a low tone down the stairs, 'Joanne! Leave Uncle Jonathan alone and come here!'

As luck would have it, the workmen had gone quiet.

'What was that?' Corinne asked. 'It sounded like a child. Do you have a child there?'

'It was the radio,' Jonathan told her.

'But I heard someone say your name.'

'I'm showing one of the gang round.'

'But—'

'This call must be costing your father a fortune. Must go now, darling. Thanks for ringing. Bye!'

Jonathan put the phone down and ran a hand over his

head. That had been close. He was going to have to be very careful. This whole situation was difficult enough without Corinne finding out.

CHAPTER THIRTY

SCARLETT woke the next morning with a curious feeling of peace. She lay on the camp-bed looking up at the sloping ceiling of the bedroom and listening to the seagulls calling outside. Reflected light from the sea came in through the uncurtained window. There was something about this apartment that soothed her. She felt right here. At home.

But it was not her home—it was Jonathan and Corinne's. For her it was only a temporary refuge. The peaceful feeling dissolved as the events of the previous day crowded in on her mind. She was homeless. She possessed nothing but the things around her that had been lent or given. Her father was dead and there was an inquest to attend and a funeral to arrange. If she did not get back to work, she had nothing to live on but a bit of family allowance. The practical difficulties of working seemed mountainous. She could do all the walking to and fro when she had only been a few streets away from the Harringtons', but now she was the far side of town from them.

Walking! With a start, she realised that the pram was

still at the Harringtons'. She would have to go back there and pick it up. She couldn't function without that pram. She tried to think about which buses she would have to catch, and whether she had enough money for the fares. Everything seemed to be such an effort. Her mind was sluggish and her emotions raw. She felt as if she had been scraped out inside and left empty and hollow.

There was a thump next door as one of the children got out of bed. They had been thrilled with the camp-beds, thinking them much better than their cots. Scarlett's spirits lifted slightly as she listened to them chattering to each other.

'Mummy!'

They both burst into her room and flung themselves at her.

'It's nice here, Mummy. You can hear seagulls. Is this our home now?' Joanne asked.

'Just for a bit,' Scarlett told her.

If only it was their home. How wonderful that would be.

'Is Grandad Vic here?'

'Grandad!' Simon repeated.

Scarlett fought back the choking tears. 'No, darlings,' she managed to whisper.

'Where is he?'

Scarlett summoned up the strength to explain once more. She tried to keep her voice level. 'He's gone to live with your Granny Joan in heaven.'

'Why?'

'Because he's…he's dead. He couldn't stay here any more. He's happy with Granny Joan.'

She could see that they didn't understand. They had

no real idea of who Granny Joan was and they certainly didn't know what death meant.

'When's he coming back?'

'He isn't coming back. When…when people die, they never come back.'

Joanne's face crumpled. 'But I want him back!'

Scarlett gathered both children to her and buried her face in their soft hair. 'So do I, darlings,' she sobbed.

They clung to her, upset by her distress.

'Don't cry, Mummy,' Joanne begged.

'I'm sorry, darlings. I'm just so sad about Grandad Vic.'

'We love you, Mummy.'

'I know, darling. And I love you. Whatever happens, we'll always have each other. You just remember that. We've got each other. That's all that matters.'

She said it to convince herself as much as Joanne and Simon, and it worked, because it was true. Somehow she managed to control her tears. She must try to make the day nearer to normal, for the children's sake. By the time Jonathan arrived, they were sitting at the table in the front window eating toast made from the bread he had left for them last night.

Scarlett felt a rush of longing as he came into the room, so much so that she couldn't speak. She just gazed at him as he stood there smiling with a pint of milk in his hand.

'How are you all this morning?' he asked. 'Here— thought you might be needing this.'

'Th-thank you. You're very kind,' she stuttered.

He was all she wanted, but he wasn't hers to have.

Jonathan shrugged. 'It's nothing. Any tea in the pot?'

Scarlett nodded. 'I'll get you some.'

She was glad to have something practical to do. Downstairs, the builders were arriving, calling out to each other and switching on their transistor radio.

Jonathan sat down at the table with them. 'Mrs Mancini says you're to go and have lunch at theirs, on the house,' he said.

Scarlett was touched. 'How kind.'

'But a word of warning—she's quite old-fashioned about things and she'll expect you to be wearing black, out of respect, you know.'

That suited Scarlett. Black matched her mood.

'I think there's something in the stuff the gang gave me.'

She braced herself for the day ahead.

The following days began to fall into a pattern. If it hadn't been for the circumstances, it would have been like a holiday, camping out in the light-filled apartment facing the sea and spending all her time with the children. Her loss brought out the best in people, and she found herself drawn back into the sea front community. Jonathan's little gang of friends and their wives and girlfriends called round in various combinations, offering help and sympathy. She weathered a difficult interview with the Harringtons when she went to fetch the pram, and arranged with her employers at the High Street pub to keep her job open.

And then she was given a date for the inquest.

'That means we can start to arrange the funeral,' Jonathan said.

Scarlett thought of her mother's funeral. It had been a terrible occasion, but there had been a great deal of comfort in it as well. They had held it at the village church and all their friends and customers had attended and said what a wonderful woman her mother had been. This time it was going to be very different. They no longer belonged to a church, so it would have to be a cold ceremony at the crematorium. And who was going to mourn her father, apart from herself and the children?

'Would you like me to come with you to the funeral director's?' Jonathan asked.

'Yes, please.' Scarlett studied him as they sat across the table from each other once more. She didn't deserve all this support, not after what she had done to him. 'You're such a rock, Jonathan. I don't know what I would have done without you.'

Jonathan looked away, staring out of the window. 'It's nothing, really. How could I abandon you at a time like this?'

'Some men might have done.'

'Well, I'm not some men, am I?'

'No, you're not.'

He was the most wonderful man in the world. She longed to wrap her arms round him, to hold him tight and never let him go. But he was still avoiding her eyes, looking at something far away over the water. Perhaps he was thinking about Corinne.

'Come on,' he said, coming back to the problem in hand and standing up. 'Get those children ready and we'll walk up to the funeral director's. Best get it over with.'

The day of the inquest arrived. Jonathan knew how much Scarlett was dreading it, and offered once again to go with her. They dropped the children off with Mrs Mancini, who was delighted to have them and sat them down at her kitchen table with ice creams, so that they hardly noticed Scarlett saying goodbye to them.

'They'll be fine there,' Jonathan said.

'I know. She's a lovely person, isn't she?' Scarlett said. He could hear her fear in her voice.

'You'll feel better once this is over,' he told her.

The whole official process was horribly intimidating and impersonal, but Scarlett appeared to stand up to it well. Jonathan felt proud of her as she answered the questions put to her with quiet dignity. The verdict was accidental death. They were free to lay Victor Smith to rest.

It was late afternoon before they arrived back, having picked up Joanne and Simon on the way. Jonathan went inside to speak to the builders before they knocked off for the day while Scarlett got the children out of the car.

He knew there was something wrong from the way the men looked at him as he walked into the building. Before he could even open his mouth to ask what was up, there was a clatter of footsteps on the stairs and Corinne appeared. A furious Corinne, eyes sparking, face flushed. She let loose a torrent of French.

'What have you been doing behind my back? You traitor! You liar! I knew there was something wrong, I knew it! All that, *There's no need to come over, you know how much you hate the ferry.* You were putting me off, weren't you? Lying to me, when all the time you had your mistress and her horrible brats in here. And don't try to deny it. I've been upstairs, I've seen it. All her things in my home, hers and those brats, in my home. How could you do this to me? How could you bring your mistress into our home?'

Acutely aware of Scarlett outside on the pavement, Jonathan tried to explain.

'Corinne, darling, it's not what it seems—'

'Oh, no? You mean she's not living here?'

'Well, she is, but I'm not living with her. I'm still at my parents'—'

'Ha! You expect me to believe that?'

'Yes, I do, because it's the truth. I offered the place to Scarlett because—'

'I don't want to know! All I know is—she has to go. Now.'

Before Jonathan could stop her, Corinne marched to the front door and erupted onto the pavement.

'You!' she screamed in her heavily accented English. She jabbed a finger at Scarlett. 'I knew it! I knew it! Is something wrong. I come here, and here is you. What you do in my house? Is *my house,* you hear? Mine, my home, not yours. And my man. This Jonathan, he is my fiancé. You understand? Mine!'

Joanne and Simon whimpered in fear and clung to Scarlett's legs, stopping her from moving. Crack! Corinne's hand slammed into Scarlett's face, whipping her head round.

'You bitch! You whore! How dare you live here? How dare you—?'

Jonathan stepped forward and grasped her wrist.

'Corinne! Stop it!'

Corinne rounded on him, screaming at him in French. 'I won't stop it till you get rid of her. You hear me? Get rid of her at once!'

She struggled to get free, but Jonathan held her tight.

'I can't. She's got nowhere to go.'

'I don't care! If you love me, you will get rid of her.'

Jonathan looked swiftly from Corinne's furious face

to Scarlett's white one to the two frightened children. This wasn't going to be solved by yelling at each other on the pavement.

'Let's go inside and talk about it sensibly,' he suggested in English.

It was Scarlett who disagreed first. 'No—really—I don't want to cause trouble—'

'You're not,' he said, and almost laughed at himself because it was so patently untrue.

'I'll wait in the car,' Scarlett told him. She looked at Corinne, who was shaking with fury. 'I'm sorry, but I had nowhere else to go. And it's not what it looks like. He's not living here with me.'

'Liar!' Corinne spat.

'Come inside,' Jonathan ordered, and pulled her after him up the steps and into the building.

The workmen had downed tools and were openly watching the show. Jonathan hesitated. If they stayed here, they had to have it out in front of the men, if they went upstairs they were going to be surrounded by the evidence of Scarlett's occupation. He decided on upstairs.

'You see, all these things of hers. Very cosy,' Corinne said, waving an arm at the makeshift home.

'Corinne, calm down, please. Let me explain—'

'Oh, yes, explain, explain! I am dying to hear this wonderful explanation!'

'Scarlett had nowhere to go. Her flat burned down. She had nothing left, nothing but what she was standing up in. And her father was killed in the fire. He was burnt to death, Corinne, and she was distraught. He was the only family she had. She has no one else, no one to turn to. Now, what did you want me to do? Tell her to go away? How could I do that? I was helping an old friend, that's all.'

He watched the conflicting emotions chasing across Corinne's face.

'Ha…well…maybe…' The generous side of her could see that he couldn't have turned Scarlett away, but she was still far too angry and jealous to let it drop. 'But you did not have to live here too, not in our home. I shall never feel the same way about it now, not after this—'

Jonathan snapped. 'For God's sake, Corinne! How many more times do I have to say it? Look around you—go on, look in the bathroom, look in the bedrooms. Can you find any of my stuff here?'

Corinne refused to look at proof.

'It doesn't matter what is here. I shall still see her here now. It will be her place, not mine. It is all spoilt.'

Jonathan raised his hands in a Gallic gesture of despair. 'So what do you want me to do?'

'Get rid of her.'

Their eyes met for a long moment, hot brown challenging cool grey in a battle of wills. Jonathan knew what he should do. Corinne was his fiancée and his future business partner. He should put her first. But he couldn't let Scarlett down.

'I can't do that,' he said.

'You can if you love me.'

'It's not as simple as that.'

'Really?'

Something in the way she said it sent a shiver down Jonathan's spine. It almost sounded as if she hated him.

'I don't think your mother and father will see it that way, and I don't think mine will, either.'

Her beautiful face was transformed into something cruel and hard.

'Is that a threat?' Jonathan asked.

'Yes,' Corinne told him. 'It is.'

CHAPTER THIRTY-ONE

SCARLETT couldn't sleep at all. She was dead tired, but the events of the day before churned around in her head, giving her no rest. The questioning and the procedure of the inquest had been bad enough, but Corinne's shock appearance had been even worse. Her face still hurt from where she had hit her, but that was nothing to the emotional pain. It made her realise that while Corinne had been safely the other side of the Channel, a small irrational part of her had dared to hope.

'They're engaged,' she said to herself as she lay on the hard camp-bed with light from the street lamps coming in through the uncurtained window. 'Their parents are backing them in buying this place.'

Jonathan was committed to his new love and his new project. However well they had been getting on these last difficult days, however sweet and kind he had been to her, however good he was with her children, still he belonged to Corinne. Scarlett groaned out loud. It made her feel quite ill with jealousy.

She tried not to think about it, to calm herself and let sleep take over, but there was nothing on which she

could rest her mind. Whichever way she looked on her
life, she met with problems. Where was she going to
live? How was she going to organise the funeral? How
could she work if she wasn't within walking distance
of the Harringtons'? When should she go and make her
peace with the Harringtons, who were very put out that
she had not gone to live with them after the fire? Top of
the list was the funeral. She wasn't even sure if anyone
would come. She had told her father's employers at The
Oaks, but she was pretty sure they wouldn't attend. She
was absolutely sure that the Harringtons wouldn't.
Maybe Mrs Jenkins and some of her old neighbours
would come, and almost certainly Bert and Nell would.
If she could get in touch with Brenda, then she would,
but she didn't even know where Brenda was living now.
But if these people did come, what would she do about
giving them tea or drinks and sandwiches afterwards?
She couldn't possibly invite them back here to a half-
furnished flat above a building site. It was so sad, so
very different from her mother's funeral. Then everyone
had been welcome back at the Red Lion afterwards.
Now she had few friends and her poor father hadn't any.
If only there was some family to support her.

Even before the funeral, she had to start looking for
somewhere else to live. Jonathan had insisted that she
waited till afterwards, but after yesterday's events, she
knew she had to start right away. She owed it to Jonathan.

Some time in the early hours of the morning,
Scarlett gave up on sleep and got up. She went down
to the living area, meaning to make a cup of tea, but
instead found herself going on down to the ground
floor. The old kitchen had been pulled out and the

rewiring was completed. The plasterers had finished in the kitchen and moved on to the restaurant area, while the tilers were covering the kitchen walls with white tiles. Scarlett had never seen so much money being spent all at once on a place, and this was only the beginning.

Now, in the quiet of the night, Scarlett stood and imagined the echoing space full of customers with a happy buzz of conversation all around. She saw herself in the midst of it, taking orders, pouring drinks, discussing the food. She knew she would be good at it. She knew that she and Jonathan would make an excellent team. Together, they could make a real success of this place. Better than anything Jonathan and Corinne could do. But without Corinne there would be no finance from her parents, and Jonathan's parents wouldn't be very happy putting money into something that Scarlett was concerned with. No Corinne, no restaurant, and the restaurant was Jonathan's dream.

She padded to the window and looked out. Far out in the deep water channel, a ship was making its way down-river. She could see its lights moving in the dark. It was time she moved too, for Jonathan's sake.

Much to her surprise, Jonathan arrived as usual the next morning. What was more, he was on his own.

'I wasn't sure if I'd see you today,' Scarlett said.

'More reason than ever to come, after the way Corinne behaved,' he said. 'I don't know what got into her. She was like a wild beast. I was shocked.'

Scarlett knew exactly what had got into her, but didn't say so.

'It was a bit of a shock for me too,' she said.

'I'm so sorry, Scarlett. After having to go to the inquest, then to have her attack you like that—'

That small spark of hope flared once more. He was concerned for her and ashamed of Corinne. But it was nothing, the situation was still the same.

'It's all right,' Scarlett told him. 'And I'm the one who's sorry. What happened when you got home?'

'Nothing much.'

It was obvious that he was lying to protect her.

'Oh, come on, I can't believe that. What did your parents say?'

'They weren't happy,' Jonathan admitted. 'But I said to them what I said to Corinne. You're to stay as long as you need to.'

Scarlett could just imagine what the Blanes had said to that. They had never liked her. Well, at least Mrs Blane had never liked her. Mr Blane had liked her far too much.

'I've caused you so much trouble,' she said. 'But I won't hang around any longer. I'll go to the council offices today and see what they can do for me.'

The children had heard Jonathan's voice and came scurrying down the stairs to see him. Joanne pulled on his hand and Simon held up his arms to be picked up. Jonathan gave them both some attention while Scarlett made tea, then he told them to go and play.

'Your Mummy and I have got things to talk about.'

Once again, they sat opposite each other at the table in the window. Jonathan insisted that Scarlett didn't have to go straight away.

'At least wait till after the funeral.'

'No, it's best that I get things started,' Scarlett said. 'And there's something else I'm going to do today. I'm going to see a solicitor and find out about getting a divorce. I'm neither one thing nor the other at the moment. I'm married, but my husband's got no intention of ever coming back or taking any interest in the children, so he's hardly a husband at all. At least once I've got a divorce I'll be a free woman.'

Even as she said it, she felt a new energy. She was going to stop being pushed around by events and take charge of her life.

Jonathan was very still, staring at her as if trying to read her mind.

'A free woman,' he repeated.

'Yes.'

'You sound very…er…very calm about it,' he said carefully.

'Yes, I am calm about it,' Scarlett said, though she felt anything but calm. 'I've made a decision. It's always better to make a decision and not flounder around wondering what to do.'

'So—you don't love him any more?'

All her good intentions of the night before went out of the window. She had to tell him. She had to.

'I never did love him,' she said. 'Not the way I love you.'

There was a long pause, while Jonathan took in the fact that she had said 'love' and not 'loved'.

'I…see…' he said slowly.

'So I think it's best to finish it as soon as possible,' she said.

'Yes, you're absolutely right,' Jonathan agreed.

Scarlett wished she had taken more trouble with her appearance. She must look as washed-out as she felt. She was wearing one of the baggy dresses that had been given to her, she had no make-up on and although she had brushed her hair it was just falling over her shoulders any old how. She didn't stand much comparison with Corinne, who always looked immaculate.

'It was wrong almost from the start. With Ricky, I mean,' she said. 'The only good things to come out of it were the children. I don't regret having them. But everything else was a disaster. It was never like it was with you and me. With you it was like…like you were the missing part of me. We thought the same thoughts. I could say anything to you. I think when you were away I went a bit mad. But that was all it was with Ricky—just a passing madness. Not the real thing at all.'

'I see,' Jonathan said again.

His face was very still, as if there was too much going on inside his head for any reaction to show through.

Scarlett took a deep breath. Her heart was beating so hard she was sure Jonathan could see it.

'I really mucked everything up, didn't I?' she said.

Jonathan didn't answer directly.

'I was very angry with you for ages,' he admitted. 'I thought that as I had waited for you, you should have done the same for me.'

Shame and regret flooded through her. It was all her fault.

'You're right. I should of,' she whispered.

'But I didn't realise—not till Graham pointed it out—that Corinne looks a lot like you. So I suppose I was still searching for you.'

Scarlett could hardly breathe.

'And—and what did you find?' she asked.

'Just someone who looks like you.' His words came

out very slowly, as if he was thinking it out as he went along. 'But, beyond the looks, she's very different. There's no one quite like you.'

Scarlett swallowed. The air between them was so charged that she was terrified of saying the wrong thing and spoiling it all for ever. What she wanted to ask was—who did he like best? But she couldn't bear to hear the wrong answer.

'In what way is she different?' she asked.

Jonathan ran his hands over his head and sighed.

'She's had a very protected life. She's an only child, she's always lived with her parents in the same apartment, she went to a nice school and church on Sundays and dancing lessons and all the rest of it, then she worked in her father's shop. She's never had to face up to things on her own like you.'

'She's very lucky,' Scarlett said.

Part of her felt an overwhelming envy of such a protected existence, but the strong part was proud of how she had survived. When it came down to it, she didn't want to be Corinne. She didn't want to be anyone but herself.

'So now,' Jonathan said, 'she expects me to protect her in the same way. Which is what husbands should do, of course.'

'Yes,' Scarlett said, thinking of Ricky. Again, Corinne was very lucky. Maybe that was how it worked. Those who expected to be looked after got what they wanted. Those who could shift for themselves carried on doing just that. 'It must be very nice to have someone to rely on like that.'

She hoped that didn't sound bitter.

Jonathan was sitting with his elbows on the table

and his hands at the back of his head. He looked at her from under his eyebrows.

'It works both ways,' he said.

Scarlett felt utterly crushed. So that was it. He felt he could rely on Corinne to stick by him. Nothing she could say could undo the fact that she had strayed while his back had been turned.

'Yes,' she said in a very small voice. 'You're right.'

She couldn't bear to look at him. When Simon came into the room crying from a bumped knee, she took him on her lap and curled round him, kissing his head. She heard Jonathan get up.

'I've got to go,' he said.

She could imagine why. Corinne couldn't have wanted him to come here by himself this morning.

'Right,' she said, still not looking at him.

His footsteps retreated down the stairs. She heard him talking to the builders, then saying goodbye to them. Suddenly, she knew she couldn't leave it at that. She set Simon down on the floor.

'Stay there,' she told him. 'Mummy won't be long.'

She raced down the stairs and through the restaurant area, catching up with Jonathan at the open door.

'Jonathan, wait!'

He turned to look at her. His face was strained and tired, but something lit his eyes as she ran towards him. Scarlett caught his hands in hers.

'I've got to say this or I'll burst,' she said. 'I know I don't deserve to be forgiven. I know it's far too late but—I love you, Jonathan. I've always loved you. There'll never be anyone else for me but you.'

Jonathan closed his eyes briefly. 'Oh, Scarlett—'

For a dreadful moment, she thought he was going to say that yes, it was far too late. But then he opened his eyes again and gazed deep into hers, pulling her towards him. With a slow, sweet inevitability, their faces came closer, their lips met, their bodies moulded together. Deeply, passionately, they kissed, wiping out the years of pain and separation and loss, reaching back to a simpler time when all that mattered was that they had each other. For a few breathless moments of soaring happiness, the world disappeared. There was just the two of them, sealed in a bubble of delight.

Scarlett didn't hear the car draw up. But she did hear the angry voices. Jonathan's lips parted from hers, though he still held her tight.

'Oh, God,' he breathed.

Dragged back from her dream, Scarlett looked towards the road. Mr and Mrs Blane and Corinne were getting out of the car and advancing on them.

CHAPTER THIRTY-TWO

THE air was full of threats and angry faces. Jonathan felt Scarlett press closer to him and tightened his grip around her waist.

'I knew it! I knew it!' Corinne was screaming in French. 'How could you do this to me, Jonathan? I'm your wife-to-be. We're going to get married!'

'What the bloody hell do you think you're playing at?' his father demanded.

'Put that grasping little gold-digger down, you stupid boy!' his mother yelled. They advanced on him like a pack of baying hounds. Corinne's face was contorted with hatred. He could see that she was about to attack Scarlett.

'Come inside,' he said above the hubbub.

With Scarlett still by his side, he led the way back through the restaurant area, past the gaping plasterers and up the stairs to the living room. The children stared at them all, wide-eyed and wary. Their small supply of second-hand toys were scattered all over the room.

'Look at all this!' his mother said. 'They've taken the place over. Like a pack of rats. Not just her, it's her brats as well. What's the matter with you, Jonathan? Can't you see what's happening? I never did trust her. Right from the start, I could see that she was trouble. Out for everything she could get.'

'Shut up, Mum. You don't know anything about it,' Jonathan told her.

Both his parents spoke together.

'Don't you talk to your mother like that.'

'I know what I can see with my own eyes—'

'You lied to me!' Corinne cut across them. 'You said she wasn't your mistress. "Oh, no, she's just a friend. I'm still living with my parents," you said. You made me believe you. Liar!'

The two children hung onto their mother and began to whimper with fear.

'I don't like the nasty lady,' Joanne wailed.

Scarlett slid out of Jonathan's grasp and bent to pick Simon up. She swung him onto her hip and laid a protective hand on Joanne's head as the little girl clung to her leg.

'You! You get out of here and take your horrible urchins with you before I—I *eat* them!' Corinne snarled at Scarlett.

The children screamed in terror and clutched even tighter at their mother.

'For God's sake, Corinne—' Jonathan said.

'It's all right. I won't let her touch you,' he heard Scarlett say.

Any minute now, it was going to get physical.

'Look, I think it's better if you do leave. This is my mess. I'll sort it out,' he said to Scarlett.

'But I don't want—' Scarlett began.

'Yes, go! Go and never come back!' Corinne shouted.

Jonathan tried to keep calm, tried to ignore all the

shouting going on and just concentrate on Scarlett. He
kept his voice steady and reasonable.

'No, Scarlett. Go now, please. It's only making everything worse.'

He could see that the children were terrified.

For a long moment she stood there, defying him. But
her children's sobs made the decision for her.

'All right,' she said. 'Come along, you two. We're
leaving these animals to get on with it.'

She left the room with her head held high.

Scarlett had managed to leave the scene of battle with
dignity. But it took some doing. By the time she reached
the downstairs kitchen area, she was choking back sobs.
The tilers, who were openly listening to the drama,
looked at her with sympathy. They liked Scarlett. She
made them tea and didn't mind a bit of backchat.

'Got a spot of bother, love?'

'Something like that,' Scarlett muttered.

'That's the Guv'nor from the Trafalgar, ain't it?
You don't want to tangle with him, love. Nasty bit of
work, he is.'

'I know,' Scarlett said.

Oh, yes, she knew all about Jonathan's father. He'd
got her turned out on the street before. Now history was
repeating itself.

'You need any help?' One of the men stood up,
scribing knife in hand.

It was tempting, but what could they do? Just going
in with some muscle wouldn't do any good. Jonathan
may have kissed her, but he hadn't said he loved her.
And now he had told her to leave.

Scarlett shook her head.

'No. Thanks all the same,' she told them and turned to the children, who were both still crying with fear.

She led them through to the yard at the back, where she kept the trusty pram in a dilapidated shed. She heaved Simon inside it and pushed round the alleyway to the sea front pavement. It was a dull autumn day with a brisk easterly wind blowing along the Promenade. She realised that they all had only their indoor things on. Simon was all right with a blanket over his knees and the hood up, but Joanne started to shiver. Scarlett took off her cardigan and put it on the little girl, rolling up the sleeves and tying a hair ribbon round it to make a belt.

'Where are we going, Mummy?' Joanne asked.

Scarlett had no idea. Perhaps they ought to go up to the council offices straight away. Looking as they did at the moment—a scruffy trio of waifs and strays with no money and nothing but what they stood up in— surely they would get some sort of accommodation? But she couldn't face it, not quite yet.

She crossed over the road and looked westwards, past the gasworks and the Golden Mile to where the pier strode out across the mud-flats to the deep water. She remembered that first day when she and Jonathan had gone up the pier. She had just lost her mother and her home then, now she had lost her father and was about to lose her temporary home. In seven years, despite all the hard work, she hadn't managed to get very far. The only difference was that then she and Jonathan had only just found each other and everything was fresh and new and full of possibilities. Now, what she and Jonathan had was coming to an end. The thought of it made her want to howl out loud.

Joanne tugged at her hand. 'Mummy?'

'All right,' Scarlett said automatically.

If she went towards the town, she could call in on the Mancinis. She would be sure of a welcome, warmth, a cup of coffee and drinks and cake for the children. But she didn't think she could bear to start explaining what was going on to anyone, even lovely motherly Mrs Mancini.

'Beach! Beach!' Simon said.

Scarlett looked at him. Poor homeless little thing. She pulled her face into something like a smile.

'All right, darling, we'll go to the beach. We'll walk along to the huts.'

Joanne perked up. 'Yes! The huts!' she said.

Scarlett turned her back to the pier and plodded along towards Thorpe Bay. The wind blew through her thin dress and brought her arms and legs up in goosebumps. Scarlett hardly cared. It was all of a piece with how she felt inside. After a while Joanne let go of the pram and started running on ahead. The baggy blue cardigan flapped around her legs. She looked like an urchin. Scarlett felt she was failing her children, letting them grow up in poverty like this. The tears that she had tried to hold back rose and flowed uncontrollably down her face.

Beyond the Halfway House pub, there were gardens instead of buildings alongside the road. Joanne stopped at the top of some stone steps down to the beach.

'Here, Mummy?' she called.

'Yes, go on,' Scarlett croaked.

She reached under the apron of the pram, pulled out a corner of the sheet and wiped her face and eyes.

'No cry, Mummy,' Simon said anxiously.

She parked up by the steps, hauled Simon out and held

his hand as he made his way ponderously down to the beach. Once there, he immediately sat down and began running his hands through the sand and pebbles, crowing with pleasure. Under the lee of the promenade wall was a long row of beach huts in ice cream colours, their little wooden steps leading up to miniature verandas. None of them was occupied on this blustery day. Beyond the breakwater, Scarlett could see Joanne waving from the top step of a pink and white hut along the beach.

'Come on, Mummy! This one's the prettiest!'

Scarlett pulled Simon up, lifted him over the break-water and trudged along to join her daughter. She sat on the veranda of Joanne's chosen hut with her feet on the step and hugged her knees. It was warmer down here, sheltered from the wind.

'We haven't got our buckets and spades,' Joanne complained.

'Never mind. You can still play houses. And you can dig with your hands. But don't go out on the mud. I haven't got a towel or clean socks or anything with me,' Scarlett told her.

Joanne wandered off to examine the other beach huts, while Simon made growling noises and crawled along pushing the sand in front of him with his hands like a bull-dozer. Scarlett clasped her legs and rested her chin on her knees and wondered what was happening back at the flat above the restaurant. What were they all saying? More to the point, what was Jonathan saying? She had a pretty good idea of what his parents and Corinne thought of her.

Where were she and the children going to sleep tonight? If things went the way she feared, she was going to have to throw herself on the mercy of the housing department and, if they didn't have anything, then she supposed she would have to go and grovel to the Harringtons. She certainly couldn't afford to go to a bed and breakfast place like the last time she'd been homeless. She could just imagine Mrs Harrington's reaction to finding them destitute on her doorstep.

She found herself looking longingly at the beach huts. They were no more than sheds on legs really, but she was sure she could make one very homely inside. But even a beach hut was out of her reach.

She sighed deeply. Maybe she should move out of Southend and start again somewhere else. The place hadn't brought her much luck. And she didn't think she would be able to bear walking along this part of the sea front ever again if it meant passing the restaurant and knowing that Jonathan was there with Corinne. She should never have phoned him up that morning after the fire. The times they had spent together since then, that window of hope, had only caused trouble for him and made it harder for her to give him up for ever. She hardly dared look ahead, the future seemed so bleak. She thought backwards instead, back to the happy days at the Red Lion, when her mother had still been alive.

'Fiddle-de-dee,' her mum always used to say if something went wrong. 'Now what would Scarlett O'Hara have done?'

What would her namesake have done in the situation she found herself in now? She would not have sat here feeling sorry for herself, that was for sure. She would have got up and done something. Scarlett racked her brains. She didn't have a Tara to go back home to. All she had was her skills as a pub manager. And then it came to her. Of course! Now that she no longer had her father to consider, she could get herself a live-in job, then she would have an income and a roof over her head. Bert and Nell would give her a good reference. They might even know of an opening. And she could go anywhere. She had no ties now, she didn't have to stay in Southend. She just had to smarten herself up and slap a smile on her face and convince someone that she was the person they needed. With a surge of energy, she stood up and brushed the sand off her skirt.

'Scarlett!'

Her heart gave a painful leap. Was it—? She spun round and gazed along the beach in the direction of the steps.

'Jonathan!'

There he was, running towards her. Scarlett clutched hold of the veranda post of the hut, hardly daring to believe this was happening. Jonathan sprang over the breakwater and dashed up to her.

'Scarlett, what are you doing hiding down here? I couldn't find you. It was only when I saw the pram—'

'I wanted to go somewhere quiet.'

For a breathless moment, they stood looking at each other. Scarlett was still hanging onto the post for dear life. She hardly dared ask the fatal question, but something in his expression gave her courage.

'What happened?'

He stepped forward and took her hand.

'There was a lot of shouting—'

'Yes, yes, I know that—'

'And Corinne was so hurt—'

A big black gulf opened up, threatening to swallow her. She nodded, unable to answer.

'—but when it came to it, there was only one thing to do. I told her I was sorry, but I couldn't spend the rest of my life with her.'

Scarlett stared at him. It took a couple of beats for his words to sink in and make sense.

'But—the restaurant—what will you do for money?'

'I'll sort it out, go to the bank—it doesn't matter. It can be fixed, somehow. There's no point in having a nice place if you're sharing it with the wrong person, and Corinne was the wrong person. It would have been a terrible mistake to go ahead with it—terrible for her as well as for me. Because you're the right person, Scarlett. You always have been, right from the start. Right from the first moment I saw you. I convinced myself that I loved Corinne, but really there's never been anyone else but you.'

Scarlett could hardly believe this was happening. Just minutes ago she had nothing, and now—this. She let go of the post and moved into Jonathan's arms.

'I loved you from that very first day too,' she said.

This time there were only the children to interrupt their kiss. Simon hung onto Scarlett's legs saying, 'Huggy, huggy!' and Joanne tried to put her arms round both of them.

'You're frozen, darling,' Jonathan said as their lips parted. He rubbed her bare arms.

'Not any more,' Scarlett said, snuggling closer. 'Not now I've got you to keep me warm.'

It felt so right there, being held by him.

Jonathan took off his jacket and slung it round her shoulders.

'Come on,' he said. 'There's nothing to stop us now. Let's go back to the flat together. Back to our home.'

As the Battle of Britain rages over the Essex coast, two teenagers fall in love…

On the bleak family farm on the Essex marshlands, Annie Cross slaves all day for her cruel father. The one thing that keeps her going is her secret meetings with Tom Featherstone.

But war steals Tom from her when he joins the RAF. Annie would love to do her bit but, stuck on the farm, she lives for Tom's letters – until they stop coming.

When, against the odds, her beloved Tom returns, he finds a different, stronger Annie to the one he left behind. But he also finds the girl he loved is carrying another man's child…

www.mirabooks.co.uk

MIRA